DARK FIRE

CHRIS D'LACEY

SCHOLASTIC INC.
NEW YORK TORONTO LONDON AUCKLAND
SYDNEY MEXICO CITY NEW DELHI HONG KONG

Also by Chris d'Lacey

The Last Dragon Chronicles

The Fire Within

Icefire

Fire Star

The Fire Eternal

The Dragons of Wayward Crescent

Gruffen

Gauge

This book was published in hardcover in the United States by Orchard Books in 2010 and in Great Britain by Orchard Books, a division of Hachette Children's Books, a Hachette Livre UK company, in 2009.

ISBN 978-0-545-10273-5

12 11 10 9 8 7 6 5 4 3 2 1   10 11 12 13 14 15/0

Printed in the U.S.A.   40

First Scholastic paperback printing, September 2010

The text type was set in Sabon.

for Lisa Ann Sandell

*Everyone at Orchard Books, both here and
overseas, knows how much I value their support
for this long, ongoing "organic" project. Trust me,
Paul, it will come to a conclusion one day; the plain
fact is, a story is as long as it needs to be. Praise and
warm regards to Catherine C., who had the tricky job
of judging my mood whilst giving, as it turned out,
valuable editorial guidance. And one wonders how many
artists would be fazed if asked to draw the language
of dragons on paper? Not so T. D. Bradshaw, who
seems to be able to turn her artistic hand to anything.
Thank you, Ptery, for inspiring the final artwork.*

*Finally, I want to thank the many thousands of fans,
worldwide, who buy these books. Without you, there
would be little point in writing them. Welcome, once
again, to the Dragons' Den.*

Hrrr . . .

I saw that in its depths there are enclosed,
Bound up with love in one eternal book,
The scattered leaves of all the universe —
Substance, and accidents, and their relations,
As though together fused in such a way
That what I speak of is a single light.
The universal form of this commingling . . .

Dante, *Paradiso*

SEAL POINT, NEAR THE INUIT VILLAGE OF SAVALIK

It had been the custom in Savalik for centuries: The old, knowing that their spirit was tired of this world, should be allowed to die in the manner of their choosing. This much Christopher Apak understood as he guided his grandfather to the sled hooked onto the back of his snowmobile. The old man, Taliriktug was his name, had been sour for weeks, ever since the great mist had fallen on the North. His face, once as ruddy as the blood of a bear, had now become as yellow as lichen. The flesh was sinking into his bones. His eyes stared inward. So, too, his toes had turned. When he walked he was like a newborn caribou, fragile, at angles, twigs for legs. But unlike the caribou, Taliriktug would never learn to stand again. The only food he had taken in this period of decline was a few sips of broth, made from muktuk, the meat of whales. Medication — the white man's penicillin — he had sneered at. Furthermore, he had put away his feathers and charms. This, people muttered, was a greater sign that his living was done with than any liverishness or tired shamanic ramblings. Even the comfort of a single bed, heated by a blanket fed by electricity, had been rejected. Taliriktug was ready to ride a sled. It was his time to sit upon the ice, he had said. In the modern way, this was forbidden. But when a raven landed on the roof of his house, the wise ones in the village had noted the omen and turned their eyes away from the laws of the South. From that moment on it was clear to all that Taliriktug would die in the ways of his fathers — alone, without help, stranded in the wilderness, there to be claimed by the spirits of the North.

"Are you comfortable, Grandfather?"

The old man pulled his furs around him. His mouth, long devoid of any consistency of enamel, with only bunched, dried wrinkles to indicate lips, did not say "yes" and did not say "no." He was sitting cross-legged, facing away from his final destination, pointing at each of the wooden shacks that were built into the land that curved around the bay, as if he were counting them, or possibly even blessing them. This place had been his home since he could first gut a fish. Yet no one stood on the shoreline, watching. That was the Savalik way.

Apak fired up the snowmobile. Gently opening the throttle, he nudged the machine forward. The rope that bound the sled jerked itself tense. Taliriktug gave a nod as they began to move. The hood of his coat slipped back a little, revealing a line of thinning black hair. Then he began to chant. A breathy, incongruous, unharmonic wail. A song for the ghosts of his ancestors. Apak let in a little more gas, keeping his gears low and his speed to a funereal constant. In the South he had heard that this was a ritual: to travel at a duck's pace to the place of burial. But his speed had little to do with respect. He was merely fearful of any sudden bumps that might ship his grandfather onto the ice too soon. That would have been a legend of embarrassment, one worthy of his own demise.

As the snowmobile eased across Savalik Bay, the north wind bled into Apak's face, cutting lines above his goggles and spiking both his nostrils and the corners of his mouth. He steered toward open ice, well away from any ridges that might be giving shelter to a hungry bear. Bears. The thought of them made him frown. Lately, they had been on everyone's tongues, especially in the news reports filling up the television screens. No one had seen Nanuk for weeks, and every day scientists would speak their piece about it. Some were making claims that bears had merely disappeared from view, lost in the cloud that had formed across the Arctic, following their observed migration north. Others were sure they had drowned. Apak did not believe this. How could the great white servant of Sedna one day be walking and the next day be not? Yet he could not deny that this very same worry had darkened the hearts of the villagers of Savalik. Peter Amitak, his neighbor, an experienced hunter, had taken out his dogs when these rumors had begun and searched the known bear runs for three complete days. He had come back saying that Nanuk was either shy or had turned himself to snow. Not a hair or a single print could be found. Some villagers, hearing this, had shut themselves away and boarded up their windows. The End of Days was upon them, they said. And no one wanted to see it.

Taliriktug had been consulted, of course. The oldest and wisest shaman in the region had studied his charms, then asked for a drum to be sounded from the highest rock at the edge of Seal Point. The beat was kept slow, to match the pace of Nanuk's heart, to encourage him to find himself, here, within the village. *Thump*. Across the ocean. *Thump*. Across the land. *Thump*. *Thump*. *Thump*. *Thump*. Like a ball bouncing from the earth to the sky. Then, during the fourteenth hour, a light had appeared in the pillows of the mist and the *inua* of the bear had come to Taliriktug. The old man had risen up and put on the bear's cloak, giving out nothing but hisses at first, before slobbering like Nanuk and speaking in his roar. This mist was a living thing, the bear said. A breathing organ. A spirit of fire. Long ago, the world had been nothing but an egg, laid from the innards of a giant bird. Now the bird had returned to its nest. And all the world was about to know it.

Apak had been present when these words had been uttered. It always chilled him to see his grandfather taken by a voice from the ancient spirit world. Afterward, when the spirit had departed, the old man had collapsed, exhausted, and Apak had left him to the care of others and stepped outside to light a cigarette. He nudged the shale around his feet with the toe of his boot. Then the tobacco caught in his throat and a great anger came upon him. He cursed and stamped the earth. It did not feel like the shell of an egg. An egg would have cracked and spilled its yellow heart. The world was solid. Real. Unbreakable. What "mist" could possibly change it?

And so, as he drove into the first wisps of vapor, two miles, maybe three, from the safety of the village, he did not let his thoughts stray far from the rifle bouncing in its harness across his back. For he could find no meaning in this talk about birds, but plenty of reasons to still believe that hungry bears roamed freely around him.

The mist closed in, quickly like a fist. Without warning, the snowmobile faltered. The engine coughed. The single yellow headlight flickered and died. Apak rubbed a glove across the frosted fuel gauge. Two points green. Juice enough. With a spit of anger he twisted the throttle grip back and forth, slapping it cruelly when it had no effect. The engine coughed again and immediately cut. Apak pulled sideways, curdling a long arc of snow as he stopped. He dropped his shoulders, cursed his maker and the makers of machinery, then looked back.

Taliriktug was not on the sled.

Apak felt a wave of panic in his chest. He knew it was the accepted tradition that the elderly should simply roll off the sled when they considered they had ridden far enough. (The sudden change of course once momentum had been lost would have prematurely aided that.) But as his mind sent roots into the origins of his fear, Apak came to realize that what he was feeling had nothing to do with his poor maneuvering. He was experiencing a primeval terror, one to do with the greater unknown. He was thinking now about his brother, Tootega, who'd been lost mysteriously out on the ice some five years before. A disappearance that gnawed at Apak's superstitious heart just as surely as the voice of the bear that had flowed out of Taliriktug's entranced mouth. He dismounted the snowmobile and looked warily around him. A bleak, unnatural darkness had descended, one that pressed against the jelly of the eyes. And though he could not conjure up a reason why, Apak felt the darkness had killed the engine. Was it the spirit of his brother, perhaps? Angry. Vengeful. Come to take them both.

"Grandfather!" he cried, but his voice seemed deadened and did not carry far. Yet the mist extended as though it had been punched, before flowing quickly back into his mouth, stroking the walls of his throat and lungs. In an instant he could feel it riding through his blood, reaching into his fingertips and toes. A living fire. As if it had possessed him.

Then, from a few paces west, he heard the faint rise and fall of chanting.

Apak unclipped his rifle and crept toward the sound. The old man's silhouette came into view. Taliriktug was sitting in the manner of a baby, swaying slightly, looking as if the merest breath of wind would topple him.

"What do you see?" Apak asked nervously, jerking the rifle to emphasize his fear. The old man was clearly wrapped in a trance.

Taliriktug spread his hands in a welcoming gesture. And then a wind did come, with such unexpected ferocity that it was Apak who was quickly blown over, to his knees. Terrified, he quickly rolled onto his back and tried to open fire at the source of the wind. Several thoughts crossed his mind in that brief unstable moment, but the strangest of them all was this: that the wind had risen from the beating of wings, as if a great bird had landed.

The trigger locked hard against its clasp, but no sound or bullet emerged from the gun. Apak squealed and tried twice more, before clumsily turning the weapon around, thinking he might use the butt like a club. Ashes of snow began to fall around him. Then the mist parted and a beast emerged. It was five times larger than a standing bear, with stout clawed feet and a rounded chest covered not in fur but in frosted scales. Its head was shaped like the skull of a dog. The eyes set into it were as violet as the brightest winter aurora. Before Apak could think to scream, two streams of light flashed out of the eyes and drilled into the center of his grandfather's palms. Taliriktug glowed for a moment, then his spirit rose out of his body. Apak saw the apparition separate cleanly, before it broke into a thousand fragments and was sucked into the light as the eye beams retracted.

Taliriktug's body slumped to one side. And Apak knew that what physically remained of his grandfather was dead.

Shaking with dread, he stared at the creature. It tilted its head and studied him a moment, as though it were trying to evaluate his worth. A plume of white smoke drained out of its nostrils, crystallizing slightly in its own flow of air. It took one pace backward, gracefully for its size, then lifted two enormous wings and with one beat summoned up another great wind that blew the gun out of Apak's hands and drove him several feet along the ice. When at last he summoned up the courage to rise, the creature had gone and tears were frostbitten onto his cheeks. His lank black hair was frozen stiff. A trail of urine had iced itself against his thigh.

In the distance a yellow light pierced the gloom, followed by the sound of an engine starting. The snow-mobile had come back to life. Apak gave a thin wail of disbelief. He hauled himself across and walked around it several times, kicking snow against it, afraid to touch. But when need overcame distrust he climbed aboard and set the thing into motion, stopping twice momen-tarily, first to pay homage to his grandfather's body, then to pick up the rifle.

Only once, emerging from the edges of the mist, did he glance back over his shoulder. The clouds were folding freely again, tucking their mysteries in. Apak spat sideways out of the wind and powered the snow-mobile's nose into the air. He raced it back to Savalik, there to tell the people that Taliriktug's prediction of the bird at the top of the world was true. This story he would come to share with all who would listen, though many would dispute his description of the creature. Yet, in time, as the story would start to filter south, the rumors would begin that the Inuk who had broken through the great north mist had seen not a bird, but something from the far side of human mythology.

And they were right.

Christopher Apak had seen the past and the future.

He had looked into the face of the ice dragon, G'Oreal.

◆ Part One ◆

Wayward Crescent

LUCY'S JOURNAL

OK, this is weird. I don't know why I'm doing this. No, hold the backspace. I sort of do. I need to get things clear. About me and what I am. Why I'm different.

I want to understand.

My name is Lucy. Lucy Pennykettle. I'm sixteen. I turn heads. I get noticed. A lot. Mainly for the bright green eyes and mass of red hair. I live in a leafy little town called Scrubbley with my mom, Liz, and her partner, Arthur, and my part-sister, Zanna, and her sweet kid, Alexa. My cat, Bonnington, is the weirdest feline you'll ever meet. We share the house with a bunch of *special* dragons, like the one sitting next to my keyboard, Gwendolen. Dragons. More about them in a mo.

Arthur (wise stepdad, sort of) told me once that people believe what they see in print. So here are a few small truths about me, just to get things into perspective:

My favorite food is vanilla-flavored yogurt.

I'm slightly scared of moths.

Squirrels break my heart.

I think I'm in love with a guy named Tam.

I'm totally in awe of the author David Rain.

I'm worried about the mist that's covering the Arctic.

I'm haunted by the shadow of beings called the Ix.

But there's one thing that keeps me awake most nights, and lately I can't wrap my head around it:

I look like a girl. I think like a girl. I walk and
talk and act like a girl.

But I was not born the way other girls are.

I hatched — from an egg.

I

AM

NOT

HUMAN

We all want to make our mark. We all want to
feel that we're some kind of hero, ready to stand
up and change the world, ready to fulfill some
kind of destiny. Mostly, we stumble onto our path,
but if what my mom has always told me is true,
my destiny was laid down way, way back.

So here it is, like I heard it in my bedtime stories, ever since I was a dot of a kid. I want to see
it in little black squiggles on paper. Then maybe
my life will begin to make sense.

Once, there were dragons on this warm, blue
world, persecuted, hunted to complete extinction.

People say they're a myth, that they never existed. No archaeological evidence to support them. I know better. I know the truth. I know what happened to dragons at the end.

When a dragon died it cried a single tear. It's known as a fire tear. Trapped inside it was the dragon's life force or auma. With the dragon's last breath, the tear would fall tamely off its snout and find its way to the Fire Eternal, right at the core of the Earth. When that happened the dragon's body simply melted away and its spirit became one with the spirit of the Earth (what Zanna, the "hip" one among us, calls "Gaia").

So far, so good.

Check.

But where do me and Mom and Gwendolen fit in? Well, that's to do with our ancestor, Guinevere, who was there when the last known dragon in the world, a male called Gawain, shed his tear. His tear didn't make it to the center of the Earth. Guinevere caught it in her outstretched hands and took it north, to what was then just a giant ocean, where she kind of . . . *preserved* it in ice. I could write a whole essay about this affair, but let's just stick with me and Mom for now.

If you touch a dragon's fire you're gonna know about it. By rights, Guinevere should have been fried. But because her heart was pure and her only intent was not to see dragons die out, she managed to absorb some of Gawain's power. It changed her, in lots of ways. One of the things she inherited from him was a dragon's ability to self-replicate. I don't know the whole procedure. It's complex. Scary. Not of this world. It involves the production of a suitable egg and a process called kindling, which has to be overseen by a wise-woman or sibyl. Guinevere did it. And so did my mom. One day, maybe I will, too.

This is strange. I feel cold. And I never feel cold. Not in this house. Not around my dragons. Yet now that the truth is here at my fingertips I find I don't want to write about it. It's all so huge. So ridiculously *daunting*. And this is just the beginning. What Mom inherited from Gawain, for instance, was the ability to make dragons, like Gwendolen, from clay. OK, any amount of sculptors can shape a blob of clay. But how many can make it come to life? Or talk to it in dragontongue? *Hrrr.* A long time ago, before I was born, Mom was given a snowball by a stranger named Bergstrom who told her it would never melt in her hands. Since then we've discovered that Bergstrom was part man, part polar bear (part Gaia, even?) and what he'd actually given Mom was a little of Gawain's auma sealed in ice. When Mom put a pinch of the snowball on her dragons it created a little fire tear inside them. That's right, Frankenstein groupies, *they live.*

And now we have lots of them, all around the house, all with different quirks or abilities. They can heal. Do spells. Grant wishes. Shape-shift. The one on the fridge in the kitchen receives messages. Gwendolen, my dragon, is good at IT. They are all little mirrors of the great Gawain. All of them fly his genetic flag. But the one, I suppose, we admire the most is called Gadzooks. He can make things happen just by writing words on the notepad he carries. He was made for our tenant, a man we came to know as David Rain. Well, I call David a man. Arthur has a different theory entirely. He thinks David was sent to us from a race of thought-beings called the Fain that exist in *a higher state of consciousness* and only make themselves known when they inhabit a physical body. The Fain are good. They seek beauty in creation. They worship dragons. Their aspiration, according to Arthur, is to become one with a dragon and be "illumined" to it. How that explains the existence of a single Fain being in Bonnington, my cat, I'm not really sure, but it's fun watching him change into other catty species (his favorite is a black panther!).

The flip side of the Fain is not so good. They are called the Ix. They invaded Arthur once, leaving him blind. I know *exactly* how scary the Ix can be. Not long ago they got into my mind and took control of me. They made me attack Mom, almost killing her and the unborn baby inside her. She's recovered now, and though there is nothing to forgive because I didn't really know what I was doing at the time, I still have nightmares about that day. I still struggle to come to terms with what happened. That's part of the reason I'm writing this, I think.

I'm hungry now. Time for a bag of chips. Chili-flavored. (Call it the dragon in me.)

So, because of what we are, because of what we know, because of our connection to the dragons of old, Arthur believes that the Pennykettle clan has a role to play in the "changes" this world is about to face. What changes? I don't know. I can't predict the future. You can talk about global warming all you like but nothing does my head in more than the thought that dragons might be coming back to this Earth. A few weeks ago, a mist descended across the Arctic ice cap. According to the news, all the polar bears migrated into it and disappeared. No one can explain it and people are saying something *alien* has taken them. All I know is there's something weird going on. Something that involves David Rain and Gadzooks. Five years ago, I saw David die at the hands of the Ix and fall into that very same, very cold ocean. Two nights ago, he turned up in the public gardens near the Scrubbley town library. Zanna saw him. Alexa *touched* him. He hasn't appeared since, but his dragon has. Last night, Arthur took a call from an old university friend in Cambridge. The guy — a professor — wanted advice. He told Arthur that a *creature*, not much bigger than a bird, had flown into his study carrying, of all things, a notepad and pencil. That was Gadzooks. We haven't the faintest idea why he was there. We'll find out tomorrow.

When we go to Cambridge.

THE ROAD TO CAMBRIDGE

"It is now twenty-two days since the so-called 'Northern Fog' arrived, and still no one has been able to comprehend it, analyze it, or in any way explain it. Meteorologists are baffled. If this is a sign of the immense climate change we're being warned about, why is the Earth's environment stable? Where are the floods, the tornados, the volcanic eruptions? It's almost as if this cloak of ice particles has taken control of the northern biosphere and reset it — just as easily as you or I might turn down a thermostat on our heating controls. But what is even more mysterious is why no one has been able to penetrate this mist since it came down. Yesterday, there were unconfirmed reports that the Russian submarine, *Sloya*, which allegedly violated

26

fishing waters off the coast of Finland, found itself there because it had lost all navigational aid as a result of trying to steer a course under the ice cap. Even the captain of the ship I'm standing on refuses to go closer than a mile to the mist because his instruments begin to fail. So, are we looking at something here that is far more extraordinary than we can possibly imagine? Are we, as a growing body of people seem to insist, being visited by something that has yet to show itself and has the power to resist being shown? Listen to the words of this Inuit man. He claims to have journeyed into the fog, and his account of what he saw there has been circling the Internet for days, receiving an astonishing two million hits per hour.

"'I was on the ice when the great bird came. It was as high as a house, with eyes like bright moons. I tried to shoot it, but my gun would not work. Its breath was cold, like the worst north wind. My grandfather, Taliriktug, predicted this. He saw it in his dreams. One day the ice would burn, he said. My people believe this bird will set it alight.'"

"Turn it off," said Lucy.

Her mother, without complaint, leaned forward and turned the car radio off. "You're very quiet," she said, casting her gaze for the fourth or fifth time into her rearview mirror.

Lucy picked at a gap in her teeth. Staring through the window at the solid green embankments of the highway she asked, "How far now?"

Hrrr, said Gwendolen. *About ten miles and approximately twenty minutes' travel, given there was traffic outside of Cambridge.* Gwendolen settled back into place beside the steering wheel. That morning, she had plugged into Lucy's computer and downloaded maps and information for the journey. She was proud to be called the best "GPS" in the world, even though she didn't quite recognize the term.

The car hummed along for another quarter mile. Then Arthur, in the passenger seat next to Liz, said, "Is there something troubling you, Lucy?"

Lucy shuffled her feet. "I was thinking about Gadzooks," she said. "I was remembering the time

Mom made him for David and how happy we were then."

Liz raised her gaze to the mirror once more.

"Sometimes I wish I was a kid again, chasing squirrels out in the garden, and David was . . ." Lucy stopped there, tears collecting in her eyes.

"Hey, what's the matter?" Liz said gently, trying hard to engage with the reflection now.

"Everything used to be so simple," said Lucy, gritting her teeth and pumping her hands. "Then David's dead and he's not dead, and we're being attacked by weird alien creatures that we can't really see, and now there might be dragons sitting in a mist at the top of the world. And I ought to be excited but I'm really, really scared, because I don't know what it means or what's going to happen or what I'm s'posed to do or . . ."

"OK, that's it." With a twist of the wheel, Liz swerved off the highway and slowed to a stop on the shoulder.

Gwendolen, busily reassessing their position, nevertheless had the presence of mind to reach sideways and touch a button, making sure the car's hazard lights began to flash.

Liz dug a tissue out of her sleeve and offered it over behind her. "Take this."

Lucy addressed her dripping nose then crumpled the tissue into a ball in her hands. "I'm sorry. I'm just trying to understand."

"Well, three heads are better than one," said Arthur.

Hrrr, added Gwendolen.

"Sorry, four."

Lucy peered down into her lap. "I've started writing this thing, a kind of journal. Sort of everything about us, and the dragons and stuff. And it's been making me think about . . . well, you know, stuff. Like, why we are what we are."

"Well, that's good," said Liz.

"No, it isn't," said Lucy, thumping her seat. "It's freaking me out. How can you be so calm about this? Me and you, we're not like other people. We're not even people! What happens to us if the dragons have come?"

Liz reached back and made sure Lucy's fingers nestled under hers. "Everyone, no matter who or what they are, asks these questions of themselves sometimes. I don't know what the future holds. All we can do is accept our life and go on with it as we've always done. Everything will be all right, I promise." She aimed the car back into the flow of traffic.

It was Arthur who picked up the dialogue again. "May I ask how far you've gotten with your journal?"

Lucy twitched her shoulders and sniffed. "I dunno. A few pages, on the computer."

"Have you written about David yet?"

For a moment, the car was heavy with silence. Lucy admitted, "No. Not really."

Arthur ran a thumb across the tips of his fingers, as if each was concealing a kernel of truth. "Then perhaps I can help you. David attended my lecture yesterday."

"Why didn't you tell us?" said Liz.

"He asked me not to. He wants to come back to each of us in his own time."

Lucy felt her bottom lip start to tremble. She had yet to see David for herself. She turned to the window to avoid her mother's eyes. "What did you talk about?"

"Physics, mostly."

Lucy sighed.

"But he did communicate something you might find worthy of inclusion in your journal."

It's the next exit, hurred Gwendolen.

Liz, looking at the signs for Cambridge, flicked a lazy blinker on. She glanced into her rearview mirror in time to see Lucy scowling. Patience had never been her daughter's strong point.

Arthur adjusted his position and said, "I know that you and Zanna have asked yourselves many times where David came from or if he's truly real."

Suddenly, Lucy found herself welling up with anger. "I wish people would stop saying that. Of course he's real! You just said he was there in your lecture. What did he tell you?"

Arthur cleared his throat. "That I am his father."

32

"What?" said Liz, almost running into the car in front of them.

Recalculating, hurred Gwendolen, who'd been concentrating so hard on Arthur's words she'd entirely lost her point of focus.

"Father? You're not his dad," said Lucy.

"Not in the conventional sense, I agree. What he meant was, it was me who made it possible for him to enter this world."

Lucy sat back, taking stock. "Is this about Gawain's claw?" Years ago, when Arthur had come to the Crescent, he had told Liz and Lucy how he'd found a claw, believed to be one of Gawain's, and used the inky substance called "ichor" inside it to write an account of David's life, even though the two men had never met.

"Yes," he said, tilting his head toward her. "When I lived as a monk on Farlowe Island and I discovered that wonderful, mysterious claw I had no idea what its true purpose was. I just let myself be guided by its power, to write about David, to create his life with you."

"And that's where he came from? Made up?! From a story?"

"In the loosest sense, yes."

Lucy shook her head in gross disbelief. "I write stories at school all the time, but none of my characters ever come to life! Hello?"

"Perhaps not," said Arthur, "but the thoughts you use to create those characters lodge themselves somewhere in the universe. There is a record in the ether of all that we imagine. However, it takes a force well beyond human comprehension to bring those images onto this plane in a physical form. Only a highly illumined being can do it."

"And that's you?"

Arthur laughed. "I may have a grasp of the finer laws of physics, but I can't animate thought, Lucy. All I did was write a human description of David. I made him look the way he does, speak the way he does, move and think and act the way he does. I gave him feelings, ambitions, memories, innocence. I invented the human vessel . . ."

"And?" Liz said, sensing one coming. Her fingers tightened around the steering wheel.

"And Alexa enabled him to fill it."

"Alexa?" Lucy almost spat out her teeth.

Arthur nodded. "She is Fain, like David — of a very high order."

"Oh, Arthur, come on," Liz said, frowning — and not just at the truck that had tried to cut her off. "We all know Alexa is extremely gifted, but she talks and behaves like a little girl, not some superbeing from another dimension."

"I agree," Arthur said. "But then, she would. Alexa is here to experience the life of a human child in order to complete her transitory path."

"Which is, like . . . what exactly?" Lucy said, still fighting to keep her cynicism at bay.

"I don't know," Arthur concluded. "David didn't share that with me. But I believe it was Alexa, in her Fain preexistence, who directed me toward the claw, so that I could describe for her the father she desired."

Lucy snorted high into the air.

At the fork in the road, veer left, hurred Gwendolen.

"But if this is right," Liz said (bearing left), "and I'm not convinced it is — why would Alexa fix on you? She could have picked anyone to find that claw."

Before Arthur could respond to that, Lucy sat back shaking her head. "This is dumb. You can't choose your own dad before you're even born!"

A thin smile ran across Arthur's lips. "Is it any stranger than you being born from an egg that might, under different circumstances, have hatched into a dragon?"

That shut Lucy up.

"So you're saying he just . . . materialized — aged twenty?" said Liz.

"Yes, in effect," said Arthur. "He stepped, ready-made, through the time rift Lucy visited in Blackburn."

A cold fire ran along Lucy's spine. She looked down at her hands where the unfortunate tissue was now just shreds of purple paper. Blackburn. Why did he have to remind her of that? She'd been trying to blank out that whole experience: the long journey to David's "home," discovering to her horror that the address he'd given when he'd moved into the Crescent didn't exist and that a dormant time rift lay over it instead, a rift being secretly monitored by the Ix. Having taken her into their clutches, they had forced her to make their darkling creature from pieces of raw, volcanic obsidian. She closed her eyes, feeling sick. She still had nightmares about that journey.

At the intersection, take a left, hurred Gwendolen.

Too busy with driving to make another comment, Liz followed the instructions, which brought them into the outskirts of the city. To her right, a shallow but reactive river was doing its best to keep up with the car. There was a sense of history in every building they passed, as though they had entered an academic fairyland. Tall spires. Mullioned windows. Porticos. Lawns. Everywhere, scholarly brick.

"I love this place," Liz said with a sigh.

Arthur turned his head. "Where are we precisely?"

Liz reached sideways and touched his knee. "We're taking the bridge — across the river."

Lucy looked at both adults in turn. Although no names or locations had been given, she realized that Arthur knew exactly where they were. Even in blindness, memories were lucid. "This is where you two met, isn't it?"

"And where Gwilanna drove us apart," he said.

For the second time in the space of a minute, Lucy found her stomach turning. Gwilanna was the "midwife" who'd overseen her birth. She labeled herself a "sibyl," though "crazy witch" would have been a better description. In one way or another she had always been part of Lucy's life, both good and bad. More often, bad.

Destination reached, Gwendolen hurred, though no one seemed to be paying much attention.

"Thank you," Liz said, giving the dragon's ears a tweak. She pulled over and switched the engine off. They had stopped outside a row of homes, each coupled to the street by a flight of concrete steps and a set of adjoining railings.

On cue, a door opened and a gangly man in a shabby tweed jacket came rheumatically down the nearest steps. He had windblown gray hair and a prominent mole on his pointed chin. He stooped as he approached the car, but it was clear that he had recognized Arthur from some feet away.

Liz dropped the passenger window. "Hello? Professor Steiner?"

"Yes, yes," he said, patting a handkerchief against his brow.

"Rupert," said Arthur, extending a hand.

Professor Steiner clamped it firmly. "Oh, my goodness. Arthur, are you blind?"

"We're his eyes," said Liz, trying to draw Lucy in. "This is Lucy. She's come along for the ride."

Lucy gave her good-girl teenager wave.

Professor Steiner nodded. "Excellent. Yes. Well, we've a great deal to talk about. Please, do come in. I —" He paused and set his gaze on Gwendolen, who by now had adopted her solid form. "Why, that's one of them," he gasped. "Just like the dragon I saw. So, there are more of them in the world. My goodness, does it . . . ?"

He flapped his hands up and down in flight.

"You saw Gadzooks flying?" said Lucy, stretching forward. "That's impossible. You —"

"Let's go inside and talk," said Liz, sending Lucy a violet-eyed warning.

Everyone stepped out of the car. As Professor Steiner led the way up the steps (with Lucy in close attendance), Liz did as she always did and settled Arthur on the crook of her arm.

"Thank you," he whispered. "How do you feel?"

"To be back in Cambridge?"

He nodded.

"Odd."

He raised his head. "I can hear the river."

"Don't," she said, pulling him closer, plucking graying hairs off his jacket lapels. "All that was a long time ago."

"I know," he said softly. "But it does have some relevance to what we were talking about in the car."

"Oh?" She walked him forward a pace.

"I didn't answer your question. Why Alexa chose me to find the claw. Why she went to the trouble that she did." He reached for Liz's hand and rested it across the slight curve of her pregnant stomach. "When Gwilanna forced us apart back then, she broke up a chain of events that the Fain had been nurturing for centuries. You and I were supposed to have a child long ago, born of genius and the auma of Gawain."

Liz shook her head, perplexed. "What are you saying?"

"David should have been our son," he said.

A MESSAGE FROM GADZOOKS

If Liz was discomfited by Arthur's revelation, she showed no outward sign of it. She merely folded the words away behind her eyes and said, "Come on. We'd better catch up with Lucy, before she starts spouting about the dragons."

Rupert Steiner was waiting at the top of the steps with a hand to guide Arthur down a hallway narrowed by two walls of bookshelves, into a room that smelled densely of tobacco. "Please, sit down. Would anyone like a window open? It can get a little stuffy in here." He hurried across the room and forced a window open anyway, fixing it on a latch heavily eaten by rust. "I've arranged for tea to be brought to us at six."

Liz glanced at the Napoleonic clock above the fire-place. Its face looked as jaded as the whites of Professor Steiner's eyes. Five thirty-five. They had made good time. She helped Arthur to a seat on a green leather sofa and sat down beside him. Lucy had taken up residence in a hand-carved chair covered loosely with an Aztec-style throw and was peering around the room as if a parakeet had escaped. A soft rebuke in dragon-tongue from her mother made her turn and fix a visitor's smile to her face.

"If it's not too impertinent a question, how long have you had your condition, Arthur?" Rupert Steiner returned to the fireplace and rested his elbow against the wooden mantel. A small depression in its outer edge suggested this was a favorite position. Liz wondered idly how many students he had spoken to from there.

"Five years," Arthur replied.

"Is it incurable?"

"The medical profession have no answers."

"What a dreadful inconvenience," Professor Steiner

43

muttered. He flapped his handkerchief like a magician. "But you're still lecturing?"

"In physics, yes."

"Good man. Good man." Steiner plunged one hand into his pocket and with the other, plucked a pipe from a nearby stand. Using its barrel as a pointer he said, "Well, now. Introductions. Elizabeth you mentioned on the telephone, of course. So I assume that this charming young lady is your daughter?"

"My daughter," said Liz.

Steiner nodded and glanced at the girl. The teenager's gaze was wandering again, rippling the spines of uncountable books. She was holding Gwendolen like a statue in her lap. Liz watched the professor's gaze settle on the dragon and noticed the apple in his neck take a pulse. "Her name is Gwendolen," she said.

That brought Lucy quickly to attention. Throughout her life it had always been taboo to talk about the dragons as anything other than ornaments. Yet here was her mother using an introductory tone of voice. She ran a finger down Gwendolen's ear. Gwendolen did as she'd always been instructed and kept to her solid pose.

Professor Steiner filled his chest with air. "Yes . . . it's remarkably like . . ." He sighed and touched one hand to his forehead.

"It's all right, Rupert," Arthur came in. "Elizabeth and Lucy can be absolutely trusted. They won't be shocked by anything you say and they won't attempt to ridicule you. Why don't you tell them what you told me on the telephone?"

A late spring breeze found its way through the window. Rupert Steiner stared at the pale pink clouds and the roofs of the colleges beyond. He put his pipe down and wiped his hand against the fabric of his trousers. "Very well. But I beg you to appreciate what a challenge this is for me. I've traveled to many exotic places and heard a great number of intoxicating stories, but that's all they've ever been before this incident: stories. What happened in this room has left me quite shaken, which is why I've sought advice from the most rational but freethinking mind I know." He glanced at Arthur briefly and then he began: "I was working at my desk a few nights ago . . ."

He nodded at it, making Lucy glance over her shoulder. It was antique, like the rest of the furniture, strewn with books, files, and manuscripts. An under-watered spider plant was throwing trails of baby spiders almost to the floor. A candleholder occupied the farthest corner, hidden by a fungal coating of wax.

". . . when, suddenly, the candle went out. There's nothing particularly unusual in that; I often work with these windows ajar, but the way the light extinguished was extremely strange. There was no flicker. The flame seemed merely to lean toward the night then disappear in a snap, as if it had been swallowed." (Lucy gave a knowing grunt.) "When I relit the wick, there was . . . the creature. A dragon, almost identical in shape and color to the one that Lucy is holding. It was sitting on the windowsill, looking like a hungry bird.

"At first, I naturally thought it was a prank. A clever stunt arranged by one of my students. I stood up to look into the quad and the next thing I knew the dragon had flown to the edge of my desk."

"I can't believe you saw him move," gasped Lucy. The dragons, when active, generally flew too fast for the human eye to follow.

Professor Steiner funneled his gaze. "It was blurred, but I definitely saw its wings spread, yes."

Liz waved Lucy quiet. "Please go on, Professor. What happened next?"

"Well, it was quite extraordinary. From somewhere — beneath a wing, I think — it produced a notepad and a pencil." Lucy gulped. She felt Gwendolen's heartbeat start. "By now I'd begun to imagine that what I was seeing was a very sophisticated radio-controlled toy, especially when it touched the pencil to the pad and appeared as though it would write something down. It had been my birthday the day before and I was expecting a fatuous greeting to appear on the pad. But then the creature changed its mind and did the most astonishing thing. It looked around the desk, raised its eye ridges, blew a rather enviable smoke ring, then put its notepad away and walked across the desk to my ink pen and blotter. It then lifted the pen, two-handed, from its stand and wrote on one of my favorite parchments." He pointed to a small stack of paper in a gilded box. "In all my years of archaeological research, in all the artifacts I've seen in Egyptian tombs and the treasures I've discovered in Turkish catacombs, I have never come across anything quite so incredible."

"Show me," Lucy demanded impatiently. "Where is it? What did he write?" She ran a hopeful eye across the desk, but saw nothing that might have come from Gadzooks.

"Lucy." Her mother's voice was soaked in fury. "You're in someone's house."

"But it's our dragon," Lucy countered. She slumped back in her chair, knocking her knees together in frustration.

Arthur quickly cleared his throat. "Elizabeth, I think now might be an appropriate moment to tell Rupert about your connection to these dragons."

Liz met the professor's gaze. "I make them," she said. "I mold them from clay. I have the ability to animate them, some of them at least. I can't and won't explain how it happens; you'll have to take that on trust. The one you saw is called Gadzooks. He was made for the young man who was my tenant for a while. You may have heard of him. His name is David Rain."

The professor fumbled through his thoughts for a moment. "No, I'm not familiar with . . ."

"He's an author, Rupert," Arthur filled in. "He writes about the environment."

"*White Fire*," said Lucy. "That's his famous book."

"Ah, is this the young man who made newspaper headlines when he disappeared in the Arctic?"

"He's back now," Lucy said, bluntly.

"And so, it seems, is his dragon," said Arthur.

Professor Steiner touched his temples as if he might be trying to unlock a memory. He gave up after a couple of seconds and wagged a finger at Gwendolen. "And does she . . . ?"

49

"Move?" said Liz. She gave a short instruction in dragontongue. Gwendolen softened her scales and turned a full circle with her wings extended.

Steiner ran a finger underneath his collar. "Miraculous," he muttered, turning dumbstruck to Liz. "Are you some kind of . . . ?"

"Potter," she said. "I'm some kind of potter. That's all that matters."

"I see. Well, I suppose I should answer Lucy's question and show you what your dragon wrote — though I warn you, it may not make much sense." He crossed over to his desk and unlocked a drawer. From it he withdrew a single sheet of paper. It appeared to be made of thick gray cotton, like a small hand towel stiffened with starch. He passed it first to Lucy, who glanced at the pen marks and said, with disappointment, "It looks like a doodle."

"Many ancient languages do," said Arthur. "If you'd never seen Japanese or Arabic writing you would probably not associate the characters with words at first. What do you make of it, Elizabeth?"

She took the paper and examined it. "I see what Lucy means. There doesn't appear to be a formal phonetic structure. Though the strokes suggest it. They're very deliberate."

"I agree," said Rupert Steiner, buoyed by her assessment, "but it's quite unlike anything I've interpreted before. I couldn't even guess at its country of origin. The frustrating thing is, I'm sure I've seen another example of this, but I can't place it."

"Could it be a drawing, perhaps?" Arthur asked.

The professor rubbed the question into his cheek. "The recording of history through storytelling and drawings was prevalent in our earliest ancestors, but even the wildest imagination couldn't pull these marks into a meaningful picture. No, I'm convinced it's a text of some kind."

"Can I have another look?" Lucy took the page onto her knees again, turning it through several angles. "It reminds me a bit of the marks I saw on a wall in that cave on the Tooth of Ragnar."

"The Tooth of Ragnar?" Steiner jerked back as if

he'd been shot. "You've been there? But that island is — or rather was — in one of the remotest parts of the Arctic. Were you taken there on a school trip or something?"

"Erm . . . something," Lucy replied, putting the sheet down on the coffee table. Her mind flashed back five years to when she'd been abducted by Gwilanna and taken to the island as part of the sibyl's bungled attempt to raise Gawain from the dead. Many times she'd been left to fend for herself, with nothing but wild mushrooms to eat and a female polar bear for company. That had been one heck of a "school trip."

"How extraordinary," Rupert said. "You must have been awfully young. You were lucky to visit it before it was destroyed by volcanic activity. The Tooth of Ragnar is a fascinating place, steeped in all sorts of Inuit myth. Why —"

"Just a moment, Professor." Liz cut him off and turned her attention to Gwendolen, who'd just given out a startled hurr. The little dragon was on the coffee table, standing by the sheet of paper.

"What's the matter?" Liz asked her.

The professor steered his gaze between the dragon and the woman. "Goodness! Can you converse with it?"

"Yes," said Liz, without looking up. "Go on, Gwendolen."

Gwendolen stepped forward and pointed to the writing. *I know how to read it,* she hurred.

"How?" said Lucy.

It's dragontongue, Gwendolen said (rather proudly).

Lucy moved her aside. "Dragontongue? I didn't even know you could write it down."

"Me neither," Liz admitted, sitting back, stunned. She glanced at Arthur, who was stroking his chin in what she always called his "pondering" mode.

"Elizabeth's dragons speak a language roughly akin to Gaelic, Rupert. It's possible to learn it, given time."

Steiner bent over the coffee table and peered at Gwendolen as if she were a prize. The dragon warily flicked her tail. She hurred again at length.

"Did she speak then? I thought I saw smoke. And did her eyes also change color?"

"You're making her nervous," said Liz. "She wouldn't normally be allowed to act this freely in human company and you shouldn't, by rights, be able to see her. Somehow, Gadzooks must have made that possible."

"Speaking of which . . ." Lucy gestured a hand.

Liz glanced at the writing again. "Gwendolen has just explained that the curves on the paper are like the way she moves her throat to make growling sounds."

"Yeah, but what does it say?" pressed Lucy.

Gwendolen gathered her eye ridges together and frowned at the markings again. It was not a word she recognized, she said, but she thought she could speak the pronunciation correctly. She cleared her throat and uttered a long, low hurr.

Lucy glanced at her mother, who gave the translation. "Scuffenbury," said Liz. She ran her fingers over the marks. "The message Gadzooks left is 'Scuffenbury.'"

ABOUT A HILL

Professor Steiner's sallow face blossomed with surprise. "Scuffenbury? Why, that's —"

"A hill," Lucy muttered, shadowing his thoughts.

"In Maine, yes. You know of it, Lucy?"

Lucy played one by one with her fingers. "It's that place where there's a white horse carved out of the grass."

"Indeed it is," Professor Steiner said, smiling. "The structural composition of Scuffenbury is a unique geological phenomenon in this part of the world. Its chalk-based foundations are far more common in England, I believe. Wouldn't you say so, Arthur?"

"Yes," he agreed. "But what's even more interesting is that a few miles from Scuffenbury is Glissington Tor, a man-made structure that looks like a large steamed pudding from the road. It's popularly known as 'dragon hill.' People say it's the burial site of a dragon."

Gwendolen pricked her ears.

"Complete nonsense, I'm afraid," Steiner laughed. "During the nineteen fifties, a large tunnel was dug into the heart of Glissington at ground level, but it revealed nothing. No bodies. No artifacts. No weapons of any kind. Certainly nothing large and scaly. Archaeologically speaking it was more lame duck than dead dragon."

"But if it's man-made, why was it constructed?" asked Liz.

"Good question," said the professor, ruffling his hair. (To Lucy's disgust, a shower of dandruff tumbled out.) "There have been many theories. A monument to celebrate an ancient deity. A lookout for encroaching raiders. A sacrificial site — in the old religions, horses were often given up to the gods. A center of natural power — it's said to lie at a vast intersection of ley lines. Or possibly just a gift to the Scuffenbury horse."

Lucy sat forward, hands between her knees. "Gift? What for?"

Professor Steiner drummed his fingers on the wall for a moment, then went to retrieve an atlas from his shelves. He flicked through it to a map of New England. "If you stand by the horse and look across the valley, you can see Glissington very easily." He turned the map and used a finger to demonstrate. "At certain times of the year, the morning sun sits on the peak of the Tor. Legend has it there was a cairn up there with some sort of keyhole structure or circle at its zenith which focused the sun on the third eye of the horse."

"Here," said Arthur, demonstrating for Lucy. He put a finger to his forehead just above the bridge of his nose.

"Quite," said Steiner. "It's what scientists call the pineal gland, often thought of as a channel of creative energy; the focus of the so-called 'sixth sense.'" He snapped the atlas shut. "There's no hard evidence to suggest the cairn actually existed, though people still climb the Tor year after year searching for fragments; the stones are supposed to have healing properties. The myth, of course, was that at certain times of the year the sun would pour through the eye of the cairn and breathe life into the horse, which could then rise up and be ridden across the hills. Some authors even claim it could fly."

"And the dragon?" asked Liz. "Where does that come in?"

"Well, the popular fable, the one you'll find in most of the textbooks, is that the dragon died at Glissington, slain by a virtuous warrior who rode the white horse against it in battle. But those of a more spiritual disposition believe the dragon was actually a protector of the horse and that when the dragon died of natural causes, the heartbroken horse lay down on Scuffenbury and simply refused to get up again."

"It's often described as 'grieving,'" said Arthur, "because of the way it holds its head low. Do you have a picture of it, Rupert?"

"I do." Steiner quickly pulled down another large book with several colored plates of the white horse and Tor.

Lucy studied it carefully. The horse wasn't what she'd expected to see. Long and graceful, its body almost flowed like a ribbon through the grass. Only one spindling leg was attached to the body and its tail dipped down out of sight into the hillside. Its head carriage, as Arthur had said, was very low. Just below the figure was an artist's impression of the Glissington cairn and the likely pathway of the sun to Scuffenbury, striking the horse in the region of its eyes.

Glissington. The name began with a G. Could there be a dragon in the ground under there?

As if he could read the girl's thoughts, Professor Steiner said, in a reverent tone of voice, "In the latter version of the myth, the one where horse and dragon are allied, the dead dragon was buried under mounds of earth freshly dug from the Vale of Scuffenbury and carried there by the local community. In the slaying account, Glissington Tor simply *is* the downed dragon, hidden by thousands of years of blown soil and grass seed. Fascinating, don't you think?"

"Very," said Liz, watching Gwendolen stroking the pictures. "So the question is, why did Gadzooks come and give you this word? All my dragons have special abilities. His is to inspire through writing."

"Well, it's obvious," said Lucy.

Steiner deflected his attention to the girl.

"David sent him. You must be important."

"Lu-cy!" Liz's cheeks shot up the thermometer scale.

The girl threw up her hands in dismay. "I wasn't being *smart*. There's got to be a connection, hasn't there?" She flapped a hand northward. "Y'know. David. Dragons. The *mist* and everything."

"Of course!" exclaimed Steiner, slapping the heels of his palms to his forehead. "Oh, what a *dummkopf* I've been." He pressed his hands together beneath his nose.

Before he could give any reason for this outburst, a bell tinkled and Steiner lurched toward the door.

Wagging a finger in promise he said, "Excuse me, that will be our refreshments."

No sooner was he out of earshot than Liz threw her full force at her daughter. "Will you *please* behave yourself!"

"What have I done?" Lucy said hotly. "I thought we were here to check out Zookie? He left a message about a place where a dragon died, Mom. He wouldn't do that for nothing, would he?"

"She's right," Arthur said, speaking in his best defusing tone of voice. "Though what I find most intriguing is why Gadzooks chose to write in dragontongue, not English."

"Yeah, way to go," Lucy said, who liked it when the genius of the family took her side.

Professor Steiner laid a tray on the table. The delicate clink of china plates made Gwendolen want to fold her ears. She was careful to stay solid while a middle-aged gentleman with neatly parted hair stepped forward carrying a silver teapot and a three-tiered cake stand. The lower tier was filled with crustless, domino-sized sandwiches. The upper ones displayed a spread of fancy cakes.

"Will that be all, Professor?"

"Yes, thank you, Hollandby."

The man drifted away without a glance and closed the door softly behind him.

"Is he your servant?" asked Lucy (just slightly impressed).

Rupert Steiner smiled. "By college tradition, there are certain privileges an academic of my status is allowed. To be waited on is by far the most pleasurable and important." With Liz's help he spread the cups and offered out the sandwiches.

Lucy bit into a salmon-and-cucumber rectangle. A little rich for her taste, but certainly preferable to wild mushrooms.

"You mentioned this mist in the Arctic, Lucy."

The girl paused midchew. Steiner was pouring the tea like a clown, giving the cups a comical amount of height. Some drops splashing freely over the tray found their way to Gwendolen's snout. The dragon quickly licked them off. She liked tea (the hotter the better) when she could get it.

"I don't know if you saw it, but there was a news report yesterday in which an Inuit hunter claimed to have penetrated the mist and seen a great bird."

Lucy exchanged a glance with her mother.

"We heard it on the radio," said Liz.

Steiner selected a sandwich for himself. "Given everything we've talked about today, I'm beginning to think the man saw a dragon."

"And what if he had?" said Arthur.

Professor Steiner looked wistfully at Arthur, as if he dearly wished his old friend could see him now. "I was right when I said I'd seen this writing before." He nodded at the parchment. "I can't be certain until I go into the college archives, but I believe there may be more examples of this dragon language down there."

"*Really?*" gasped Lucy.

"Possibly," he cautioned her. "Your reference to the Arctic fog has triggered a memory which I've been struggling to bring to mind about this writing. What I'm about to tell you won't present a motive for Gadzooks's message, but there are connections to the Tooth of Ragnar and some strange parallels with the experiences of the author you mentioned, David Rain."

Lucy's clothing seemed to crackle as she sat up to listen.

Steiner took a bite of his sandwich and set it aside. "In the early part of the last century, a party of Norwegian scientists and explorers ventured out on an expedition to a place called the Hella glacier, which is geographically in the same region as the Tooth of Ragnar. The mission was cut short when one member of the party disappeared in mysterious circumstances, thought to have been mauled and dragged away by a polar bear. Apparently, he'd encountered the same male bear the day before and had distracted it by placing his pocket watch on the ice, cleverly making his escape while the animal pored over the ticking object. Tragically, he returned to the area the next day in search of his watch and on this occasion wasn't so lucky, for he was never seen again. I'm sorry, this must sound terribly gory. Let me continue to the relevant part.

"The scientist who disappeared was a brilliant young man with an exceptionally promising future — geologist, archaeologist, even physicist, I think; he had no fixed specialization. The day before his ill-fated demise he'd been exploring the mountains through which the glacier ran and had taken photographs of rock formations there. When the film was developed, some of the photographs highlighted a series of unusual marks in the rocks. They were thought to be simple stress fractures at first or smudges caused by water erosion, no one could really tell — and by this time, of course, the man who'd shot the film was missing, presumed dead.

"Several decades later, the photographs were sent to me — in a plain brown envelope with no return address and a short note saying what they were and where they had been taken. The sender expressed a hope they might be 'useful.' I had just published an academic paper about Inuit mythology and somehow this man had latched on to it and found me. I was puzzled by the photographs, enough to do some background research on the history of expeditions to Hella, and discovered the material was indeed genuine.

"My immediate impression was that I was looking at some form of writing, but despite months of effort I could find no way to interpret it." He reached forward and picked up the sheet. "Thanks to you, the door has now opened a crack. If these photographs turn out to be recordings of what you call 'dragon-tongue' burned into the rocks, then everything we thought we understood about our history might have to be reassessed."

"This correspondent," said Arthur, "the one who sent the shots? Did he leave any clue to his identity?"

"He signed the note," Rupert Steiner said. "But all I could make out were his initials: HB."

"Hhh!" gasped Lucy. "I know who it is!"

"Don't be silly," said Liz. "There must be millions of people with the initials HB."

"Not with a room full of books about the Arctic who lives next door to *us*, Mom."

A glint of interest lit Professor Steiner's eyes.

"She's referring to our neighbor, Henry Bacon," Liz explained. "He's a librarian and a collector of books about the Arctic."

"David and Gadzooks used to stay with him," said Lucy.

"And I happen to know," Arthur said quietly, drawing on the memories that David had exchanged with him, "that Henry Bacon's grandfather was a surviving member of the party that explored the Hella glacier."

"Good Lord," said Steiner. "What an amazing series of coincidences."

Arthur leaned forward, gazing blindly into space. "Rupert, you need to find those photographs. If there is dragontongue written in the Hella mountains, we need to know what it says. Gadzooks has come here to give you the key to translate that discovery. I suspect that you are meant to publish what you find, so that the academic world will give credible weight to the idea that dragons are not a myth."

"There must be more to it than that," said Liz. "Gadzooks could have written an alphabet on that sheet. Why did he choose that particular word: 'Scuffenbury'?"

"That will surely come out in the translation," said Arthur. "But in the meantime, I think we should run this by someone who'll know far more about the subject than I will."

"Not . . . ?" Lucy dropped her shoulders and sighed.

"Yes, Zanna," said Arthur.

A MEETING WITH DAVID

Back on Wayward Crescent, Zanna was blissfully unaware that her name had been praised by Arthur — or taken in vain under Lucy's breath. Intrigued though she was by the trip to Cambridge, Zanna had chosen to stay at home and catch up on some domestic tasks, one of which was bathing her daughter, Alexa.

The five-year-old loved water and had learned to swim at the age of two. The only things allowed to swim at bath time, however, were Alexa's impressive collection of toys. Dolphins, fish, mermaids, and turtles all shared the tub whenever she got in. Each had a name. Each had a story. Today it was the turn of Dempsey, the duck.

"Where do you think Dempsey's voice is, Mommy?"

Zanna closed the bathroom cabinet and came to kneel by the side of the bath. The story of Dempsey, the duck who'd lost his quack, was Alexa's latest creation. Zanna picked up a sponge and dipped it into the water. "Oh, I don't know. Trapped in a soap bubble?"

Alexa scooped a few into her palms. "No," she said, splatting her hands together.

A rogue bubble splashed across a female dragon sitting by the taps. She flicked the suds away and gave a moody snort. Her name was Gretel. Her ability was making up potions from flowers. At the moment, she was simply monitoring the tea lights that Zanna had set up around the bath.

"Perhaps it went up one of the spouts?" said Zanna. "It might whoosh out if we turn on the taps."

Alexa picked up the unfortunate mute and sailed him down toward her feet. She shook her head.

"Well, how about . . . the sponge? Sponges are full of tiny holes and tunnels. Lots of places for a voice to hide. If we squeeze it, you might hear a quiet quack."

Alexa's eyes grew very wide.

"I'll need to hold the sponge to your ear, of course."

The child moved her dark curls out of the way.

"Ready, set . . . squeeze!" said Zanna, emptying a cascade of water over Alexa's head.

"Oh, Mommy! Plurrgghh!"

"Sit up." Zanna laughed. "Let me wash your back." She lifted the sponge again, but as she brought it close to Alexa's neck her attention was caught by a rivulet of water running down the little girl's shoulder. She stopped the bead with a prod of her finger. "Lexie, have you been scratching?"

"No," she answered.

"Are you sure?"

"Yes."

Zanna picked up a towel and pressed it against the

rose-white skin. Concentric to the curve of the child's shoulder blade was a faint pattern of reddish blotches. They were present on the other side as well.

Zanna traced a finger slowly along them. The texture of the skin was distinctly bumpy and the tissues underneath moved like gel when she applied even modest pressure. Water vapor swelling the pores, perhaps? "Does this hurt?"

Alexa shook her long black curls.

"Is it itchy?"

"Only when I've got a sweater on."

A clothes rash? An allergy to wool, perhaps? Zanna laid the towel aside. "Well, we'll put something on that when we're done."

Ten minutes later, once her hair had been washed, Alexa was in her Peter Rabbit robe with her hair tied up in a soft blue towel (because all the women in the house did that). Dempsey's quack had thankfully turned up in the linen closet. Leaving Alexa playing with him, Zanna went downstairs to find some cream to apply to the girl's back. Zanna owned and ran a "New Age" shop and therefore knew a wide range of natural remedies. Confident she might have some chickweed balm that would soothe Alexa's itching, she was on her way to her room to get it when she stopped abruptly at the entrance to the hall and looked down it into the kitchen.

David was sitting at the table, reading a paper. Faded leather boots, stonewashed jeans, battered black coat, shoulder-length hair. Take away the *X-Files* T-shirt and he might have passed as a modern Doc Holliday. He even had the chain of an old-fashioned fob watch dangling from a pocket of his dark blue waistcoat.

Zanna steadied her nerves and came to the doorway. "Well, well. The wanderer returns. And how did you get in?" She darted a glance at the listening dragon that sat on the fridge top, wondering why it hadn't sent a message to Gretel. It twitched its uncommonly large ears and blew a hesitant smoke ring.

"Interesting article," David said.

Zanna glanced at the paper as he put it down. She frowned when she saw that what he'd been reading was a story about Apak's "vision" in the Arctic. Part of the headline was obscured by a fold, but the word "dragons?" was bold and prominent and there was an artist's impression of what Apak had seen. It looked frighteningly realistic. But what really took her breath was the name of the journalist who'd written the article. Tam Farrell. The man who'd tried to investigate David's disappearance and just about stolen Lucy's heart in the process. Tam. The irony was almost chilling.

"I repeat," she said, scooping up the paper and throwing it into the recycling bin. (She didn't want Lucy seeing that.) "How did you get in?"

David moved his hand palm down across the table and lifted it to reveal a key. "I used to live here, remember?"

She stared at the key as if she'd like to melt it. "It would have been polite to knock."

"I did. Gruffen let me in. He was on the windowsill by the door — where Gwillan used to sit." He nodded at a small dragon sitting on the table. Unlike the others, it was gray and lifeless.

Zanna threw open a cupboard door, glad to put a screen between them for now. Like it or not, he still scooped hollows out of her heart. She brought down a box in which Liz kept a basic first-aid kit. Band-Aids, scissors, antiseptic ointments. Nothing she'd ideally use for Alexa, but useful props to maintain her composure. She closed the cupboard door and turned to face him. That moment of hidden calm had helped.

"Mommy, are you coming yet?" Alexa's voice drifted down the stairs.

"In a minute, sweetie, just stay there."

David's gaze settled on the tube she was holding. "Problem?"

"She has a rash on her back. Don't act like you care."

"She's my daughter, too, remember?"

A small volcanic rush of emotion tried to escape through Zanna's mouth. She clamped her tongue and let the anger out physically, pushing the first-aid box aside, almost knocking over a wooden block of knives.

"The front door sticks. Make sure you close it tight when you leave."

She turned abruptly, but had hardly taken a step when he said, "I couldn't help what happened to me, Zanna."

Somehow, his voice seemed to clamp her to the spot.

"I went to the Arctic to protect you and Lucy. How could I have known what was waiting for me there?"

Shivers. Why did he make her shiver? She turned fiercely and addressed him again. "Five years you were gone."

"I didn't know that."

"Five Christmases, five birthdays, five Father's Days, five . . . Valentine's." Five letters, she was thinking bitterly, remembering how she'd always written one to him on that day in mid-February, the anniversary of his apparent "death." "And then you just turn up out of nowhere?"

"I couldn't help it," he repeated. "The Fain took me back. Into the world they call Ki:mera, a place where time is meaningless."

"Not to me." She forced her pretty face forward. "Just go, David. Disappear into your weird Fain world. Leave me alone to look after my child."

"I can't. She's part of this."

"Part of what?"

At that moment, the cat flap opened and Bonnington trotted in. With a purr of recognition, he leaped onto David's lap.

Zanna scowled at the cat, and briefly again at the listening dragon, as if they had both betrayed her trust. "Is this what you are, now: king of beasts? Dominion over dragons, polar bears, and cats? What's it like being up there on a level with Gawain?"

"Like breathing in several degrees of the sun," he said. He stroked Bonnington's head, smiling as the Fain being trapped inside the cat came to commingle in joyous greeting. "This world is on the edge of a change, Zanna. There isn't time to explain the history or the reasons but the planet is ready to accept a new species; I have to make sure that the wrong species is not allowed in."

Zanna shook her head. "What brand of science fiction is this?"

"Neither fiction nor science," he said, evenly. "Think about it — you live in an extraordinary household. A physics genius. Two women descended from the last known dragon on Earth. A daughter with the power to draw the future. A cat that can shape-shift into any feline species it chooses. You — a young sibyl — capable of all kinds of magicks."

"And your point is?"

"My point is you can't keep it out of Alexa's life. But you can help me keep her away from danger. No matter what you feel about me as a parent, isn't her safety our first priority?"

"Mommy?! Are you coming?"

"Yes, darling! I'm on my way!"

Zanna folded her arms. Several bangles clinked around her wrists. "All right, what is it you want? You didn't come here to talk custody agreements."

"I need to know where Gwilanna is. My sources tell me she took his fire tear." He nodded at Gwillan again.

"He's not dead, Zanna, he's in a kind of stasis. I intend to help him, but first I need to know all the facts. I understand you fought the Ix here? Tell me what happened."

Zanna sighed and touched the wall beside her. That day in the garden. That dreadful day. So often she'd tried to blot it from her mind, so often it came back to haunt her dreams. "Lucy came to us, possessed by the Ix. She had a knife with her, made from obsidian. She claims it was the heart of a creature called a darkling, some monster the Ix had forced her to make. She scratched it right across Liz's back. Liz was poisoned. We thought she was dead. Gwillan saw her body and was deeply traumatized. He shed his fire tear and it seemed to transfer itself into the knife. I don't know how. I threw the knife away not knowing what it was. It broke into three clean pieces. One of them had the tear inside it. Gwilanna took it and disappeared. That's it. End of story. That's all I know. Now, if you don't mind, my — our — daughter needs my attention."

"Gwillan's fire tear has suffered an inversion."

Once again, Zanna stopped midturn. He was middle-distancing, calculating outcomes. Briefly, very briefly, she saw something of the man she loved in the soft blue focus of those languid eyes. She shuddered and looked away.

"Obsidian has the power to draw negative energy. The greater the energy, the easier the transfer. The sight of Liz dying would have created a powerful auma shift in her dragons, particularly one as sensitive as Gwillan."

On the fridge top, the listener tremored.

"And what's an inversion?"

"What it implies. All the love and devotion Gwillan felt for Liz has been transformed into fear. His fire has turned from white to black. His tear is now dark. It's harmless if it stays within the obsidian."

"And if it doesn't?"

David chose not to answer that.

Zanna gave a sigh. Through gritted teeth she said, "I don't know where Gwilanna is. Surely you can find her?"

"She's covering herself. It's a sibyl trait — but you can trace her." He nodded at her arm.

Zanna let her eyes drift sideways to a jagged three-lined scar on her forearm; a "gift" of magicks from Gwilanna after a clash with the sibyl many years earlier.

"Lay your fingers across the scars," David said. "Look for her in your mind. She's the only other sibyl you know. It should be easy."

Zanna swept her glossy black hair behind her ears. "I know how it works, David. If I find her, what then?"

"Just get her location. Leave the rest to me."

A child's gasp broke the conversation there and Alexa came running in to join her father.

"Daddy!"

Bonnington jumped down in search of his food bowl. Alexa replaced him on David's lap. Her towel was slipping off her head. He gathered it and gently patted her hair.

"How are you, baby?"

"Clean and sparkly."

"Did you wash behind your ears?"

"Yes!"

"And between your toes?"

"Yes!"

"And up your nose?"

"Daddy!" She beat a fist against his knee.

Zanna, watching this, began to feel another, deeper form of betrayal. One that amounted to a kind of exclusion. How could David and Alexa bond so well? How could this man walk into her life and override five years of diligent motherhood? As if he could do no wrong?

"Alexa?"

The child turned around. She saw tears collecting in her mother's eyes.

"I want you to be good, OK?"

"Zanna?" said David. "What are you doing?"

She was tying back her hair: a sign of action. "I was responsible for losing Gwillan's tear. It's up to me to do something about it. Time for you to be a father, David. You'd better protect that little girl with your life."

"Zanna!"

But she had already laid her fingers into her scars. For barely a second they glowed bright blue. Then the whole of her body seemed to vaporize and shimmer before compressing into a single point. The tube of ointment she'd been holding clattered to the floor.

The listening dragon leaned warily forward, put on his glasses, and peered into the empty space. No Zanna.

Gone.

THE SPIDER AND THE FLY

Bleak. Eerie. Cold. Uninviting. Fitting, Zanna thought, that she should land in a place that might be adequately described by words she could also apply to Gwilanna.

She had materialized in the middle of a large stone circle, on what she guessed must be Farlowe Island. Although she had never been to this place, in her dialogues with Arthur the home of the monks had often been described. It was, as Arthur had always suggested, at the hostile edge of faith. Apart from the stones and the reedy grassland and the hollow gray sky choking out the sun there was nothing else visible in any direction. She couldn't even hear the sea.

Nauseous from the effects of the shift, she dropped to her knees and added a few threads of semiclear bile to the indigenous dampness of the flattened grass. Great. Now there was barf in her hair and her favorite jeans were filthy. Two more reasons to curse Gwilanna.

"Well, well." And there was the voice. That old, familiar, cynical drawl.

She appeared from behind the largest stone, ambling around the outside of the circle. She was barefoot, in sackcloth, and looked like a throwback to stone-age times. Her hair, easily as thick as Liz's, was falling down her back in gray-green straggles. Feathers and moss were caught up in the knots. A black beetle was exploring close to her ear. "Not quite the fly I'd hoped for," she said, scraping her fingernails across the nearest stone. From the hand still hidden by her body, something liquid seemed to be falling.

"You know what?" Zanna said, having to turn to direct her speech (and growing rapidly annoyed because of it; the giddiness was being slow to wear off). "If you were a spider, I'd care more about you. Stand still, you old crone. Didn't anybody teach you it's impolite to walk away while someone's speaking to you?"

"Where's the boy?" Gwilanna snapped. Caustic, even by her standards. Someone had definitely stepped out of the wrong side of the cave this morning.

"On the steep learning curve of fatherhood. And call me paranoid, but I'm keen to get home to make sure he's playing the part. So let's get down to business, witch. I want that piece of obsidian you stole."

At that moment, Zanna heard a squawk behind her. Looking over her shoulder, she saw that a raven had landed on the tallest crooked finger of stone. Two stones away, another of the large black birds set down.

"You seem to have attracted some attention," Gwilanna said.

The blueberry eyes of the ravens swiveled. They stared at the scars on Zanna's arm. One of them shifted sideways a step and opened its beak, as if snarling at her.

Zanna lowered her sleeves. "Just give me the knife and go play with your birds. I've got better things to do than stay for this pantomime."

"Always such disrespect," Gwilanna said. "If you were half the sibyl you could be, I'd admire you, girl."

"Yeah? Well, here's the thing," Zanna said, pressing forward. "I never could stand bullies, show-offs, or people with bad grooming." She raised her hand, planning to snatch a clump of Gwilanna's hair, only to find that her movements were blocked. The sibyl had set up some kind of force field. The result was the same at the next space along.

Two more ravens landed on the stones. And now Zanna could see what was really attracting them. The liquid Gwilanna was trailing from her hand was green in color. Ichor. The "juice" from a dragon's scale. Only then did Zanna remember that Gwilanna had made off with another trophy from Wayward Crescent. She had Gawain's isoscele, the triangular scale from the point of his tail. A rare and treasured Pennykettle artifact — and a potent source of magicks in the hands of a sibyl.

"How is Elizabeth?" Gwilanna said airily, still trailing around the circle. "I miss her. How's her unborn son? Is his heart still beating in triples? There may be dragon inside him yet. Ah, the triple slip of the hybrid valve. Unmistakable, if you know what to listen for. Really, child, I could have taught you so much."

"What are you doing?" said Zanna, following the ichor.

"Sending a warning," Gwilanna said. "It should have been David in the circle, not you, but the result will be the same. He'll come looking. He'll be angry. The message will go back to his dragon masters. One way or another, I'll get what I want."

Zanna pushed at the spaces again, but it was like trying to beat through thickened plastic. She drew back her sleeve.

"I wouldn't bother," Gwilanna scoffed. "Your useless grasp of magicks could never compete with mine. I put a lock on the rift. You won't be able to travel back through it. And by the time you've exhausted your limited mind trying to work out how I created the barrier, I will be at the final stone and the beacon will be lit."

"Beacon?" Zanna twisted on her heels, looking for any sign of a fire to kindle.

Then, to her horror, she noticed something. On the plinthlike rock at the center of the circle was the thing she'd come to recover: Gwillan's fire tear, still trapped in its prism of obsidian. She ran to it and tried to snatch it up, but it had been cemented by magicks to the plinth. Inside the obsidian, a dark fire burned.

"What do you want?" Zanna hissed, whipping around again. Gwilanna had only three stones left to go past and the ichor was showing no sign of running out. Zanna ran to the back of the circle where she noticed that a line of the dragon's blood had been spilled inside the ring as well. An arrowhead of green was pointing to the plinth, its shaft curving back to the gateway of stones at the east of the circle. It appeared that Gwilanna had started at the plinth and worked her way outward, before luring her victim in.

"Ah, you've seen the pattern," the sibyl drawled, pausing briefly to watch Zanna's face. "In the times when dragons were bred at this aerie, the shape was commonplace. It's carved into stones all over the island. The monks even have it on the walls of their chapel. How ironic is that?"

"What pattern?"

"Don't be ridiculous, girl. This is not a time to disappoint me. You probably only have moments to live. You're surrounded by one of the most powerful symbols in the universe. That fickle charlatan in clay you call Gretel even has it carved into the base of her tail — at my insistence, I might add; I was present when Elizabeth made her. Don't tell me you've never seen it?"

"The letter *G*," said Zanna, wishing more than anything she'd brought Gretel with her. The potions dragon would have been working on escape routes from the start. Moments to live? What was the crazed witch talking about?

"Not just any *G*," Gwilanna drawled on. "A *G* curling into an isoscele. It represents the tail of their creator, the she-dragon, Godith. Haven't you ever wondered why dragons copy it into their names? To have the sign of Godith on your breath is a mark of respect. Really, girl, you're such a waste. You could have learned so much from me." She sighed and started her journey again.

"You still haven't told me what you want." Zanna threw the words up into the air. She was pacing around now, considering her options. A glance at the ravens (still arriving) reminded her she'd once used magicks to adopt their shape. She looked at the sky. *Did the force field tent across the stones?* she wondered.

"I want what my mother never had," said Gwilanna. "I want illumination to a dragon."

Zanna stopped and pressed her fingers into her scars. "What dragon in its right mind would want to be with you?" In an instant, she became a raven and flew upward as swiftly and vertically as she could. She rose well above the height of the stones and it seemed at first that she might get away, to lose herself among the squawking flock. But the force field closed with such intensity around her that her wings were stretched to their widest limit and almost torn away at the shoulder.

She tumbled back to Earth, having just enough cohesive wit to remain a bird as she hit the plinth. She rolled over, becoming human again. Pain was searing through her upper arms.

"Fool!" squawked Gwilanna, shaking a fist. Several droplets of the ichor of Gawain sprayed against the ancient stones. The ravens there clamored to be touched by its power. Beaks and claws were displayed. One bird took a squealing stab to its belly. Fights were breaking out all around the circle.

Zanna pushed herself up against the plinth, coughing blood into the corner of her mouth. She swept it away with her tongue. Gwilanna had reached the final stone and was just a few steps from completing her *G*. "What happens when you finish the pattern?"

"The beacon will light," Gwilanna repeated, letting her hand drop loosely to her side. Ichor continued to drip from her fist. Vengeance clouded her feral eyes. She swept her gaze toward the plinth. "There is an echo of the dragon Ghislaine in this ring. Its spirit still cries for my mother. I need to put it out of its misery."

"How?" said Zanna, watching the drips. Each time Gwilanna moved, drops of the ichor moved randomly with her. The right drop at the wrong time and the spell would be cast.

"Fire," said the sibyl, brooding again. She laughed to herself. The ravens above her cawed for blood. "The circle will magnify the spark behind you and the Fain will see it from here to Ki:mera. By the time they arrive, I will be gone — with the obsidian — and my terms will be written in your blood across the stones: Give me illumination — or I take the dark fire to the Ix."

Zanna swallowed hard. Though the old woman was a distance away, she could see that a black light was flickering in her eyes. "You're not a killer, Gwilanna. Why do you need a sacrifice?"

"To remind the Fain what the Ix will do to this world if they once again possess dark fire. I'm sorry it turned out to be you, girl. It should have been that irritating boy — fitting retribution for everything he's put me through."

"Stop!" Zanna cried, scrabbling to her feet.

The old woman dropped her hand. "It's useless trying to appeal to me, girl. My needs are worth more than your pathetic life. I've waited centuries for my rightful inheritance."

"Listen to me, you lunatic, sibyl to sibyl. Back away from the stones. It's time to sit down, peel a mushroom, and have a nice herb tea. You know that if anything happens to me, David is going to track you down, tear off your head, and feed it in strips to the crow brigade here."

"David." She gave a scornful snort. "He's a construct of the Fain. You think he cares about you?"

A needle of hurt pierced Zanna's heart. She healed it over quickly and said, "He cares that I'm the mother of his little girl. If any part of you can relate to that then let me out of the circle, now. You had a mother yourself, once. Think about her. Would she have approved of this?"

A soft rain began to fall, beading the ugly twists in Gwilanna's hair. "There was an egg put aside for me once," she mumbled, looking decidedly crazed but soulful. "It was destroyed when my mother was killed in the last encounter between the Fain and the Ix."

"Gwilanna, let me go," Zanna pleaded, coming right to the threshold of the gateway. Just above her, the largest of the ravens sharpened its beak against the moody gray stone. "You've been tainted by the fire. If you let me go, I promise I'll persuade David to help you."

Their eyes met.

"He knows you saved Liz from the Ix's poison. He'll reward you for that."

Gwilanna shook her head.

"Think about it!" Zanna yelled. "People are saying there are dragons in the Arctic. Maybe another egg — for you?"

Wretchedness tore through Gwilanna's eyes. "But I should have been a daughter of Ghislaine!" she cried, and beat her fist against the rock.

With that movement, the last drop of ichor found its spot.

"Hhh!" gasped Zanna, jumping back as the pattern

ran with fire. Gwilanna, her hand still raised, disappeared behind a wall of bright green flame.

It was around the circle in seconds. With a roar it rushed straight to its target: the plinth.

Zanna fell against one of the stones, fearing a fireball or possibly even blindness as the base of the plinth began to throb with light. It was Gwilanna's voice saying, "No! That can't be right!" that made Zanna realize: First, she wasn't dead; second, she was still in mortal danger.

She uncovered her face.

Something was growing around the obsidian. Something muscular and disturbingly dark. Its torso — chest and back — formed first, in layers of translucent, thickening plasma. Then, as two stumpy legs appeared, the piece of obsidian was lifted off the plinth and turned over and around until it hovered at the very heart of the being. Zanna recoiled in terror. She could see the obsidian pumping, sending the light inside it crashing against its glassy black walls. The heart was trying to burst — inside the body of a birthing darkling.

A Dragon's Return

Within seconds, the creature's shape was complete. The darkling flexed its thickset wings and stacked them half-height against its back. Its eyes bulged forth from a gruesome face that would have petrified even the most hideous of gargoyles. A circlet of dark rays strobed from its eyes, probing every raven present. The birds squealed in dread and took to the skies, but could not flee the kite strings of light. Then, just as quickly, the probes disappeared. The birds broke free and came together in a ramshackle flock, landing several fields away.

The heart inside the darkling continued to pump. The eyes swiveled and picked out Zanna.

"No!" she screamed, feeling for her arm.

But before the beast could turn its dark rays upon her, its head snapped back and it barked at the sky. A large, bilateral shadow was falling. Zanna heard Gwilanna scream, "No! No! No!" It was a shout of intense annoyance, as though she was about to lose all control of the situation — which she was. A torrent of fire streamed down toward Zanna. In the shadow behind it, before she passed out, the young sibyl thought she could see a dragon.

From her point of view, it was impossible to describe what happened next. A short time passed, then she simply became aware of being conscious again. She fell forward onto her hands and knees, spitting small pieces of grit from her mouth. She was still on the island, still within the circle, but the grass and the plinth and the monster that had somehow emerged on the plinth were now reduced to a sheet of charcoal. The smell of it, the heat of it, made her retch, producing more grit from the back of her throat. Powdered fragments were lining the cracks of her knuckles. It was in her ears and around her collar. Everywhere. Like sand.

"Take it steady. Let me move you back." A hand touched her arm. Frightened, Zanna beat it aside and scrabbled for the sanctuary of the nearest stone.

"What are you doing here?" she said, coughing. "I left you with Alexa."

David walked forward, leaving smoking footprints in the ashes. "Alexa's safe. Please, let me help you. If you stay inside the circle, the air will become uncomfortable to breathe."

Zanna mussed her hair. The dust of a thousand ages fell out.

"Send the shampoo bill to Gwilanna," he added. "She saw the dragon coming and cast you into one of the stones. She was trying to save you. Unnecessary, as it happened, but it's the thought that counts. You were screaming. Your mouth was open, hence the —"

"Shut up!" Zanna tried to kick him but missed. She staggered to her feet. "Where is she? I'm gonna kill her.

Several times over." She looked down at her jeans. Unrecoverable. Ruined.

"She got away," said David, "fortunately without this." He held up the piece of obsidian rock. Gwillan's tear was intact inside it. "She's going to be one very unhappy sibyl now."

Zanna whirled around and stared at the place where the darkling had been.

"It's dead," said David. "Never really alive. I'm guessing that Gwilanna was trying to call Ghislaine. Somehow, she managed to get the auma of a darkling I thought I'd destroyed here once."

Zanna dragged the back of her hand across her face. "How did the heart survive?"

David looked across the circle. "The darkling was an echo of the monster Lucy was forced to make when the Ix brought her here, to the island. It materialized at a different vibrational level around the obsidian block, but was trying to find a match through living auma on the same plane. Thankfully it probed the birds, not you." He turned the heart like a paperweight.

"One cool thing you learn about dragons if you're around them long enough is that they have the ability to modify their flame to the melting point of whatever they want to destroy or preserve. He followed my orders pretty well. He was smart."

"He?"

David took her hand and drew her to the other side of the stones. In the fields, some forty yards away, grazing gently on the grass, was a magnificent bronze-colored dragon.

"Grockle?" Zanna gasped.

Hrrr? growled the creature, pricking its ears.

"Not now. We've got to go," David said, preventing her from moving closer to the beast. "Any ripple in the space-time continuum leaves an echo. If I was able to trace you, the Ix could, too. This little episode won't go unnoticed. The moment will come when you can reunite properly with Grockle, I promise." He turned and gave a sharp command.

Grockle raised his head. All the classic dragon features were there: jeweled eyes, small horns, indescribably scary teeth. He extended his neck, setting off a ripple of color that began behind his ears and ran to his shoulder. Tilting left and right, he peered at Zanna. Whatever structures composed his eyes shifted like a set of tectonic plates. He was capturing an image. He knew her. She could feel it. Grockle: the young male dragon born from an egg that she herself had quickened five years ago.

With what appeared to be a snort of reluctance, Grockle shortened his neck, opened his wings, and took to the sky. He was a point on the far horizon before the island grasses had ceased to waft.

"Where will he go?" Zanna asked, cupping her eyes.

"North," said David, casually adding, "until I need him again."

She threw him a sideways glance.

"A fire star has opened over the Arctic. A dragon colony — a Wearle — is being established there."

"Then it's right, what Apak saw?"

"They come in peace," he said, detecting her concern.

"Hidden? Inside a mist?"

He nodded. "It's better that way for now. The Wearle are cloaking the region till the climate is right and the Earth is ready to accept them back. They'll reveal themselves gradually to minimize the shock. It would be far too traumatizing if millions of people suddenly had to come face-to-face with what they've generally assumed to be nothing but a myth. Now, please, take my hand, we have to go. Better that you travel with me this time." He clicked his fingers and a small white dragon named Groyne materialized on his palm. More birdlike than Liz's sculptures, Groyne was recognizably dragon nonetheless. He had been created by an Inuit shaman and was a shape-shifter of extraordinary means. He made a smooth transition into a piece of narwhal tusk. In this form, he was able to move whoever was holding him through space and time.

Realizing she had little choice, Zanna stretched her arm and let David clasp her fingers. "There's one thing you haven't told me," she said. She waited until she had eye contact with him. "Why are the dragons coming back at all?"

"Later," he said. "Hold tight." He raised the hand containing the tusk and shook it three times.

In an instant they had all disappeared and peace had returned to Farlowe Island. The sun broke through the low-lying clouds. An easterly breeze blew in off the sea, sweeping anonymously across the stone circle, stirring and layering the harmless ashes.

But in the field where the party of ravens had landed, all was not well. They were staggering through the grasses as if they'd been drugged.

The first bird to change was the dominant male. He was tossing his head back and forth when, suddenly, his skull swelled to twice its size and ears appeared where ears had never been before. His beak collapsed into a sawed-off nose, complete with flared and dribbling nostrils. At the same time his striking blue-black wings shortened dramatically and thickened at the shoulder. Next to go were his spindling legs, replaced by muscle and bulleted claws.

The raven had become a tiny monster.

Leader of a flock of eleven semidarklings.

CATCHING UP

David and Zanna arrived back in the garden, near the rockery. They were still holding hands. Zanna immediately cast his aside and stalked toward the house with her arms tightly folded. She was met by Liz, back from Cambridge, who stopped her on the porch with a horrified gasp.

"My goodness! What happened to you?"

"Ask him," said Zanna. "I need a bath."

Liz's gaze lingered over David for a moment. The son she'd never had, returned to her. "No, wait," she said, calling Zanna back. "There's something I need to tell you — both of you."

"What's the matter?" David said. In a couple of

strides he was at Liz's shoulder. Tears had dried in runs on her cheeks.

"While you were gone, Henry had a stroke."

"What?" Zanna said.

David's eyes fell shut. When he opened them again he let his gaze rise over the garden fence and settle kindly on the house next door, the scene of so many domestic adventures.

Zanna shook her head, looking confused. "Is he OK?"

"He was taken to the hospital about half an hour ago. It doesn't look good, I'm sorry. Alexa seems fine though."

"Alexa?" said Zanna. "I don't understand."

"She was with him when it happened," Liz said. "They were feeding Henry's fish when he sat down and went 'a bit wuzzly,' apparently. She held his hand until she heard us come home. She sang dragon lullabies to him. Rather touching, really."

Zanna's dark eyes drilled into David's. "You left her with Henry? He's not been well for weeks!"

David spread his hands. "How was I to know? Anyway, I thought it was important to come after you."

"Some father you are!"

"I saved your life," he reminded her, calmly.

But Zanna just glared at him and swept away.

"Oh, dear," sighed Liz. "That's not a good start." She looked him up and down, then stepped forward and draped her arms around his neck. "I don't want to know how you were able to come back or how any of this is possible; I just want to know that you'll stay with us — please?"

He hugged her sweetly. "For as long as I can. It's so good to see you again."

She pulled away. "Alexa said something about you going to find Gwilanna?"

"Yes. I managed to retrieve this." He lifted the obsidian out of his pocket. "Be careful, it's fragile." He handed it over.

Turning it like a kaleidoscope, Liz said, "Is this light inside it really Gwillan's tear?"

David shook his head. "The complete antithesis. What you have in there is pure evil."

"But it came from one of my dragons. From a beautiful creature that wouldn't harm a fly."

"That's what makes it so dangerous," he said. "Innocence, turned on its head. That is a spark of dark fire, Liz, the most destructive force in the universe. If the Ix got hold of it, they'd harm a lot more than flies."

Even so, she caressed it softly. "All I want is peace — and Gwillan back. Is there any hope for him, David? Can this . . . thing be reversed? Can his life be restored?"

David returned the block safely to his pocket. "I'll need to seek advice on that." He quickly changed the subject. "How's the baby?"

"Baby?" Liz looked down at herself as if she were surprised to remember she was pregnant. "How did you know?"

He pointed at her tummy and made the shape of a curve with his hand.

"Oh, yes. Silly me." She tossed her mane of hair. "He's fine."

"Him?"

"It's a boy — according to Gwilanna."

"Interesting. Got a name for him yet?"

"Joseph. Joseph Henry," she said. "But we're trying to keep it a secret for now." She smiled and tilted her head toward the house.

Lucy had just stepped out of the kitchen. She came walking down the garden with her arms tightly crossed and her mouth puckered inward, as if trying to work out what she should do. How did you greet someone you loved when everyone around you had been saying for the past five years that he was dead? Two yards from him she cast all that aside and launched herself forward. He caught her and lifted her clean off the porch.

"Oh," was all she could say.

He said, "Wow, you've grown."

He smiled at Liz. Her bright green eyes were glistening again. She patted his arm. "Come to dinner." She made it sound like a hopeful question.

With a puff, David set Lucy down. She put her fingers underneath her nose, embarrassed by the drip that was forming there. She threw up her hands, briefly lost for words. "We went to Cambridge," she blurted, as if it was an alternative form of hello. "Why did you send Gadzooks to that professor?"

His gaze shifted sideways and he shrugged. "I didn't."

"But . . . there was a dragon in his room that wrote things down."

"The description Professor Steiner gave us sounded very much like Zookie," said Liz.

"Oh, I'm sure it was him," said David, moving his toe against the ground. "But he wasn't sent to Cambridge on my orders. For the moment, he's in the service of a dragon called G'Oreal."

"Who's G'Oreal?" Liz and Lucy spoke together.

David smiled and looked at them in turn. Give or take a few wrinkles, they could have been twins. "He's an ice dragon, the leader of a colony that's settling in the Arctic. What message did Gadzooks leave?"

"Scuffenbury," said Lucy, in a quiet voice. "Do you know where it is?"

David looked inside himself, recalling something distant. "Yes. There's a dragon hidden there."

"Oh?" said Liz.

"Hidden? Not dead?" asked Lucy.

"In stasis," David said. "It's one of the last twelve."

Liz and Lucy exchanged a glance. They knew the legend of the last twelve dragons very well, but to be suddenly confronted with evidence of it . . .

"Are the others in stasis as well?" Liz asked, massaging her arms with the tips of her fingers.

"And why has Gadzooks told us about this one?" added Lucy.

A green light pulsed from David's pocket. "Let's talk about it over dinner," he said.

"What's that light?" Lucy couldn't help herself.

"A message," he said.

Lucy bent forward to peek. "From your watch?" She could see the light glowing around the rim of the casing.

Liz intervened then and took her arm. "Come on, Lucy. It's none of your business." She turned the girl away and said over her shoulder, "Dinner. Tonight. Seven thirty."

He watched them go back to the house. When they'd stepped inside the kitchen he flipped the watch open. An endless tract of space appeared where a regular watch face would have been. As David stared into it his eyes seemed to mirror it, until he was part of its spinning matrix. It took him into the aura of a dragon. A dragon that the Inuit Apak had seen. A dragon that David knew as G'Oreal.

The jeweled eyes of the illumined creature poured their telepathic gifts into his mind. *The Wearle awaits news of your progress, G'lant.*

David turned away from the house. Despite its powerful connection to dragons, it felt odd to be looking at its sunlit windows while he was being addressed by the name he'd been given in the Fain world, Ki:mera. Thinking in dragontongue he replied, *The sibyl, Gwilanna, is still at large.*

G'Oreal angled his nostrils inward. A gradation of blue shades rippled across his neck. *Do you need the help of the Wearle to trace her?*

David bowed his head. *I am confident of success.*

Then proceed, swiftly, came G'Oreal's reply. *Find the dark fire and bring it to the colony. The Ix are probing. It must be destroyed.*

David paused a moment to think. During the course of the conversation his eyes had adopted the familiar scalene shape of a dragon's. He turned their force fully northward. *What if the darkness could be transmuted?*

A rumble could be heard as G'Oreal breathed in. A strong indicator of impatience — or displeasure. *Your mission is clear,* the dragon transmitted, and though he wasn't using his vocal cords, smoke still jetted from the sides of his mouth. *No tear, once inverted, has ever been reclaimed. Find it.* The jeweled eyes burned with intent. *Find it and deliver it north.*

A JOB FOR GWENDOLEN

"Knock, knock. Can I come in?"

Lucy swiveled in her chair, instinctively reaching back to her computer to clear the screen of words. Her wallpaper image of Stonehenge took the place of her latest journal entry.

As the door was half-open, David allowed himself entry anyway. "Hi. Am I interrupting anything?"

She shook her head. "Just . . . homework and stuff."

He glanced at Gwendolen, sitting by the keyboard. The IT dragon blushed and swished her tail. "Can we chat?"

Lucy curled her mouth. "Is it about last night?" The family "dinner" had not gone well. Despite Liz's plea for everyone to relax and enjoy the "reunion,"

114

Zanna had eventually gotten fed up with David and had stormed out, taking Alexa with her.

"No," he said, peering idly at the bookshelves. Amid Lucy's impressive collection of fiction were several copies of his own two books: *Snigger and the Nutbeast* and *White Fire*. He smiled and said, "Got a pen?"

She fished one out of a candy tin and handed it over. He pulled a pristine copy of *White Fire* off her shelf, opened the book at its title page, and began to write an inscription.

Frowning, she asked, "What are you doing?"

"Signing. Makes them more collectible," he said. He handed it to her to read.

For Lucy, I'm sorry you had to wait so long. Thank you for believing. David Rain xx

A tear escaped from the cusp of her eyelid.

"Hey," he said softly, crouching down. "I know I'm nearly famous, but don't you think this is over the top? The mascara police will be around at any moment."

Laughing, wet-eyed, she slapped his shoulder. "I thought you'd never come back."

"But I did," he said, tapping his thumbs together.

She plucked a tissue from a box decorated with photographs of hedgehogs and squirrels. For a moment, all she could do was stare at him. Then she asked, "Are you one of them, now?"

"Them?" he prompted.

Her gaze jumped nervously away from his face.

"I'm just David," he said. "Like I always was." He gave her back the pen. "Listen, I want you to help me, if you will."

She sniffed and made an eye patch with her hand. "How?"

"Zanna told me about the attack on your mom."

"David, I couldn't help it. Honest."

"I know. It's OK." He touched her arm. "I just need to ask you something."

Her face went through a series of contortions. "Is this about the Ix?"

"Partly, yes."

116

"I hate them," she said, slamming the pen back into the tin. "They're always there in a corner of my mind. Pushing me. Taunting me. As if I'm theirs." She wiped her mouth. "I hate what they made me do to Mom. Sometimes I can't go to sleep at night because I'm so scared they'll come back and get me."

"Listen to me," he said. He picked up her hands. "They're not inside you. Not anymore. But because they work in the planes of thought, your memory of them makes them feel active. You can learn to control that. You might even be able to use your feelings against them."

"How?" She didn't look convinced.

"You'll be able to sense their presence, long before anyone else can."

She shivered and said, "I don't want them near me."

He gave a nod of understanding. "Then just answer this. On Farlowe, when the Ix forced you to sculpt a model of their darkling, you left out the heart. You made the creature deliberately flawed, is that right?"

"Yes," she said.

He hummed in thought. "Can you remember what you were thinking when you made that decision?"

Lucy rolled her head to one side. "Do we have to talk about this?"

"It might help me to understand Gwillan's condition. These are highly intelligent beings, Lucy. Yet somehow you managed to fool them into believing the darkling was whole. Did you call on the auma of Gawain, for instance?"

Lucy crossed her legs and flicked out a foot. "All I remember about the heart was that I didn't want to put it into anything evil because a heart is supposed to be . . . a receptacle for love. While I was making it I tried to fill it with all the happy thoughts I could so that the darkling could never be entirely evil. I did think about Gawain, because he's strong and good. Then I sort of had the idea not to put the heart in the darkling's body anyway and . . . I just got away with it, I s'pose. Maybe the Ix aren't as smart as you think?"

David smiled at her. "Maybe not." He stood up quickly. "Thanks. That's really helpful. Oh, there's something else I want to ask you as well. A really big favor, actually."

"OK," she said, a little warily. She ran a hand inside her sweater and rubbed her shoulder.

"I want you to go to Scuffenbury Hill."

"Scuffenbury? Why?"

"There's a dragon there, remember?"

"So . . . ?" She spread her hands.

"I want someone I can trust to go and check it out."

A laugh escaped like a hiccup from her throat. "Erm . . ."

"I'll check with your mom. You'll be chaperoned, I promise."

"By you?"

"Uh-uh. I was thinking Tam Farrell."

Her jaw almost hit her knees. "Tam? Do you know him?"

"We've met — he kind of owes me a favor."

She chewed her upper lip. "I can't go anywhere with Tam."

David stared at her silently.

"No," she emphasized, looking uncomfortable. "Can't you go?"

He shook his head. "This is a job for a journalist — and a red-haired daughter of Guinevere."

Lucy played with a bouncy twist of that hair as if she'd just pulled a very short straw. "You're serious, aren't you?"

"Yes," he said.

But she laughed again, as if he must be teasing her. All the same she asked, "Is the dragon going to wake?"

"Maybe. If it's time."

"So . . . what would I have to do?"

"Observe. That's all."

She stretched her arms into the valley of her knees. "I don't know. That's kind of scary."

"Lucy, can you come down here, please? And if David's with you, tell him I'm ready."

"You don't have to think about it now," he said. He knuckled her arm and stepped toward the door. "Your mom and I are going to see Henry. Do you want to come?"

Grimacing, she dug her hands between her thighs. "I don't like hospitals much."

"That's all right. No pressure. See you later."

"David, wait. Can I ask you something?"

"Anything. Sure."

"Yesterday, in the garden, when that light went off on your watch, you looked like the white rabbit in *Alice in Wonderland* — sort of anxious."

He lifted his shoulders. "Maybe I was late for a very important date."

"It's not an ordinary watch though — is it?"

He turned and answered truthfully, "No. It's a communications device. It keeps me in touch."

"With the dragons? In the Arctic?"

"With the universe," he said, giving nothing away. "Just like you use that." He nodded at the computer. "I'll tell your mom you're busy with your homework."

Again she stopped him. "It's not homework," she blurted. She traced a finger over the keyboard. Committed now, she met his gaze. His eyes were like a dragon's: mesmerizing. "Would you be mad if I told you I was writing things?"

Gwendolen took in a gulp of air.

He looked at the computer screen, going through updates. "A story?"

"No. A sort of journal. About us. Gawain. The dragons. You."

He glanced at Gwendolen, swishing her tail again. "No, I'd have no objection to that. I think it's good for people to write things down. Helps you make sense of the jumble up here." He tapped the side of his head.

"Lucy, have you been abducted by aliens or what?" Liz called.

Lucy's feistiness returned at light speed. "Ugh, mothers! They're such a pain." Her hand moved purposefully over the mouse as she began to close the computer down. "Tell me I won't grow up to be like her."

David laughed. "On the contrary, I hope you'll grow up to be exactly like her. Can I read some of your journal? Just an extract, perhaps?"

Lucy gritted her teeth. From a tray beside the

computer she picked up a couple of sheets of paper. "All right, there's a bit here. But if you laugh at it I'll never speak to you again." She slapped it to his chest and swept from the room.

Gwendolen immediately made to follow, but a thought impulse from David kept her by the keyboard. He cast his eyes over the writing:

Last night, before dinner, we lit a candle for our neighbor, Henry Bacon. We kept a minute's silence in honor of his memory. Not that Henry's dead, just . . . close to it, Mom says. She went to the hospital to see him yesterday. She said he was like a pale pink eggshell, still and fragile, waiting to crack. The thought of it fills my chest with pain. I can't say Henry was a nice man. He was grumpy and annoying — and he HATED squirrels. But I will miss him all the same if he dies. Mom always said that his heart was in the right place, but Mom tends to see the best in everyone. He did let David stay with him once and he gave

Alexa some fairy pictures. OK, he thinks the sun shines out of Zanna, but anyone can make a mistake.

The thing I don't get about Henry is this: Somehow, he's managed to play a vital part in our understanding of dragons, despite the fact he's never believed in them. David talked about it over dinner last night. He said we shouldn't underestimate Henry's "contribution." For instance, on Henry's study wall is a blown-up photo of a polar bear looking up from the ice. The photo was taken by Henry's grandfather, and the bear, according to David, is none other than the one that Anders Bergstrom met/was part of/turned into. Bergstrom. Snowball. Icefire . . . dun dun dun. And now we find out that Henry had some photographs of dragontongue that had been burned into the walls of a cave on the Hella glacier. In other words, the grouchy old curmudgeon (love that word) had proof of the existence of dragons for years. Pity he might not live to know it.

At the end of the last dragon era, it came to a point where there were just twelve left. Driven from their aeries by wild-hearted men who knew no better than to kill a creature they couldn't tolerate and didn't understand, the dragons came together and decided to surrender. They didn't give themselves up for capture or sacrifice; they just refused to fight anymore. This, to me, is the saddest story ever. I grow tired of people who only think of dragons as fire-breathing, maiden-snatching, cave-dwelling monsters. Dragons had heart. Morals. Courage. Zanna always says they were the spiritual guardians of the Earth, and for once I agree with her. We don't really know what happened to the twelve. The legend is they separated and flew away to isolated places, remote volcanic islands and the like, where they could live out their lives in peace, and where they could eventually die in peace. Up until yesterday, the only location I knew about was the Tooth of Ragnar, where Gawain set down. Now, if David is telling the truth, there's one hidden underneath Glissington Tor, close to Scuffenbury Hill, not a million miles from here. Arthur, being the scientist he is, was skeptical about it. He reminded David that Glissington Tor was excavated, a tunnel dug into its center. How could they miss anything the size of a dragon, he said? David had a really cute answer. He made his shape-shifting dragon, Groyne, stand on all fours the way a natural dragon would, then he rolled a pea between Groyne's front legs. Voilà. The archaeologists dug under him. It's kind of funny when you think about it. . . .

David rested the pages back beside the keyboard.

Hrrr? said Gwendolen. Could she go now?

"No. I want you to do something," he said. "It has to remain a secret, Gwendolen."

The little dragon gulped as she felt his auma wave.

"Download the whole file and translate it into dragontongue. From the beginning. All of it."

Then what? the little dragon hurred.

"Store it — until Lucy's ready."

Gwendolen tilted her head.

"She's going to put it out on the Internet," he said.

A JOURNEY NORTH

Henry Bacon, by virtue of his prudent investments in a long-term personal health plan, had been given his own room at the exclusive, private hospital, Lightways, just a few miles south of Scrubbley. Liz and David arrived in the early afternoon and were immediately met in the reception area by a nurse who'd been attending to Henry the day before. Liz's smile of recognition quickly dissolved when she saw the look of professional sympathy on the nurse's face. Greeting them quietly, the nurse took them aside and said, "I'm sorry to tell you that Henry's condition has become considerably worse overnight. We don't expect him to see the day out."

Liz steepled her hands beneath her nose.

The nurse touched her arm. "I'm so sorry."

"Can we see him?" asked David.

"Yes, of course," the nurse said. "Just be aware that because he's very frail we may have to come in if things . . . develop. By the way, his sister, Agatha, is here. She was in Henry's room a few minutes ago, but I think she may have gone to find a sandwich."

"Thank you," Liz said, fighting off a sniff. She linked her arm through David's and pointed down a corridor. "This way."

Henry's bed was located on the first floor. A flowering cherry tree blocked most of the view from his double-paned window, but the room was light and airy nevertheless.

Henry was lying peacefully on his back, his head supported by the tilt of the bed and a cluster of plain white pillows. He was dressed in a hospital gown and his arms, which lay to either side of him, were bare from the elbow down. Some kind of breathing apparatus was plugged into his nose and he appeared to be connected to a machine that was silently monitoring his heartbeat in waves, though the exact point of contact was hidden by the gown.

Liz approached him first. She said, "Hello, Henry," and stroked his hair across his forehead. When he didn't respond she turned to the vase of flowers on his table and began to extract any dead leaves or stems. "This must be odd for you," she said, as David came up and peered at the sallow-faced old man. "Do you remember the last time you saw him?"

David nodded. "Just before I went to the Arctic." He laid the back of his hand against Henry's temple — and smiled.

"What's the matter?" said Liz.

"He's dreaming of polar bears. Take his hand. I'll show you."

Although her look suggested she was a little unsure, Liz slid her fingers over Henry's knuckles, surprised at how taut and bony they were.

"Now mine," said David, reaching across the bed.

The instant Liz touched him her mind was set free on a stunning landscape of cracked ice floes and pressure ridges flooded by a burnt orange sun. "Oh, my goodness, where are we?" she gasped.

"In Henry's imagination," said David, speaking directly into her mind. "In search of an answer to a riddle, I think. Relax. Let the images come to you. I'm going to guide him."

A moment later, Henry's awareness opened up fully and his voice, as clear as the polar sky, floated into the scene. "Ah, Hella," he said.

"Yes," said David. "Dream it, Henry." And using the power of his Fain teaching, he let Henry's thoughts pan back from the ocean, where the gigantic Hella glacier cut a path through the coastal mountains on its long imperceptible slide to the sea.

Henry rested a moment in the cold, watching a shower of Arctic terns arrowing west toward the mainland. "I hear ticking," he said.

"Then follow it," said David.

And in his mind Henry trudged toward the sound, ice crunching to the beat of his footsteps.

In a single, shifting moment of time David guided him to an untidy icescape, which could have been the ground-level ruins of a castle had the blocks not been chiseled by water and wind. At its farthest point was a mis-shapen arch. Under the arch sat a large male polar bear. The ticking was coming from between its front paws.

Suddenly, into the scene stepped a man. He wore waxed brown trousers, a thickly padded jacket, a cream balaclava, snowshoes, and gloves. Despite the bulkiness of his Arctic clothing it was easy to see that he was tall and physically well-proportioned. At his hip, he carried a rifle. The bear turned its rigid gaze on the man. It showed no sign of suspicion or distress.

The man drew to within twenty feet of it and stopped. He lowered his gun, then pushed back the fraying hood of his jacket and tore off his balaclava. He shook his hair loosely about his shoulders. It was straggly, almost golden, highlighted by catches of glinting frost. "You have my watch," he said.

The bear cast its almond eyes down at the time-piece — a pocket watch, still ticking despite the cold. "You may have it back if you come with me, Anders Bergstrom."

The golden-haired man looked all around him, before returning his focus to the bear. "Are you a spirit?"

"Sometimes," the bear said, lifting its chin. "I am Thoran, the first bear to walk this ice."

"And what is it you want with me — Thoran?"

"To commingle with your auma. So that you might take me to the hearts of men. I will show you great wonders in return."

The man called Anders Bergstrom switched his rifle to the opposite hand. "Why me?"

"Because of what you have seen."

"The writings in the caves? They are writings, aren't they?"

The bear pointed its black-tipped snout into the wind. "They are a record of a meeting. They are the words of dragons."

Anders Bergstrom laughed. Every fold of his clothing crackled as he crouched down and laid his gun upon the ice. With a finger, he drew three lines in the snow. "What does this symbol mean? I see it everywhere. Why do the Inuit fear it?"

The polar bear shuffled its shaggy-haired feet. "There is power in the symbol. It can be used for good or evil. Once, it caused a war across the ice and came to be known as the mark of Oomara. The lines represent the lives of men, bears, and dragons. But they are not in harmony. This is why they do not meet. Yet the force which keeps the lines apart also holds them close, so that each always dreams of alliance with the others."

"What is this force?" the man asked boldly.

The polar bear raised its snout. "You might call it consciousness, Anders Bergstrom. Bears would point to the colors in the sky and call it the dancing spirit of the North. Dragons would call it the breath of Godith."

Bergstrom ran the knuckles of his glove across his chin. "Will the lines ever meet?"

The bear took a breath. It seemed to create the first hint of a blizzard, which ruffled the hairs around its stubby little ears. "Take off your glove," it said.

Bergstrom leveled his gaze.

The bear grunted and nodded at the symbol of Oomara. The lines were beginning to glow.

The explorer pulled off his glove. Without waiting to be asked, he laid three fingers into the lines. His hand quickly turned a bright translucent blue and the ice all around him shook. "Unity will come through fire," he whispered. "Fire? In the ice? How can that be?"

"Come with me," said Thoran. He was standing in the archway, pointing north. Air billowed over his shoulder as he spoke. "All you have to do is pick up the watch."

Anders Bergstrom looked back the way he'd come. He looked for the shapes and colors of his camp, but the wind had been busy, covering his tracks.

When he turned again, Thoran was padding away.

Bergstrom knelt down and picked up the timepiece. He set it on his hand like a shining jewel. In shape it was nothing but a standard pocket watch. But where there had once been an antique clock face there was now an impression of a solar system whirling around inside the casing. Bergstrom snapped it shut. The ice upon his eyebrows cracked with the eager movements of his thoughts. Once more, he stared ahead at the bear. Then he threw away his other glove and stepped through the arch.

"Mmm," a voice grunted. It was Henry Bacon.

David's thought waves surged toward him. "Now you know what happened in the watch story, Henry. Now your mind can be at peace."

Henry grunted again. Then (to Liz's shock) he appeared in the scene, dressed in trousers and a golfing sweater and the spotted tie that was his everyday trademark.

Somewhere on the periphery of their entwined thoughts, a machine began to beep.

A shift of time took Henry to the brink. One more step and he would find himself on the far side of the ice. In the distance, Thoran was waiting.

"Henry?" Liz said, projecting her worries into her thoughts.

"Time I was off, Mrs. P.," he said, speaking back as if he could see her. He smiled and rubbed his hands together.

From far away came the sound of people running.

The old man's eyes rose up to meet David's. "Good to see you, boy. Hair's a disgrace. Get yourself to a barber, eh?"

"I'll attend to it," David said. "Go forward, Henry. Take your freedom. Explore, like you've always wanted to. Look through the archway, into the light."

Henry took a deep snort of polar air. "You'll remember me to Suzanna?"

"Yes, I will."

"Mmm. Don't forget to feed my fish."

With that, Henry Bacon stepped through the arch. David squeezed Liz's hand and let her go.

The dreaming broke.

Almost immediately they were bundled aside by a nurse and a young Asian doctor.

"His heart's stopped," said the nurse.

"Call a team. We'll need a defib — now," the doctor said, pulling the covers off Henry's chest.

"No, you will leave him," a stern voice said from the back of the room.

Everyone turned to look at the elderly woman standing in the doorway. "He is at peace. Let him go." She looked pointedly at David, kindly at Liz. "You must be Elizabeth," she said. "I am Agatha, Henry's sister." Her gaze ran the length of the figure in the bed.

The doctor checked the monitor, looked at Henry, looked at Agatha, and obediently accepted the situation.

Liz turned away with tears in her eyes.

Henry Bacon, her neighbor of some fifteen years, was no more.

FUNERAL BLUES

Agatha Bacon turned out to be every bit as organized as her late brother. In the hospital, she gave her thanks to Liz and David for visiting Henry, but asked to be alone with him at his hour of passing. They did not hear from her again until later that evening when a card was dropped into number forty-two explaining that a modest funeral ceremony would be held at St. Augustine's Church in a few days. Henry would be buried in the graveyard there. The family were invited to pay their last respects.

Come the day, Lucy, who loved the chance to dress up for anything, wore a knee-length skirt with a matching black crossover top. Her wild red hair was pinned up in a clip, the odd strand winding a stalactite path toward her shoulders. Her mother, a little more conservative, chose a simple skirt and blouse. Black and cream. Pearl brooch at the neck. Both of the Pennykettle women were impressive, but they were each about to be eclipsed by Zanna.

The young mother stepped out of the house in a chic black dress, belted at the waist. It flared slightly just below her knees and swept around each hip and curve with the design and grace of a very expensive Italian sports car. For the first time in many years she had applied an amount of dark makeup to her eyes, reinventing her gothic roots. Her glossy heels took her to over six feet. She was the only member of the family to wear a hat: a modest lace affair, tilted at a thin Saturnian angle.

"Anyone would think she'd won an Oscar," Lucy tutted, watching her part sister working the catwalk that was the Pennykettles' driveway. "I bet she's only done it to tick David off."

"Don't be unkind. She looks fabulous," said Liz.

The chauffeur sent to pick them up clearly thought so, too. His jaw was almost dragging on the pavement as he rushed to open the door for her.

Zanna got in discreetly, holding her hat. The weather was breezy. Pollen in the air. Henry himself would have probably said it was the perfect day for his own funeral.

Alexa, in stark contrast to her mother, was dressed entirely in white. She had a cardboard fairy pinned to her shoulder (her personal tribute to Henry). She jumped into the backseat alongside Zanna, full of excitement for the forthcoming ride.

Lucy glanced down the driveway at David, who was guiding Arthur toward the car. "Wow, you look weird," she said.

David smiled and handed Arthur into the care of the driver. "I was hoping for 'smart but casual,' to be honest."

"Is that one of Arthur's suits?"

David struck a pose. "This year's must-have fashion."

"You look very handsome," said Liz, adjusting his lapels and brushing a speck or two of cotton off the jacket. "I'd be proud . . . to call you my son."

That remark produced a grimace from Lucy, who turned her head to look at Agatha Bacon and the plump-suited gentleman accompanying her. They had just stepped out of Henry's house and were taking the leading car.

"What's she like?" asked Lucy.

"A female version of Henry," Liz replied.

"Should be a fun party afterward, then."

That earned Lucy an icy glare. "Get into the car. Now."

St. Augustine's Church was a well-preserved eighteenth-century building halfway up the rise of Croxley Hill, looking back over the south side of Scrubbley. To Liz's surprise their party of six was the largest present. Apart from a few colleagues from the town library, where Henry had worked for most of his life, there were no other friends or family besides Agatha (who, Lucy said, reminded her of Miss Havisham, "the old mad cow" from *Great Expectations*). But just as the service was about to begin, another figure strolled through the arched doorway. A woman in a two-piece business suit.

"Oh, no. What's she doing here?" Liz gasped.

Zanna lifted her head from her prayers. Gwilanna was walking toward the altar.

David, standing with Lucy in the pew behind Zanna, gripped Zanna's arm to prevent her from moving. "No. Not here."

"Get off me," Zanna hissed, shaking him away. She glared at the sibyl, who nodded at her coolly and slid into a pew on the opposite side.

"Dear friends . . . ," the minister began, over a wisp of organ music.

"Not for long," Lucy said below her breath. *Might be a fun party after all,* she thought.

The service was short and passed without incident. The small congregation then followed Henry's coffin through the graveyard. As they shuffled down a path between the gravestones and the yew trees, Liz, puffy-eyed but still together, gave a firm order that no one was to engage Gwilanna until they were out of the church grounds. The sibyl had tagged on to the rear of the mourners, but well away from the Pennykettle family. Zanna, a hurricane bound in black, walked tall behind the figurehead of Agatha Bacon, dragging Alexa along at her side like a teddy bear with an outstretched paw.

At the back of the family group, Lucy was sticking close to David. She was peering over her shoulder through the trees. "Leave it," he said. "I'll deal with Gwilanna afterward."

"It's not her. I'm looking at the church," Lucy muttered. "Why do they always have gargoyles? They make me crawl. They remind me of . . ."

"Darklings?" David said.

Lucy moved a little closer, taking reassurance from the brush of his shoulder. "What is a darkling? I've never understood how I was able to make one. I'd never even seen one before the Ix got me."

David checked ahead. They were still some way from the mound of earth that marked Henry's burial site. "That's not strictly true."

Lucy threw him a quizzical look.

So he explained: "Long ago, when the Ix became a breakaway part of the Fain, they began to seek control of the medium of the universe that Arthur would call dark matter. To do that, they needed to combat the dragons. So they developed a template for what might be called an antidragon or darkling. A darkling is far smaller and less graceful than a dragon, but extremely robust and agile nonetheless."

"Can they kill dragons?"

"In a straight fight, no. That's because the Ix have never been able to create the dark fire to delumine one. If they did, a darkling would be a thousand times more deadly. The only way to create dark fire is to invert a source of spiritual purity, such as you might find in a dragon like Gwillan or a selfless act of love or a moment of inspired creativity. That's kind of where you come in."

"Me?"

"Humankind — well, near-human in your case. Apart from dolphins, dragons, and a couple of other species, humans are the only sentient creatures capable of displaying the altruistic emotions that might, under the right circumstances, be inverted into dark fire.

"Thousands of years ago, the Ix tried an experiment in cumulative terror. Knowing that humans had a fantastic capacity for imaginative reconstruction, the Ix planted the image of a near-perfect darkling into the murkiest corners of our psyche and let it ferment in the playground of our thoughts."

"So we'd see it in our nightmares?"

"Nightmares, stories, dimly held beliefs. People have been dragging the gargoyle — or the grotesque, to give it its correct name — from their memories ever since and reviving it on churches and in works of art. This is how you were able to create the monster out of obsidian during your capture. You simply found that elemental seed in your mind."

"OK, stop now, you're making me feel sick."

David looked up. The mourners were beginning to gather around the grave. He placed a hand lightly on Lucy's arm and stopped her walking. "One last thing. About your journal. I thought the bit you showed me was excellent."

"Oh, cool," she said, blushing like a plum. Now she, too, was glancing ahead. "Shouldn't we talk about this later?" She could see her mother wondering why she was dallying. The four men carrying Henry's coffin were preparing to lower it into the ground.

David toyed with a loose cuff link. "Why don't you put it on my Web site as a blog — coded, perhaps, by Gwendolen?"

"What?" Lucy wrinkled her nose as if she'd just sniffed a lemon. "Don't be dumb. I can't put stuff about our dragons on there. People read it, David. They'd think we were freaks."

"Not if they were like-minded people," he said.

Once again she threw him a questioning look.

"You're not alone, Lucy. Whatever Gwilanna may have told you" — he glanced back the way they'd

147

come; there was no sign of the sibyl for the moment — "you and your mom are not the only living daughters of Guinevere."

Lucy gulped. Her upper body began to shake.

He picked up her hand and kissed it softly. "Pretty soon dragons will be commonplace," he said. "Trust me, you're no freak. You're a wonder of creation." He tipped his head back. "Just like your sisters."

Lucy had been dreading the final part of the service and David's revelation didn't make it any easier. Even so, she managed to compose herself for the burial itself. It was surreal, she thought, to watch a box containing the remains of a man she'd known for all but a few months of her life being lowered into a hole in the ground. She fought back a tear when her mom followed Agatha Bacon's lead and threw a handful of earth onto the coffin. But what finally set her off was the sight of a gray squirrel, sitting in the grand horse chestnut tree whose branches swept out over the hole. It was only there a moment before it chirruped and ran away. Alexa saw it, too, and pointed it out. A single five-thumbed chestnut leaf tumbled gently into the grave, burying with it the age-old squabbles Lucy had had with Henry over the right to have squirrels running free in the Crescent. At that point, she broke down in her mother's arms. David, meanwhile, looked across the plot at Zanna. She was strikingly wistful, lost in her own cherished memories of the neighbor who had helped her so wisely, so often. Arthur was bent in prayer, and Agatha Bacon was standing at the foot of the grave like royalty. She neither wept nor seemed to take breath, her gaze fixed firmly on the coffin name-plate, gradually being concealed by soil. Her companion, showing a respectful solemnity, puckered his lips and stood just behind her, the way he'd done for the entire proceedings.

Eventually, it was Agatha herself who broke rank and went around the grave, shaking hands and greeting the mourners. The only one she failed to acknowledge was Gwilanna. The sibyl had stayed in the sanctuary of the trees throughout the burial rite. But as Agatha led the walk back to the cars, David dropped off the pace and started sidling back toward the grave. Gwilanna was over it, sifting her own handful of dirt.

He was about to challenge her when Zanna's voice suddenly reared behind him. "You!" David caught her as she tried to sweep past, on her way to do murder, by the look of it. "Give me one good reason why I shouldn't push you in there as well, you witch, even if it would be a sacrilege against a decent man!"

"I will give you three good reasons," said Gwilanna, with her typical arrogant zeal. "First, I still have this" — she twisted Gawain's isoscele through her fingers — "which I could use to cast a spell that would boil your blood if you dared to attack me." She swiped her palms. "Second, Elizabeth's child will die at birth if I am not present. Third, I want to make a deal."

Zanna pushed forward again, still held tight in David's grip. "You can go and play with the mushroom fairies. I will never make a deal with you!"

"I was talking to the boy wonder!" Gwilanna snapped.

David finally pulled Zanna away, pushing her several yards farther up the path. "No deals," he said.

The sibyl's face contorted with fury. "Then you'll die," she snarled. "All of you. Is that what you want for your pretty little daughter? They'll come for her, when they know what she is."

David turned his back and walked away.

"If the darklings find her she won't have a chance! Not even Gawain himself could protect her. You're nothing but a meddler and a common thief, boy. Give the fire back to me!"

David whipped around to face her again. "You're the one in danger," he said, with menace. "Leave the isoscele where you stand. It won't be long before Gawain will be looking for that."

"You can't raise him," she hissed. "He's stone, broken."

"Not while his ichor is dripping through your fingers.

He's in Liz's dragons. In the ice. In me. Leave the isoscele. Run. Hide. There are dragons who would willingly see you dead. I repeat, there are no deals."

"Fool," Gwilanna growled, closing her fingers in a fist around the scale. "You're right, boy. The auma of Gawain is deep inside you — I can feel your heart resisting my squeeze. But for how long? Even a dragon has to sleep. It's only a matter of time." And with that the air bubbled and the sibyl was gone.

"What was all that about?" Zanna demanded as David came sloping up the path toward her. She banged his shoulder to make him stop.

"Nothing. It's just talk."

"Don't lie to me." Zanna slapped his face, leaving him looking at the grass verge beside them. "What did she mean?"

"She has no control over me, Zanna."

"I'm not talking about you. I'm talking about Alexa."

"Excuse me."

The warring couple looked up.

Agatha Bacon was waiting on the path. Black dress, black boots, black laced gloves. She looked like a phantom, Zanna decided. An old Victorian ghost.

"The cars are ready to return us to the Crescent. And your charming daughter seems anxious to see you."

"Yes, forgive me," Zanna said, flustered. She moved her clutch bag from one hand to the other, straightened her dress, and walked on quickly.

David followed a little more sedately, stopping momentarily as he came shoulder-to-shoulder with Agatha.

"You —?" he began.

"The cars," she said, refusing to engage him.

He nodded and continued up the path. When he reached the church and Alexa's eager hand, Agatha Bacon was still among the trees, looking back at the spot where Gwilanna had been.

LAST WILL AND TESTAMENT

The only people to return to Henry's house were the Pennykettle clan, Agatha, and her companion. Several plates of food had been set out on the table, waiting to be uncovered. Liz, with Agatha's approval, adopted her usual motherly role and handed out paper plates and napkins. A few minutes later everyone, barring Zanna, was eating. Zanna had taken a seat on the end of the sofa and was directing operations with Alexa, primarily the avoidance of chicken drumsticks beating greasy rhythms on the child's dress.

Agatha Bacon, eating a piece of mushroom quiche, sat very properly in the armchair opposite Henry's favorite. That position was occupied by her over-round companion, whom she finally introduced once everyone was settled.

"This is my brother's lawyer. He is a partner in the firm of Hamilton, Portley, and Smythe."

"Are they local?" asked Arthur.

"They are from where I live and where my brother was born."

"So are you Mr. Port —?"

"Hedley Hamilton," he said, cutting Lucy off. He maneuvered like a bloated rodent and from the floor beside him picked up the most distressed leather briefcase Liz had ever seen.

"Hedley is here to read Henry's will," said Agatha. "Of which you are all beneficiaries to some extent."

Lucy spat a droplet of tea at the fish tank. "You're joking," she said, inviting a warning glare from her mother. "I'm in Henry's will?" After all the arguments they'd had? He'd probably left her his favorite rattrap.

Agatha's gaze moved sideways to Liz. "Henry always

spoke fondly of your family. He often talked about your pottery creations. I would like to see one — if I may?"

"I'm afraid they're all next door," said Liz.

"I can fetch one!" said Alexa, jumping up. She looked hopefully over her shoulder at Liz.

"Lexie, sit down," said Zanna.

"No." Agatha's voice overruled her. "Come closer, child, let me look at you."

Zanna cast a concerned glance at David, but he remained sitting calmly, sipping a cup of tea.

Alexa came up and almost curtsied before the old woman.

A ragged pattern of wrinkles formed around Agatha's prune-colored eyes. She reached out and lifted Alexa's chin. "You are a delightful creature," she said. "I see you're wearing a fairy, child. Do you like fairies?"

"Yes," said Alexa.

Agatha said, "My brother liked fairies."

"What?" Lucy again. She left her mouth open for

added effect. "Mr. Bacon thought anything like that was weird."

"Of course he did," Agatha said. "The men in our families have never been able to come to terms with the etheric world, but they can never quite step away from it either. One only has to look at Henry's collection of books to know it. Everything from Native American legends to the Loch Ness Monster to the works of Bram Stoker. He was drawn to 'weirdness.' He just didn't know why. It frustrated him all his life."

"Who are you?" said Zanna, broaching the question that Lucy had been dying to ask.

Agatha responded with a hairline smile. "You of all people should know the answer to that."

"You're a sibyl," said Arthur.

Liz brought her cup down onto her saucer.

David broke a cheese straw in half. He placed one end in his mouth and said nothing.

"Yes," said Agatha, "just like Suzanna and the woman in the graveyard."

"She's my aunty Gwyneth," said Alexa before Zanna could speak out and stop her.

"Is she now?" Agatha said. She didn't seem the least bit surprised. "Yes, I can understand why 'Aunty Gwyneth' would be quite attached to you."

"What's that supposed to mean?" said Zanna.

Agatha cast her regal gaze over her. "You don't trust me, do you, girl? Understandable. I was young and headstrong once. But given there is an invisible spirit — probably a small dragon — watching my every move, and that the exceedingly quiet young man to my right has scanned me several times for any signs of wickedness — and found none — I think you can assume I wish you no harm." She turned again to Liz. "Tell me, did your 'aunt' ever visit this house?"

"Occasionally," said Liz, still in shock. "She and Henry . . ." But what could she say? That Gwilanna was another piece of "weirdness" he'd been attracted to?

Agatha raised a hand, indicating Liz need go no further. "I think it's time we heard Henry's will. Hedley!"

"What? Oh, yes. Yes, of course." Mr. Hamilton reached for his briefcase again. From it, he drew out a legal-looking document and a glasses case even more battered than his bag.

He put on his spectacles, cleared his throat, and started to speak. "Well, now. Yes, here we are. Mr. Bacon — Henry Augustus Charles — left a remarkably concise will, to which he added one or two significant codicils over the years. He was unmarried, as you know, and therefore without dependents. He was a thrifty man who looked after his investments and inheritances wisely. By late middle age he would have had no real need to work. I suspect it was his love of books and his desire to be of service to the people of Scrubbley that kept him at his library desk. He died a wealthy man.

"It will come as no surprise perhaps to learn that he has left a sum of twenty thousand dollars to the town council to aid the redevelopment of the children's library area overlooking the public gardens. He was very fond of promoting reading among young people."

"Oh, Henry," Liz said. Arthur patted her hand.

Mr. Hamilton turned a page. "There are one or two other minor bequests but I'll skip to the main part of the will, the paragraphs which concern those present." He coughed like a boiler in need of service. "'To my dear sister, Agatha Bacon, I leave the sum of fifty thousand dollars, plus any items of sentimental value which she might wish to take, at her absolute discretion, from my house.'"

"Wow," whistled Lucy. She knocked her fists together. "He never even bought me a flipping ice cream."

"Lucy, be quiet! Show some respect!" Liz shook her head in dismay. "Sorry, Mr. Hamilton. Please go on."

Hedley raised his gaze above his spectacles. "'To my neighbor, Mrs. Elizabeth Pennykettle, I also leave the sum of fifty thousand dollars —'"

"What?!" screeched Lucy, jumping out of her seat.

This time, her mother was just as voluble. "Oh, my goodness! That can't be right. Read it again. There's been a mistake."

"My brother never made mistakes," said Agatha. "Not with matters of a legal nature. Go on, Hedley."

"'— of which an appropriate sum will be set aside for the education of Lucy Pennykettle, through the best university obtainable.'"

Zanna opened her bag and took out a tissue. She was practically in tears.

Hedley Hamilton turned his gaze toward David. "'To my one-time tenant, David Rain, I leave my entire collection of books and Arctic memorabilia in the hope they might further his literary career, this to be modified by any claim Agatha might wish to have on said items.'"

"I have none," said Agatha brusquely.

Mr. Hamilton noted it. He tapped the document and peered at David. "There is, however, a slight condition attached to this bequest. Mr. Bacon wishes for these items to remain intact, in the house library upstairs, if the new owner is in agreement."

"But how's that going to work?" said Liz. "Won't the property be sold? It would be unfair to expect the buyer to preserve a whole library."

"Well, that brings me to the final announcement," Hedley Hamilton said. He turned another page. "'To Suzanna Martindale, I leave my house and its entire contents —'"

"Hhh!" gasped Liz and Lucy together (Alexa joined in for good measure). David merely smiled and glanced at Zanna, who was shocked into a state of motionless beauty.

"' — barring any claims as stated above, for the upkeep of herself and her daughter, Miss Alexa Martindale, plus the residue of my estate.'" Mr. Hamilton produced a sheet of figures. "Which, after legal expenses, executor's fees, and the payment of outstanding utility bills will amount, I suspect, to somewhere in the region of thirty-eight thousand dollars. Congratulations, Ms. Martindale. I can tell you from personal acquaintance with Henry that he held you in the deepest, most gentlemanly regard."

"No," said Zanna, running with tears. She stood up and gaped at the ceiling, as if she was appealing to Henry's spirit. "Henry, you can't do this."

Liz stood up and put her arms around her. "Sweetheart, it's OK. Come on. Sit down."

"No," Zanna said, shaking fiercely. "I mean, I know he was kind, but —"

Mr. Hamilton recleared his throat. "Erm, there is one other inclusion attached to your bequest, Ms. Martindale. It has no monetary bearing, but I'm legally obliged to mention it to you."

Liz waved a hand at him. "Yes, go on."

Hedley tapped his polished black brogues against the carpet. "This concerns you as well, Mr. Rain."

David tilted his head.

"I understand you've been away for some while?"

"I have," said David, careful to look at no one but the lawyer.

"Mmm. Your return prompted Henry to add a short, but . . . urgent codicil to his will, which was also done in light of the knowledge about the unfortunate state of his health."

"Oh, Hedley, do stop bumbling and get on with it!" snapped Agatha.

"Yes, of course," said Mr. Hamilton, pushing his glasses a little higher up his nose. "Well, it's simply this. Although the deeds of this property will be transferred into Ms. Martindale's name and will be entirely at her disposal, Henry wished that his library remain in place in the hope that you two, erm, rekindle your relationship and perhaps eventually ... marry one day?"

"What?" said Zanna, whirling around, almost elbowing Liz in the ribs.

"Wow," muttered Lucy, under her breath. "Everybody back to the church ..."

Alexa bounded straight to her father, bouncing energetically off his knees. "Hhh! Are you getting married, Daddy?"

He looked up, hoping to engage Zanna's eyes, but by then the new owner of number 41 Wayward Crescent was heading out the door.

AN AUDIENCE
WITH AGATHA

Agatha Bacon and Hedley Hamilton announced they would stay for another two days, Agatha's primary objective being the management of Henry's outstanding affairs. But this she achieved with the minimum of fuss by four o'clock on the first afternoon: another testament, she said, to Henry's skills of organization. So, having some time to spare, she spent the early evening in Liz and Arthur's company, mainly admiring the Dragons' Den. She said little else about her talents as a sibyl and did not push for any more information from Liz. But on the second day, the telephone rang in Liz's kitchen and Zanna was the one to pick it up.

"Hello."

"I would like to see you." It was Agatha's voice.

Zanna did her best to stall. Since the unveiling of Henry's will, all she'd wanted to do was shut herself away — and think. "Well, I'm . . ."

"Eleven o'clock," said Agatha. "Here. Alone."

The phone went down.

Zanna glanced at Gauge. The timing dragon showed her ten thirty-five. She sighed and looked out across the garden. Now, thanks to Henry, she could be the mistress of her own home. If she decided to stay. Somewhere upstairs, she could hear Liz and Lucy arguing. Arthur was at work and Alexa was playing. And David? Out with the shadows again. At least he'd done the decent thing and stayed out of her way.

Leaving Gretel with instructions to entertain Alexa, Zanna got ready to go next door. She was walking down the hallway, shouldering her bag, when Lucy came thundering down the stairs.

"You going out?"

"Next door, to see Agatha. Not that it's any business of yours."

Even so, the news seemed to please the girl. "Where's David?" She was bubbling over with excitement, the kind associated with the advantage of holding a secret.

"How should I know?" Zanna said curtly.

"Well, you're his fiancée, aren't you?"

The temperature in the hall dropped several degrees. Gruffen, fearing violence, shot away to fetch Liz.

Zanna rounded the foot of the stairs and backed Lucy up them another two steps. "Don't you dare taunt me. Not unless you want to feel the power of this . . ." She dragged three purple-colored fingernails back and forth across the mark of Oomara.

"Zanna?" Liz was quickly on the top step, her hand reaching down into the well for calm. "Zanna? Honey? What's the matter?"

The young sibyl pulled away, her dark eyes drilling into Lucy's terror.

And the girl, despite her fright, should have left the argument there. But the ability to concede with minimal loss of face had never been part of her makeup. So she chose to blurt out, "He won't want you anyway when I tell him what's happened."

And Zanna, her heart in enough cruel shreds, should have known better than to listen to this taunt. Instead, she swung around and faced the girl again. "What? What's happened?"

Thereafter, the victory was Lucy's. "I've received an e-mail for him." She paused, long enough to enjoy the flicker of doubt in Zanna's eyes and to revel in her own superiority. "From Africa. From Sophie."

"Oh, Lucy . . . ," Liz groaned, but Zanna had already turned the doorknob and gone out in a blur of anger, before there was any chance of making amends.

Outside, she fell back against the door in a wretched state of tightened muscles and unshed tears. It took her fully ninety seconds to maneuver the heartache into the least disruptive channel and draw down calm into her mind again. She blew her nose and looked at the Crescent. It was a normal, slightly overcast spring day in Scrubbley. A young woman was wobbling by on a bike. A whistling postman was doing his rounds. It was a world away from dragons and Arctic mists. Zanna drew a breath and righted herself, then set off for number forty-one, unaware she was being watched by two large black birds in the sycamore tree just across the street. . . .

Agatha Bacon sensed at once that the young woman before her was in some kind of turmoil.

"I'd rather not talk about it," Zanna said as she settled once again on the end of the sofa. Her sofa. She briefly explored the leather with her fingers.

Agatha, slightly less imposing today in a pale pink blouse and shapeless skirt, poured tea. "Affairs of the heart can be the undoing of any sibyl. You are at the age where that discovery is becoming most painful. Women like you and I rarely find love. This man —"

"He's not a man," Zanna heard herself saying.

"David," Agatha continued, "is unlike anyone I've ever met."

"You can say that again."

169

Agatha snapped her fingers. Zanna felt her neck muscles lock. Just like that, the old woman had thrown a physical spell. "Listen to me, girl. And listen well. I've brought you here today to give you advice. You're strong in spirit but weak in resolve. You must learn to control your wildness or at least channel it. That mark on your arm has extraordinary power and you have a grave responsibility to use it wisely. It will destroy you if you don't. What use would you be to your exquisite daughter then?"

Zanna felt the spell loosen. Rubbing the back of her neck she said, "I think I do a pretty good job with Alexa. I'm bringing her up as a normal child, as far away from . . ."

"People like me?" Agatha took a sip of tea.

". . . magicks as I can reasonably get. I don't want her playing with . . ."

"Her powers? What exactly can she do?"

Zanna glanced at the fish, weaving their own spells around the aquarium architecture. "She seems to be able to draw the future. And we think she's telepathic."

"With you?"

"No, her father. She usually knows his whereabouts, unless he blocks her."

"Fascinating," said Agatha, looking into a distant corner of the room. The fish, Zanna noticed, all turned and swam in the direction of her gaze. "What else can you tell me about the girl?"

Zanna lifted her shoulders. "Nothing. She's just a happy, carefree little girl."

"Living in a house of flying clay."

Zanna sighed and said, "So you know that some of them have a spark of white fire?"

Agatha Bacon gave her nostrils some exercise. She slanted her eyes as if the naïvete of this statement was quite beyond belief. "In the graveyard, you argued bitterly with her father after the sibyl Gwyneth had told you something."

"Gwilanna," said Zanna, grating her teeth. "Her real name's Gwilanna. She only calls herself Gwyneth in 'lowly human company.' She seems to have been around since the dawn of time; she's certainly got the skin tone for it. She was screaming that evil forces would come for Alexa once they knew what she was. But that's Gwilanna for you, always talking out of her antique butt."

Agatha Bacon pressed her hands together, making her green veins pulse. "That woman is a poor role model, I grant you, but she is by no means a fool. She is not to be underestimated. Like me, she detects something in your daughter's auma that sets the girl apart from sibyls, shamans, and other 'weird' folk as my brother might have said. Yet you cannot see it and neither can I. Perhaps Gwilanna can. The child's father must certainly know."

Zanna started to chew her lip. She abandoned the action when she realized her anger might result in the need for a couple of stitches. She thought back to what David had said in the kitchen. *This world is ready to accept a new species.* "I ought to get back to her."

"Wait." Agatha beckoned her close. "I want to give you something before you leave."

Zanna looped her hair and came across the room.

"Your arm. Show me the scar."

Though wary, Zanna drew back her sleeve.

"How advanced are you in the healing arts?"

"Some," said Zanna. "I have a potions dragon, and a shop that deals in natural remedies. We've been closed for several days, because of Henry. That's something else I ought to get back to."

Agatha raised one hand and placed it carefully over the scar. Her fingers were as strong and as able as a chimp's. "Don't flinch," she said. "Let me assess the power. Call upon your inner strength if it pains you."

"What are you doing?"

"Improving your education, girl. I don't have the time to spend teaching you my skills, but I can transfer some of them through this. Was it Gwilanna who marked you?"

"Who else?"

Agatha raised her gaze. Another don't-talk-disrespectfully look. "Believe it or not, in a perverse kind of way, she wants you to progress to the highest levels."

Zanna raised a doubtful eyebrow. Then, despite Agatha's instructions, she couldn't help but gasp again as a pulse of energy raced up her arm and around her neck to the spinal cord. The effect was like a firecracker shooting color and wisdom into her brain. When it stopped, Zanna was aware that sections of her mind she'd never thought present had suddenly opened, and all were ripe with healing knowledge.

"Do not delve now," Agatha advised her. "You will only make yourself faint. Let the learning come when you need it. I'd like to leave you my card." She flourished a hand and the card was there. "If I can ever be of assistance, please contact me."

The card was blank. But when Zanna ran her thumb across it, a picture of Agatha appeared.

"Let me tell you something about Henry," said the sibyl. "He once confided to me that if he could have had a daughter, you would be her. I approve of his choice. Wild you may be, but there is a beautiful integrity in your auma. Take care of this house and it will take care of you. Go carefully, girl. I sense danger ahead. You will meet the sibyl Gwilanna again. Do not seek her out. She will come to you — probably in a guise you trust. Stay within the company of dragons, Suzanna" — she paused and squeezed the young woman's hand — "and make your peace with David."

THE BIRDS

David aside, making peace with Liz was the first thing on Zanna's mind when she returned to number forty-two. But that had never been a problem in the past, and neither did it prove to be on this occasion. As soon as the two women saw each other there were smiles and a hug of common understanding.

"I'm sorry," Liz whispered, swinging Zanna lightly as though she were a pendulum of her own dismay. "You'd think Lucy would have grown more sensible over the years, but there's still a huge slice of brat inside her."

"Where is she?" said Zanna, putting down her bag.

"Grounded. In her room. Probably plotting our mutual destruction."

Zanna laughed. "I'll go and talk to her."

"No." Liz held her arm. "I appreciate the thought, but she needs to learn a lesson."

Zanna gave a nod of understanding. "In that case, I think I'll go and open the shop for a couple of hours. My poor customers must be wondering where I've gone."

"Good idea," said Liz. "Take Lexie with you. She'd appreciate a change of scenery, I think."

Zanna turned toward her room, hesitated, and looked back. "On the subject of me and Lexie, I've been doing a lot of thinking in the past few days. I've decided that I'd like us to live in Henry's house. You've been so kind, but we can't go on being your tenants forever. If it's OK with you we'll move out right away. It's not like we've very far to go, is it? Thank you for everything you've done for us, Liz."

Liz opened her arms and they hugged again. "Everyone in this house has been shocked by Henry's death, but to have you as a neighbor in his place is a blessing. Anytime you need me, just . . ."

"Knock on the wall?"

"Exactly." They separated, smiling again. But then Liz's face grew slowly more pensive until Zanna was eventually forced to ask her, "What?"

"I know this is difficult, considering the will, but what are your thoughts about David?"

Zanna sighed quietly and gathered one half of her hair into her fist. "Well, every cloud . . . as they say. When I've transferred my things next door, he can have his old room back, can't he?"

Some ten minutes later, Zanna ushered Alexa into the hall, buttoned her into a coat, and told her they were going into town. Gretel decided she was bored and wanted to go, too. Zanna zipped the dragon into her bag. Then with a wave at Liz, who was cuddling a rather sleepy-looking Bonnington, the party of three went out.

Zanna usually drove the mile-long journey to The Healing Touch, a shop she had bought just a couple of years before, but on this occasion she took Alexa by the hand and headed for the pedestrian route they called North Walk. This was a wide asphalt path that cut through the professional heart of Scrubbley. The houses that ran along one side were mostly occupied by lawyers or accountants. Zanna adored the architecture of them and liked to imagine herself sipping morning coffee on the neat, railed balconies or holding dinner parties in the high-curtained stately rooms.

Alexa preferred the other side of North Walk. There were houses and offices along here, too, and a fine museum of art. But dotted between the buildings were squares and rectangles of urban grassland, shaded by vast maple and oak trees. Lucy had once written a story for school about two squirrels that lived on the edge of such a square. The name of the story was "Bodger and Fuffle from Twenty-three Along." The number twenty-three referred to the broken glass lantern, on the twenty-third lamppost from the top end of the

Walk, where the squirrels had built their home. One of Alexa's favorite games was to count the lampposts aloud, even though she knew exactly which one (by the double-mouthed blue mailbox just beyond the museum) was home to the legendary squirrels.

So Zanna was happy to let her bowl ahead, zigzagging wildly across the path, slapping each post in turn. Fortunately, there were few other people about, so no one was in danger of sustaining an injury from a collision with the enviable zest of youth. As they reached eighteen along and turned the slight bend that would bring them to within distant sight of the High Road and the town, they had the path to themselves. This was Zanna's favorite stretch. The path narrowed here and the branches of the trees came together in an arch. On a sunlit afternoon, the ground was always covered in dappled shadows. And for a moment or two, that was just how it was: idyllic. Then the leaves rustled and four things happened at once.

In the distance Alexa said, "Mommy . . . ?"

The zipper on Zanna's bag began to urgently rattle.

A spill of unnatural darkness blotted out the checkerboard of light and foliage.

A raven's cark rent the air.

Zanna whipped around to see a large bird descending. It was coming for her, claws out, angled like a bat. She ducked and it swept by, spitting venom. Then a second bird came in the slipstream of the first. This time Zanna swung her bag at it, caught the bird's breast, and sent it spinning. It crashed into a bench and looked defeated for a second, its wing jammed between two slats, dislocated. But then, to her horror, it withdrew the wing as though it were a knife in butter. It reset the joint with an ugly-sounding snap and turned to face the girl again.

It was hideous. Black-eyed. Awkward. Cruel. It appeared to have teeth. Hard fragments of bony material, nestling around a squirming tongue. Yes, it was a bird. But not a raven. More like a mutant of avian evolution. "Gargoyle" was the closest name Zanna could give to it. "Evil" was the generalization she preferred.

"Alexa!" She was already running toward the girl

when another bird sank its claws into her shoulder, forcing her to drop her bag and sink to her knees. She threw back her head in pain and the thorny protuberances on the bird's body became grossly entangled in her hair. The bird thrashed about among the long black strands, trying to deliver a blow with its beak. Zanna was not to know, but one stab deep into her ear canal would have caused an incurable infection and rotted her cerebellum in seconds. This was how close she came to death that day.

"Lexie, RUN!" She drew back her sleeve.

High in the trees, a third creature, the alpha male bird, stared at Zanna and zoomed in on the mark of Oomara. Without making a sound, it dropped through the chinks of light and clamped itself to Zanna's right hand before she could fasten her fingers to her arm. She screamed in agony and rolled over with it, her cheekbone grazing against the path. The bird tore a strip of flesh between the tendons of her hand and even took one finger into its beak. Deep at its base, she felt the prickling teeth gnaw through to her bone. It was all she could do to stop from passing out.

And all this time she was aware of a terrible scrabbling beside her. Three birds, maybe four, were scratching at her bag, trying to tear through the lining to get inside. Suddenly it broke and Gretel was loose.

Fly, Zanna mouthed, through a blur of hair and saliva and pain.

Instead, Gretel froze. She had flowers in the quiver she carried across her back. A knockout potion would have been easy to administer, if she'd had time to make it up. But she was surrounded and wholly outnumbered. She'd be dead, she knew, if she touched a stem.

She raised her paws in surrender. The half-darkling ravens sneered. And then something happened that terrified even Gretel beyond her wildest nightmares. One by one, the birds changed shape. Until they were her shape. Four black Gretels. Four monstrous inversions of herself.

Gretel felt something move inside her body. An

auma shift. Deep within. And though she had always believed she would be far too strong to ever reach this state, she identified the feeling right away: the moment before a dragon sheds its fire tear.

She was about to die.

RESCUE

But in an instant everything changed. A new and longer shadow fell across the path. Human. A man. Tall. Strong.

The birds around Gretel turned their heads in concert and quickly reassumed their darkling shape. Chattering aggressively, they backed away from the oncoming figure, spread their wings, and scattered to the trees. The alpha male was not so fearful. It threw out its wings and lifted away from Zanna, but hovered for a moment assessing the battle strength of the intruder. One swift scan of the visitor's auma warned it that engagement was not an option. It glanced at the darkling trapped in Zanna's hair. The thing was beating out a message of distress. The alpha male flew to the trees, where it

185

could observe its companion's fate. The human figure stepped forward, put his hand around the bird's neck, and squeezed the darkness out of it. It turned as white as ice, from teeth to tail, then collapsed inward in a gush of water that trickled down the path and found a drain.

The alpha male recorded this and wisely flew away.

"David . . . ?" Sensing the sanctuary of the human form behind her, Zanna rolled over and stretched a bloodied hand.

A firm hand took it. "Not this time, sorry."

That voice. That soft Scottish accent. Zanna raised her eyes. "You?" she gasped, before she finally fainted.

Her rescuer was the journalist, Tam Farrell.

When she came around (a waft of scented flowers from Gretel) he had moved her to a quiet, shaded bench and was already securing a makeshift bandage, torn from his shirt, around her injured hand. She pushed him away with a startled breath and swept Alexa up in a desperate hug. "Are you all right? They didn't touch you?"

Alexa shook her head.

Mouthing a silent prayer, Zanna steadied her by the shoulders and stroked her face. "Gretel? Are you OK?"

The potions dragon gave a nervous *hrrr*.

"Sit back," said Tam. "Please. You're hurt."

Zanna's dark eyes faded into his. "Where did you come from? Why were you even here?"

He shifted to the front of the bench and attended to her injured hand again. "Long story."

"Fine. I'm all ears," she growled.

He tied the bandage off. "I was coming to the house, spotted you and Alexa, guessed you might be heading for the shop, and tagged on behind. Lucky I did." He looked at her kindly. "We should get you home."

"My hair's wet," she said, feeling the ends. "Have I got the blood of those things on me?"

He shook his head. "Just melted ice."

"And where did a journalist from *The National Endeavor* learn to turn gargoyles into ice?" She grabbed his wrist and turned his palm up. Under the skin was the faint translucent image of a polar bear.

"That's another long story," he said, and put her hands back into her lap. "I'll get your bag."

It was lying, torn, on the far side of the path. Tam gathered up the contents and handed it to her. "They've made a real mess of it. Was it expensive?"

"Don't ask," she said, chin in the air.

So Tam spoke not a word on the entire journey back to the Crescent. But as they approached the gate of number forty-two, Zanna stopped him with a hand to his chest. "You've never met Liz, have you?"

He shook his head. "She was ill in bed when I was here before."

"Well, she's not ill now. Bear in mind she's Lucy's mother, OK?"

"Am I unwelcome?"

"We're about to find out."

* * *

As usual, Liz's first priority was for Zanna's and Alexa's welfare. She bundled them into the kitchen, where Agatha Bacon was admiring the dragons and enjoying a farewell cup of tea.

Agatha unwrapped the wounded hand. "What caused this?"

"Birds," Zanna told her. "Like mutant ravens."

Liz stepped back with one hand across her mouth. "Didn't you say you saw ravens on Farlowe Island?"

Zanna, looking harrowed, didn't reply.

"This is infected," Agatha said. "In most cases I would prescribe a poultice of geranium and calendula root." She raised a hand as Gretel looked set to fly. "Wait," she commanded. "The flowers may not be necessary." She rested Zanna's palm on hers. "Look inside yourself, girl. The remedy is in your mind, is it not?"

Zanna focused her concentration. "I can see it, yes. Geranium and —"

"For others, certainly," Agatha cut in. "But you are a sibyl. Concentrate harder. Think of the remedy; look at the wounds."

They were a frightful mess, made worse, Zanna suspected, by the bloodstains smeared and caked around the knuckles. But as she brought her sibyl mind to work on them, she understood what Agatha was getting at. As she focused her thoughts on the image of a clean, undamaged hand, the blood loss from the darkling's bite was staunched and the severed tissues began to reknit. Within a minute, she had healed herself.

"Oh, my goodness," gasped Liz. "I've never seen anything like that in my life."

Zanna turned her hand as if it were new. Her fingers were bloodied but painless to move.

"Excellent," said Agatha, bristling with pride. "You have progressed at a speed I would not have thought possible. But that was before I visited this house and its colorful occupants, of which we now appear to be grateful for one more." She studied Tam Farrell carefully. He was standing, out of the way, by the fridge.

"I just happened to be in the right place at the right time," he said modestly.

"He frightened the nasty birds off," said Alexa, going to sit on her mother's knee.

"And not by flashing his smile," said Zanna. "Why didn't the darklings go for you? What were they afraid of, T —?"

"Tam?!" Lucy's voice was louder, more insistent.

"Hello, Lucy," he said, turning.

She stopped at the kitchen door and pulled a strand of loose hair into her mouth. He was still just as handsome as ever, even with a slim gold chain around his neck (she hated "bling" on guys) and unworldly dark brown eyes.

"You're supposed to be in your room," Liz said.

Which did not go over well with her daughter. "Oh, why don't you just tell me I'm not going to get any dinner tonight either? Let's go for total embarrassment, why don't we?"

"I think I'd better go," Tam said quietly.

"Thought you had a story to tell me?" Zanna threw him a penetrating look.

191

"It can wait," he said.

"But you'll be back?" Liz said, hurriedly, hopefully.

Tam offered her his Lowlands smile.

"You'll be welcome, Tam."

"Thank you," he said, smiling at Alexa as she waved him off.

As he stepped toward the hall, Lucy flattened herself against the door to let him past. "Bye," she whispered as he angled himself to face her.

He looked kindly into her over-round eyes. A moment later, he was gone.

Outside, at the top of the path, Tam checked his cell phone and found he had a new voice mail waiting. The message was breathless, spoken with an anglicized German accent. "Mr. Farrell, please call me. I have a story for you. One which is going to change the world."

Tam snapped his phone shut and opened the gate. Over the creak a voice said, "Steiner?"

David was approaching along the sidewalk.

Tam gave a nod of recognition. "I'm guessing he's translated the photographs."

"Good. Then you know what you have to do."

"The shell of the article is already written. I'm just waiting for Steiner's input."

David nodded and looked anxiously at the house. "What happened?"

"Birds. About double the size of a normal raven. Not full darklings, but close enough to matter. Liz mentioned they were there on Farlowe?"

"Yes," said David, thinking back, showing in the merest tightening of his lips that he'd made a mistake in letting them go. "How many were there?"

Tam shrugged. "Half a dozen."

David looked away. Six. He'd remembered more than that. "What's your assessment? What would Kailar say?"

Tam turned his right palm up, where the image of the polar bear David was referring to was glowing luminescently under his skin. "He'd say things were going to get worse. That the enemy are learning fast what they're up against. That they'll step up their efforts to achieve what they want. Maybe attack on different fronts." He glanced at the house. Gwendolen was watching from Lucy's window. "You need to know something, David. Zanna was badly hurt in the attack, but she's recovered, through her own magicks."

"And Alexa?"

"Untouched. The birds didn't come for Alexa. I believe they came to scare Gretel. My guess is they were looking for another tear to invert. You need to deal with that piece of obsidian, or none of what we're doing is going to matter."

David nodded again. "Did you speak to Lucy?"

Tam moved the toe of his boot across the ground. "I didn't think the moment was right. You really want me to chaperone her to Scuffenbury?"

David glanced at Tam's left hand, at the second bear image imprinted there. It was younger than the bear on his right hand, with a far more intelligent profile. What it brought to Tam were memories of the Arctic; every story of the North was right there, in his palm. David said, "Isn't that what the Teller of Ways would desire: to be present when a dragon rises out of stasis? You did well, Tam. Stay close. I'll call you." And with that he clapped the young Scot once on the shoulder and walked away silently toward the house.

KITCHEN TALK

For a while, it was a time of comings and goings. As soon as David walked in he was updated with the news of what had happened on North Walk. Shortly afterward, Agatha Bacon left in a taxi, Alexa went into her mother's room to play, and Liz announced she was going to the university to collect Arthur.

"After what happened to Zanna?" Lucy said.

Liz glanced at David. "They won't touch you," he said.

"Oh, you are such a piece of work!" Despite the soothing qualities of a mug of chamomile tea, Zanna couldn't keep an angry snarl out of her voice. "You waltz in thirty minutes after the event and assure us

196

everything's fine and dandy. How can you be so blasé about this?"

"They want a dragon," he said. "Another Gwillan."

Every dragon in the room shrank back in fear.

Zanna glared at him for a full three seconds. "If you'd been there, feeling their claws ripping into your skin, you wouldn't be coming out with a cheap remark like that."

"I'm not saying you weren't in danger," said David. "But you weren't the real target. Tell her, Gretel."

But the potions dragon, in a fierce display of solidarity, flew to Zanna's shoulder and refused to say a word.

Liz sighed and picked her car keys out of the fruit bowl. "I'll be careful, I promise. Please be kind to each other while I'm gone. A bit of TLC all around wouldn't hurt." She checked her hair in the mirror and set off toward the hall. On her way out, she paused and said to David, "These creatures: Will they attack us here?"

David glanced at the listening dragon. Its tall frail body was shaking in time to the refrigerator pump. He sent it a calming impulse and said, "I doubt it. The house is too well guarded. And we're wise to them now. If I'm not here, Zanna and Bonnington will keep them at bay." As if by magic, Bonnington popped in through his cat flap and rubbed himself against David's shins.

Zanna banged her mug down and swept straight out. "I've got some packing to do," she said.

The door to her room slammed shut.

"Behold, TLC in action," Lucy muttered.

Moments later, alone in the kitchen with Lucy, David slipped into a chair and said to the girl, "So, what did you decide about Scuffenbury?"

Lucy sat down uneasily beside him. "How come you're friends with Tam?"

"I told you, he owes me a favor."

She tilted her head, expecting more.

He took a banana out of the fruit bowl, studying its symmetry as he peeled it. "I rescued him from the Ix."

Them again. Lucy funneled a sigh. "Zanna hates him," she said, musing to herself. "Not long ago he tried to use her to get some information on you. He wanted to write in his magazine about you. He thought you weren't real and your books were written by someone else. Zanna went crazy when she found out. She branded her sibyl mark across his heart. She's scary sometimes. Crazier than Gwilanna. Is Tam a male sibyl now or something? Is that why the birds weren't scared of him?"

David placed a foot on the bar of her chair. "He's just a friend. Someone you'd want near you in times of trouble. Anyway, you haven't answered my question. Would you be happy traveling to Scuffenbury with him?"

"Happy," thought Lucy, was hardly the word. Scared. Astonished. Ecstatic. Any of those might have fit. "Will we be camping? I was trying to remember where my tent was yesterday."

"The attic?" he suggested. "It was there the last time I looked."

"That was a long time ago," she said, tying her fingers into knots. He'd gone up there in search of her old rabbit hutch, to make a trap to catch the one-eyed squirrel, Conker, whom he'd later immortalized in print. Everything had been so wonderful then. Conker. Mr. Bacon being grumpy. Gadzooks on David's windowsill. The birthday gift of *Snigger and the Nutbeast*. The library gardens. Sophie.

"Hhh!" Lucy popped upright in her chair.

"Anyway, you won't need your tent," he said. "Tam will organize a B&B or something."

"No, it's not that. I got an e-mail for you — from Sophie."

He took his foot off the chair. "From Africa?"

"I guess."

"Saying?"

"She tried your cell phone but got nothing. So she found the Web site I did for your books and e-mailed me through that."

"Clever girl. What did she say?"

"Hi to all of us, some stuff about the wildlife hospital she works at, and . . . she wants to talk to you. It sounded a bit . . . important."

Hrrr, went a voice behind Lucy's ear. Gwendolen, sitting on the rim of a plant pot.

"Oh, yeah. She wrote that she thinks Grace's ears keep moving."

David looked at her hard for a moment. He put the banana aside and shot a glance at the listening dragon. "Has Grace made contact?"

The listener shook its head.

"When did this e-mail arrive, Lucy?"

She chewed her lip again. "Erm, a few hours ago. But I didn't check my e-mail until —"

He stood up quickly, just as Zanna emerged from her room looking flustered.

"Don't be mad," Lucy begged, sensing that he might be. "I was going to tell you as soon as you came in. And I did. Almost. Didn't I? David?"

But by then he was heading for the hallway, with the narwhal tusk in his hand once more.

"Don't disappear, I need to talk to you," said Zanna.

"Not now."

"This is about Alexa. The rest of the world can wait."

"No, it can't," he said, and bundled past.

"What's more important than your daughter, David?"

"Right now, Sophie Prentice . . . ," he said.

AN OLD FRIEND

Eyes. They're, like . . . the weirdest thing. How can two balls of colored jelly make you feel so wanted or so . . . deserted? I can do green. I can do violet. It's the dragon inside me, according to Mom. It began to show properly after the age of eleven, when my hair turned red as well. Green: I'm just gorgeous. Violet: deadly. Maybe I should have turned the violet on him? That look in the hall. What did it mean? Why didn't he speak? Why didn't he acknowledge me? It only takes a second to say "How are you?" . . . doesn't it? All he had to do was part his lips. Maybe he's not the Tam I knew? He's different. His eyes. So brown. Like a bear's. Or maybe he's still got a thing for

Zanna. Even after what she did to him. Why does everything whirl around ZANNA? Why couldn't David have stayed with Sophie, instead of letting MORTICIA dig her purple nails into —

Normally, when the phone rang, Lucy ignored it, especially when she was immersed in her journal. She hated landlines. What was the point of them in this age of cell phones? But with her mother and Arthur still not home and Zanna taking Alexa next door and a convenient break in the playlist on her iPod, she felt she had no choice but to answer the thing. With a huff, she pushed her keyboard aside, took out her earbuds, and went into her mom's room to pick up the call.

"Yes?" she drawled, with her characteristic lack of social grace.

"Is that Lucy?" A girl's voice. Breathy. Teen.

"Yep."

"Omigosh!"

"Who's this?" asked Lucy, puzzled by the burst

of enthusiasm. No one she knew ever talked to her like that.

"Don't you know?"

Lucy tried not to tut. "If I did, I wouldn't be asking, would I?"

"Dragons . . . ?" said the girl, letting the question hang. "We used to talk about them for HOURS on our sleepovers — when I lived on Orchid Close."

Orchid Close, just around the corner from the end of the Crescent.

"Melanie? Melanie Cartwright?!"

"Lucy Pennykettle," the other girl said, as cheery as a chipmunk. "Long time no hurr, huh? Mom rustled up your number from the back of some old notebook. They come in useful, don't they, moms?"

Lucy flopped down on her own mother's bed, her stunned reflection looking back from the dressing table mirror. Around her knees, the dangling earbuds began to throw out a loud, tinny beat. She switched off her iPod and said, "Where are you?"

"Erm, on the other end of the phone?"

"Yeah, I know that. Have you moved back to Scrubbley?"

"No. Me and Mom are still in Plymouth. It's not the best. And school is, like, the pits. But it's good for Dad. He works on ships, remember? Captain Cartwright, yo ho ho. By the way, my granddad died."

"Oh, sorry," Lucy murmured. When she and Melanie had been friends as young girls, "Pop," Melanie's grandfather, had been a sickly but lively old man.

"It's OK," Melanie said. "It was ages ago, just after we moved. I was going to write to you, but, you know . . ."

Lucy grunted, thinking of Mr. Bacon. Melanie had known him slightly. Not enough to mention his passing. "So why are you calling? I mean, it's cool and everything, but . . ."

There was a pause while Melanie gathered her thoughts. "It's about Glade."

Lucy felt her stomach curdle. Many years ago, her mother had made a string of special dragons that went to live with people who'd bought them from the

Pennykettles' market stall or that sometimes had just been gifted by Liz. Glade was one such example. She was a mood dragon, who carried a scarf of ivy leaves around her neck, which changed color depending on how she, or those around her, were feeling. The practice of giving special dragons away had ended with the creation of Gadzooks. This had come as some relief to Lucy, who had always thought it dangerous. For though it was difficult for normal people to see the dragons moving, they were nevertheless capable of getting up to mischief or even being broken while in their solid state. It was this more than anything that Lucy feared as she asked, "What about Glade?"

"Well, it's not about her, really —"

"Is she OK? What color's her ivy?"

"Green. She hasn't changed today. She's sitting on my desk. Hey, you know what's weird about her?"

Lucy held her breath.

"She never gets dusty. Anyway, like I said, it's not really about her, it's about the one that's been on TV. Is it one of your mom's?"

"TV?" said Lucy. "What are you talking about?"

Melanie almost choked with disbelief. "What am I talking about? What the whole world's talking about. What planet have you been on?"

"I don't watch much TV," Lucy replied. That was a lie. She did. But not lately. Not since Henry and Apak and everything.

"Then get on the Net, like . . . now, 'cause this is mega."

Chained by wire to a phone, Lucy opted to go with conversation. "Can't you just tell me?"

"OK!" Melanie said. "Well, you must have heard about this mist in the Arctic and how everyone is saying there are dragons hiding under it?"

"Are they?"

"Lu-cy! Where have you been? The world's on the edge. There's, like, the Spanish Armada cruising around the Arctic waiting to blast whatever comes out of the fog."

"The Spanish Armada?"

"Warships. Big ones. Kinda scary, don't you think? Oh, and no one's seen a polar bear for, like, two months and there's this theory, right, that the dragons are actually feeding on them."

"That's gross," said Lucy. "Dragons wouldn't do that. They . . ." But how could she tell Melanie in the space of a phone call the history of the Arctic, Gawain, Thoran? No way would dragons attack the bears. But it was something to ask David about when she saw him next.

"Anyway," Melanie rattled on regardless, "people are reporting sightings of scaly beasts everywhere. There was a photo on the news of one that was snapped in the sky over Scotland. People are calling it the Loch Ness Dragon 'cause you can't really tell if it's a giant kite or a blowup of a bird. But it looks totally real. A little like a pterodactyl. Horns. Spiky tale. Claws. Everything. And everyone, I mean everyone, is talking about it. You know when someone sees a UFO whizzing about and then zillions of others say they saw one, too?"

"Yeah?"

"That's what it's like. Except there's been no real proof — until now."

"So . . . what's happened?"

"Well, this is where you come in."

"I haven't done anything!"

"No, but . . . Oh, just . . . shut up and let me spill, OK?"

Lucy rolled her eyes. Ten minutes ago would have been good. If blabbing was an Olympic sport, Melanie would have won medals every time.

"There's this place in Canada, some sort of big meditation stroke healing center. A little 'out there,' you know? Anyway, they were having this kind of conference about peace and love and healing, whatever, and it was being filmed by one of the networks. So it gets to this bit where some guy in a none-too-fetching white robe is about to bless this lady in a wheelchair and there's a gasp from the crowd and a dragon materializes on the lectern thingy."

"What?"

"I know. Awesome, isn't it? It was just sitting there, like a bird." ·

"What color was it?" Lucy asked, thinking of the ravens Zanna had described.

"Green, duh. It looked like Glade. That's the point. Well, not exactly like Glade. But like one of your mom's. But it was living, 'cause they filmed it before it flew off. When I showed Glade the reruns her ivy went crazy. Rainbows. All the colors you could think of. Weird."

Lucy slid the phone from her ear to her shoulder, but when Melanie's vibrating, squeaking voice was in danger of burning holes in her flesh she raised it again and asked, "Did it do anything? The dragon on the TV?"

Melanie blew an exaggerated sigh. "Well, people are saying it was a trick — but if it was it was a really, really neat one. It grabbed a light pen they use for showing messages on a screen and it drew something. Well, it made squiggles. Some people think it's a word in an ancient language. Go on the Net. You can see it everywhere. It's the biggest thing since Harry. Bigger!"

"Harry?"

"Potter. Are you alive today or what?"

Once again, the conversation stalled. Then, in a voice muted by a note of awe, Melanie asked, "Is she real, Lucy? Is Glade like the one on the TV?"

Lucy glanced at her reflection again. A red-haired dragon princess. A descendant of Guinevere. Crumpling up in fear, on a comforter, on a bed. "I have to go," she said, hearing the front door opening. "Can I e-mail you?"

Melanie gave an easy-to-remember address. "Lucy?"

"Um?"

"Please answer my question. I'm looking at Glade now and her ivy's glowing gold. How does it happen? How does —?"

"She's just clay and fancy glaze," Lucy cut in, hating herself for denying the truth. "Look after her, won't you?"

"I guess," said Melanie, disappointment crumbling her voice into shreds. "You still there?"

"Lucy?"

"That's my mom. Gotta go."

"Wait. Just tell me what you think. I mean, we always said how great it would be to have actual dragons flying about, didn't we? It's creepy, but sort of exciting as well. It's like, everyone's looking at the sky for a miracle. We want it to happen, but we're not quite sure. Do you think they will come?"

There was a two-second pause. "Yes," said Lucy, and put the phone onto its cradle. She noticed as she did so her hand was trembling.

"Lu-cy?"

The eleventh commandment rang out once more: the abbreviated form of thou wilt come down and speak to thy mother. Sighing, Lucy glided to the landing.

She was about to swing onto the flight of stairs when she saw her mother going into the front room clucking, "She's not home. Probably next door with Zanna. Maybe that's just as well."

"You can't keep this from her," Arthur replied. "Rupert is describing the Hella writings as the most important document in the history of mankind. Now that he has the full translation he'll publish the transcript of the photographs. When he does, the whole world is going to know. She'll pick it up off the Internet anyway. Far better that it comes from you."

Lucy crept down a few steps. Over the top of the front-room door she could see Arthur, sitting down, stroking Bonnington. Her mother was out of sight.

"I need time to think it through. It has to be broken to her gently."

"Do you think so? I think she's mature enough to understand Gawain's motives."

Motives? thought Lucy as her mother went on, "Arthur, she's been brought up to believe that Gawain was a magnificent, peaceful dragon, completely incapable of any kind of aggression. How am I going to tell her that he was on the verge of destroying — what? What's the matter?"

"Nothing, go on," Arthur said.

"You jumped."

"Bonnington dug in a claw."

"What's he staring at?" Liz marched to the door and yanked it open.

But by then, Lucy had had the foresight to put in her earbuds and come plodding downstairs. "What?" she said as she reached the bottom. She clicked her iPod off.

Liz stared at her suspiciously. "I called you. Twice."

Lucy wafted by with a casual shrug. "The god that is Pod called louder. Sorry." She stepped into the kitchen and opened the fridge. "What's with you anyway? You look whiter than this stuff." She took a swig from a carton of milk. *But then you would look pale, wouldn't you, Mother, because you're keeping something from me, aren't you?* And it was obvious that Lucy had a right to know. But to ask would have only blown her charade. For now, she was enjoying the buzz of being one up on the old and the "wise," even though she was burning to know the truth. Gawain was ready to destroy what, exactly? She'd find out later. There were ways.

In true parental fashion, Liz avoided the question. "How come you're alone? Is Zanna next door?"

Lucy offered up a vacuous grin. "Dunno. S'pose we'll have to get used to not having her around here from now on, won't we?"

"And David?"

That was Lucy's undoing. One twitch of concern around the mouth was enough to hand the advantage to her mother.

Issuing one of those I-can't-leave-you-alone-for-five-minutes kind of sighs, Liz said, "Has there been trouble while I've been out?"

"I don't know."

"Stop saying you 'don't know.'"

"He's gone," snapped Lucy, hurling the milk back into the fridge. The listener, long practiced in the art of jumping, did so again as she slammed the door.

"Again? Where to?"

"Mom?! I'm not his secretary! I don't know." But she did, of course. And if the truth be told it was worrying her, the way he'd left so suddenly. "Oh, all right, he's gone to Africa," she muttered.

"Where?!"

"Africa!" This time, Lucy stamped her foot. Her eyelashes, slightly moist, were gluing together. "He's gone to see Sophie."

Liz glanced at the listening dragon.

Hrrr, it confirmed. That was the implication of David's last words.

"Does Zanna know?"

"Who cares?" Lucy growled. And she jammed her earbuds in, turned her iPod up loud, and stomped away upstairs again.

AFRICA

Smoke. Spiraling upward like a weak tornado, dragging west in the breeze across the outlying flood plain and blotting out the early evening sun. The whole site was ablaze: one large building, which David took to be the veterinary hospital, plus an arc of five or six smaller thatched huts. The spit and crackle of burning wood was as loud as the voices calling through the smoke. A barefooted woman, in T-shirt and shorts, was screaming at a male colleague to leave the water pumps and go to the animals. From mesh pens just beyond the burning huts, the cries of distressed wildlife added to the general chaos.

David started after the woman, who by now had abandoned her colleague and was staggering toward the veterinary center, shielding her smoke-stained face from the heat. She was caught by a slender African man, who pushed her back and told her there was nothing, nothing to be done. As she argued with him, the central portion of the roof collapsed and glass exploded inside the center. The man clutched the woman to his chest and together they fell to the hard-baked earth. Orange flames tipped with angry black crests sailed six feet out of a shattered window. The woman began to scream and sob.

"Work, darn you!"

To David's right, the white man by the water pumps slapped his hand against the failed machinery, then stood back and kicked one, making it clank. He swept around, eyes as wild as the fire. "Who are you?" he barked, catching sight of David.

"A friend of Sophie Prentice. What happened here? What caused this?"

"What does it matter?" said the man, in a deeply shaken South African accent. Sweat was pouring off his broad, bare shoulders. Smoke streaks were dabbed like war paint on his cheeks. He looked around in an agony of despair. "It's all gone, man. It's all gone."

"Pieter! The tower!" somebody shouted.

The man looked urgently toward the pens. An observation tower, wrapped in high-kicking tendrils of fire, had cracked a wooden stanchion and was keeling toward an enclosure of terrified impala.

Uttering a string of profanities, Pieter dragged a scorched arm across his forehead and sprinted to the enclosure nearest the tower to grapple with the locked mesh gates. Using a swatch of his vest to protect his hands against the heat from the bolt, he rattled the gates open and ran inside, clapping the animals out. Three impala quickly escaped, swerving erratically through the smoke. A fourth animal, a half-blind female zebra named Jinnie, had pressed herself into a corner.

"Jinnie, come on, girl," Pieter shouted. He raced in and slapped its hindquarters hard. The zebra whinnied and flashed its tail, but planted its juvenile hooves to the ground. All around it in adjoining pens, wild cats and wetland birds voiced their torment. Other volunteers were racing to their aid. Splinters of fizzing timber were all the while falling, sparking where they landed in the grassy enclosures.

"Pieter!" someone shouted. "Get out of there, man!"

A colleague in the adjacent pen pointed to the platform of fire above them. Pieter looked up at the raging timbers, gradually losing their rigidity and structure. He made an assessment and gritted his teeth. "Not without you," he said to Jinnie and threw a muscular arm around her neck, hoping he could physically pull her clear. She put out a foot. "That's it," he shouted. "Come on, girl, you can do this!"

The young zebra bayed in fear.

At that moment, a devastating snap of wood forced Pieter to look up over his shoulder. One of the crossed-beam sections that formed the four walls of the observation platform had broken free and was plummeting toward him. Too committed to dive away from Jinnie, he draped himself over her, protecting her head. The wood hurtled down like a giant branding iron, trailing tails of crackling embers. Pieter filled his lungs with what he knew might be his dying breath. But seconds before impact, something came to save both man and beast — an updraft of air so huge that Pieter felt as if his clothes were being ripped off his skin. The heat was blistering. The sound deafening. Gravity delivered the beams to their target, but the weight of their impact was strangely negligible. The cellulose and lignin that had given the wood its strength appeared to have been sucked right out of its fibers. The timbers broke across Jinnie's back in a cloud of hot, papery ash. The fire consuming them had been put out.

This time Jinnie bolted, throwing her shaken helper to the ground. Pieter rolled back against the blown mesh fence and looked once more at the observation tower. It was standing like a spent and blackened match, still bent but mostly intact, odd fragments being chipped off in the breeze. Suddenly, there was a scream across the far side of the site. Spitting the taste of charcoal off his tongue, Pieter looked toward the source of the yell and saw something he had only thought possible in dreams or nightmares or comic books or movies. There was a dragon in the middle of the compound. It had just ingested the last of the fires.

Terror, incredulity, or blind astonishment — something hauled Pieter Montgomery to his feet. His hands went through the motions of dusting down his clothing, but his eyes never left the shape of the beast. It was incredible, well over twelve feet tall. Bronzed. Powerful. Irresistibly primeval. He glanced at one of the animals it had saved and the team had been unable to free: Kanga, the arthritic lion. The so-called king of the beasts was standing transfixed at the front of its pen, its muscles so locked that it appeared to have entered the shock of rigor mortis. But Pieter could see the improbable wonder in Kanga's eyes. And when the dragon spread its wings and took to the sky, scattering shattered debris in its wake, Kanga's eyes followed it in slow, slow motion and continued to stare at the yellow horizon long after the creature was out of sight.

Through the cloud of the dragon's departure, David Rain appeared.

"Who are you?" Pieter hissed.

Before they could make any further exchanges, their attention was drawn by a torrent of deep, heart-wrenching sobs. Over by the hospital entrance, one of the women was weeping inconsolably into the arms of two of her colleagues. The African man was trying to shepherd a small gathering away from a body, laid out under a sheet by the steps.

"Oh, no," said Pieter, checking the faces, looking at the sheet. "No, no, no!" He ran past David, past the man, and dropped to his knees beside the body. He pulled the sheet back, exposing the face of a serene young woman. Despite the superficial burns to her skin and the wreckage clinging to her close-cropped hair, her grace and beauty were easy to see.

"No," moaned Pieter. His shaking fingers settled on her lips. "No. Oh, no." He sank into a deeper, anguished heap as David came to kneel beside him.

The dead woman was Sophie Prentice, David Rain's first girlfriend.

DAVID'S WARNING

I couldn't stop her."

Just behind David, another young woman with dark brown hair in a stunted ponytail brought her hands together in prayer. Tears were rolling down her chubby, red face. Her fingers crumpled inward as she spoke. "She insisted on going back into her hut. I told her it was stupid but she wouldn't listen." The woman sobbed and pressed her hands to her head. "Please, someone tell me. What was that monster?" She looked around in vacant distress. "Am I going crazy? We all saw it, didn't we?"

David stood up intending to explain. But as he reached out to take the woman's arm, she let out a squeal of fright and stepped back, pointing at the body on the earth. A small green dragon with fragile ears had appeared as if from nowhere on Sophie's chest. Pieter gasped and drew back his hand to strike it.

"No," said David, clamping his wrist. The two men exchanged sharp looks. "That's what she went back for, Pieter. She wouldn't thank you for harming it. Look carefully. You know this dragon, don't you?"

"Grace," he muttered. "She called it Grace." His gaze fell again on Sophie. "But how did it get here?"

By now, the beautiful listening dragon was on Sophie's shoulder, close to her chin. She had abandoned all the rules and was moving freely. Only David could really see her stroking Sophie's cheek and whimpering in dragontongue into Sophie's ear, but the shocked woman said, "It looks upset. And its eyes have changed color. Is it . . . alive?"

David knelt down again. "Grace," he said, in soft dragontongue, running a finger down her spine. The dragon would not take its gaze off Sophie. By now the first hint of moisture was present in the scalene duct in the corner of its eyes.

"I want everyone to leave here," David said. "There may be great danger present."

"There is." The clack of a rifle bolt brought a slice of cold reality to David's words. The African man had a gun at his waist. He was tilting the barrel upward a little.

"Mutu, what are you doing?" Pieter followed the man's hardened gaze. On the stripped, scorched walls of the hospital building sat a dark and ugly shape. For a moment, it appeared to be nothing more than a hideous artifact of the blaze. But with a nauseating crack of bones, it unlatched its wings and turned its grisly head toward the humans.

One of the women screamed. The rest of the crowd backed away in fear.

Not Mutu. "I saw this beast begin the fire," he said, his words thickened by thirty years of dust. "It is a spirit of darkness."

"Don't try to shoot it," David warned.

But Mutu, with slow and calculated malice, raised the gun to his shoulder and fired.

There was a thud as the bullet struck home. The creature's chest muscles buckled inward and it was slammed back against a blackened timber. The lids that protected its blueberry eyes closed for a second, then half-opened. Its beak parted and it shook its neck as though about to choke on a knot of mucus. From its throat came a hostile gurgling sound and a substance, as thick and black as molasses, pooled around its swollen, retracted tongue.

Mutu lowered his gun.

But the bird was far from dead. Lifting a foot, it steered a demonic claw into the hole the bullet had made. Someone was sick behind David as the tip of the claw was heard scraping the base of the shell. Then, in one movement, the muscles around the wound contracted and the bullet appeared to be sucked farther in. The bird withdrew the claw, leaving a trail of grotesque fluid stringing between its tip and the hole. Its eyelids opened fully.

"What in Our Lord's name is that?" said Mutu. He cocked the rifle again.

"Stop," hissed David. "You can't kill it with lead. You'll only make it stronger. Get back, all of you."

"I'm not leaving Sophie to that thing," said Pieter.

But as he tried to push forward, David rapped an arm across the middle of his chest. "It's not Sophie it wants," he growled. He glanced at Grace. She was going through the motions of final closure, about to shed her fire tear. And just like the birds on North Walk, the black creature was beginning to mimic her shape, cruelly elongating its ears.

"If that fiend began the fire, it killed my fiancée," Pieter insisted. "And it can take me as well, but not before it's tasted this." From his belt, he produced a hunting knife. Forcing David aside, he stepped forward, shouting at the thing to come on.

The half-darkling flared its teeth. In one peculiar grinding movement, it raised itself up and rippled its chest in a vertical flow of muscle. Its wings went out to their maximum extent and it brought them down with a single rapid beat, creating a thrust of air in its windpipe.

With a cry of pain, Pieter was knocked forcefully onto his back. His hand went to a wound in his chest. A red stain was spreading through the cotton of his vest.

"It's shot him," someone gasped.

With the same bullet Mutu had used, spat out of the mouth at speed.

Once more, the dark wings lifted. With a cry that lay somewhere between triumph and death, the creature turned its gaze on the only other quarry between itself and Grace.

David calmly put a hand into his pocket and drew out the piece of obsidian. He held it aloft for the bird to see. The black spiders of light inside it dashed themselves against the outer walls.

The creature let out a vile snarl. Its eyes swiveled greedily between the obsidian and Grace. A tear glittered on the young dragon's eye and slowly tipped over onto her snout.

"Come on," whispered David. "Make your decision."

The darkling was swaying in angry confusion. Dark fire or undefiled tear?

With a roar it launched itself at the obsidian.

David stood his ground. When the bird was just an arm's length in front of his face, he raised an almost preternatural hand and took the creature by the throat. The speed of the catch made everyone gasp. The darkling raven flashed its claws and struggled to discharge whatever bile it could muster. A bubble of foul-smelling vitriolic filth popped at the hinge of its cracking beak and dribbled pathetically down its neck. David's grip, as strong as a bear's, deadened any chance of it spewing further.

"Struggle and you choke," he told it. Wisely, the creature calmed. Then, drawing it so close to his face that its wild eyes bulged as it read the power inherent in his, David continued, "I ought to turn you to dust for what you've done." He looked down at Sophie's body and shuddered. Grace, head lowered, wings folded, was still. "But I won't be responsible for giving the Ix more grief to chew on. So listen to me, bird, and I'll let you live. Go back to your masters and tell them to halt the raven inversion or the Fain will wipe the mutation out. My dragon will be following your auma trail. Don't fly away thinking you've escaped me. Oh, and one last thing." He tightened his fist again, forcing another squawk higher up the register and turning the darkling's head pure white. "Tell them they'll get nothing from the Pennykettle dragons."

With that, he attempted to throw the bird into the sky. But at the moment he released his grip, Pieter leaped up and drove his knife deep into the darkling's belly. The creature screamed and twisted against the blade, oozing hot black juice down Pieter's arm. Enraged beyond all hope of redemption, it razored its claws against his chest. It had torn his skin into hanging shreds before David, with one swift blow, could turn the bird to exploding ice.

Pieter dropped to the ground. His colleagues, dedicated coworkers and friends, rushed to his aid. His final act was to raise an arm and let it fall against Sophie's body. He was dead before he could whisper good-bye.

Half an hour after the cleanup had started, Mutu came to seek David out. David was sitting in the shade of a spreading acacia tree, staring across the great green flood plain. The dragon known as Grace was between his feet.

"What should I tell them?" Mutu asked. "The newspapers and the police are here. They are asking what happened. They wish to know if Pieter was mauled by a lion. No one is willing to talk about the wonders or the horrors they saw."

David flicked a piece of grass aside. "Let the police believe what they will. Right now, they won't believe anything else."

Mutu crouched down and picked up a piece of broken acacia. "I need to show you something." He started scratching in the dust. "Just after the blaze began I thought I saw a spirit, dancing in the heat. She was flowing, like this."

"She?" said David. Mutu had drawn a snake.

"It might have been a woman," the African said.

A fly landed on David's knee. He watched it change position three times before he swatted it away. "Can you tell me anything more about her? Was she old? Long-haired perhaps?"

"Someone called out to me," Mutu continued. "I looked away and looked back and the figure was gone. I'm sorry I cannot help you further." He wiped his scratchings out, then gestured a tender brown hand toward Grace. "What will you do with this object, David Rain?"

David turned his head to look at the man. "How do you know my name?"

Mutu gave a bucktoothed smile. Rocking back and forth on his haunches he said, "Sophie spoke of you fondly. She told me once that this . . . creation reminded her of home. Of a loving family. Of a garden. Of you. Will you weep for her, David?"

David turned his face to the sky. That was the one thing he couldn't do: weep. Right now, that thought was breaking his heart.

Mutu tossed the branch aside and stood up, dusting his palms. He placed a warm hand on the mysterious man's shoulder, then started on the short walk back to the center.

"Mutu, wait."

He turned.

"I didn't tell you what I would do with the dragon."

Somewhere in the distance an egret called. Mutu looked toward the sound, pulling a piece of thatching grass through his fingers. "And what will you do with the dragon?"

"Give her this." A few inches above David's open palm, something tiny, like a flashing star, hovered.

"What is it?"

"Life, Mutu."

A slightly high-pitched hum escaped from the gap between Mutu's lips. "The greatest gift of all," he said.

"Good-bye, David Rain." And this time, when he turned toward the ruined buildings, his journey was not interrupted.

When Mutu was out of sight, David said quietly in dragontongue, "Show."

Groyne materialized on his palm. He was holding Grace's sparkling fire tear.

"You did well," said David. "Did she sense you beside her?"

Groyne shook his head. *What now?* he hurred, looking at the wondrous treasure he had caught.

David pulled the obsidian from his pocket. He spiraled it close to the tear, watching the dark fire splash against its walls like an angry wave. "We take Grace back to the Crescent," he said, "and we see what we can do about this . . ."

HOME

David came in to find Liz and Alexa at the kitchen table, busy with clay and modeling paints. Alexa ran to her father at once, wearing a smock that Liz had made for her. She clamped her arms around him in a misshapen hug, leaving clay smears clinging to the sides of his jacket.

"Hello, baby," he said, mussing her shining wavy black hair.

"Aunty Liz is going to let me make a dragon, Daddy."

"Is that right?"

Alexa grinned like a fish. "Shall I make a listener — like yours?" She pointed at Grace. "She's very pretty."

"She's not mine," he said quietly. "You should make what you see in here." He tapped the crown of Alexa's head. "Isn't that right, 'Aunty'?"

"Yes," Liz muttered, alarmed to see Grace, quite lifeless, in his hands. "Why is Grace with you? Lucy said you went to Africa. Is everything all right?"

David put Grace down on the table. Her bright green scales were beginning to fade to the same washed-out gray as Gwillan's. Her wonderful ears, normally so upright and alert, were bent and fixed forward. Gruffen flew down from his perch on the windowsill and landed beside her. He tapped her snout. There was no response.

"She's shed her tear," said David. He nodded at the counter where Groyne had just materialized, holding it. "I'm sorry, Liz. I couldn't prevent it."

Bewilderment tore at the lines of Liz's face. She turned Grace left and right, then stood up quickly and went to Groyne. "Why has he got it? What on Earth happened? For a healthy dragon to shed its tear it has to be deeply —" She paused midsentence. "Sophie." She fixed her former tenant with a harrowed look. "No." She backed away, flapping her hands. "Not my beautiful Sophie. No."

"Sophie," said Alexa, as if she'd just picked up a piece of a puzzle. "Oh."

David kissed the tips of his fingers and touched them to the top of the little girl's head, then he went straight to Liz. Fighting to steady her flailing arms, he shook her and made her look into his eyes. "There was nothing I could do. She was dead before I arrived in Africa."

There was a sudden thump in the hall doorway.

Lucy had just fainted in a heap on the floor.

Gretel brought her around with a delicate potion of lemon balm, lavender, and almond essence. For several minutes, all Lucy could do was sit with her head against her mother's palm and sob. Eventually, she turned her gaze toward David, who was standing with Alexa, holding the child's hand.

I'm sorry, she mouthed, tears bunching at the corners of her eyes.

"It's not your fault," he said.

"But if I'd told you about the e-mail sooner?"

He came over and placed his hand on her forehead, letting it slip to support her cheek. "It's not your fault."

She squirmed around to look at Groyne. "Will Grace be OK?"

"I hope so," he said. "Why don't you go and lie down for a while? I need to talk to your mom. Gretel." He snapped his fingers. The potions dragon landed on Lucy's knee. "Take her upstairs and make her calm. Lexie, you go, too."

"We can do stories," Alexa said, slipping her fingers into Lucy's.

The pale-faced teenager looked at her mom.

"Go on," Liz whispered. "I'll be up soon."

*   *   *

When the girls were a creak of footsteps on the landing, David dropped into a seat at the table and explained the events in Africa to Liz.

Her eyes picked out a tile in the center of the floor. "This is awful, David. You must be devastated."

He passed a hand halfway through his hair. It still carried the scent of smoke and death. Haunted by the image of Sophie's face, he let his gaze and his thoughts dip solemnly toward Grace. "I knew she would cry her tear. If I'd tried to interrupt I'd have lost concentration and given the raven a chance to absorb her grief. So I instructed Groyne to turn invisible and catch the tear, knowing it was Grace's best chance of survival. She might not thank me for it. Without Sophie, there will always be a gray shadow in her auma."

Liz pressed her lips together and cupped one hand around Grace's body, as if she might warm her back to life. "I remember the day I made her," she said, unable to suppress the wobble in her voice. The usual sparkles of green in her eyes were all but misted over and lost. "It was a beautiful August afternoon, the year before you came to the house. She was unusual because I already had the listener on the fridge and I could see no reason she should come into being. But she seemed content enough just to sit in the den and meditate, as they do sometimes. I could tell she was waiting for someone special. I thought when you came it was going to be you. But she told me on the first day you were not the one. She knew, David. She knew Sophie was coming. And now these creatures have . . ."

She broke down freely then. David gathered her into his arms and held her till her grief had subsided. When she was ready he said to her calmly, "I've instructed Grockle to hunt the birds down."

"Grockle?"

"Yes. He's at my command. He'll trace them and destroy them. I owe Sophie that." He sat again, holding his face in his hands. "It may not seem like it, but at the moment these ravens are acting without real purpose, compelled to follow their quest for dark fire by the memory of what they saw on Farlowe. What troubles me is how they latched on to Grace. An isolated dragon was always going to be an easier target than any in the Crescent, but I think I unwittingly led them to her."

"How?" said Liz.

"When Zanna went to Farlowe I ordered Groyne to track her. He took a fix off your listener and another off Grace. Anyone with the means to eavesdrop those signals could have easily identified Grace's coordinates."

"Would these birds be capable of that?"

"I don't know," David said, musing on it. "Maybe they had help. The man I spoke to, Mutu, told me he thought he saw a woman at the center, just before the blaze began."

"Gwilanna? In Africa?"

"She did threaten us at the church. And she has the isoscele of Gawain, remember. That gives her a direct conduit into every dragon you've ever created. Grace would have been a little beacon of his auma. Not difficult for a sibyl like her to detect."

Liz sighed and shook her head. "Brutal destruction is not Gwilanna's way."

David picked up a place mat and tapped it against the tabletop. "She wants illumination to a dragon, Liz. Maybe she'll do anything to get it? Anyway, the answer to the problem is pretty basic: What we need to do is remove the prize. If we neutralize the dark fire in the obsidian, we won't have to worry about any more negative outcomes."

"Neutralize it? How would that affect Gwillan?"

Before David could answer, the front door opened and Zanna came sailing into the kitchen. "Liz, can I borrow your scissors, please?" Knowing she needed no real permission, she went to the utensils drawer and yanked it open. With a brief, slightly puzzled glance at Groyne, she whipped the scissors out and bumped the drawer closed with her hip. "Short vacation. Lousy tan. How was your girlfriend, David?" Sweeping back toward the hall, she told Liz she'd have the scissors back within the hour. She'd put one foot across the floor bar separating kitchen from hall when David said quietly, "She's dead."

Zanna froze. She turned around and stared at him. "Dead?"

"Please," Liz begged. "You two. Not now."

David got up and slid his chair under the table. He picked up a modeling stick and drilled it into the unworked clay. He nodded at Groyne, who dematerialized with the fire tear. "Bring the icefire up to the den," he said to Liz. And picking up Grace, he brushed past Zanna without another word.

A few minutes later the door of the Dragons' Den creaked open and footsteps sounded across the wooden floor.

David was sitting at Liz's workbench. Grace and Gwillan were on the bench in front of him and Groyne was on the potter's turntable, enjoying the sensation of pressing his toes into a loose bit of clay. He was still holding the fire tear.

The visitor, Zanna, perched herself on a tall wooden stool just within David's peripheral vision. "Liz has told me, briefly, what happened in Africa. I'm sorry — about Sophie. And for what I said."

All around the room dragons shuffled their feet. Bonnington, lying on a shelf on a roughed-up blanket, moved his ears forward then went back to sleep.

"The ravens are growing in confidence," said David, as far away as his gaze implied. "It's possible Gwilanna is controlling them. If that's so, sooner or later the kind of devastation I saw in Africa is going to come here, unless we're united against it. I've put some procedures into place to deal with the threat. The best apology you can give me is to help me see them through. I need you on my side, Zanna. We all do."

A small lump formed in Zanna's throat. She gulped it down, half-hoping he wouldn't hear it, half-hoping he would. Stretching her body shape long and slim, she stared at the lonely gray figures of Gwillan and Grace.

On the shelf beside her, G'reth the wishing dragon was pressing his wonderful paws together. Gollygosh, right next to him, was sitting on the special tool kit he carried. "All right, I'm willing to work with you. But I want a few answers first."

David leveled his gaze at her.

Her perfect mouth trembled a little but she said, "You can begin by telling me why my daughter appears to have wings growing out of her back...."

ABOUT ALEXA

She's a messenger," David said, as casually as if he was telling her the time or remarking on the weather or bending down to tie his shoelace. He seemed to have been expecting the question for weeks.

"A messenger?" The scorn returned to Zanna's voice in a flash.

"Alexa is a synthesis of dragon and human — or rather, illumined Fain and human. People will look at her and see an angel. She will be a symbol of harmony and hope."

"Whoa. Whoa. Whoa." Zanna stood up and walked a full circle, digging her hands into her jeans' back pockets. "Where on the curriculum of motherhood was this?"

David swung around to face her directly, allowing himself a moment to observe how stunning she looked whenever she was tense. "She knows what she needs. Just follow your instincts."

"Oh, easy for you to say, Daddy. Bringing up an angel isn't exactly top of the list in parenting class, you know! How's she going to live in this world? She'll be an outcast. She'll be . . ."

"I told you, this world is changing," he said. "The Earth is ready to accept a new species."

Zanna fixed him with an ice-cold glare. "My daughter is not a species. She's not something to be put into a jar, or poked or prodded or classified for scientific reference. I thought you were talking about dragons anyway?"

"Dragons are hardly new," he said. "This is their world. It always was. When everything is ready, they will colonize again. Only this time, things will be different."

"Oh? Surprise me?" She folded her arms.

Now it was David's turn to stretch. With their body

language almost mirrored he said, "The last human dragon era didn't end well. Any day now, *The National Endeavor* will remind the world of that."

"*The National Endeavor*? Tam Farrell's magazine?"

"Rupert Steiner is ready to publish his interpretation of The Last Dragon Chronicles."

Zanna looked as if she needed to pinch herself. "You're working with Tam?"

"Let's just say he's part of the team; you learned as much on North Walk, I think."

"Oh, I'm learning a lot of things," said Zanna. She swept back to the stool again. "In fact, I've got a small revelation for you. When the Wicked Witch of Scrubbley was last around, healing Liz of the obsidian poison, we had a revealing sibyl-to-sibyl chat. She told me it was your kind who bungled the last age of dragons."

"My kind?"

"Oh, sorry, didn't you know? She refers to you as a Fain 'construct.' That was pleasant, by the way — for me to learn I'd had a child by someone who wasn't completely human."

"Alexa isn't human — completely," he reminded her. "But you love her — the way you loved me at the time."

"Don't play that game with me," she said, grinding the sentence into spittle. "The pledge I just made is entirely platonic. Never lose sight of that."

He held up his hands. "So what do you want to know?"

"Oh, let me think." She snapped her fingers repeatedly by her ear. "A word beginning with *E* . . . ?"

Everything? hurred G'reth, just beating Gruffen to the answer.

"Thank you," Zanna said to the wisher. "Well?" She glared at David again.

"How much did Gwilanna tell you?"

"Doesn't matter. I want to hear it from the dragon's mouth. The full story, not the spaces in between. Particularly the bits that concern my angel."

David ran his hands along his thighs, patting them as he reached his knees. "OK. The history is straightforward enough: When the Fain commingled with the earliest humans they made a terrible error of judgment. They had no idea that their hosts would compete against each other for superiority, then turn on the indigenous community of dragons and try to wipe them out. From that aggression the Ix were spawned. There has been darkness in this sector of the universe ever since. The Fain are attempting to put things right. By recolonizing the Earth with a new dragon population, they plan to draw the Ix back to their point of origin — and deal with the problem once and for all."

"So this Arctic wheeze is a trap?"

"In a sense."

"What happens when they throw back the mist?"

G'reth rolled his eyes toward David.

"We open the Fire Eternal and the transformation of the Ix begins."

"Transformation?" Zanna's gothic eyes flashed like knives. "Why don't I like the sound of this?" She got up and turned away, nodding tautly. "So what are you going to do? Drill a big hole in the Arctic ice cap and sweep the nasty thought-beings down into a barbecue at the center of the Earth while the human race looks on and goes 'ooh'? Is that it?"

"Nice image. Bit more complex than that."

"Too right," she said, making her ponytail kick. "I may not have your Fain insights, but I'm smart enough to know that you can't defeat evil, you can only rise above it. It's part of what keeps the universe in balance. Ask Arthur about the fifth force sometime."

"Arthur and I are united," said David. "And you're right, the Ix can't be defeated as such — but their negative auma can be transmuted."

"Oh, yeah? Tell that to Lucy. She's still scared out of her wits by them."

"I have talked to Lucy," he said. His gaze drifted sideways, compressing into bitterness. "She was attacked by an Ix:risor, a highly intensified Ix grouping, sometimes called a Comm:Ix or a Cluster. When they're concentrated into a conglomerate like that they become almost impossible for the human mind to resist. But that's exactly the state we need them in: one huge cluster. It's getting them there that's the difficult part."

"And whose finger will be on the trigger when you do? I'd never seen that mangy crone Gwilanna scared until she talked about you meddling with the Fire Eternal."

"It won't be me," he said, and looked at her hard.

Slowly, the implication in his gaze began to register. "No," she said, covering the scars on her arm. "If you put Alexa in any kind of danger, I'll —"

"Alexa is already in danger," he said, with a calmness she found unsettling. To her deeper dismay, she realized she was trying hard not to cry.

"Listen to me," he said, his eyes as violet as Gruffen's or G'reth's. "Alexa's been protected since before she was born. Her auma has been watched over by many guardians. The reason the ravens didn't go for her on North Walk is because the Ix have no idea what she is."

"But Gwilanna does," Zanna said pointedly, the graveyard threat still ringing in her ears.

David nodded and drew himself up. "Gwilanna is a menace. But she's not stupid enough to sell her soul to the Ix. She wants to bond with a dragon, not a darkling. It's far more likely she'll provoke the conflict to bring the dragons into play. That was always her aim on Farlowe."

"And in Africa?"

"I don't know yet if she was even there. I think that sibyls around the world are being drawn to sites of activity because they can sense the dragon auma in the North. But Gwilanna could still be a real threat. I want you to trace her again for me. It would be good to know which bit of the ointment my fly is in."

Zanna gave a disgruntled *hmph*. "I've tried. She's wise to me, David. She's marked me up like a piece of spam. But I can promise you this: If she goes near Alexa, I'll kill her. Stone dead."

"Then you might have to get in a line," he said. "And I'm not just talking about me and you. Alexa is the key to everything. She will be the light that people will be drawn to, a new breath of life for this ailing planet. The Ix are not the only threat to human development. In the last forty years, the Earth has undergone dramatic environmental changes. We believe the climate scientists have got their predictions seriously muddled. If things are allowed to go on as they are, you might not see the Arctic ice melt away gradually in thirty or forty years, it could happen suddenly, within as little as a twelve-month period. The results will be cataclysmic, and the real sadness is that the human race is beginning not to think about preventing the melt, but how they're going to cope with the aftermath. The dragons can change all that. Once people come to terms with the benefits of having a dragon culture here, the human race — and Gaia — will enter a new phase of spiritual evolution."

"Assuming it all goes to plan," Zanna said. "What's to stop mankind attacking the dragons like they did before?"

"Alexa." He glanced at the dragons around him, blowing their smoke rings and swishing their tails. "She was ... imagined," he said carefully, "to be a bridge between the two cultures. For humans, she represents the promise of what can be achieved —"

"A race of six and a half billion angels?"

David shook his head. "Only a small fraction of humans will ever achieve Alexa's level of illumination."

"And what happens to the rest?"

"In time, the same thing that's happened to the polar bears."

Zanna squinted at him, not unlike a bear.

"They'll enter Ki:mera," he said.

A HAMMER BLOW

Ki:mera? The Fain world?" Zanna stared at him blankly. "Every single bear has been taken there?"

"Not taken. Crossed over. Into another dimension. When the climate is stable, as many bears as want to will return. It's a journey into freedom, Zanna. Whatever good mankind, or bearkind, can imagine — in Ki:mera, they can achieve it."

At that moment, Liz tapped the door and walked in. "Hope I'm not interrupting anything?"

"Just the future of the human race," Zanna muttered.

"Well, I'm glad to see you're getting along," Liz said. She held out a plastic container to David. "Here's the icefire, what there is left of it."

David took the box from her and opened it. Inside was a small fraction of the snowball, given to Liz long ago, still glistening with Gawain's auma. *The fire that melts no ice,* David thought. He could feel it resonating in his heart. He placed it on the workbench next to Gwillan, then stood the obsidian chunk beside that and called Gollygosh and G'reth off their shelf. Groyne folded his wings and rubbed his toes against his leg scales to clean them of clay.

"What is that he's holding?" Zanna asked.

"Grace's fire tear," David said. "I want to try a mutual auma shift with it."

She threw him a withering glance. "And for those of us who flunked our *Star Trek* master class . . . ?"

"If we open the obsidian and bring the tears together, I believe that we can neutralize the dark fire, especially if we add the ice into the mix."

"Open it?" Liz's expression paled. "Won't that be dangerous?"

David's silence assured her there was no other way.

She moved up behind him, clutching at her arms to

hold herself together. "Assuming the procedure works, what then?"

David looked at the two gray dragons. "We divide the neutralized tear between them."

"You're gonna split it?" Zanna railed back, puzzled. "But this is their life force. Their whole personality is determined by their tears. Surely this will mean that neither will be the individual they were before?"

She exchanged a glance with Liz, who said, "How will you open the obsidian, David?"

"We'll leave that to him." He nodded at Gollygosh.

The healing dragon stepped forward and studied the problem, then put down his tool box beside the obsidian. The cantilever flaps opened up right away and an asterisk of purple light zipped out. It settled in his hand and turned into a small magnifying glass.

David raised an eyebrow. "It appears he intends to draw it out."

Hrrrrr, said Golly, frowning thoughtfully as he circled the chunk.

"And focus it onto Grace's tear. Groyne, when this happens, the tears should naturally commingle. When I give the word, I want you to pass them over to G'reth. We're going to need to make a wish."

The wishing dragon flexed his paws in readiness.

"Why the two steps?" asked Zanna. "Why can't G'reth hold Grace's tear and the dark fire be focused straight toward him?"

David tapped his foot. "Because if anything goes wrong, Groyne can dematerialize and take the tears with him."

"And go where?"

"Into the heart of the Fire Eternal."

All eyes turned toward the shape-shifting dragon.

"I feel faint," said Liz, covering her mouth.

Zanna showed her to the stool. "Sit down." She put a hand on Liz's forehead. It was already clammy. "So that would be three of them gone, then: Gwillan, Grace, and Groyne?"

David shook his head. "Groyne's skillful; he'll drop the tears and escape. But Gwillan and Grace, they won't survive, no."

"This is madness," said Zanna, toying with her sleeve. "This whole procedure is incredibly risky. What if they end up changing gender? There has to be another way."

"Magicks are not going to solve this," said David, raising his voice to a mild command. "I'm already going out on a limb here, Zanna. The best you can do is put a cloak around the den to shield it from prying eyes — and trust that this works." He swung toward Liz. "Liz, when G'reth takes charge of the tears, I want you to adopt the frame of mind you'd be in if you were making a special dragon, then put the icefire into his paws. Your auma is the key to success. Only an act of loving creation can truly rise above the darkness. When you're done, I'm going to commingle with G'reth and make a wish for Gwillan and Grace to be restored. Are you OK with that?"

"Yes," she said, with a nervous nod. "What do you mean you're going out on a limb?"

"Never mind," he said, cradling her hands. "Golly, are you ready?"

Strangely, Gollygosh failed to respond. But what was even more bizarre was that G'reth at that moment launched himself forward and bundled the healer onto his back, spilling a jar of paintbrushes in the tumble. Liz and Zanna both jumped in shock. And though David barked a stern rebuke, G'reth would not resign the attack. None of the humans had seen what he had seen. None, he thought, was aware of the danger.

While David had been speaking, the wishing dragon had been watching Gollygosh twisting and turning his magnifying glass, calculating the likeliest path through which the dark fire might leave the obsidian. But in doing so the healer had allowed himself to be exposed to the malevolent gluttony of the fire, which had spun back into the depths of his eye and corrupted his creative auma, causing an inversion of his natural healing instinct. The first and only indication of this was when the magnifying glass suddenly changed its form — and morphed into the shape of a small hammer.

The flurry of activity behind the turntable was brief. Wings flapped. Claws flashed. Growls were issued. Gollygosh had never been a fighting dragon, but empowered by the force of temporary madness, he dug his isoscele into G'reth's left knee and punched the wisher hard on the jaw, sending him reeling across the bench. Then he stood up and swung the hammer.

The obsidian exploded: every which way from its evil center. Splinters of the volcanic magma it was made from showered the room and all its occupants. Liz screamed, and in trying to cover her face toppled sideways off the stool and collided with a shelf of plain clay dragons, causing several to fall to the floor and break. From the bedroom next door, a terrified Lucy yelled, "Mom?! What's happening? Mom?!" Footsteps sounded on the landing.

"Zanna, keep Lucy out of here," hissed David, as a snarling Bonnington appeared beside him in the form of a strapping, violet-eyed panther. The cat's gaze was fixed on a point above the workbench — where Gwillan's fire tear was hovering like a small eclipsed sun.

Gollygosh by now had broken free of its spell but was gaping openmouthed at the incredible floating object. His eyes were like the atmospheres of alien planets, swirling gas clouds of violet and green.

"Get away, both of you," David whispered.

G'reth, recognizing this order was really aimed at him, hobbled forward, grabbed the startled healer by the tail, and yanked him off the bench to hide amid the debris on the floor. Groyne, meanwhile, had instinctively dematerialized the moment the hammer had struck. On a telepathic order from David he remained invisible on the windowsill, guarding Grace's fire tear.

The dark fire pulsed and seemed to wrinkle the air around it, distorting the visual dimensions of the room as if it were gathering up a sheet by its middle. Suddenly it moved, recentering over Gwillan.

"Don't let that thing go near him!" cried Liz, stumbling forward through broken clay.

David, who'd assumed that Liz had left the room with Zanna, took his eye off the tear for a moment. In that moment, Bonnington lunged. His plan was simple: swallow his prey whole. Let the Fain entity commingled with his brain do battle with the darkness, even if it tore his mind apart.

But even Bonnington wasn't quick enough on this occasion. The dark fire evaded his leap and closed in on Liz. It struck her directly in the center of the forehead and dissolved smoothly under the skin. She crashed against the wall and slid down to the floor, her head lolling as if her neck had been severed. She began to blow a series of short, shallow breaths.

"Liz!" David was with her in an instant, cradling her face to make her look at him. "Can you speak?"

Her eyelids closed with a heavy flutter and her head thumped back against the wall.

At that moment, Zanna burst in. "Oh, my goodness, what happened?" She dropped to her knees and gripped Liz's hand.

"The dark fire has gone into her."

"*What?* But, it'll kill her. And . . . and what about the baby?"

"Let's get her to the bedroom," David said. He picked Liz up and carried her to the landing.

There he was met by a frantic Lucy. Zanna immediately took the girl's hand and whipped it down hard to gain her attention. "Come with me," she said plainly. "Your mom's had an accident. She needs you. So do I. But you have to be calm. I'll explain everything when David's got her settled."

Lucy closed her gibbering mouth and nodded. Together they turned toward Liz's room, passing Alexa on the way. The child was in the doorway of Lucy's room, looking like something from a horror movie. Still, ghostly, totally silent. One of Lucy's old plush toys was dangling from her small white hand. But it was her eyes that Zanna found most disturbing. They were angled upward, like a doll's, as if she was tracking the mysterious power that was now a part of Elizabeth Pennykettle.

A MISSION FOR LUCY

Leaving Liz in Zanna's care, David telephoned the university to inform Arthur what had happened. He kept the details sparse, adopting the approach that Zanna had taken when calming Lucy. Arthur arrived in a taxi shortly afterward and went straight to the bedroom. Meanwhile, David took Alexa to the Dragons' Den and together they made the room tidy. When all was done, David called the little girl across to the workbench and ordered Groyne to show himself again. This time, David allowed Alexa to hold Grace's fire tear, encouraging her to feel the power of its natural creativity and love. Then, taking up the last of the icefire, which despite the commotion still remained unmelted in its box, he touched it onto Grace's snout and used the auma of Gawain inside him to help it soften the membranes of her nose. When Grace was ready, he invited Alexa to reintroduce the tear to her. The spark was engulfed as if a light had blinked off. Grace spluttered and shivered and almost fell over. A worried Gollygosh put down his tool box. The flaps opened and the usual asterisk of light turned itself into a small blanket that he draped around Grace's slender shoulders. David looked at Liz's dragon Guinevere and sent her a message in dragonthought. Alexa gasped as Guinevere opened her eyes and two violet rays of life-giving energy poured out and wrapped another kind of blanket around the ailing listener.

David took Alexa's hand. "What do you feel?" he asked her.

"Grace and Gwillan are going to get better," she said.

He squeezed her hand until she looked up at him. "Do you dream it? That Gwillan will live?"

But Alexa just shrugged and led him downstairs.

By now she was her happy self again, content to play

with the clay on the kitchen table. As David watched her building "something" (as yet undescribed) he made his second telephone call. "It's time," was all he said and placed the phone back on its stand.

A short while later, Tam Farrell was in the house.

Leaving Alexa at work on her creation, David drew Tam outside to talk.

"OK, what's wrong?" the young Scot asked. "Usually when I come here the house is overflowing with good-looking women. Where are they all?"

"Upstairs. We had an accident," David said. "It hasn't been a great day." He explained what had happened in Africa and the den.

Tam's breath whistled through the air at pace. He looked down the garden, absently nodding. "Pretty place, this. Lovely plum tree. My grandma used to have one just like it." He slid his hands into the pockets of his jacket. "Who'd have thought that a quaint little garden in suburban Scrubbley might be the setting for an interdimensional war?"

"There's no reason that should happen," David said. "We can contain this. You, me — Zanna."

Tam's expression failed to match that view. "Come on, David. You messed up, big-time. You should have taken the fire north when you had the chance. Isn't that what the dragon clan wanted?"

David's eyes slipped into their scalene profile. "If I'd gone north, they would have cast whatever was left of Gwillan into the Fire Eternal. I couldn't let that happen. I owe a great debt to Liz and Lucy. They taught me what it's like to feel human, Tam." His eyeline fell upon the rockery and its alpines, the scene of so much domestic adventure: the squirrels, Caractacus the crow, Henry Bacon. But even as the happy times flooded back, the sadness overwhelmed him again. For all of those memories only led one way: back to Sophie Prentice. David closed his eyes and recentered himself. "The Wayward Crescent dragons are practically my kin. How could I not try to save Gwillan's life? The attempt to commingle the dark fire with Grace's tear was valid. If nothing else, it would have proved that the Ix can be easily transmuted."

"If it had worked," Tam pointed out. "Surely all it's shown you is a greater danger? It might be more than Gwillan you have to sacrifice now. What's the situation with Liz?"

Before David could answer, the back door opened and Arthur's voice called out to him.

"Coming!" David replied. Then in a quieter voice to Tam, "Do you have everything you need from Steiner?"

Tam nodded. "'The Chronicles of the Last Twelve Dragons' comes bursting off the pages on Friday morning. Pretty mind-blowing stuff. Got a draft in my bag if you want to see it."

David shook his head. "I want you to take Lucy to Scuffenbury before publication, before the crowds descend. I want her well away from here, in case we have problems."

"Lucy's not going to leave if her mother's in danger."

"Then we'll have to persuade her somehow. Come on."

"One more thing." Tam caught his arm. "Gadzooks has been sighted again. He turned up in India and left another message."

"A new location?"

"Yeah. Steiner's translated it. Somewhere on Svalbard this time. I've got a team of reporters and two film crews heading up there, and to Fujiyama to record whatever happens there. But something's puzzling me about all this. Why did Gadzooks choose Scuffenbury as the main focus of awareness for Steiner? I mean, it's an interesting place, but compared to a dormant Japanese volcano or some remote Norwegian archipelago it's a modest little hill in Maine for a dragon to pop out of — by newsreel standards. If you're going to make a splash, make a big one, is what I'm saying."

David glanced toward the kitchen. Arthur was standing there, cradling Bonnington. Gretel had just buzzed by, snatching the heads off several flowers. "Gadzooks has always been a step ahead of time. If he chose Scuffenbury, he chose it for a reason. Keep your camera handy. *The National Endeavor* might be on the brink of another big scoop."

With that, David led Tam back to the kitchen and introduced him, in brief, to Arthur. "How's Liz?" they both asked.

Arthur felt for the countertop and leaned back against it. Still cradling Bonnington, he said, "She appears to be stable, but in some kind of semiconscious state."

"And the baby?" asked David.

"Zanna believes it's unaffected — for now."

"For now?" Tam said.

Arthur's strokes over Bonnington's head became shaky. "Would I not be right in thinking, David, that because of Liz's ancestry my son has the potential to be dragon under the right — or possibly the wrong — conditions? And if a dragon could develop, then given the nature of the 'spark' that entered his mother, surely a darkling could, too?"

Before David could answer, Alexa ran in as chirpy as ever. "Daddy?"

David trapped her absently against his hip. "Not now, sweetie." His gaze was on Arthur. The professor, his "father," was looking pale and disoriented.

"But I made something." She pointed to a figure beside the mound of clay.

Arthur angled Bonnington's head toward it.

"A horse?" said Tam.

Not just any old horse. It had a ribbonlike body and tapering neck. Its legs were so thin it was a wonder how Alexa had ever made it stand.

A bedraggled-looking Lucy came in behind the child. Though her breath was briefly taken by the sight of Tam, she made no attempt to tidy her appearance. "That's the Scuffenbury horse," she said, sounding tired. "How did you learn about that?"

Alexa, as always, gave no answer. She bent forward and stroked the horse's nose, then marched across to Tam and took his left hand. "You touch it," she said.

"Oh, I'm clumsy," said Tam. "I might knock it over."

"No you won't," said Alexa and drew him toward it.

On a nod from David, Tam touched his finger to the horse's back. To Lucy's amazement, a spark ignited in the region of its heart and radiated slowly outward, turning the bland gray clay the crystalline white of Arctic ice. "How did you do that?" she gasped.

Alexa clapped in glee. "I'm going to show Mommy." She scooted away with her prize.

David signaled to Lucy to get her attention. "Tam's going to take you to the real horse, Lucy. I want you to pack, right now."

She looked at Tam. "Don't be dumb. Mom needs me."

"Scuffenbury might be where she needs you the most."

Surprisingly, this notion gathered further support from Arthur. "It seems appropriate," he put in, "that Alexa should create a replica white horse at a time when the Scuffenbury dragon might rise. She appears to be picking up on something. Considering Elizabeth's current condition it falls to me as Lucy's guardian to make a decision: I give my blessing for the journey."

"Arthur!" The girl dropped her hands onto her hips.

"Go," he said, with an audible gulp. "Find whatever powers might help your mother." A film of moisture sliding across his eyes made them appear more eerie than ever.

"My car's outside," Tam said quietly. "I'll . . . well, I'll be waiting, OK?" For the second time in a matter of days, he went past Lucy making only eye contact.

The girl skewed a hand across her forehead. "This is crazy," she said. "I can't leave now." She switched her stressed gaze back to David.

"Your mom will have all the protection I can give her," he said. "There's nothing you can do here, Lucy. Arthur's right: Scuffenbury might hold the answers. Tam will look after you. He'll make the arrangements."

Lucy twirled a nest of red hair in her hand. "Can I take Gwendolen?"

"Yes, of course."

"You really think this will help Mom?"

"It's what she would have wanted for you," David said carefully.

"What will you tell her when she wakes?"

"That you're obeying your birthright."

That was enough to make Lucy squeeze herself into a private huddle. David made a move to comfort her, but she shook a hand in his face and stumbled away. Halfway up the stairs, he heard her burst into tears.

When all was quiet again Arthur said, "That wasn't easy for me, David. I assume you wanted my support for this venture. I'm placing a lot of trust in you."

David drifted back into the kitchen. "Tell me something," he said, running a thumb inside Bonnington's ear. "Do the others know you can see through his eyes?"

Looking grim, in the manner of an exposed schoolboy, Arthur shook his head.

"Then let it be our secret," David said. He tilted up Bonnington's chin. "I'm going to take my old room back. That's as far away from Liz as I'll be from now on."

Arthur nodded silently and walked out of the room.

With a jarring note of dragontongue, David called for Groyne.

The shape-shifter appeared on the table beside him.

"I want all the house dragons on full alert — except Grace; she needs to rest. Tell them to report anything unusual, no matter how trivial, to me."

Hrrr, went Groyne, and dematerialized again.

David picked up a modeling stick and twisted it through his restless fingers. *Heck of an afternoon,* he thought. *Heck of a life.*

But unbeknownst to him, that life was about to get worse. For as Groyne reappeared in the Dragons' Den and began to give the special dragons their orders, he glanced at the blanketed Grace and noticed she had gone into her solid state. Should he report it? No. Dragons often rested in semistasis. Besides, Grace was recuperating, wasn't she?

Later, however, like Golly with the hammer, Groyne would come to blame himself for much of what followed. For if the shape-shifting dragon had investigated closely, he would have seen there was something very wrong about Grace. She was standing on the workbench, partly in shadow. What Groyne had failed to see was on her unlit side, under the blanket. She was being touched by the isoscele of another dragon. Grace was solid for a reason, but it wasn't for rest.

Her auma was being drained through the tail of Gwillan.

PART TWO

SCUFFENBURY HILL

THE ROAD TO SCUFFENBURY

"OK," said Tam. "Tell me what I have to do to make this work."

Lucy threw him a moody glance.

"We've been driving for an hour and you haven't said a word."

"Wrong. I said 'thank you' for this." She raised up a bottle of carbonated water, put the neck to her lips, and took a long swig.

"I don't think you'll find 'uh' in the dictionary," he corrected her. "Technically, it's not an expression of gratitude, it's a grunt."

"You're the journalist," she said.

"Oh, is that what it is? You still don't trust me because I tried to run a feature on David once?"

"I'm cold," she said, refusing to answer. She pulled her sweater sleeves over her palms. "Can't we turn the heat up?"

Tam turned the dial a little, flipping the vent settings so that warm air was blowing around her feet. To compensate, he opened the driver's side window.

"What's the point of doing that?" she railed.

"I feel more comfortable with a cool air flow."

"Yeah, well, I get hay fever. Hello?"

"And I get headaches — and I'm driving," he countered.

She sighed, crossed her arms, and slumped to one side.

He touched a button and narrowed the air gap at his window. "Haven't changed much, have you?"

"This is so boring," Lucy said, not about to enter a discussion that might have any possibility of including the word "teenager." Instead, she stared at the never-ending landscape of rural New England. The green rolling hills. The empty gray sky. It had been the same view for the last twenty minutes. And barely another vehicle had passed them.

"It's a military zone," Tam said, beeping the GPS. "Some of it's restricted. The military uses these fields for training exercises. Favorite place for UFO spotters as well."

Lucy capped her water and put it away. "Oh, that's really comforting, thanks. So if I don't get squashed by a tank or blasted by a missile there's always the chance I'll be abducted by aliens?"

"As opposed to being abducted by a Scot in a Range Rover? What are the chances, eh?"

She clamped her teeth together and grimaced.

"Come on, talk to me," he said, after a few more minutes of annoyed silence. "We need to trust each other, Lucy. If I'm going to take care of you, it would help me to know just what you're thinking."

"Thought you could read my mind?" she sniffed, staring ahead at the unfolding road, a snide reference to the time when Gwendolen had "spiked" him with information about the Pennykettle family, to wake him from a mind-blanking spell that Zanna had cast.

"Memories," he said. "I've got nothing more than memories. I have a journalist's intuition, but I'm not telepathic."

"*Hmph,*" she replied, and drew in her lips. "How did you do that thing with the horse?"

"Ah," he said. "Well, that's thanks to David."

"Your pal."

"My . . . well, I don't know what he is, really. After he came to my rescue on Farlowe, I just seemed to qualify as part of the . . ."

"Clan?"

"Team."

"There's a difference?"

"I'd say so. I don't have dragon auma running through my veins."

"You've got something," she said, remembering Zanna's description of the way he'd dispatched the raven on North Walk. "If you want me to trust you, you'd better talk."

The Range Rover flashed past a blue parking sign. Tam signaled and pulled over onto the shoulder. He yanked on the brake but left the engine running. "OK, you've had some experience with polar bears, haven't you?"

"I've talked to them," she said, somewhat smugly.

He turned his dark brown eyes on her.

"You're not a bear," she said, with a condescending cluck. All the same, his gaze made her shudder.

"Not the way David is — or can be," he said. "But ever since I met him, I have been able to call upon the auma of two of them." He turned up his palms.

Lucy shriveled back slightly as their faces appeared like watery reflections under his skin.

"This is Avrel, the Teller of Ways," he said, flexing his left hand until the image rippled. "And this is Kailar, a fighting bear, on the right. He's the one who doesn't like ravens."

Lucy wrinkled her nose and gulped. "Next time I have a Halloween party, remind me to invite you."

He went back to the wheel, let the clutch in, and

drove on. They had traveled half a mile before he asked, "Are you shocked?"

She shook her head.

He looked over, making her catch his gaze. Eventually, she spoke again. "If you've got a Teller's auma inside you that means you've got the legends of the Arctic in your head."

"Pretty much. Why? Do you want to hear a story?"

"Tell me about the last twelve dragons," she said.

"I can do better than that." Keeping a careful eye on the road, he reached over to the backseat, pulled a bag forward, and dropped it in her lap. "There's a copy of the latest *Endeavor* in there. You'll find a full translation of the writings Anders Bergstrom discovered on the Hella glacier in 1913."

Lucy rested her fingers on the bag as if she'd just found the Holy Grail. "I heard Mom and Arthur discussing this. She didn't want to tell me. It's bad, isn't it?"

"It's history," said Tam. "Your history. Open it."

Doing her best to remain poised, Lucy undid the buckles and drew out the magazine. On the cover was a stunning close-up of a dragon's eye. "I've seen this before," she said.

"The cover image?"

"Yes."

"I doubt it. The artwork was commissioned entirely in-house."

Lucy moved her head from side to side. "Next time you come to our kitchen, look on the wall above the countertop. Alexa drew this. The same triangular-shaped eye, with three extensions like a comet's tail at the back. Even the scales are the same shade of green, all arranged like overlapping roof slates. I'm telling you, Alexa drew this."

Tam shrugged. "Well, she is David's kid. Go on, take a look. The whole edition is dedicated to the Hella findings. There are lots of maps and expedition pieces, plus digital reproductions of all of Bergstrom's original photographs. The bit you'll want is the center spread."

Lucy flipped to it. In a scripted font against a back-drop of stone, to give the impression that you were reading something off a cave wall, were two spreads of patchy writing.

"There are two translations," Tam informed her, pulling in to give a clanking farm vehicle room to roll past. "The one you're looking at is based on the exact photographic evidence with no further interpretation from Steiner. It's been laid out to match the way the original marks were burned into the stone. It's quite difficult to make sense of because it's not laid down in anything we'd recognize as a structured system. Steiner is confident it's the work of one dragon, because the shapes and strengths of the inflections are consistent. He's written a pretty dense article about how he thinks it should be read. He believes the dragons don't read methodically left to right or top to bottom or even in a circular shape; he thinks they just take in the pattern as a whole. If you flip over a couple of pages you'll find a more grammatical account, with Steiner's conti-nuity suggestions. Like most languages, dragontongue has a unique syntax. By the weekend, scholars all over the world are going to be putting their own twist on it, but the crucial elements are very clear: The dragons were threatened with extinction and they set out a plan to deal with their enemy. It's powerful stuff. Take your time."

Lucy slanted her gaze downward. The first thing she noticed were some of the names: Galen, Gessine, Gyrrhon, G'larne — which was the first indication of authenticity for her. They all began with G. Anything like "Ember" or "Elrond the Red" would have seen the magazine flying straight out of the window. She took her time, as Tam had suggested, picking out phrases, reading snippets, digesting unusual sequences of words. Yet somehow, despite the need to know, her eyes kept jumping over the script without being able to settle, as if it required a special kind of concentration just to acknowledge the words were there. She thought about sharing the task with Gwendolen. But the little dragon was asleep in her bag and it would have been unfair to wake her.

So Lucy changed her approach and searched for the one word she knew would be meaningful. When she found it, however, it tore a small strip of surprise from her heart. The name Gawaine leapt out several times, but the word always ended with an *e*, suggesting a feminine gender. Maybe it was the way the dragons spoke back then, like olde worlde Englishe when Shakespeare was alive? Gawain, female? That was silly. Impossible. She studied the context where his name occurred. The word "chosen" appeared and also "receiver." In another, much denser section, she read "drinker of tears, gatherer of fire." And suddenly it struck her what this meant. The other dragons, the remaining eleven of the "Wearle" (that word was evident throughout) had shed their tears through "the unnatural eye" (whatever that meant) and Gawain had . . . she drew back a little. Ingested them? If that was correct then Gawain would have had the auma of twelve fire tears sparking through his body, including his own. He'd be like a ticking bomb. With that thought in mind, she focused her attention on the one outstanding section where his name was mentioned, right at the very center of the script. The text here was dark and heavily compacted, but she read it three times just to be sure. And each time it made her cry a little more.

She wasn't aware as she closed the magazine that the car had rolled to a halt again.

"Hey," said Tam. He moved his hand across hers.

For several seconds she could not speak. Only when she pulled away needing a tissue did she ask him, "What's the matter? Why have we stopped?" They were in the middle of a much smaller road, on a slight downward incline, with a row of hedges and grassy shoulders to either side.

He pointed up through her side of the windshield.

Beyond the hedges was a whole ridge of hills, stretching away under a string of low cloud. One of them, Lucy noticed, looked out of place. It was bumpy. More like a wart than a part of the natural landscape.

"That's Glissington Tor," said Tam.

Lucy closed her hands around the tissue she was holding. From the way he'd spoken, she guessed this was only part one of the tour manifesto. She was right. As her eyes panned across to the opposite side of the road, Tam leaned well back in his seat. And there, through his window, she saw what they had come for.

The flowing body of the Scuffenbury white horse.

THE OLD GRAY DRAGON

What now?" Lucy asked, as a few drops of light drizzle began to spot the windshield.

Tam reached into his jacket and pulled out a business card. He flipped it toward her like a folded banknote. "I've booked us in here."

"The Old Gray Dragon?"

"It's a guesthouse," he said. "Bed-and-breakfast. Right on the side of the Tor. It says in their blurb that on a still night you can hear the dragon snoring. I thought it might make you feel at home." He paused, waiting for her to dip into her usual bag of cynicisms. Her fingers were stroking the picture of the dragon. "You OK, Lucy?"

She put the magazine back into the bag. "Yeah. Let's go."

Beeping the GPS, Tam took the Range Rover on. They swept along a twisting country lane, farther and farther into the hills. By now the odd cottage was beginning to appear. A mailbox fixed to a drystone wall. Tractors, off-road. Cows. A bicycle. The suggestion of life, albeit minimal. Then, as they crested a ragged stone bridge over a deeply bouldered stream, Glissington Tor was huge in front of them, just like a strange green bubble in the Earth.

Tam dropped through the gears and powered the car up and around the bottom of the Tor. The steepness of the ascent was making Lucy dizzy and she was grateful when, after a couple of bends, Tam swung off onto an access road where a large Victorian redbrick house, half-hidden by its sloping garden and the retinal branches of a cadaverous tree, awaited them.

"This is it," he said, pulling up. He turned up his collar and quickly got out. Through her rain-spattered window Lucy could see a flight of rough, weed-ridden steps, climbing through what looked like the sort of garden where people grew their own vegetables or herbs. She spotted a cloche and that settled it for her: They had come to a hippie house. Its deep-set austere windows were just visible beyond the slope, the glass crisscrossed with strips of lead. Nothing about the place appealed to Lucy, until she caught sight of a smoky gray cat tucked up in a furry bundle on the steps. It turned its head and stared lazily at her, more concerned with soaking up the pillars of sunshine that the tree and the rain had not been able to block.

Behind her, the rear door opened and Tam started pulling out their bags. "Lovely rainbow over the vale. You going to sit there all day or what?"

He slammed the door shut before she could answer.

By way of reply she got out, marched around to the back of the vehicle, hoisted her travel bag onto her shoulder, stuck out her tongue at him, ignored the rainbow, and mounted the steps. As she reached the cat, she crouched down to stroke its dewy fur. It stared fixedly ahead, unfazed by the contact, as if it had known her all its life. But when Tam approached, the cat got up and quickly, but unfussily, disappeared behind a tent of beanpoles generously endowed with twining, heart-shaped scarlet runner leaves. Sounding a small note of triumph, Lucy walked on.

They crossed a gravel pathway (where someone had left a wheelbarrow and some long-handled tools) into a short porch. The multipaneled guesthouse door was already half-open. Tam pressed the bell. After a few moments the door swung back and they were greeted by a short, carefully dressed woman who Lucy guessed was roughly the same age as her mom.

"Mr. Farrell?" the woman asked, beaming through a pair of dark designer spectacles, whose top edges flared like the fins of a rocket.

He let loose his killer smile. "Tam."

"Lovely. And this must be your niece?"

"N—?" Lucy began. She let the word soften to "nice to meet you." Niece was more acceptable than sister, she supposed, and certainly less open to question than "friend."

"My," said the woman, "what lovely red hair you've got."

Lucy smiled aimlessly. She was used to being complimented about her hair. But for some reason — maybe because of the way this woman was staring so intently at her, making her feel like a museum exhibit — she was tempted to say, "All the better to clog up your vacuum with, Grandma." (She didn't, of course.)

"I'm Hannah," said the woman, as she invited them into a generous hallway with a stunning mosaic floor. "Two single rooms, for just the two nights, is it?"

"If the rooms are available we may stay longer," said Tam. "It rather depends how things pan out. I'm on a working vacation. Lucy's come along to see the sights and generally explore the area with me. I'm a historical writer, researching a piece about dragons."

"Well, you've come to the right place," said Hannah. "There's an enormous amount of history attached to Glissington. You know about the legend, I assume?"

"Is the dragon meant to be gray?" Lucy had picked up a leaflet that gave some history of the guesthouse. Despite what had happened to Gwillan and Grace, a gray dragon didn't seem right to her. Green. Ice blue. Red. Gold. Definitely. But gray? She was prepared to debunk the myth there and then until Hannah said, with brusque authority:

"The color of wet clay — or so I'm told." Her closed mouth formed a tight-lipped smile. "We've got more leaflets over there on the sideboard. And Clive, my husband, would be happy to fill you in with anything you don't already know. He's got every book ever written on Glissington. He's in the guest lounge watching the television, I think. He ought to be outside harvesting some food — we grow our own organic vegetables here — but there's been some news about this mist thing in the Arctic and he can't seem to drag himself away. Clive?" She marched across the hall and pushed open a door. What sounded like a news broadcast filtered out. "Clive, come and meet our new guests." She beckoned Tam and Lucy over.

"Welcome to the Old Gray Dragon," Clive said, wiping his hand across the seat of his jeans before holding it out for Tam to shake. He looked a little organic himself, Lucy thought, with Medusa black hair cascading onto his blousy white shirt. "Been following this?" he asked. His boyish blue eyes were full of wonder. "It's absolutely astonishing."

"What's happened?" said Lucy. "Has the mist gone?"

Clive shook his head. "Late last night there were reports of seismic disturbances in the high Arctic. Really got the ships on full alert. Around ten this morning, an enormous island of ice floated out of the mist. Since then, several more have appeared in different geographical locations. The mist has receded, but it's still covering the central polar region — and they still can't breach it."

"What have they found on the islands?" asked Tam.

Please, let it be bears, thought Lucy.

Clive chuckled at the question. "I don't suppose they'll let on until the military have been all over them.

Hannah's cousin is on one of the ships. It's all very hush-hush, isn't it, Han?"

She clamped her hands together and spoke to Tam. "Let me show you to your rooms. You can sign in later, once you're settled. We're very relaxed about everything here. There's only one other guest. An elderly lady, Ms. Gee. She's been here for several weeks. She's practically a resident."

Tam picked up his bag. "With all this talk about dragons I'm surprised you're not putting people up in sleeping bags in the grounds."

"Yes, it's very quiet," Hannah said. "Almost ominously so. Do follow me."

As they recrossed the hall Lucy thought to ask, "What's the name of your cat?"

"Cat? We don't have a cat," Hannah replied.

"Oh, but I saw one in the garden. Smoky-colored fur."

The rocketlike spectacles almost fizzed. "Really? Well, it wouldn't be ours. Clive's allergic to anything with fur. There's a private house a little higher up the road. They have animals. It probably strayed down from there."

Turning swiftly, Hannah led them up a wide-angled staircase, beautifully carpeted in checkered beige. At the top she offered them a choice of rooms, but in the same breath decided that Lucy should have what she called "the rose." It was obvious what she meant the moment they entered. The walls were papered a delicate shade of pink, and everything from the towels in the bathroom to the cushions on the chairs and the floral bedspread matched it. "Lovely view from here," said Hannah, marching to the window and opening the shutters. "Right across the vale."

"Can you see the horse?" asked Tam, stopping by a fireplace as tall as his shoulder to examine a fist-sized lump of rock on the mantelpiece. It was the same grayish texture as the boulders they'd seen in the stream.

"No, you'd have to climb the Tor for that," said Hannah, stepping aside to let Lucy look out, "but it's only fifteen minutes to the top from here, right out of our kitchen door."

"There!" Lucy suddenly sprang onto her toes.

"What?" said Tam.

She pointed through the window. "That cat I saw. It's staring at me."

He came to her shoulder to see. But just like before, the animal had slunk away before he could catch sight of it.

"It's somewhere near that tree," Lucy tutted, annoyed that she'd lost it again.

"Well, it's just a cat," said Tam. Looking back at Hannah he asked, "Is it dead? The tree, I mean?"

"Since the seventeenth century," Hannah replied. "There's a rather grisly story attached to it. A woman was hanged there."

"A woman?" Tam was shocked.

"Was she a witch?" gulped Lucy.

Hannah's face became serious. "That depends on your definition of 'witch.' The woman lived by the laws of the natural world. She would certainly have believed in dragons." She swung her gaze to the window. "People say we ought to have the tree cut down, but it adds a kind of mystique to the place. It hasn't rotted in all this time. And who am I to uproot history?" She stepped forward, stared at the tree for a moment, then half-closed the shutters.

Tam returned to the rock on the mantel. "What's this?"

"Part of the Glissington cairn," said Hannah. "Clive will tell you —"

"Yeah, we know about it," Lucy cut in, smiling kindly to hide her irritation. She just wanted to be alone now to crash for a while. The countryside was tiring (and scary), she'd decided.

But Hannah could read Lucy better than she thought. "People say it never existed," she said, as if she felt the need to defend her private heritage. "But if you find the right stone — and this is one of them — you can feel the ancient vibrations from it. We encourage our guests to put it under their bed at night. It keeps you in touch with the spirit of the dragon."

"Cool," said Lucy.

Tam raised a warning eyebrow at her. "So, it's just fifteen minutes from here, then, Hannah?"

"To the top of the Tor, yes."

Tam slid his cell phone open and shut. "Excellent. Nothing like a brisk walk to work up an appetite."

"I'm not going up there now," said Lucy. "Anyway, I need to phone home."

"You'll get a better signal outside," said Hannah.

Touché. Lucy's resistance failed.

"I'll go and change my shoes," said Tam.

Out of the back door, through a strangely untidy garden (rabbit hutches, ferrets, sacks of potatoes, an incongruous man-made water feature) and they were on Glissington Tor, just as Hannah had said. Nothing above them but a hump of grass. What had looked reasonably smooth from the road turned out to be the worst walk Lucy had ever experienced. It was like climbing a hill of golfer's divots.

"Oh, I hate this!" she exclaimed the fifth time she stumbled, narrowly missing yet another cow pie. "Some uncle you are! You'd better carry me, Farrell, if I twist an ankle!"

He roared with laughter. "That's actually quite witty."

And perhaps it was the auma of the ice bear within him, but as he helped her up he tugged a little too hard and she fell in so close that he had to put an arm around her waist to steady her. For a moment, their eyes met in something other than sparring mode.

"Do I look windswept?" she said.

He cleared a few strands of hair off her nose, loosened his hold, and backed away. "It's safer if you stick to the path."

So it was that some ten minutes later they were standing on the summit where Lucy got her second look at the horse. It was in her line of vision now, ready to gallop across Scuffenbury Hill. It seemed a lot closer than it actually was and made her think that if her step was large enough, she could probably mount it. That made her glance down, wary of what she might be standing on, disappointed that she didn't really feel anything. No beating heart. No rumbling breath. No auma of dragon at all. The ground here was bare, scorched by bonfires. In those places where the odd rock jutted from the soil, visitors — pilgrims — had carved their names. How many times had people come here trying to raise the spirit of the dragon? She wondered. Maybe her time would be just one more. Perhaps there was no dragon here at all.

As if he shared her disillusion, Tam checked his watch, grimaced into the wind, and said, "Come on. We'll come back tomorrow, at dawn."

Dawn? she mouthed to his disappearing back. She spread her hands and appealed to the horse. *Take me away from here.*

Great "vacation."

Thanks to her grumpiness, Lucy had forgotten to take her phone onto the Tor. But back at the guesthouse, she found a weak signal and managed to call home. She spoke for a few crackly minutes to Zanna, feeling for once that they were sharing the crisis like real sisters. There was no change in Liz's condition. Stable, but sleeping. Everything was calm.

After she'd showered, Tam took her out for something to eat. They spent the evening in a small country pub. Lucy couldn't finish her "hunter's pie" and was ready to go long before Tam was ordering dessert. They drove back to the Old Gray Dragon in silence.

Before bidding her good night, Tam reminded her exactly where he was.

"I know," she said, chewing her lip, stopping him from having to say he'd hear her calls if anything was wrong or she could rap the wall if she needed him. She stepped into her room unable to look at him. She pressed back against the closing door, felt for the key, and turned it.

She thought about another shower — maybe a bath. There were plenty of rose-scented oils to choose from. She thought about TV. She thought about cocoa. Most of all, she thought about her mom. Before she got into bed, she settled on her knees and tried to pray. She had gotten as far as "deliver us from evil" before she broke down and sobbed, burying her face chin deep into the blanket so that Tam would not hear her; she knew he'd be listening.

And then, from across the room, came the most comforting sound ever.

Hrrr.

Lucy gasped and hurried to her bag. Gwendolen! Poor Gwendolen! Stuck in there all day.

Fortunately, the little dragon didn't seem to mind. After investigating every aspect of the room (she liked the cairn rock; it did have a faint dragon auma, she said) she fluttered to the bedside table where she always sat at home and settled down under the pretty lace lampshade.

Lucy leaned over and kissed her. Now she could sleep in peace.

In bed, she did as she always did: checked her cell phone for messages. There were none, but it occurred to her she'd forgotten to e-mail Melanie before she left home. No problem. She could send a message through the phone instead.

MEL, she tapped in. GOOD 2 HEAR FRM U. SOZ 4 DELAY. GOT TIED UP. WON'T BELIEVE WHERE I AM. She paused to think. If she was going to pretend that she'd been "tied up," she might as well tell the whole white lie. She deleted "I am." I'VE BEEN, she wrote. B&B ON THE SIDE OF A DRAGON HILL!! HRRR! CAN'T BLAB NOW. WILL TELL ALL SOON. MISS U. STAY COOL. LUV2GLADE. LUCY XXX

She pressed SEND. Almost immediately a FAILED message came up. One more thing to hate about the countryside: signal-blocking hills. "Can you boost this?" she said to Gwendolen.

The little IT dragon thought about it. *Hrrr-r-rr*, she chattered.

"Plug in and bounce it off the listener at home?" *Hrrr!*

Lucy shrugged. "If you say so." She opened up one of the IT ports so that Gwendolen could push her isoscele into it. On a nod from the dragon, Lucy pressed SEND again. There was a flash of blue light and the scales around Gwendolen's tail began to rattle. Streams of green data poured down the screen, but to Lucy's satisfaction it came back with a SENT response.

"Smart," she exclaimed, and tossed the phone aside. "You're a genius. Night-night." She blew Gwendolen a kiss and slipped under the covers. Gwendolen, looking proud of her achievement, rose up and flicked off the light, plunging the room into near darkness.

Despite the unfamiliar shadows and the sounds of snoring (Tam, she guessed, not the dragon) Lucy dropped off to sleep very quickly. As her waking thoughts passed into fantasy and dreams, she saw herself on Glissington Tor again. Across the vale, the white horse rippled like a sail, but still it did not rise from the hillside. "What do I have to do to wake you?" Lucy asked it. "Tell me what I have to do."

As her dream state played with methods of communication, so she imagined the old gray dragon rising from the hill and plugging its isoscele into the earth in the same way that Gwendolen had worked the phone. Swathes of energy fizzed across the vale, lighting the ley lines electric blue. Storm clouds gathered. Rain hammered down over Scuffenbury Hill. The white horse woke up and reared into the storm, neighing at twelve dragons circling overhead. Then, bizarrely, Gwillan appeared, sitting in the branches of the hanging tree like some kind of haunted owl. Lucy felt herself twitch. He looked different. Undead. Like some kind of zombie. He was gray-scaled, hollow-eyed, and struggling to move, as though he were controlled by some outside force. Frightened, she tried to blank him out. But he peered deep inside her, into her dreams. To her horror he pricked his ears like a bat. No, not a bat. Like Grace. Like a listener.

Her hands clutched the blanket and drew it around her. Suddenly, something landed with a thud on the bed. Its presence was enough to force her eyes open.

Next to where she'd left her phone, the smoky gray cat was holding something dark and limp in its mouth. It took a pace forward and dropped the kill on her chest.

A mutant raven — with Gwillan's face.

At that point, Lucy screamed.

An Encounter with Ms. Gee

Lucy!" Tam was outside her door in seconds. The aged oak panels shuddered as he beat them. She saw the handle rattle. He called her name again.

"What is it? What's the matter? I thought I heard a scream?" Hannah's wiry voice joined in.

"Stand back!" Tam shouted. "I'm going to break it down."

"What? No! We have spare keys for all the rooms. Mr. Farrell? N —!"

At that moment, Lucy opened the door.

Tam rushed in and gathered her into his arms. "You all right? What happened?" His eyes scanned the room. Nothing. Just the blanket trailing across the floor.

Clive came up the stairs, tying a bathrobe. "What is it? What's happened?"

"It would appear that Lucy's had a nightmare," Hannah said, looking rather coldly at Tam. She almost pinched Lucy's arm. "Is that right?"

"Um," Lucy grunted, into Tam's shoulder.

Hannah folded her arms. "A little extreme, your reaction, don't you think?" She drew Tam's eyeline back toward the door. "I do understand that bad dreams are very frightening, but they're hardly worth damaging hinges for. And please be aware that we do have another guest in the house. Ms. Gee is in the room right above this." She pointed to the ceiling. "Drama over, I think. We'll leave you to comfort Lucy in peace." She turned and marched out, dragging a meek-looking Clive away with her.

Tam closed the door, guided Lucy to a chair, and sat her down.

"I want to call home," she said.

He nodded, but didn't reach for his phone. "What did you see?"

"It wasn't a dream."

She waited for his gaze to scour the room.

"The cat came," she said. "With a dead raven. It was horrible. It dropped it on top of me."

"On the bedspread?"

"Um."

He examined it for bloodstains or feathers or cat hairs.

"It was here," she said, suspecting he would find no trace. "And there's something wrong with Gwillan. He was in my head, reading me, like a listener. Something's happened. We've got to call David."

She stood up and paced around, looking for her phone.

"Whoa, whoa, wait." Tam caught her arm. "Speak to him for sure, but he won't come, Lucy. He won't leave the house, not after what happened to your mom. Besides, if there was something going down in the Crescent, he'd know about it, wouldn't he? Why don't we ask Gwendolen what she saw? If the cat was here, she couldn't have missed it."

Lucy glanced toward the bedside table. Gwendolen, who'd caught the gist of Tam's words, shrugged apologetically and hurred to say she'd been drowsy and hadn't seen anything much, just Lucy tossing and turning a bit — the way she did sometimes at home.

The girl sank miserably onto the bed. "But it was so real," she insisted, slapping the bedspread. "It must use magicks to cloak itself when it moves about. And why would it bring me a raven?"

Tam rested two fingers on her shoulder and rocked her back and forth. "Look, why don't you get back into bed and I'll sit in the chair and keep watch."

"No way," she said, pulling the robe closed at the neck. "I'm not having you in my room. Me and Gwendolen can look after ourselves."

He backed away, raising his hands. "OK. But this time you leave your door unlocked. Is that fair?"

She gave a reluctant nod.

"Good." He stepped sideways and checked the window (closed and locked), the old fireplace (a possible point of entry, but where were the sooty prints?), and the bathroom (barring one small spider, empty). By the time he'd finished Lucy was sitting in bed with her knees drawn up. "Can I get you anything?" he asked.

"Phone," she muttered. It had fallen to the floor when she'd dragged the bedspread over her again.

He lobbed it onto the bed. "Call David," he said, "if it will make you feel better."

She toyed with the phone and put it aside. What could David say that Tam hadn't? She slid down as if a ghost had tugged her ankles, soaking herself in the warmth and security of compacted polyester and a goose feather pillow. "Turn off the light when you go out — please."

"Sleep well," he said. "Early start, remember?"

She gave an unappreciative grunt. Tam smiled, flicked the switch, and closed the door.

On the landing, he paused a moment. The house was all but silent, its historic heart beating to the characteristic thrum of heated water traveling through tubes of metal. But as he turned toward his room, the ceiling above him suddenly creaked. A swift assessment of the architecture of the stairs told him that the sound must have come from the landing above. He climbed five stairs and looked up. A gray-haired lady in a dark green quilted gown met his gaze. Her nostrils flared. She clasped the gown tight at her neck.

"Oh, I'm sorry," Tam said. "I was . . ." Well, why not tell the truth? ". . . looking for a cat. You must be Ms. Gee?"

The old woman's mouth grew tight and wrinkled. Her top lip protruded over the bottom, making her look a little like a duck. "I was not aware there were any such animals in the house." She propped a hand under her tightly-pinned hair, wound at her neck like a ball of wire wool. "Now, if you don't mind, I should like to visit the bathroom — in private. I was woken rather suddenly by that awful girl's shriek."

Tam nodded in apology. "Won't happen again." He lowered his weight onto the next stair down. "Bathroom?" he queried. "The rooms are all en suite, aren't they?"

"Not on this floor," Ms. Gee said, in a voice that could have tarnished metal. She continued along the landing. And the only other thing Tam noticed about her was that she was barefoot.

Had he crouched down and stayed in hiding, however, instead of going back to his bed, he would have been far more suspicious of the slipperless Ms. Gee and might have been tempted to knock down her door with all the strength of the ice bear, Kailar. She remained in the bathroom for less than a minute before shuffling back to her room, whereupon she began a strange, and apparently one-sided, conversation.

"So, the girl is genuine. Interesting."

(pause)

"What? What about the sculpture?"

(pause)

"Don't be foolish. How could it be her familiar? It's a poor imitation of a dragon, nothing more. Even so, it seems we are not alone. What do you make of her handsome guardian?"

(pause)

"He smells of bears? Have you lost your senses entirely?"

(pause)

"What? Are you certain? Where?"

(pause)

"Don't tax my patience. I meant, where does he carry the mark?"

(pause)

"Then they are powerful, and we must act before they do. The girl cannot be allowed to imprint on the dragon."

(pause)

"Impertinent creature! There is no such thing as a rightful 'heir.' And you will do my bidding or suffer!"

(pause)

"That's better. Now, come here. Comfort me. Such excitement isn't good for my heart — or yours."

(pause)

"Be quiet. I'm not interested to know about the girl's dreams. I don't like ravens. Especially dead ones."

(pause)

"I said, be quiet!"

And there the "conversation" ended, but for a particular sound rising and falling through the silence.

Purring.

GWILLAN WAKES

How is she?" David came into the bedroom and stood beside Zanna, who was staring down wistfully at Liz.

A day and a half had passed since the accident and Liz was still stretched out asleep beneath the covers, her beautiful red hair splaying across the pillow like the roots of a small tree. Several dragons were in attendance, most notably Gretel, who had a tray of small dishes containing seeds and flower heads and strange-colored liquids laid out in the empty space at Liz's side. On the bedside table next to her was Alexa's white horse.

"No change," Zanna said, moving a strand of black hair off her brow. A hint of defeat had seeped into her voice. Dark rings were appearing under her eyes. "Gretel's prepared some diagnostic potions from samples of Liz's hair and saliva. The good news is there's nothing to indicate distress in either mother or baby. No infection. No signs of abnormal development. The bad news is we can't wake her. We've tried to stimulate her, but she's just not responding. Her brain is very active, though. Look at her eyes."

David glanced down. Liz's eyelids were fluttering rapidly. "Dreaming?"

Zanna nodded. "She's been channeling something ever since you brought her in. Arthur thinks she's transmitting thought waves. Where to is anyone's guess."

David moved around behind her and sat in the wicker chair vacated by Arthur. The professor, having spent the entire night there, had gone downstairs to telephone his office. "You need to rest, Zanna."

The young sibyl twisted her knees and let herself perch on the end of the bed. She laid a hand on the region of Liz's ankles. "I'm worried that she might not break out of this, David. I've used every technique that

Agatha taught me, but nothing's working. The thought has crossed my mind that Gwilanna could have left a 'thorn' in Liz's back when she was treating the obsidian. Some spell that only she could remove. She was pretty definite in the graveyard about the child not surviving without her."

David leaned forward, making the legs of the wicker chair creak. "Gwilanna's an expert in double-talk. Don't lose faith. Liz is strong — in body and in spirit. Let's wait a while longer and see how she progresses."

Disbelief flickered across Zanna's face. "David, she's carrying the dark fire. Anything could be happening, to her or the child."

"I know," he said, acknowledging her concern. "And I've been thinking about that." He stared into the cradle of his hands for a moment, then stood up and turned toward the window. A still gray light had settled over the Crescent, a fine drizzle beading the leaves of the trees. It made him wonder about the conditions at Scuffenbury. "Don't forget this is Gwillan's tear. He's part of Liz. Just like Gretel and the others. You said you've detected no trauma. So it's possible Liz's body is assimilating the threat. I'm wondering if she's got some kind of immunity. For all we know, when Gwilanna cured Liz of the obsidian poison, far from damaging her, she might have actually strengthened Liz's resistance. I say we wait and monitor her carefully."

Zanna bobbed her head as if she wasn't quite sure. "OK, but I hope you're right. I don't trust that witch one bit."

"I'm always right," he joked. He came over and cupped a warm hand around her arm, wishing so much that he could kiss her head. "You're doing a fantastic job. I promise you, if you feel you can't cope then —"

He stopped speaking as Groyne materialized on the bed in front of them.

"What is it?" David demanded. The shape-shifter's tail was flipping like a rudder.

Hrrr! went Groyne. *It's Gwillan,* he said.

The house dragon was moving.

The dragons that had been in the bedroom with Liz reached the den first, so there was already a cluster of activity around Gwillan when David and Zanna hurried in. To their amazement, color had returned to the house dragon's scales, and though his eyes were nothing like the intense shade of violet that would indicate a full charge (for want of a better description from G'reth), he was nevertheless active, if a little woozy.

"Gwillan?" David crouched in front of him, speaking the name in dragontongue. He touched his fingers to the sensitive regions just behind the dragon's ear, like a doctor might feel for raised glands in the throat of a child.

"Well?" said Zanna, clutching tightly at her arms. This whole business was spooking her a little.

"Strange," David muttered, drawing his hands away. "That was Liz's auma."

"Liz?"

"Yes. It's like a scent or a signature. He's reaching out to her — or her to him. It's hard to tell."

"They're commingling, you mean? How can that happen? I didn't know it was possible over a distance."

David glanced at Grace. He saw she had closed down but thought nothing of it. "Neither did I," he muttered, rubbing the ends of his fingers together. "But he was reading me — or trying to. I could feel the energy racing through my fingertips. He was drawing on the auma of Gawain inside me."

At that moment, Gwillan gave out a thin wail. It was not unknown for the Pennykettle dragons to make sounds above the pitch of their normal hurrs. But when they did, their companions were usually quite startled, which was the case now. Every dragon jumped, barring Gretel (and Grace). The potions dragon sighed and tapped her foot. She blew a funnel of smoke at Gruffen. Some guard dragon he was. Hmph.

"That sounded like a cry for mommy," Zanna said. "Should we take him to her, do you think?"

Before David could speak, there came another interruption. This one did make Gretel apprehensive. The doorbell had rung. The dragons turned their heads toward the sound.

"If that's Gwilanna," Zanna said, narrowing her eyes, "you'd better decide whose side you're on."

Gwilanna wouldn't ring a doorbell, David thought. But the first time he'd met her, that was exactly what she'd done. Turned up at a crucial moment, on a drizzly day like this, when Liz had been going through the kindling process that had ultimately spawned Grockle. "Keep a watch on Gwillan," he said to Groyne, and moved to the door of the den.

Downstairs, he could hear Arthur talking to a woman. To his relief it wasn't Gwilanna.

"Well, I'm afraid Lucy's not here," Arthur was saying, "and Elizabeth . . ."

"If it's difficult, we'll come back another time," said the woman.

"Mo-om?" A young girl's voice rang out. "We've come all the way from Plymouth! That's, like, zillions of miles. We can't just 'come back' when it's more convenient!"

"Who is it?" Zanna hissed, coming so close to David's shoulder that he could take in the scent of her hair.

"Not sure. Someone who knows the Pennykettles, though."

At that moment, Alexa joined in the conversation. "Hhh! You've got a dragon!"

"Yep," said the girl. "Are you Lucy's sister?"

"I'm Alexa," said Alexa. "What's your dragon's name?"

"Glade."

"Liz made her," the woman explained.

"Then I think you'd better come in," said Arthur.

"This gonna be a problem?" Zanna whispered. She looked back at the workbench. Groyne was instructing the other dragons to stand well clear of Gwillan. The house dragon, still unsteady on his feet, had wrapped his tail around Groyne to support himself.

"The girl's got one of Liz's dragons," muttered

David. "I didn't know there were others besides Grace outside the house."

Zanna, none the wiser, pushed up her sleeves. "Well, let's go and investigate, then. Time to observe the most ancient of Pennykettle traditions."

David looked at her blankly.

"Kettle," she said, tapping his cheek.

A New Dragon
in the House

In the kitchen it transpired that Rachel Cartwright and her daughter, Melanie, had not made a specific journey to the Crescent, but had pulled in en route to seeing relatives nearby.

"Such a drag that Lucy's not here," Melanie said, wringing out her disappointment through the last few inches of her pale pink T-shirt. "She'll be so upset that she didn't see Glade." She ran her fingers down the dragon's spine. Despite what must have been the great excitement of returning to her "birth" place and seeing other Pennykettle dragons around her, Glade remained solid, though the scarf of sculpted ivy around her neck had turned from green to a warm shade of gold. "That means she feels welcome," Melanie said to David, who was sitting in the chair opposite, juggling Alexa on his knee. "She's a mood dragon. She likes you. Who are you anyway?"

"Melanie!" her mother gave an exasperated squeak. Rachel Cartwright, a slim, slightly sad-eyed woman, who wasn't aged by a polo neck sweater and small pearl earrings, looked apologetically at everyone present. "You have to forgive us. None of you were here when Melanie and Lucy were just little girls. It was a bit impolite turning up like we did, but we hoped Lucy might be back from her vacation by now."

Zanna put a tray of cups and saucers on the table. "Vacation?"

"Visiting some dragon hill," said Melanie, shrinking from the enquiring faces. "I got a text from her phone. Past tense."

"She's still there," David explained. "She might be gone for another few days, I'm afraid."

Melanie wormed her mouth into a pout.

"I take it Liz is with her, then?" Rachel said. She began to help Zanna put out the cups.

"Elizabeth's not very well," said Arthur. "She's upstairs, in bed — asleep."

"Oh, dear. I'm sorry. Nothing serious, I hope?"

"Is it dragon pox?" asked Melanie, sitting on her hands. She noticed the lines around Zanna's eyes sharpen. "It's what we used to say when we were kids. Just a joke."

"Daddy, the dragon changed color." Alexa sat up erect. Glade's ivy had just drifted across the spectrum, running from gold through watery green to blue.

"That means she's sad," said Melanie, shaking her head so her bob fell into place. "She'll be upset about Lucy's mom. Weird, isn't it, the way she changes?"

Alexa clearly agreed. Before anyone could stop her, she began to comfort Glade in dragontongue.

"Gracious, that's a nasty cough," said Rachel.

"No, it's not," hooted Melanie. "Mom, you're such a wuss. It's a game. Me and Lucy used to play it all the time. It was our secret language for talking to the dragons. Lucy was scarily good at it. I'll show you." Leaning toward Glade she cried, "Arraarrgh!"

On the fridge top, the startled listening dragon closed the flap of its ear canal. Arthur raised an eyebrow and Alexa opened her mouth into an O to accommodate the change in air pressure.

Glade's ivy did not change color.

"Yeah, like I say. Lucy was the queen at that game," said Melanie.

"Tea?" asked Zanna, wearing a grin as wide as a saucer.

Melanie picked up the milk jug. "Thanks. What's that noise?"

"Just the cat flap," Zanna said. It rattled behind her.

"Oh, course, you've got a cat! Don't tell me, his name's a bit strange, isn't it? Bonbon or something?"

"Bonnington," said Alexa, looking down.

That was the moment the niceties ended. Quick to realize there might be a problem, Zanna tried to shoo Bonnington back the way he'd come. But the cat just chattered and swerved right past her, stopping to look up and frown at the visitors.

Melanie Cartwright screamed. The milk she was holding sprayed across the table, a good portion of it drenching Glade. And whether the tension just got too much or she felt she was in the appropriate environment anyway, Glade raised her scales until she looked like a pinecone and shook herself dry. Milk droplets flew in all directions. Some of them, of course, went Bonnington's way. He gratefully began to lick his fur clean. But it had somehow never felt right to him, drinking milk in the form of a tiger. So he morphed back into a tabby cat.

And Melanie Cartwright morphed into a faint.

"Mel?" cried her mom, reaching to support the girl as she slumped. Zanna went swiftly to her aid as well, mouthing a quick, *Do something!* at David.

He moved Alexa off his knee. "Go and fetch Gretel," he whispered to her. The child hurried away. David turned to Rachel and spoke her name.

"What happened?" she asked.

"Nothing you need concern yourself about," he said. His eyes ran to violet and he dazzled her in a moment. Her head nodded forward and she fell fast asleep.

"Well, this is priceless," Zanna carped.

"I take it that's two less for tea?" asked Arthur, confirming it for himself when Bonnington jumped onto his lap. He turned the cat's gaze onto Glade.

"It's all right," David reassured her in dragontongue. "Don't be alarmed. Your humans won't be hurt and neither will you."

Glade tilted her ears and sniffed at him. *You're dragon,* she hurred. Zanna sighed and looked away. Glade's ivy sparkled like a set of Christmas lights.

"Sometimes," said David. "Will you do something for me?"

Zanna half-expected the mood dragon to curtsy, but the moment was broken when Alexa returned with Gretel on her shoulder.

The potions dragon fluttered onto the table and took a long and dangerous look at Glade.

"Gretel, don't frighten her," Zanna said, as a

shimmer of defensive red now became the ivy's dominant color. "What is it you want Glade to do?" she asked David.

David put out his hand, encouraging Glade to hop onto it. "Would you like to see Liz and the Dragons' Den again?"

Hrrr, she went. Her violet eyes widened.

"Good," he said, smoothing her wings. "Gretel, make sure our visitors don't wake up."

With a *hmph* of servitude, the potions dragon reached into her quiver for the necessary flowers.

At the far side of the kitchen, Arthur cleared his throat. "Would I be of more use here?"

"No, you go up," Zanna said to him quickly, knowing full well that he wanted to. Lately, he'd felt a little worthless, she thought. "I'll stay here with Lexie."

"But I want to see Glade," the little girl sighed.

"Later," said Zanna, ripping off a piece of paper towel. "You can help Mommy clean up the kitchen. You can start by dabbing the milk off our guests . . ."

*   *   *

David took Glade to the bedroom first. The little dragon flew straight to Liz's pillow. It reached out a paw and stroked her hair. Sympathetic shades of blue from the ivy began to reflect off Liz's pale skin.

"Don't be upset. She's only sleeping," David said, as a whimpering hurr escaped Glade's throat. "Glade, listen to me carefully for a moment."

The dragon turned her head.

"I know you read moods. What else can you do?"

She lifted her wings. *Grow things,* she hurred.

"Plants?"

She nodded.

"You look after them at home?"

Hrrr, she said brightly. None of her humans knew it, but yes.

Arthur's mouth opened with a watery smack. "One of Gwillan's cherished duties," he said.

David sat down and felt for Liz's hand. It was slightly cold, but not dangerously so. "Do you know what dark fire is, Glade?"

The mood dragon brought her eye ridges together. From a distant part of her innate memories the answer came to her. It made her shudder.

"It's within Liz," David told her.

Glade looked at Liz's body and gulped.

"I want you to read her mood, and her child's if you can. Put aside how you feel about seeing her like this and just show what you find. If it becomes too much, break away and read me instead. Do you understand?"

Glade shifted her gaze toward Liz, and nodded.

"Good. Off you go."

The dragon found a comfortable dent in the pillow. Then drawing in a puff of her exhaled smoke, she squeezed her eyes shut and fell into a huddle of concentration. To Arthur's immediate relief, the ivy scales began to show warmer colors, until they'd settled somewhere in the amber zone. "Are you reading Elizabeth now?" he asked. Liz's eyelids, he noticed, were no longer fluttering. It was the calmest she'd been all day.

Glade gave out a lengthy *hrrrrr*.

"Are you altering her mood? Are you capable of that?"

Glade frowned, flexed her shoulders, and spoke a burst of dragontongue, far too quick for Arthur to translate.

David leaned toward him and said, "She says she's not consciously soothing Liz, but that Liz is somehow exploring her abilities and using them to level her mood."

"Like a meditation state?"

"Sounds like it, yes. Can you pick up the baby's auma, Glade?"

The semicircular scales underneath Glade's eyes tightened as she redirected her senses. She held this pose for several seconds before giving a sudden jerk and flicking out her wings to steady herself.

"Go carefully," David whispered. "Feel it from a distance if you need to."

The dragon tried again. A few seconds passed. Her tail beat a syncopated rhythm against the pillow. Then, with a snort, she opened her eyes. Her ivy had not changed color.

"Well?" David asked.

Glade sank down, frowning. She spoke a few words of dragontongue: *hrrr*.

Arthur stepped back, cupping Bonnington's throat. "She sounds confused. Is the baby all right?"

Hrrr! went Glade. The ivy rustled as she moved her head.

David released his grip on Liz's hand. "She says the baby is 'growing' properly, but there's something unusual about its mood. Its auma is not where it's supposed to be."

"What?" said Arthur.

"I think you'd better come with me," David said. He picked Glade up and hurried to the den.

Sweeping a path through the enquiring dragons, most of whom had never seen a mood dragon before (though Gruffen remembered her from many years ago), David put Glade on the workbench next to

Gwillan, who had his head bowed low like a dragon in prayer. "Any change?" he asked Groyne.

There was no reply.

"Groyne!"

The shape-shifter shook himself conscious.

"What's the matter? What are you doing? I told you to watch him."

Groyne scratched his head and blushed a deep green. He must have fallen asleep, he said.

David sighed and returned his attention to Glade. The assembled dragons were staring in awe at her mood-detecting ivy, which had flared a deep violet when they'd all leaned toward her. But now that her attention was focused on Gwillan, the ivy leaves were glowing black and white, alternating swiftly between the two.

"Tell me what you're reading," David said.

Glade picked up the end of her scarf. She seemed as mesmerized as anyone by the changes in the leaves. *Hrrr-rr*, she replied.

"What's happening?" said Arthur, coming to stand by David's shoulder.

"Something extraordinary," David said. He pointed at the workbench. "Glade has detected your son's auma in Gwillan. It appears that Joseph Henry would like to be a dragon, after all."

ORDERS

He's done *what*?" Zanna dropped a piece of paper towel into the garbage and gathered Alexa to her. Melanie and her mother were still fast asleep, being watched over by Gretel. "I don't understand. Do you mean the baby's *transferred* his auma?"

"Extended it would be more accurate," David said. "Somehow his consciousness has reached out to Gwillan and brought him out of stasis, which means the commingling is more advanced than I thought. The boy's drawing on the power of Gwillan's tear. He's manipulating the dark fire to his own ends."

"How is that possible?"

"I really don't know."

"You think he's dangerous?"

"I think he's clever, which amounts to the same thing. Glade read his mood as 'playful' and 'indecisive,' and that's not something I can afford to be anymore."

Zanna stared at him hard.

"The dragon colony wants the dark fire destroyed. I was sent here to retrieve it. My orders were to take it north as soon as I'd reclaimed it from Gwilanna. I held out, hoping I might save Gwillan. Now, the situation has become unpredictable. I need to act."

"And do what?" Zanna's voice was like the clang of steel. Even Alexa looked at her father with stern disenchantment strengthening her curls.

"I'm going to take Liz and Gwillan to Ki:mera."

"Oh, good. Get another gallon of milk while you're out."

"Zanna, this is serious."

"Too right," she said. "When Liz wakes up, she's going to want a cup of tea. She's going nowhere, David."

"You can't argue this," he pressed. "Even by Fain

standards what the boy's done is way off the radar. There's no knowing what will happen if Gwillan starts to roam."

"He was a house dragon," Zanna hit back. "He watered plants, he dusted, he fed the cat. He had no special abilities other than kindness. What's the worst he's going to do? A bit of extreme ironing? You told me yourself not an hour ago that Liz might be dealing with the crisis in her own way. You made me believe it; now it's your turn. Seek advice from the Fain if you want to, I have no issue with that. But Liz is my patient. She's mine to watch over. I'll fight you if you try to take her from me — so will Arthur."

"No fighting," said Alexa, stamping her foot.

David sighed and looked at the ceiling. He was about to come back with another point when Melanie Cartwright raised her head and groaned. Gretel, who'd been distracted from her duties by the argument, gave an irritated snort and wafted her flowers under Melanie's nose. The girl's head jerked back, as if she'd been punched.

Zanna winced, as if she'd just watched a public execution. "And this situation is plain ridiculous. How long are we meant to hold these two hostage?"

David glanced at the visitors. Melanie had a face like a ventriloquist's dummy and Rachel was snoring like Bonnington on a full stomach. Quietly he said to Gretel, "Bring them around."

The potions dragon pulled her quiver forward. She stared dourly at Melanie. That was one good tranquilizing flower wasted.

David's gaze swept across the kitchen to Gauge, who signaled it was twenty-five minutes past two. Time, thought David, was something he no longer had. He looked at Zanna again. She had her arms draped over Alexa's shoulders. "They'll come, Zanna — the Fain, the dragons — if I don't deliver the fire to them soon. They'll work it out and take Gwillan and Liz by force, if necessary. That's not what I want. It's not what I came for."

Zanna tightened her grip around Alexa. "And neither, it seems, were we."

"That's not true," David said to her, looking pained. "I can't ignore this situation. I'll talk to G'Oreal, try to stall. I might have to travel to the colony tonight."

Hearing this, Alexa broke free of her mother and ran across the kitchen into David's arms.

Zanna raised her chin. Her body was shaking, her thoughts awash with unresolved angst. But the feeling tearing a hole in her chest she realized, to her dismay, was regret. She folded her arms to protect herself against it. She hadn't been expecting to react like this.

"I'm sorry, did I miss something?" Rachel Cartwright sat up suddenly. She blinked a couple of times, looking as fresh and rosy as ever.

Zanna reached for the teapot. "Another cup?" she asked, even though the pots were all untouched.

"Oh, no, thank you," Rachel said. "Gosh, look at the time. We really should be —"

"Urr . . ." Melanie's head rolled and her eyes crossed. In a slurred voice she said, "The gorilla's burned the sausages . . ."

"What?" said her mother.

On the windowsill, Gretel shook her head and sighed.

Rachel shook her daughter's arm. "Wake up, sleepy. You sound like you've gone ten rounds in the boxing ring."

"I was in the jungle, with tigers the size of cats."

"Tigers are cats," her mother said. "And this is Wayward Crescent — and we're in company."

Melanie scratched her head. "Where's Glade?"

"I think you must have left her in the den," said David. He tapped Alexa, who ran to fetch her.

Rachel searched her memories. "Did we go into the den?"

"Well, Glade didn't fly there," David said. Across the kitchen, he saw Zanna grimace. *I carried her, didn't I?* he mouthed to her.

"I suppose not," Rachel laughed, looking around. "And, erm, Arthur?"

"Gone upstairs to see if Liz can be woken."

"No, please. Don't disturb her," Rachel said, looking slightly horrified at the idea. "Let the poor woman rest." Alexa came hurrying in with Glade and put her on the table in front of Melanie. Glade's ivy, David noticed, was variegated green, just as it had been when she'd arrived. She was settled again. Happy. Proud she'd been of help. As the guests were rising to leave, David sent her an impulse, thanking her. She rolled her eyes toward him and blushed very slightly. He smiled and said to her, *Take care, Glade.* And although there was no forewarning in those words, it did worry him to think she would be out there unguarded. He made a mental note to ask Lucy next time if there were any more Pennykettle dragons beyond the Crescent. Even so, he saw no reason to frighten Glade with warnings of possible attacks by the ravens. Unlike Grace, she wouldn't be beaming messages around the world. In that sense she was largely "invisible." She would be safe if she stayed at home with the Cartwrights.

"Well, thank you for a lovely afternoon," said Rachel as Zanna shepherded them down the hall. "Is it me, or did it seem to go in a bit of a blur?"

"Oh, you know what they say," said Zanna, "time flies when . . ." *you're zapped by a potions dragon.*

Rachel smiled and buttoned her coat. "I'm so sorry about Liz. I hope she's better soon. Tell her you're all welcome to visit us in Plymouth."

"Yeah, and tell Lucy to call me," said Melanie.

"The moment she gets back from Scuff —" Zanna paused and bit her tongue, wondering if she'd given too much away. She was relieved when David showed no sign of wanting to zap their visitors again.

"Scuffenbury?" Rachel stopped pulling on her gloves. "Is that where she's gone? Scuffenbury Hill? Wonderful place. Very atmospheric. I went there once with my first boyfriend."

"Mo-om?" Melanie gave her a look.

"He was quite cute," Rachel said, fondly. "He played a tune on his panpipes for me."

"That's gross," her daughter complained.

"What's Lucy doing there? Not off with a boyfriend, I hope?"

"Project for school — on dragons," said David. This time he did react, clamping a hand across Alexa's mouth.

"Yes, well, they're very topical, aren't they?" said Rachel. "I can't help thinking this TV coverage is all a bit hysterical, though. I mean, dragons never really existed, did they? 'Imprinted memories of dinosaurs,' that's what I read the other day. Mind you, I wouldn't want a Tyrannosaurus rex trampling through town. Imagine what our insurance premiums would be like!"

Melanie looked into the rain and groaned. "Mother, you're being embarrassing. Let's go." She set off at a brisk pace up the drive.

Been a pleasure to meet you, Rachel mouthed.

And you, Zanna mouthed back, waving good-bye.

At last, the door closed. Zanna sank back against it and sighed. "Oh, that was weird."

A leopard that might have been Bonnington trotted past.

David chose to make no comment.

"So, what now?" Zanna asked him. She flicked her head toward the stairs.

"About Gwillan? We watch him."

"We? I thought you were leaving us — again?"

"Can I watch him?" said Alexa, springing up on her toes.

Zanna crouched down and stroked the child's hair. "No, sweetie. Gwillan . . ."

"She'll be all right," said David. "The other dragons are with him. If there'd been any problems we'd have heard the rumpus." He made Alexa stand on the second step of the stairs. "If he's not too tired, talk to him, Lexie. Come and tell me what he says, OK?"

She gave an enthusiastic nod. Then her gaze dipped toward his waistcoat pocket and she put her hand into it and drew out his watch. A green light was chasing around its circumference. Alexa held it out at arm's length like a present.

David took it off her palm and touched her on the nose. "No commingling. Just talking. Promise."

"I promise," she said and hurried upstairs.

Zanna, watching stiffly from the shadows of the hall, turned and walked silently into the kitchen.

When she was gone, David stepped out into the rain, hesitantly tapping the casing of the watch. To ignore this call would arouse suspicion and might bring a gathering of dragons to the Crescent. To answer it might have the same result. He thought carefully before he flipped the case open.

The star patterns cleared and the face of G'Oreal swirled into view. The dragon's astonishing kaleidoscopic eyes drilled their patterns into David's mind. "We await news of your progress, G'lant."

David gave a slight nod of his head. "The daughter of Guinevere has been sent to her location and the angel child is safe," he replied.

G'Oreal's nostrils contracted a little. "Are you now in possession of the fire?"

"The fire is contained, yes."

"Then bring it to the colony. Why do you wait?"

David let his gaze slant away to one side. This was

the question he'd been hoping to avoid. "The creator of the dragon whose tear was inverted believes she may be able to restore it."

The picture glittered, as though G'Oreal was communicating through a blizzard. The image zoomed back and two new dragons could be seen to either side of him. One was almost entirely white with translucent blue bands on the ventral edges of its planished scales. When it moved against the icy background it resembled a cloud of floating lights. The other was a magnificent purple beast, slimmer of face, with dramatic green eyes and a prominent carina. A pattern of semiradiant fins, as precise and threatening as the thorns on rose stems, followed the outlines of its skull, growing larger in size as they ran to its neck. It peered thoughtfully at David, churning small furrows in the ice with its claws. It dipped its head to listen to G'Oreal.

G'Oreal consulted both dragons at length before bringing the transmission back to himself. "This is a dangerous development. The decision of the Wearle was that the fire be destroyed. We are still detecting random concentrations of Ix in your sector. We do not judge it wise to leave a burst of dark fire exposed if the Ix are Clustering."

"I can answer this," David said. "When I recovered the fire, several birds were corrupted by the image of a darkling. My i:sola, Grockle, is hunting them down."

The scales around G'Oreal's temples darkened. "A delicate task to entrust to one so recently ascended."

"The threat from these birds is minimal," David was forced to say, though it pained him to have to block images of Africa from his mind, lest the trio detect them. The purple dragon was a Ci:pherel, a reader. Had he been entirely human, it would have known he was lying. He switched the conversation back to the situation in the Crescent. "We agreed before I returned to this plane that the clay dragons initiated by the spark of Gawain were worthy of special consideration."

G'Oreal's eyes slid closed for a moment. Two antennaelike projections above his eye ridges twisted inward and seemed to give off a slight static charge. "The importance of these figures is still to be assessed."

"I agree, but they are as allied to Godith as any dragon of the Wearle. The entity I named Gadzooks has served you well, has he not?"

Once again, G'Oreal reined the image back. The Ci:pherel nodded. The white dragon spoke in a whisper to him. "His ability to manipulate dark matter through language continues to intrigue us."

David smiled and wiped the rain off his face.

"This amuses you?" G'Oreal's eye ridges narrowed.

David lowered his head. His eyes adopted a more subservient slant. "Forgive me, I mean no disrespect. The writing dragon intrigues me, also. My instincts tell me that these creations are highly significant to the outcome of our plans. Even though we have detected other daughters of Guinevere and countless sibyls among the humans, these figures are unique. They are touched by the power of twelve distilled fire tears. I do not think we should forget that."

"And you," G'Oreal transmitted, "should not forget your mission — or your position within the Wearle."

The seriousness of this statement was not lost on David, who bowed his head again and said, "I ask the Wearle for more time. If the restoration fails, I will deliver the dark fire to you."

G'Oreal consulted left and right. "The awakening of the old Wearle is ready to begin. As each flies north they will draw the Ix with them toward the Fire Eternal. Nothing must endanger their sacrifice. Nothing."

"I understand," said David, tasting the rain on his tongue.

G'Oreal's image faded a little. "When the twelfth dragon rises, your time among the humans is done. You have until then to complete your purpose."

The picture disappeared in a horizontal shimmer.

Without looking at the watch again, David snapped it shut. For a moment, he raised his eyes to the Crescent, taking in the arrangement of houses and trees, as if the scene would be lost to him forever if he failed to commit it to his heart right then. With water dripping off the ends of his hair, he turned toward the house and looked at the number on the wall beside the door.

Forty-two. Five years earlier he had stood right here, a shabbily dressed student, and done the same thing, unaware of what he was or what he would come to be. And it occurred to him then, in that exact instant, of how easy it was to miss the very obvious. For painted on the number plate of the house — tiny, but never forgotten, once noticed — was a squirrel. It was gray and it was sitting up, smiling. A tear pricked the corner of David's eye. And it took every measure of his Fain awareness to draw it back within himself and master his destiny. He put the watch away and stepped back into the house, knowing that he might have crossed that threshold for the very last time.

THE SECRET OF
SCUFFENBURY

I— AM— FREEZING!" Lucy complained, as she
struggled to keep pace with Tam Farrell's eager stride.

"You can't be cold. It's May," he said, picking the
best route over the tourist-trodden pathway that would
eventually take them to the tail end of the Scuffenbury
horse. Even here, in the charcoal light before the dawn,
he could see white patches of chalk between the grass.

"It's damp. I can't feel my toes," grumbled Lucy.
"And it's, like, four in the morning. I've never been
awake this early in my life!"

"Well, you daughters of Guinevere must be delicate," he said, "'cause I don't feel the cold much." He
stopped and offered his hand in support. She was

wearing her yellow raincoat like a straitjacket, hands (though gloved) tucked into her sleeves.

"It's all right for you; you've got polar bear blood!" Spurning his help, she scrambled past. A few knots of loose shale tumbled down the path as she sought to get a better foothold. "I thought we were going up the Tor again, not hiking across half the county?" Her thighs were aching. Her lungs were burning. White flags of surrender were probably fluttering from her ankles by now.

"I want to see the sun rise over the Tor — from here, in relation to the horse," he said. "Besides, if Glissington's going to spew out a dragon it might be wise to be some distance away." He grabbed her arm and drew her toward him. "Quick. Look at that."

A slim rail of amber light had risen up and stroked the far horizon, casting blood orange spokes across the downs. "Isn't that fantastic?" He ripped the Velcro seal on his camera case.

Lucy, annoyed that she'd lost her momentum, blew

sighs of condensed air into the ground and tramped on. "How far do we have to go?"

"To the horse's head."

She looked up to assess their position. The horse was some three hundred yards away, cut at a relatively shallow angle out of the grassy escarpment facing Glissington. It didn't look anything special from here, nothing like as impressive as it had done from the Tor. She sighed and sought out a course. Thanks to the oncoming daylight, she could see that the pathway offered her options. One fork would take her to the brow of the hill, where she'd be able to look down the slope and see the entire horse from above; the other would take her directly to it. She chose the direct route.

Half a minute later, her energetic chaperone came bounding alongside. "I think we've chosen a really good day. The sun's going to rise directly behind the Tor, which means if we get our skates on we'll see how its rays fall across the horse when it crests the peak."

"Fab."

He sighed at her disregard. "You should take joy in this, Lucy. It's a wonder of nature."

"It's a wonder I don't fall flat on my face." She tutted as her shoes betrayed her again. What she wouldn't give for a decent pair of boots. She found some slightly better ground and forged on ahead, only to hear him say, "That's interesting."

"What? Me falling over? Thanks."

"No, this."

She stopped to catch her breath. He was bending down to pick up a stone.

"It's a stone," she said.

He flicked a bit of dirt off its surface. "Cairn stone. Like the one in your room. Look, they're everywhere." He pointed to them, dotted about in the grass.

"So?"

"So it's a chalk-based hill. How did these get here?"

"If I answer correctly do I get a drink of water?"

He reached into his coat pocket, pulled out a plastic bottle, and tossed it to her. "Keep it. I don't need it."

She split the seal on the cap with a crack that seemed to carry right across the vale. She watched him lob the stone back onto the hill, as if he were returning a pebble to the sea. "Maybe the dragon was building a rockery and he dropped them here?"

Tam's silence suggested that was just plain silly. He stared at the mound that was Glissington Tor, backlit by the emerging sun. "Come on, we've got ten minutes, if that."

He walked on, shaking his head in dismay. Somewhere inside, that hurt Lucy deeply. *OK*, she told herself, *just for today be Guinevere, not Barbie.* She tilted the water bottle with purpose to her mouth and let her gaze slant toward the Tor. To her surprise, she thought she could see a figure on the peak. "Tam?"

"Come on, you're going to miss it." He was already twenty yards ahead.

"I think there's someone on the Tor."

His footsteps halted. She saw him squint in that scary polar bear fashion, just the way David sometimes did. "Probably a tourist. People come here all the time."

He started along the path again, almost bounding where it hollowed out into a dip.

Lucy scrabbled after him, glancing at the figure every now and then. Comparatively speaking it was nothing but a matchstick, but Lucy, blessed with the eyesight of youth, could still work out its basic movements. She saw the arms come parallel with the shoulders. Half-stretched, not full, as if the person might be cupping their hands above their eyes. Or holding a pair of binoculars.

"Tam, I think they're watching us."

"Amazing," he muttered, not hearing her. He was at the white horse's head by now, placing his palm on the hard, dry chalk.

Lucy quickened her step and practically jogged the last thirty yards. She glanced at the horse as she walked its length. Impressive. A whole creature, branded in the grass.

"What do you make of that?" Tam said. He was on his haunches, pointing to a region just beyond the head where there was an unusual density of the cairn-type stones. They were tightly packed together and barely grassed over. Many were scratched and badly chipped where tourists had tried to excavate them, apparently with little success.

"Let me borrow your camera," Lucy said. She dragged it off his arm. "How do you zoom it?"

"Hey, give me that!" He snatched the camera back. Suddenly he was towering over her, angry.

In her defense she snapped, "Just look at the Tor!"

In his own time he put the camera to his eye. Lucy followed the whirr of the lens. The figure on the Tor had made a *Y* with its arms and was catching an arc of sunlight between them.

Tam lowered the camera. "I think that's Ms. Gee."

An inexplicable shred of fear rippled across Lucy Pennykettle's chest. "Can you see what she's doing?"

He shook his head. "Praying? Celebrating the return of the sun?"

The wind tugged at Lucy's raincoat and something rustled in the grass around her feet. "Erm, Tam . . . ?"

"What?"

"The stones are moving."

"What?"

"The *stones*. They're rolling down the hill."

More than that, Tam noticed: They were leaving the ground. Whatever force was moving the stones was strong enough to pluck them out of the earth and leave a small pile of exploded dirt. As each one gathered momentum, it lifted off Scuffenbury Hill and started spinning toward the Tor. Tam glanced at Ms. Gee again. Her arms were still raised as though she was calling all the rocks to her. "Get down!" he shouted, pulling Lucy flat. A small boulder came hurtling toward them. It deflected off his shoulder with a bruising thump. The impact knocked him back a few feet. Lucy squealed as shale began to swirl around her head, catching and pulling at her wild red hair.

"Help! Something's digging into me!" she cried.

Tam could feel it, too. Stones, underneath them, rising out of the ground. If they didn't move quickly, they'd be thrown into the air or turned into sieves.

"Slide!" he shouted. "Get onto the horse! We'll be safe on the open chalk." And summoning up the strength of the ice bear, Kailar, he slid down the hillside hauling Lucy with him until she was flat against the horse's shoulder.

For several minutes he held her in place, until the rush of air had stopped and he judged there was no more danger. She was dirty and shaken, but mostly unharmed: one minor graze on the side of her chin. Tam rolled onto his back and sat up quickly, training his camera on the Tor again. But this time he didn't really need a lens. In the place where Ms. Gee had stood was a monument, easily visible to the naked eye. She had rebuilt the Glissington cairn: a tall, tapering pillar of stone with a diamond-shaped extension at its zenith. Cut out of the diamond was a hole roughly the shape of a teardrop, waiting to catch the rising sun.

But that wasn't all. Lucy was the first to notice what had been uncovered on Scuffenbury Hill. Not the scars in the earth — the hundreds, probably thousands of pockmarks in the soil, as if a plague of moles or rabbits had escaped — but the region by the horse's head where all the sunken stones had been. They were gone, torn away to their places in the cairn, leaving behind a long, twisting spiral of chalk. Lucy's hand began to shake as she pointed to it. "Tam, this is not a horse."

He looked over and saw what she could see.

"It's a unicorn," she said.

THE LEGEND OF THE VALE

Impressive," said a voice.

Ms. Gee whipped around. A little way below her, dressed in green rain boots and an unflattering weather-proof top, was Hannah.

The old woman cursed and stretched a long finger, as though about to turn the intruder to dust. Hannah was quick to raise her hands in submission.

"Please. I'm no threat to you. I have no powers. Please."

Ms. Gee kept her finger aimed at Hannah's heart. "Why are you here?"

"To see the dawn." Hannah approached the cairn. She closed her eyes and pressed her face against the stones, caressing them as if they were alive. "I come up here to worship the sun, to be part of this landscape and all that it is. I've had a passion for dragons ever since I was a child. And now you've shown me this — and the unicorn as well. With one flick of your fingers you've vindicated all my beliefs. If you look back far enough into the history of this area it's written that people like you have always existed. Women able to control the elemental forces. I never dreamed I'd be lucky enough to witness the restoration of the cairn — or meet a genuine sibyl."

Ms. Gee lowered her hand. She was wearing a woolen tweed suit all the colors of vegetable soup and a pair of dull brown shoes. "I don't have time for this prattle. Your insignificant presence is of little interest to me. In a matter of moments the sun will be aligned with the eye of the cairn and what is hidden beneath these hills will be mine to command. Worship all you like. You will be consumed in the dragon's first breath."

"Oh, I don't think so."

"You dare to defy me?"

Hannah shook her head. "I'm simply questioning what you think you know."

A stream of air flew into the sibyl's nostrils.

"Wait! I didn't mean to insult you. All my life I've wanted to see the dragon and the unicorn risen, but this isn't how it happens. Look across the vale. Where's the shadow of the cairn?"

Ms. Gee turned sharply on her sensible heels. "I can't see it," she snapped.

"And you won't," said Hannah. "It's written in the legends that the 'horse' will wake and call the dragon when a teardrop of flame is framed beneath its eye. But that can never be. The angle of the sun is always wrong. That version of the legend is a cover for the real one."

"Then pray tell me what is right?" the sibyl demanded.

Hannah let her gaze roam over the stones and plucked something barely visible from them. "It's all to do with this," she said, holding up a single red hair.

"The girl," said Ms. Gee, curling her fingers. Her gaze flashed across the valley, but there was no sign of movement on Scuffenbury Hill.

Hannah nodded. "A red-haired innocent, to tame the unicorn. But she must be touched by the spirit of dragons — and she must be prepared."

The sibyl's mouth snapped like a hunting trap. "How?"

Hannah chewed her lip. "I can arrange it, but I want something from you in return."

"Oh, really? Then have this." Ms. Gee twisted her hand. A streak of energy flew from her fingers, striking Hannah in the center of her chest. The younger woman fell to her knees in pain. Her glasses shattered.

Ms. Gee's soft and callous footsteps stopped a few yards in front of her victim. "Tell me what you know, or your eyeballs will be next."

Hannah leaned forward, spreading her hands on the warming earth. "Gaia, Earth goddess, guide me," she breathed. She spat a trail of thick saliva from her mouth. "My family are no strangers to persecution, Ms. Gee. My grandmother, six times removed, was left dangling like a bauble from the tree in my garden, all for the truth she refused to give up, a secret entrusted through the generations to her. The tree died with her and her spirit still haunts it. You would do well to remember that. Those who took Mary Cauldwell's life tore down the cairn in frustration and vengeance and covered the unicorn's horn with its stones. That was over four hundred years ago. Do you really want to wait that long again, sibyl? Do you want to see your clever spell wasted?"

"Very well," said Ms. Gee. "What are your terms?"

"I want a gift," said Hannah. She removed the frames of her useless glasses and threw them aside. "In ancient times, a scale or a claw, given by a dragon to those in its service, would endow the receiver with creative integrity and purity of heart."

"How wearisome." Ms. Gee stifled a yawn.

"What you do when she wakes is your concern,"

snapped Hannah. "All I ask for my part in her rising is to be blessed with a token of her glorious body so I might do great things in her name."

"She?" Ms. Gee seemed to freeze to the spot. "Did you say . . . she?"

"My, you really don't know, do you?" For a moment, Hannah's laughter filled the vale. She struggled to her feet and looked at Ms. Gee with bitter contempt. "I always knew that a sibyl would be drawn to this place, but I had hoped it might be one that could cope. Are you sure you want to learn the truth, Ms. Gee? Are you sure you want to wake the beast in this hill? The dragon underneath our feet is a queen. One of the fiercest matriarchs ever known. She came here when the vale was a natural forest, tired, wounded, and about to give birth. She was seeking a creature of her own legends, a white horned horse that might heal her injuries and grant her time to rear her unborn young. The storytellers say she was far beyond help, but the unicorn still did its best to save her. It failed. In its distress, it lay down on Scuffenbury Hill to die. If the queen hadn't shared the last of her fire and let them both go into stasis, it would have. They are locked together, Ms. Gee. Wake one, you wake them both — the last of the healing horses, Teramelle, and the greatest dragon of her age, Gawaine."

ABOUT UNICORNS

Morning. What do you know about unicorns?"

Zanna swept into the Pennykettles' kitchen, picked up the kettle, and filled it at the sink. The whole movement was flawlessly smooth, as if she'd had it programmed into her at birth. "Well, that's a good one as early morning greetings go. I suppose it beats 'Did you sleep well, Zanna?' or 'Did you manage to get our daughter to nod off, eventually?' knowing she was upset that Daddy might flit away to the boys in the colony at any moment." She clamped the lid on the kettle and plugged it in. "You're still here, then — Daddy?" She opened a cupboard and took out some mugs.

"Wayward Crescent is my home," he said, hoping she would turn and see the sincerity in his eyes. She was wearing a hair band and very little makeup. He liked her like this. Stark, pale-faced, achingly beautiful. Yet still untouchable — for now. "That communication yesterday: I've been given more time to take the dark fire to the Arctic."

"How great for you." She swung a teaspoon idly. "Not terrific as bedtime stories go, but Alexa would have appreciated hearing it all the same."

"I needed time alone to think. I'll do my best to make it up to her, I promise, but the situation remains unchanged. When the dragons are ready, Alexa will come into play. There is nothing you or I can do to stop it. It's what she chose. It doesn't mean we can't be with her."

Zanna closed the cupboard door and stared at it. "Then answer me this: If her destiny is written, why is she so upset when her father ignores her?"

He lowered his head and sighed. "Where is she this morning?"

"Parked in the front room, watching TV."

"OK. I'll go and talk to her in a minute. Liz is unchanged, by the way. I sat with her through the night to give Arthur a rest. He's with her now."

"And Gwillan?"

"In the den, still asleep, I imagine. I sent Gretel up yesterday afternoon to make sure he didn't get up to any mischief overnight. I'll have her wake him shortly. Do you know if Alexa spoke to him?"

Zanna opened the teapot and dropped in two bags. "She said he was 'making friends' yesterday. He's become good pals with Groyne, apparently. They spent the afternoon playing hide-and-seek. She also told me that at one point Golly opened his tool box and brought out some sort of board game for them."

"A version of Mousetrap," David said, bemused. "I heard about it from G'reth. Gwillan won every time, he said. Hide-and-seek? None of them mentioned that — slightly unfair if Groyne was 'it'?"

"I find it creepy," said Zanna. "Just a bit surreal. I'm not sure I like the idea of Alexa spending so much time with him." She shuddered and set her black hair dancing against the bare skin of her pale white shoulders. She was wearing a red-striped, scooped-neck top and a pair of blue jeans with decorative stitching on one rear pocket. "Pass me the milk, will you?"

David dragged his eyes away from her and opened the fridge. He said a quick hurr of greeting to the listening dragon, which gave a sleepy blink and barely raised its ears. "Tell me about unicorns." He gave her the milk.

"White horses — flowing manes, horns. What about them?"

"There's one on Scuffenbury Hill."

"What?" She put the kettle down.

"I had a phone call from Tam. He and Lucy were on the hill at dawn when they witnessed the restoration of the Glissington cairn, he thinks by a sibyl who's staying at the guesthouse he's booked them into."

"Another sibyl?"

"One sniff of a dragon and they're out of the ground like worms — no offense."

She resisted a caustic comeback. "What happened?"

"Nothing. The sun came up, shone through the eye of the cairn, and moved on around the sky. Shortly afterward, Lucy saw the cairn disappear. Tam thinks the sibyl may have cloaked it to prevent unwanted attention from locals or tourists."

"And the unicorn? Where does that fit in?"

"The sibyl used magicks to draw the cairn stones from the countryside around them. A bunch had been used to hide the unicorn's horn. That, Tam says, the sibyl hasn't cloaked."

Zanna frowned darkly and started plonking mugs onto a tray.

"So, unicorns are good, right?"

"Unicorns," she said, "are generally taken to be the most wholesome, spiritual creatures in the universe. That doesn't mean they'd be a pushover in a fight." She opened another cupboard and took out some sugar. "They've been romanticized by storytellers for centuries, generally dressed up as icons of purity by children's books and the film industry. The chaste white horse is the image that's become fixed in people's minds; the carving on Scuffenbury would seem to support that. But if you look back far enough the picture wasn't always quite as rosy. In ancient Greek texts you'll find unicorns described as having the feet of elephants or the head of a lion."

"Not an animal you'd want to mess with, then?"

"Definitely not. I think the horse depiction is generally accurate, but if provoked they can probably appear as ferocious as a lion or as daunting as an elephant. Maybe they physically change. I don't know." She nodded at Bonnington, who had just swaggered in, crying for food. "Maybe they're like him? Interesting hosts for the Fain, wouldn't you say?"

David chose not to comment. "What about magicks? What abilities do they have?"

Zanna flicked the kettle on to boil. "Unicorns were persecuted, one assumes to extinction, because it was believed that their horns could enable spells, usually medicinal ones — there's a theory that magic wands are really just dried and shriveled unicorn horns. The literature I've read always suggests that the creature can't wield any power of its own, but can be made capable of acts of healing if it's first tamed by . . ." She stopped and stared at the wall. Bonnington wrapped himself around her ankles.

"Go on," David said.

"A red-haired maiden."

"Lucy."

"Yes. She fits the profile perfectly. If it's there and Lucy gains its trust, she would be an extremely power-ful young lady — and an instant target for anyone, or any 'thing,' with malevolent intent."

The conversation swerved into silence for a moment. Zanna busied herself with brewing the tea and feeding Bonnington while David stood by the window, musing. It was Zanna who eventually spoke again. "This sibyl. If she's anything like Gwilanna, she's up to no good. Is it possible that she was the woman who was seen in Africa?"

David ran his hand across his mouth. "I don't know."

"Well, she knows about the Glissington dragon and now she's got the bonus of a unicorn, too. That's a dangerous mix, David. Maybe you should go and check it out?"

He turned away, tumbling his phone through his hands. "I daren't leave here till I'm certain there's no threat to you from the dark fire. Lucy's in safe hands with Tam. Tell me something: Why do you think the sunrise had no effect when it hit the cairn?"

Zanna crouched down and put a spilled piece of *Chunky Chunks* back into Bonnington's bowl. She went to the sink, looking down at the water as she washed her hands. "Legends are the worst form of Telephone; they change over time until the truth is barely recognizable. I'll do some research for you on Lucy's computer, but my guess is the sun has nothing to do with waking the unicorn." She turned, drying her hands on a towel. "They're traditionally associated with the moon."

David nodded, taking this in. "Can you find out when the moon rises over Scuffenbury?"

She shrugged. "Late afternoon, at a guess. Arthur's got an almanac. I'll look it up."

"Good. Let me know — to within half an hour, if possible. As long as everything here remains stable, I'll stay with you till then. I want to catch this sibyl in the act. Right now, though . . . I'm going to take a shower."

"*Hmph*, none too soon," she muttered. She opened his jacket and let it fall. "Don't you have anything else to wear besides this sharpshooter outfit? You look like you just got off the *Deadwood* stage."

"What's wrong with the gunslinger look? I'm told all the goth girls go for it."

She gave him a cheesy grin. "Leave your stuff on the landing, I'll put it in the machine. Borrow one of Arthur's robes for now. Maybe some fresh underwear, too, mmm?"

He made a gun barrel with his fingers and fired a blank shot. "Thank you, ma'am. Hold the fort. I won't be long."

*   *   *

In the bathroom, he piled everything outside the door except his waistcoat, which he draped across the back of a chair, lest there be any messages from the North.

The shower was warm and relaxing. David closed his eyes and let the water pour down, allowing himself these moments of comfort in which his worries could temporarily drain away. But as the bathroom filled with steam, he was unaware that underneath the window, on the soft cork lid of the utility box where Liz kept her spare supply of toilet rolls, something small had suddenly punctured the mist: a dragon, materializing. It looked warily at the silhouette behind the shower curtain, saw it raise its hands to its head and start to rub. The visitor tapped its foot. Cleverly adapting its eyes to the increasing density of water vapor, it shifted its gaze around the room. Its eyes widened when it spotted the waistcoat. It spread its wings and flew to the chair. Silently, it reached into the pocket and pulled out the watch, freezing as the silver chain clinked against the casing. It looked sharply at the curtain. The silhouette rubbed on and even began to sing. Taking no more chances, the dragon pulled the waistcoat over itself. Then it flicked the watch open.

The star patterns began to form at once, but they were far from complete when the dragon flipped its tail, dug its isoscele into a port on the side of the casing, and twisted it. There was a flash and the screen went from green to gray. The dragon frowned and twisted its tail again. Something whirred (quietly) and although no image appeared on the screen, the streaks of light converging at its center were a clear indication that information was crossing the airwaves — or the thought planes. Had Gwendolen the IT dragon been present, she would have identified the data as coordinates. She would have pinpointed them also, and probably reported her findings to Lucy. And she would, most certainly, have raised the alarm. For the dragon in the bathroom was none other than Gwillan, though how he'd been able to get through a locked door would surely have puzzled any dragon other than Groyne. But aside from this, the thing that would have truly disturbed Gwendolen was the image waxing like a shadow in the watch face: first dragon, then darkling. Darkling then dragon. Bone for bone. Scale for scale. Jeweled eyes; blueberry eyes. Interchangeable. It was just as if Gwillan — or more precisely the boy, Joseph Henry, controlling Gwillan — could not decide which of these creatures appealed to him the most. . . .

A CLOSE ENCOUNTER OF
THE FURRED KIND

Cats. They had always been the one creature the Pennykettle dragons were wary of. Unlike the vast majority of humans, cats had an uncanny sense of spotting a dragon's movements or knowing they were alive — even in their solid state. Not that a cat was any real threat. Bonnington, for instance, had learned long ago that if he pounced on any of the Pennykettle dragons his reward would be a sharp spike of clay in his paw. And Groyne often told an amusing story about the time he'd been forced to scorch a kitten's whiskers when he'd been on a mission at Tam Farrell's apartment. Even so, cats were best avoided, which was why Gwendolen found herself slightly miffed to be left in the guesthouse at four in the morning and told to keep a lookout for "that cat" when Tam and Lucy had gone to explore Scuffenbury Hill.

She didn't expect to see the cat, of course, and after ten minutes of guarding nothing but dust she'd grown weary of the task, closed her eyes, and gone to sleep.

So it was quite a surprise when she woke suddenly to see the cat standing on Lucy's pillow, its smoky gray face looking directly into hers. It was studying her carefully and must have seen her eyes blink open, for it drew its nose back with the slightest of jerks and the pupils of its green eyes widened like saucers.

Gwendolen froze as solidly as she could, but when the cat stretched a leg and tried to paw her snout, her only option, she believed, was to defend herself. She issued a jet of smoke. The cat spluttered, reared up, and hissed in anger. This time its paw was not so gentle. It flashed at Gwendolen with claws extended. But by then, Gwendolen had flown to the mantelpiece, too high, she thought, for the cat to jump up.

With an irritated sneeze, the cat turned its head to see where she had gone. It found her on the mantelpiece and glared. Taking as much time as it needed, it trod across the bed, leaving deep and purposeful prints in the bedspread, then dropped to the floor and stalked toward the fireplace. As it reached the hearth it tilted its head back to check on Gwendolen's position. Gwendolen leaned forward and waved at it, then put her shoulder to the cairn stone Tam had examined the day before and pushed it off the shelf. The cat leaped sideways, just in time to avoid its head being crushed. The stone bounced on the hearth tiles and rolled onto the carpet. The cat stared at it and swished its tail.

Then something quite extraordinary happened. The cat's eyes turned purple and the stone lifted slowly off the floor. When it reached a height level with the mantelpiece, Gwendolen panicked and flew to the mini chandelier in the ceiling, fearful that the cat was going to hurl the stone at her. Instead, she saw the stone wobble slightly and travel back to its place on the shelf, where it was set down with an awkward clunk. The cat then jumped onto the foot of the bed — and started to wash itself.

Gwendolen was confused. Did the cat want to attack her or not? She changed position to get a better view of the bed and gripped one of the chandelier's candle-shaped bulbs. A string of glass diamonds underneath it tinkled. The whole thing tilted and began to swing. The cat raised its eyes but continued washing, as though it had now become bored of the chase. But a moment later it turned its gaze to the light switch on the wall and the chandelier suddenly lit up. Gwendolen fled to the window shutters, rocking precariously on the top of one. The cat yawned, then focused its glare at the shutters until the one next to Gwendolen banged itself shut. Shaken, Gwendolen returned to the mantelpiece, where the cat fixed her with an imperious gaze.

What do you want? Gwendolen hurred, confident the stupid creature wouldn't understand. But the cat jerked violently and pricked its ears.

Me-ow? it said, at length.

Gwendolen twizzled her snout. Now she was really puzzled. The cat's meow had come from genuine feline vocal cords, there was no question of that. But there was something more familiar mixed in with the sound. She'd had enough practice at home with Bonnington to recognize certain catty inflections, but this was different, more advanced. And whereas Bonnington never progressed beyond a few random snorts and chunters, this cat seemed to know she was speaking a language and not just grunting. It was trying to communicate.

Hrrr? she said. *Can you speak dragon?*

The cat tilted its head and meowed again, this time in a lower register.

Still the sounds made no obvious sense, but an idea had now occurred to Gwendolen. She was famed for her powers of translation, most commonly employed in transferring digital data into human words on a screen for Lucy. When this happened, Lucy had a habit of speaking the words out loud as they appeared. Gwendolen had learned the language of humans by matching the shapes Lucy made with her lips to the downloaded data. For that reason it occurred to her to watch the cat's mouth.

Speak again, she hurred, making mouth movements with her paws.

Downstairs, a door slammed. The cat sat up. Its fur stood on end. It poured off the bed like molten lava. It trotted to the door and was clearly going to pass right through like a ghost when it stopped, looked over its shoulder, and meowed one final time.

Though the creature was slightly farther away, Gwendolen could still identify the shapes its mouth was making. The words were unpolished but the sentence was clear: *My name is Bella.* Spoken like a human, out of the body of a cat . . .

TIPPED OFF

What do you mean, it's not a cat?"

While Gwendolen was explaining, there was a knock at the door. Lucy raised a finger to her lips and called, "Who is it?"

"Hannah. I wondered how you were this morning."

Lucy glanced at her mud-stained raincoat and quickly took it to the bathroom and dropped it in the tub. She checked her hair hurriedly then opened the door. "Hi. I'm fine, thanks. I slept OK once you'd gone."

"Well, that's a relief." Hannah, a picture of middle-aged efficiency in sharply creased slacks and a plain beige T-shirt, smiled and looked the girl up and down, her gaze coming to rest on the last two inches of her sodden jeans. "Have you been out already?"

"Erm, yeah," Lucy said, wondering if this was some kind of honesty test. After the incident on Scuffenbury Hill, she and Tam had quickly gone back to the car and driven around the area of the Tor for a while, eventually returning to the house about seven a.m. No one had seen them come in, but Hannah (or Clive) could easily have spotted their shoes in the foyer. "Me and T — Uncle Tam went to see the sunrise."

"Really?" Hannah's shrill voice dropped to a whisper. She looked toward the upward flight of stairs. "Did you see what happened?"

Lucy, playing dumb, lifted her shoulders.

"You haven't seen the change in the horse?"

"We weren't on the Tor," Lucy said truthfully. "We just . . . went for a drive."

Upstairs, a door banged shut.

"That's Ms. Gee," hissed Hannah. She gripped the girl's arm and drew her close. "I can't explain now, but be wary of that woman. She's not what she seems.

I need to speak to you and your uncle privately after breakfast. It's terribly important." She touched Lucy's hair and pulled the door closed.

Lucy quickly pressed her ear to the wood, listening to the women making small talk on the stairs. When the voices dwindled, she slipped out onto the landing and burst into Tam Farrell's room without knocking.

"Hello, niece," he said calmly. He was barefoot, but dressed, and buttoning up his shirt. Lucy allowed herself one blushing peek at the contours of his chest before sitting down quickly on the edge of the bed with her hands tucked firmly between her knees.

"I got quizzed by Hannah."

Tam folded back a sleeve. "What about?"

"I'm not sure. I didn't tell her anything, but she warned me to stay away from Ms. Gee. And she knows about the unicorn, I think."

"You think?"

"There wasn't time to talk. The old bag was coming downstairs. She obviously got back before us. And while we were out, the cat was here again."

"I thought we'd established that —?"

"Tam, just shut up and listen. It came to my room to check out Gwendolen. It's got magicks. It can move things about. It's not a cat."

He turned to the mirror to comb his hair. "Then —?"

"It's a girl."

"*What?*"

"Her name's Bella. She and Gwendolen almost talked."

"Almost?"

Lucy spread her hands. "It's a *cat*." How many meaningful conversations did anyone have with Bonnington? She sat back, allowing Tam time to think. As he did, her gaze toured his square-cut chin and handsome profile, the shining spikes of wetness in his hair, the perfect indent his throat made at the neck of his shirt. When her eyes arrived at his muscular forearms she could bear it no longer and blurted out, "This is scary. We should tell David."

"I called him about the unicorn before I got into the shower."

"What did he say?"

"To be careful. He's going to get Zanna to check it out. By the way, they had a surprise visitor at the house. Some girl named Melanie and her mom."

"Melanie Cartwright?"

"That sounds right. He said they brought a dragon with them."

Lucy nodded. Glade.

"David wants you to compile a list of any other special dragons you remember that might be outside Wayward Crescent, particularly any listeners."

Lucy sank back a little and frowned. "There were loads. Mom would know more than —"

"Your mom's still sleeping," he said gently. He tossed the comb aside. "Anyway, for the moment, let's concentrate on the situation here. Get yourself ready for breakfast. Act like nothing weird has happened."

"What about the flying stones? What if someone asks?"

"We were holed up in the car. Weirdest hailstorm
we'd ever seen. We'll hear what Hannah has to say and
we'll just observe for now."

"But —"

"No 'buts.' I'm here to keep you out of trouble, Lucy."

"But," she persisted anyway, "if Bella tells Ms. Gee
we've got Gwendolen —"

"Then she'll know we're not to be underestimated.
She's played her hand and failed to raise the dragon.
Now she'll watch and wait as well. She doesn't know
the key to it; she might think we do."

"But . . . *we* don't know how to raise the dragon —
do we?"

Tam opened the wardrobe and took out a sweater.
"No, but Gadzooks and David want us here for a reason. I'm pretty sure we're going to find out. *The
National Endeavor* is published this morning. Our
findings are going to be all over the news. This is the

day the Earth's history changes. It could be a long one. Might be dramatic. You want my advice, Lucy Pennykettle?"

She looked up openly.

"Start it on a decent breakfast."

BREAKFAST FOR THREE

There were four tables in the guesthouse dining area. Ms. Gee had taken the best one by the window. She was sitting perfectly upright, as if she'd been born with a pole for a spine. She didn't look up when Tam and Lucy entered, but just slid her eyes sideways to note where they were sitting. Tam chose a table by the oak-paneled wall, underneath an aerial photograph of Scuffenbury. He flapped out a napkin and wished Ms. Gee good morning. The old woman stiffened. She raised a triangle of dry toast to her mouth and snapped off the corner, as if she'd like to do the same to his head. Tam smiled and picked up the breakfast menu. "Cooked or continental?" he said to Lucy.

She glanced at Ms. Gee. Mushrooms. The old bag was eating Gwilanna's favorite dish. "Continental," she said, and went across to a long sideboard where Hannah had laid out fruit, yogurts, cereals, and a variety of cold meats.

And croissants, a pastry never seen in the Pennykettle household. Lucy was considering whether she should try one (and how best to eat one) when Clive breezed in and switched on a small, wall-mounted TV. "Good morning, everyone. Forgive me if I appear rude, but I thought you'd all like to see this."

The screen unfolded on an outside broadcast from somewhere coastal and icy.

"Svalbard," said Clive, pointing at the banner of information scrolling across the bottom of the screen. "Norway." He was almost panting with excitement. "In the early hours of this morning there were reports from a research station on one of the eastern islands — Nordaustlandet, I think — of significant activity on one of the surging glaciers there."

Tam stood up to get closer to the screen.

"What's a surging glacier?" asked Lucy.

"One that's capable of moving at an extraordinary speed," Tam muttered.

"Not as fast as this," Clive said. "Something large exploded out of this baby. It caused a small tidal wave of icebergs and showered the mountains either side of it in ice. The precipitation is still coming down."

On the screen, a reporter was jabbering away under a golf umbrella. Lucy risked a glance at Ms. Gee. The sibyl wore a stern expression while sipping her tea, apparently uninterested.

"But that's only part of it," Clive went on. "They'll show the footage again in a minute."

Tam looked at him quizzically.

"A marine environmentalist stationed there managed to get some film. It's hard to see the creature because of the blizzard it caused when it broke out, but it's unmistakably a dragon. Gold-colored. Fabulous. Massive wingspan. You get a glimpse of its eye — slit, like a reptile. And it's been tracked."

"Tracked?" Lucy squeezed her napkin tight.

Clive spoke over his shoulder to her. "Naval radar. They followed it to one of the Arctic islands. One of those that came out of the mist."

"What triggered this, do we know?" asked Tam.

Clive lifted his shoulders. "Your guess is as good as mine. They're saying that a comet was visible in those skies last night —"

A fire star? Lucy mouthed at Tam.

"Or maybe these creatures have simply got a very long-lived biological clock. Look, here comes the film. The beginning's a bit shaky 'cause the guy's climbing to get a better shot, but if you stick with it —"

"Switch it off."

The polished floor squeaked as Clive turned to Ms. Gee. "But this is the most extraordinary event since —"

"I don't wish to see it."

There was a crackle and the screen went dead.

"What the —?" Clive whacked the set. "Oh, how's that for timing?"

Dead on, thought Tam, *if you were hiding something.* He slid back into his chair, acknowledging Ms. Gee with a carefully weighted smile. "It's OK, Clive. We'll catch up with the news later, no doubt. Whether there be dragons on the Earth or not, a guy still needs his breakfast. Wouldn't you say so, Ms. Gee?"

The old woman turned to the window, her wizened face draped in shadow. She ate the last of her mushrooms (with her fingers, Lucy noticed), dabbed her mouth, and exited the room.

To Lucy's great annoyance she was forced to spend the next quarter of an hour eating (when she really wanted to be talking to Tam), because Clive insisted on fiddling with the TV. Eventually he left in a bluster of frustration and Hannah came in to clear the plates and cups. She put everything onto a tray, but instead of going to the kitchen with them she placed the tray on the sideboard, slid the doors to the kitchen annex shut, and joined Tam and Lucy at their table. "Have you told your uncle about our conversation?"

Lucy shrugged and rolled her lip. "Some of it, yes."

"Do you mind if I ask you a question?" said Tam. "Why aren't you wearing your glasses?"

"Small accident," she said. "I've got my contact lenses in. Listen, I need to know that I can trust you." She covered Lucy's hand but kept her focus on Tam. "Both of you."

"That depends what you want of us," he said. "Lucy tells me you warned her about Ms. Gee. Why?"

Hannah sat back and spread her hands across the table, smoothing out creases in the tablecloth. "Do you believe in witchcraft, Mr. Farrell?"

He folded his arms. "Are you accusing Ms. Gee of being a witch?"

"Yes, I am."

Lucy curled her hands into her lap.

"Yesterday morning, I went into her room to make her bed and I found something disturbing."

A bag of bones? A straw effigy? A book of spells? Lucy had imagined all of these things before Hannah explained: "There was a loose sock on the floor."

"A sock?!" Lucy spluttered.

"Please, keep your voice down," Hannah said. "I picked it up and should have just left it on the bed. But for some reason I opened a drawer instead, and there, to my amazement, I found a dragon artifact."

"Oh?" said Lucy, much quieter now.

"It was yellowish white, crusted with some kind of bacterial residue; I think it was a tooth."

"How do you know it's from a dragon?" asked Tam.

Hannah sat back smiling. "Come on, Mr. Farrell. Meet me halfway. It's no coincidence that you've come to Scuffenbury at a time when the whole world is talking about dragons and on the day before the white horse is shown to be a unicorn — I take it you've checked the hill by now?"

"Erm, yeah," said Lucy. "We looked before breakfast, didn't we — Uncle Tam?"

"Go on," he said to Hannah.

"Bringing with you a beautiful red-haired child . . ."

The significance of that was lost on Lucy, but she let it pass.

"... and expect me to believe you're not here to claim the dragon, like Ms. Gee surely is?"

"Claim it?" Lucy wrinkled her nose.

"We're here to witness its waking," said Tam. He picked up a saltcellar and relocated it behind the vinegar, as if he'd just checked Hannah's king at chess. "That's all."

She sat back, her face filling up with disappointment. "Then we're doomed," she said. "If Ms. Gee gets to the dragon first, I dread to think what will happen. I can assure you she's not here to enjoy the scenery. She's going to bring darkness upon us all."

Tam let his chair rock back on two legs. "And let's just say we wanted to stop her. What would you propose we do?"

Hannah leaned forward again. "Take Lucy directly to the dragon. She needs to be the one. She's the innocent the legends predict."

Lucy was confused. She looked restlessly at Tam and noticed he was drawing the fingers of his left hand across his left palm, as if he was trying to access all the memories of the Teller of Ways.

"All right, I'll tell you what we know," he said, leaning forward on his elbows. "Lucy is descended from a long dragon ancestry and we do expect her to commingle with the creature in stasis here, but we thought it would happen after the dragon emerged from the hill. From what you're saying we can short-circuit that?"

Hannah nodded excitedly, her hopes restored. "Yes. There's still time. Before Ms. Gee completes her prep-arations." She leaned in. Her hair smelled of rosemary and mint. "Listen carefully. The secret I'm about to share with you has been preserved by my family for centuries. It's very short and very simple but very pow-erful: The creature can be woken by the song of an innocent red-headed girl — but she must be in physical contact with it."

Tam flicked his gaze at Lucy, who seemed anything

but ready for such a daunting prospect. "It's buried. How would we get to it?"

From the pocket of her apron, Hannah drew out a map and unfolded it in front of them. "This is a diagram of the exploratory excavations that were made on Glissington some years ago. Clive's father was one of the geologists involved. As you can see, they were a lot more extensive than was reported in the press. They found nothing and the main tunnel was eventually backfilled for several yards and the entrance sealed. The rest they left untouched. Shortly after the project was canceled, however, a subsidiary tunnel was started . . . here." She pointed to an area on the side of the Tor nearest the guesthouse.

"Your cellar?" Tam guessed.

"Clive's father was a believer, like us," said Hannah. "He was convinced there was something in this hill, but he died before he could prove anything. For years, Clive has continued his work. He's completed a link between the cellar and the original excavations, and he's explored and extended many of the branches the geologists left behind. Progress has been slow, but last week he struck gold — or should I say, green."

Lucy gasped out loud. "He uncovered the dragon?"

Hannah raised a finger to her lips. "Part of the tail, we think. If you do as I've suggested, we'll know for certain."

Tam sounded a note of caution. "And . . . how do we avoid Ms. Gee's 'preparations'?"

Hannah folded the map away. "She's following the path of the accepted legend, which means she won't make her next move until the moon rises. I was out walking early this morning and saw her do something quite extraordinary. She cast a spell to rebuild the Glissington cairn, then made it invisible somehow. I believe she'll uncover it when the moon comes up. If she knows the incantations, and I'm sure she does, when the moon shines into the eye of the cairn she'll turn its light back onto Scuffenbury Hill and fill the body of the unicorn with it, making it live again."

"What about the dragon?" said Lucy.

"That version of the legend says that if the unicorn is calmed by a red-headed maiden, it will point its horn at the Tor and crack it open with a bolt of moonlight, allowing the maiden to claim the dragon. Maybe Ms. Gee had a way of getting around that, but you turning up completes the fairy tale and gives her options — or poses an unexpected threat. Either way, I think you're in danger. Trust me, we have to get to the dragon before her. Ms. Gee sleeps in the early afternoon. Meet me in the kitchen at one o'clock and I'll guide you through the tunnels. They're complex. Lots of branches. You'd never find the way to Clive's discovery on your own. Are we agreed?"

Without looking at Lucy, Tam said, "Sounds like it might be quite an adventure."

"Oh, indeed," said Hannah. And gathering the tray off the sideboard she slid the doors to the kitchen annex open and left her guests to finish their breakfast in peace.

415

A MEMORY OF DRAGONS

Mommy, there are BIG dragons on the TV."

Alexa pottered into Lucy's room, where her mother was poring over the computer. Without turning away from the densely texted screen, Zanna stretched an arm and drew the girl to her. Her palm slid across the emerging wing butts. They seemed to grow more prominent by the hour. "You could always switch channels," she muttered.

Alexa shook her head. "The dragons are on ALL the buttons." She put something down beside the keyboard. Zanna half-expected to see a mangled TV remote. Instead, it was Alexa's white horse.

"Why have you brought that in?"

"I'm going to show Gwillan."

Zanna took off her dark-framed reading glasses. She touched the sculpture's forehead. Smooth, like a horse. "How is Gwillan?"

"Sad," said the girl.

"Oh, why's that?"

"Daddy won't let him come out of the den."

Zanna suppressed a *hmph*. She sat back, chewing on the earpiece of her glasses.

"The others have come out," Alexa added.

"Others? The other dragons? I thought they were all playing."

"That was yesterday," Alexa said. "G'reth has gone downstairs. He's watering the plants."

Zanna burst out laughing. G'reth, watering plants? The wishing dragon's lethargy was legendary. Bringing his paws together to meditate was about as active as he usually got. "Why's he doing that?"

Alexa closed her mouth and thought about it. "It was Gwillan's job."

"Oh, of course." Zanna clicked her tongue. "G'reth's helping him, then?"

"Yes."

"That's very sweet."

"Mmm," said the girl. "Will you come downstairs and see the dragons now?"

"Well, I'm sort of busy here, darling."

"But . . . there isn't long," Alexa said, an undercurrent of frustration in her voice.

Zanna reached absently for the child's hand, accidentally clipping the head of the horse. The shock of almost knocking it onto the floor brought her attention back to the girl. "For what, baby? There isn't long for what?"

Alexa picked up her sculpture and stroked it. "Nothing," she said. Her mood lifted again. "A dragon came out of a mountain in Japan."

"Really? You could see it?"

"Yes. But it was very smoky. There were lots of rocks and puffly clouds and some . . . fire spilled out."

"I expect that was lava. Did it flow down the mountain?" Zanna made a river with her fingers.

"Mmm."

"Well, that must have been very exciting." *And frightening for the local community*, Zanna thought. She pulled the girl closer until their hips bumped. "What did you mean 'there isn't long'?"

Alexa swung her body left and right. "Before all the dragons come out."

"Oh? And what happens then?"

The girl shrugged as if she was a little embarrassed. Then lifting her chin she blurted out brightly, "His name's Gyrrhon."

"Who is?" asked Zanna. "The horse?"

The little girl sighed. "No, the dragon that flew out of the mountain."

Zanna squeezed her waist. "How do you know that?"

Alexa took a second or two to think. "I remember him," she muttered.

Her mother's blood ran cold. "You remember him?"

"From a long time ago. Mommy, what are you doing?"

"I . . . erm." Temporarily stunned, Zanna couldn't

think of anything to say. She replaced her glasses and ran a hand through her hair. "I'm finding some information for Daddy about..." She looked at the horse again and clicked the keyboard. An image of a unicorn appeared. "Do you know what this is?"

"A magic horse." Alexa's smile lit the room.

"Do you ... remember anything about them?"

Alexa thought hard. She touched the horse's forehead, like her mother had done. "You're going to see one," she said, which chilled Zanna almost as much as the previous statement about the dragon.

At that moment David walked in, carrying a rolled-up magazine. "Hi, how's it going?" He stood behind Alexa and placed the palm of his hand on her forehead, making her hair froth over his fingers. The child's face became a picture of absolute serenity. Her skin glowed as brightly as the computer screen.

"What are you doing?" Zanna asked him, tensing up.

He let his hand slip away. "Just saying hello. You find anything?"

She moved her fingers back to the keyboard. "Not really. I've managed to unearth some contradictory legends about Scuffenbury, but none of them mention a unicorn. It's either a hoax or a closely guarded secret. To be honest, I don't understand why a creature like that would stay at a place like Scuffenbury anyway, even if there was a dragon there."

"You told me once it was covered by ley lines."

"Yeah, but so are hundreds of other sites. If the legend is true, there has to be a very strong reason for that unicorn's presence, but I don't know what it is or why — oh, grrr! There's another message." She pointed to a box in the corner of the screen. "That's about a dozen this morning. Lucy doesn't have that many friends, does she?"

"Put them up," David said.

Zanna frowned at him darkly. "No. They're personal."

"Just the subject lines. I'm curious. Arrange them — by address."

Zanna tutted and opened the software. "They're coming from two girls, mainly." She turned the screen slightly. "One of them is mailing from Australia. Who would Lucy know in Oz?"

"Her siblings," David said, after a pause.

For the third time in the space of five minutes, Zanna found her body temperature dropping. "Siblings? What are you talking about?"

"Lucy's been writing a journal," he said. "All about what she is and what she knows. Before she left for Scuffenbury I asked her to put it up on the Net. I think this is the result." He nodded at the screen. "Check out the subject lines."

Zanna read a couple.

IF **GAWAINE** MEANS ANYTHING TO YOU, PLS, PLS RESPOND.

TWELVE DAUGHTERS. I'M HERE. YOU ARE NOT ALONE.

"They could be cranks," she said. "And the top one can't spell."

David shook his head. "They're not cranks. When

the press report the stories of the dragons tomorrow there will be one significant factor linking them: a red-haired girl will have been close by. Liz and Lucy are not unique. What you're looking at is more of their extended family, other daughters of Guinevere. Contact one of the girls: They may know something about how their dragon is triggered. It might help us understand the setup at Scuffenbury."

"No way." Zanna put the mouse through a series of clicks. The computer's closing-down jingle rang out. "I don't care who they are; I won't invade Lucy's privacy." She stood up, resting her arm around Alexa. All this time the child had been quietly singing to her horse. "How come you and your friends in the North don't know the triggering process anyway?"

David stood away. He dropped the magazine, the latest copy of *The National Endeavor*, faceup, onto the bed. "Arthur ordered it," he said. "He wants you to read the relevant passages to him. When you do, you might think again about reading those e-mails."

Zanna threw him a quizzical look.

"Until Bergstrom discovered the writings on Hella we had no idea how the last Earth colony of dragons expired. The Fain abandoned them, remember? Even with the Chronicles, the narrative is sketchy. All we're clear about is that twelve adult dragons went to their final resting places with a plan to defeat the Ix. One of them, possibly the most important of all, settled at Scuffenbury. Among the new Wearle of dragons in the Arctic is a type called a Ci:pherel. It detected the resting locations by scanning for traces of live dragon auma from around the world. Barring the Tooth of Ragnar, the signal was at its strongest on Glissington Tor, where, to the Ci:pherel's surprise, it found a female — which the writings identify as being named Gawaine."

"Gawain?"

"It's not the one you're thinking of. The name's pronounced roughly the same, 'Ga-wen,' but the spelling is different; there's an *e* on the end."

"I'm going to play with Gwillan," said Alexa, slipping away.

Zanna let her go. "A female? You mean, all this time . . . ?"

"No," said David. "We think this is the mother of the one that Liz and Lucy revere. Their Gawain, her son, did live and die in what we now call the Arctic. When the Ci:pherel scanned the polar ice cap the auma trail there was off the scale, which is why the new Wearle were keen to secure it — hence the mist.

"We're pretty sure Gawaine — the mother — transferred most of her power to her son before she went into stasis, and that's how something as huge as the ice cap came to be created when he shed his fire tear into the ocean. It's an awesome feat, even though the dragons that made it possible might have deemed it wasteful. But when you think of the influence the ice cap has had, not just on the climate, but on the variety and density of life this planet supports, then Gawain has at least fulfilled the most basic principle of dragon ideology: Through him dragons have commingled with Gaia and earned their right to be called the spiritual guardians of the Earth. The only thing that's really in debate is whether the outcome was accidental or altruistic."

"And I suppose you've got a theory on that?"

"Not yet. We'll know more when the old Wearle has risen."

Zanna rubbed the back of her neck. So many questions she wanted answered, not least what would happen to Alexa when the "old Wearle," as David put it, was brought back. "What did you mean when you said that the other dragons made it possible for Gawain to create the ice cap?"

"Have a look at the magazine. Steiner's translation gives a pretty good account of their final meeting. At the end of the last colonization, eleven male dragons came together on Hella and cried their fire tears through their unnatural eye, into a hollow in the floor of a cave. I should explain that all dragons have a defect in the duct in one eye, a kind of sac that won't allow the whole tear to pass. It's considered to be a kind of safety mechanism, a second-chance blessing from Godith; a dragon shedding its tear in this way will always retain a little of its spark. The eleven who went through with this ritual wouldn't have been able to function for long on the modest amounts of energy they'd be left with, but they would have had enough to enable them to fly to a mountaintop and hibernate for a few thousand years, by which time their tears would regenerate. The supreme tear as it came to be called, the one they'd pooled, was given to Gawaine. Steiner's translation has her drinking it, but it's more likely she would have just snorted it up through her nose. Whatever the means, it would have endowed her with enormous power."

"But the tear wasn't meant to end up in the ocean, surely?"

"No," David said. "Gawaine's task was to use it to destroy the Ix."

"How?" Zanna asked, framing the word carefully.

David sighed and looked around the room, as if everything in it were a treasure to him. "We think her Wearle had adopted the same approach as ours. She was probably expected to open herself for illumination, with the idea of drawing the Ix to her. Such a vast amount of power would have pulled them all in. Once the Ix had commingled with her, she'd have sacrificed herself in the Fire Eternal. End of dragons. End of Ix."

"But instead we have an ice cap, and the Ix are still around."

He nodded, looking serious. "For some reason the transcendence never came about and Gawaine went into stasis instead, giving birth to a son along the way. Maybe it was something to do with him. Or maybe she just couldn't cope with the moral consequences of what she'd been asked to do." Stepping forward, he touched Zanna's arm, letting his hand slide down to her elbow. "We know that the Ix were fond of commingling with chosen members of the human race, inciting them to acts of aggression against the dragons. The Wearle on Hella must have been prepared to accept there would be human casualties if their plan to defeat the Ix went ahead. But if the Ix got wind of their intended fate they could have tried to shelter themselves by commingling en masse with human hosts, forcing Gawaine into a dreadful dilemma: kill her natural enemy, yes — but wipe out their largely innocent hosts as well."

Zanna looked away. "This is what Liz wouldn't talk about to Lucy. She hinted something to me when you came back from Africa."

David nodded again. "Liz learned of it when Steiner called Arthur at his office a few days ago to tell him the translation was done. She didn't know, of course, that the Gawaine Steiner spoke about was their Gawain's mother."

"And you didn't think to set them straight?"

David opened his hands. "What difference would it have made? The knowledge is just as hurtful either way. As I said, we'll know the full story when Gawaine rises from Glissington."

"And then what?" Zanna turned toward the door. "The Wearle tries again? With better odds? Keeping their scaly claws crossed there aren't six and a half billion Ix out there so they can leave a few worthless human survivors behind?"

"It's not like that," David said, but she had already stormed away.

He threw his head back and looked at the ceiling, at the luminescent stars he'd once helped Lucy stick up there. Sometimes he wished he could be nothing more than a speck of cosmic dust among them.

In those few small seconds of gloom, he missed the entrance of Gruffen — and would have probably missed him entirely were it not for the sound of the guard dragon's coughing.

David saw him hovering by Lucy's lampshade. "Gruffen, what are you doing?"

Hrrr! said the dragon. *Cleaning.* He produced a small feather duster and proceeded to demonstrate. A cloud of dust flew up off the lampshade.

David shook his head. *This whole house is going crazy,* he thought. "Gwillan would be proud of you," he said, not realizing, as he walked away, just how much truth lay in those words. . . .

INTO THE TOR

At exactly one o'clock, Tam and Lucy turned up in the kitchen where Hannah was already waiting for them, dressed in the clothes she'd walked out in at dawn. Handing them both a flashlight, she beckoned them across the room to a sturdy farmhouse door. She rattled it off its latch and switched on a light. The cold sigh of dampness entered the kitchen. Lucy glanced into the open doorway. At the bottom of a flight of redbrick steps she saw the outline of a wine rack. Beyond that, only shadows.

"Close the door behind you," Hannah whispered to Tam. She was down the steps in seconds like a ferret, warning them to crouch when they reached the actual cellar. Lucy went down gingerly and sideways, yet still managed to slip halfway and crack flakes of white-washed plaster off the walls.

"Sorry," she muttered, stepping onto a concrete floor that rang like the slap of a wet pavement.

Hannah took her hand and drew her into the light. "That's the hardest part done with. Now, follow me."

She led them in single file past the wine rack, into a small utility area lit by a row of bulkhead lights heavy with spiderwebs and condensation. At the cellar end she put her flashlight into her pocket and called Tam forward, asking him to move aside a large section of tongue and grooved timber propped against the wall. Another gasp of stale air blew into the cellar as his efforts uncovered a hole in the brickwork behind the wood. With the air came a whistling moan. The scent of dampness intensified. Lucy's heartbeat rose. A drip of water crowned her shoulder, making her give a little peep of fear.

Hannah said quietly, "Don't be concerned about rats, we haven't seen one down here for weeks."

Lucy, undecided about whether her mouth wanted to construct the question "Rats?" or "Weeks?", merely gulped.

Hannah smiled and flicked another switch, and there before them lay a rough-hewn tunnel, cut upward from floor level to a height of about five feet. It was lit by a string of candle-shaped bulbs, stapled to the wooden beams, which held back the earth to either side and above. It continued for some twenty yards into the hill before the trail curved away to the left.

"Welcome to our best-kept secret," said Hannah.

"Doesn't look very safe," said Tam, nodding at the slews of fallen dirt that banked the pathway on either side.

Hannah shone her flashlight into his face. "All adventures carry a little danger, Mr. Farrell. Not getting cold feet already, are you?" She didn't give him the option to respond. "Watch where you're going. It's very slippery until we reach the excavations. Aim your lights down for now."

"Does Clive know we're doing this?"

Hannah had already stooped into the entrance and had to twist back to answer Tam's question. She smiled like a widemouthed frog. "He's keeping watch upstairs."

Without waiting for a comment she continued forward.

Tam held Lucy back for a second. "Be careful. Stay close. Just in case . . ."

"In case what?" she hissed anxiously. Any moment, Hannah would turn and question the delay.

In case it's a trap, he wanted to say. The auma from his right hand was urging caution. But all he said was, "Anytime you want to go back, just say."

She frowned, then bent down and followed Hannah.

Thankfully, the backbreaking trot only lasted for about a minute. After that, even Tam was able to straighten up fully as Clive's makeshift tunnel broke through into a professionally dug one. The area was well lit and stocked with a number of kerosene lamps, digging implements, rope, and several boxes of Lucy knew not what. (She imagined the possibility of dynamite, and shuddered.) The new tunnel stretched left and right for a few yards before plunging into darkness both ways. Hannah handed each of them a kerosene lamp, explaining they would light them farther ahead and leave them as markers. She then took a sharp left turn, warning them to expect sheer blackness for a while and suggesting that they group together and pool their flashlight as best they could. Lucy dropped in beside Tam, letting her light glance off the wall so she wouldn't crash into the framework of beams. Every now and then more bulkhead light fittings glinted at her like the cat's-eye reflectors that guided motorists in the road at night. She wondered why they couldn't be switched on, but was afraid she'd just seem silly if she asked. Instead, she did something that Hannah had advised against and looked back the way they'd come. Seeing nothing but the diminishing tawny glow at the junction, she was suddenly struck by the closeness of the earth pressing in and her insignificant mass compared to that of the Tor.

"I'm scared," she said to Tam. "It's hard to breathe." His nod acknowledged the truth of this. The air was plentiful enough but its texture was thick with decomposition and, despite the omnipresent tick of dripping water, it now lacked humidity.

"How far do we have to go?" he asked Hannah, offering Lucy his arm for support.

Hannah's light wobbled and veered to the right. "Stop here." Her lamp clanked as she crouched down. Within seconds she had removed the glass and lit it. She positioned it on a ledge that seemed to have been deliberately constructed for the purpose. Lucy was never more thankful to see Tam's face. He was looking ahead, throwing his flashlight into the shadows.

"Is this a fork?" he asked.

"One of several," said Hannah. "Go left and you'll find a dead end. The diggers created many, usually where they struck rock. Clive filled most of them in with the soil he needed to displace; the soil from the cellar tunnel went to make the water feature in our back garden."

Tam moved his flashlight around. "I thought this was purely an earth mound, no rock?"

"You'd have to ask Clive; I'm not a geologist," said Hannah. "Shall we go on?"

Lucy, who'd recovered a little from the break in walking, nodded.

Twice more they stopped to light marker lamps. By then, the route had narrowed again in those places where Clive had continued his personal explorations. Before they set off on the final leg, Lucy realized she was beginning to shake. Not that it was cold. Quite the opposite, in fact. Like the cave she'd spent time in on the Tooth of Ragnar, the air here was surprisingly warm. What was getting to her now was the weight of responsibility that came with her ancestry. They had to be close to the dragon.

Hannah saw this in her face and said, "Maybe now would be a good time to sing?"

Tam rested a hand on Lucy's arm. "No one's talked

about the danger of the tunnels collapsing, Hannah. Assuming Lucy is able to wake the creature, there's going to be a large amount of earth dislodged." His mind was going back to the TV scenes from Svalbard.

"She won't be fully active right away," Hannah said. "She'll need time to spread her spark throughout her body. By then we'll be out of here."

"She?" said Lucy. "You mean it's a female?"

"According to the legends, it's a queen. Is that a problem?"

"Did you know this?" Lucy threw a glance at Tam.

He shook his head. "Only that a female existed. It's in the article. I didn't know we'd find her here."

"Sing, Lucy," Hannah encouraged her. Her fingers scraped along the tunnel wall.

Lucy wiped a hand across her mouth. Her skin was puckered and tasted of mud. Never had she felt less like singing. And the acoustics in this warren were hardly good. Every footstep sounded like the thump of an iron on an ironing board. Even so, she parted her lips and let her throat do the work of producing a sound. Out came a sweet, comforting tune, somewhere just below the pitch of birdsong. It was what her mother called "The Song of Guinevere." Lucy had fallen asleep to it many times, always dreaming of dragons when she did so. Long ago, their red-haired ancestor had wooed Gawain with it, easing the shedding of his fire tear. Now its melody swept through the darkness, almost moving the air like a sail.

"That's beautiful," said Tam. "I never knew you could do that. Listen, it's going everywhere. It's like the tendrils of a plant."

"Remarkable," said Hannah, looking suitably impressed. She came to a halt and turned toward them. "Don't stop, girl. Your moment has arrived." She flipped her flashlight sideways.

Less than twenty feet ahead the tunnel ended in a hollowed-out chamber, where it was clear that a huge amount of excavation work had taken place. Tam approached the entrance and explored it with his flashlight. "After you," he said to Hannah.

Her spectral features recorded a smile. With Lucy's dragonsong still weaving its spell, she dipped her head and stepped inside, holding her flashlight at shoulder height like a javelin. "There," she said, as Tam came to join her.

Tam doubled the beam and saw, to his amazement, a run of what appeared to be overlapping scales. They were dark green, just as Hannah had described, and set in the wall like a row of large tiles. He traced the color sideways and noted there were other contiguous patches standing out here and there from the chamber wall. If this was a dragon's tail, it was curving, not straight.

By now, Lucy had seen it as well. Tam caught his breath as he watched her stretch on tiptoe and fix her fingers around one of the scales. The volume of her song increased. He noticed Hannah put her flashlight down so she could press her hands together in prayer. He thought he could hear her asking for forgiveness but the chance to ask her what she meant by that was overtaken by a sudden thump from deep within the hill.

He aimed his light toward the ceiling. A few grains of earth rained down from a fissure.

Lucy stopped singing. The thump came again. "That's a heartbeat," she said. "It is a dragon. I can feel her auma."

Hannah's hands went up to her mouth. "Then it's . . . true," she gasped. She staggered back and fell against the chamber entrance. "You've actually woken her."

"Wasn't that the intention?" said Tam. He moved toward Lucy as more earth fell. "OK. Job done. Time to get out of here."

Grabbing the girl's arm, he dragged her away and pushed her into the tunnels again. He trained his flashlight back onto Hannah, who hadn't moved. "Hannah, come on. What are you waiting for?" Her eyes were filled with awe, her brow beaded with sweat.

"She's alive," she breathed.

"Apparently so. Now lead us out."

Hannah took a deep breath and looked at him blankly. "My flashlight. I left it on the floor of the chamber."

Tam panned his light back in. He couldn't see it. "All right, go to Lucy. I'll find it. Hurry."

Hannah stepped out into Lucy's flashlight beam.

"What's happening? Where's Tam?" the girl demanded.

Hannah merely shook her head.

At that moment, a wind raced along the tunnel with the same kind of swirling intensity Lucy had experienced when waiting for an underground train to arrive. She whipped around and stared into the darkness. One by one, the bulkhead lights came on. The figure of Ms. Gee appeared between them almost floating along the path.

"Tam!" Lucy screamed. But by then Ms. Gee had raised her hand and uttered a spell. The Tor rumbled and a great mass of earth crashed down from the chamber roof, plugging it completely.

Tam. Lucy screamed his name again and ran to the mud face, clawing at it with her cold, bare hands.

"What have you done?" she yelled, already thick with tears. "Get him out! Get him out!"

"Save your breath, child. He's already dead," said Ms. Gee.

"You!" Lucy snarled. "You made him go back into the chamber!" She threw herself at the traitorous Hannah, looking to squeeze her scrawny neck. A bolt of energy from Ms. Gee made her fall away, breathless. As she slumped against the mound of earth burying Tam, something briefly eclipsed one of the low-level bulkhead lights. It was the cat, Bella.

Now it was Hannah's turn to question the sibyl. "You've killed him," she panted, traumatized into instant repentance. "That wasn't the arrangement. You told me he'd only be imprisoned, not murdered!"

Ms. Gee snorted. "He was a threat. Besides, do you think the dragon would have spared him? In my opinion, I did the fool a favor. And now it is time to be rid of you."

The Tor beat again. Hannah felt the ground quake. She stumbled away, her eyes darting at the fine cracks appearing in the ceiling. The wooden support she was clinging to creaked. In places along the rumbling walls, rivulets of water were spurting through the mud and turning to steam. "I pray the queen doesn't spare you, witch . . ." She dipped into her pocket and pulled out the skeleton of a tiny hand. She threw it at Ms. Gee, who caught it, gave a repugnant sneer, and crushed it instantly to dust.

"That belonged to my ancestor, Mary Cauldwell," Hannah said, stumbling backward away from the sibyl. "Anyone who touches it is cursed. Welcome to a nasty death, Ms. Gee. I hope you get the chance to look into Gawaine's eyes before she sears the flesh off your bones."

"Curses?" scoffed the sibyl, dusting her hands off. "I'd be more concerned about a stone in my shoe." With that, she lifted her hand again and another bolt of energy took Hannah off her feet and sent her flying down the tunnel.

Ms. Gee raised her chin, expecting to hear the satisfying crunch of disintegrating ribs as Hannah's body struck a solid wall of earth. Instead, there was a sickly mulching noise. A death moan escaped from Hannah's throat. Ms. Gee frowned, looking puzzled. To her surprise, Hannah was pinned to the wall and not in a crumpled heap on the floor. The sibyl, bizarrely, put on her glasses. Her confusion quickly cleared along with her myopia. Hannah's body was skewered in three neat places, buttoned from her breast to her groin by talons. Her corpse squelched as the talons expanded further into three fully extended claws, pushing her internal organs out. Ms. Gee stepped back. For once in her life she almost vomited as she watched the claws contract into a fist.

Dry-mouthed, she said, "Girl, get up."

There was no response from the tunnel floor.

"Get up, I said!" Ms. Gee whipped around.

But Lucy — and the smoky gray Bella — had gone.

TERROR ON THE ROAD

Mom, where are we going?" Melanie Cartwright said.

Rachel's mouth curled into a secretive smile. "On a little detour."

Melanie glanced at the GPS screen, which had been "recalculating" their route for the last half hour. "Not more relatives?" She crossed her arms and sighed. How many cheek pinches and hairy-lipped kisses could a girl take?

"Be patient. It's not far now," said her mom. "In fact, we really ought to see it soon."

Melanie looked through the window. Fields and trees. "Please tell me we're not going to another garden center?" She slumped into her seat. What was it with people when they hit their forties? Why did shops that sell plant pots suddenly become so attractive?

Overwhelmed by her daughter's mounting apathy, Rachel finally caved in. "All right, I'll tell you — as we're slightly lost and I think I'll have to tap the name into the GPS anyway." She pulled over and brought up the keyboard screen. "Where would you most like to have been today?"

"At home, watching TV," Melanie said drily. "We're missing all the dragon stuff."

Her mother grinned, looking youthful and pretty. "What if we weren't — missing the 'dragon stuff,' I mean?" She turned the screen.

Melanie gave out a loud gasp. "Scuffenbury?!"

Rachel hit SEARCH and set the car in motion. "I realized yesterday that your aunt Jane lives only about sixty miles from the site. I thought it would be a treat for you. A sweet way to end our 'tour.' You never know, we might bump into Lucy."

447

The voice of the GPS crackled.

Melanie pointed threateningly at it. "Do NOT break now."

Rachel leaned forward and tapped it. "Strange. It's always been pretty reliable before — apart from that time it led us onto a construction site instead of a parking garage." She followed the arrow and took a right turn. "You'll like Scuffenbury. It has a wonderful atmosphere."

"Can we climb the Tor?"

"Oh, I think that's obligatory."

Melanie rustled in a shopping bag by her feet. She resurfaced holding Glade. "Can she come with us?"

"As long as you don't drop her. She'll be in several pieces at the bottom if you do. I — oh, what's that?"

The sound of the small car's engine thickened and it slowed to a quarter of its speed.

A large black bird was standing in the road ahead.

Rachel hooted the horn. "Shoo, silly thing."

"Just drive at it," Melanie said. "It'll fly off when you get too close. I'll scare it away with Glade." She brought the mood dragon up to the window and made one of her customary *grrr*s.

Right away, Glade's ivy turned completely black and she seemed to fly out of Melanie's hands. Melanie saw a blur of motion and whipped around to face the rear of the car. Her coat, which she'd thrown onto the backseat, appeared to be hiding a trembling bump.

"Mom, w-what just happened?" she said.

Rachel was staring at the GPS screen. On it was an image of a snarling raven. She slammed her foot down hard on the gas.

A split second later something dark impacted with a *whump* on the windshield. Both females screamed as the glass cracked into a many-pointed star. With a screech of tires the car slid off the road and onto a dirt track between the hedges, where it collided with the post of a gate before coming to a halt, nose down and steaming.

"Mel?" gasped her mother, fumbling for her seat belt and reaching across to free Melanie from hers. "Are you all right? Are you hurt?"

Before Melanie could respond, something struck at the windshield again, breaking a hole the size of a tennis ball in it. The head of a bird punched through the gap. It was the ugliest thing Melanie had ever seen. She screamed and drew her hands and feet into her body, ducking as the raven spat. It left a glob of phlegm on the headrest behind her, which quickly began to dissolve away the cloth. With a snort, it whipped its head toward Rachel. It bared a set of miniature fangs, filling the car with the hideous odor of raw, undigested meat. Rachel wasn't slow to react. Snatching the GPS off the dashboard she struck the bird twice with as much sideways force as she could muster. Its eye was almost punctured on a spike of glass; the same spike skewered its cheek instead. The creature shrieked and thrashed its wings, its hooked claws squealing on the hood of the car. Then, in a movement that must have caused enduring pain, it sawed its head back and forth against the jags, gashing its mouth as it freed itself. A pencil line of black blood ran down the inner surface of the glass and dripped into the air vent at the bottom. And yet, despite its appalling wounds, the bird was able to flog the glass again with even greater force. Suddenly, the entire windshield disintegrated. The bird's evil eyes glowered at its two adversaries. Wings spread, it was now as wide as the car.

"Mel, get out!" Rachel yelled, and was grateful to see the passenger door open and her daughter fall onto the grass shoulder beside it. But her own door, wrenched and buckled by the crash, stayed jammed. In an instant the bird had forced its way in. It clamped Rachel Cartwright's face in its claws and knocked her head against the frame of the car. It would surely have gone on to fracture her skull if a voice hadn't called out in the tongue of dragons: *Stop!*

The raven paused. Rachel's blood was warm between its claws. In one swift movement it let go of the broken, unconscious human and snatched up the little mood dragon instead, dragging Glade out onto the hood of the car.

"No-oo."

The raven turned its head. The human that had not

tried to challenge it was huddled up and crying at the side of the road. For a moment it considered terminating the girl, wondering if the tiny life quaking in its claws could be made to shed its fire tear. But the dragon had been brave to give itself up and was therefore unlikely to demonstrate weakness. And there was no time to waste in idle speculation, not when the rest of the raven flock had been turned to water — or lately to ash — by a dragon many times the size of this.

And so the last of the ravens that would be a darkling took to the skies with its delicate hostage, spreading its shadow in premature triumph over the image of the horned white horse, before pitching toward the hill from where the dragon auma was steadily rising. There it set down — in the branches of a dead tree beside an old house — and concealed itself in shadow, awaiting developments, unaware that the dragon imprisoned in its grasp was not quite as helpless as it might have seemed. For Glade was doing innately what all Pennykettle dragons were capable of: She was sending out a message to a listening dragon. Her signal of distress was beaming across the Vale of Scuffenbury all the way back to Wayward Crescent, where it was indeed being heard — but not by the listener on top of the fridge or even by Grace, still in semistasis on the workbench in the den. Both of those dragons had now been superseded by one with fast-growing, superior powers. His name, albeit arbitrary, was Gwillan.

And his time had come.

ESCAPE

Though her lungs were bursting and tears continued to cloud her vision, Lucy ran and ran down the Glissington tunnels, driven on by fear and the rumbling groans of the shifting Tor. Every few yards a shower of earth fell. The air was now dreadfully choked with heat and soiled with an awful, fetid smell that was beginning to sting the lining of her nostrils, something foul she knew she could have identified if she'd taken the time to try. But time was something she didn't have. Ms. Gee could not be far behind.

On the path, lit by the lights at floor level, Bella was leading the escape. While the sibyl and Hannah had been arguing by the chamber, the cat had padded up, pawed Lucy's hand, and together they had drifted away. So far Bella had guided them faithfully, past two of the kerosene marker lamps, but as they approached the intersection of tunnels she skidded to a halt and disappeared suddenly into the shadows. Confused, and fearing more treachery, Lucy at first prepared to run on. A warning yowl from the cat made her stop and reconsider. It was then she heard what Bella must have heard: Clive's voice, farther along the tunnel, calling out in search of Hannah. If Clive and Hannah were working together, Lucy needed to hide. Looking back and seeing no sign of Ms. Gee, she followed Bella's cry and found herself in a backfilled side tunnel, scrabbling up a mound of earth until she was several feet higher than the path and swallowed up in a knot of darkness.

It wasn't long before Clive and Ms. Gee came together. Lucy had managed to draw herself up with Bella's warm body pressed against her shins. Although they could not be readily seen, Lucy's concern was that they might be heard. The cat was making small gagging noises, her sensitive nose tortured by the putrid odors and the heat. Lucy silently gathered her up, just as Clive swept past with a flashlight. A few yards down the tunnel, he stopped. "Ms. Gee? What the —? Has Hannah brought you here? What's going on?"

"Where's the girl?" said Ms. Gee, with a sandpaper snarl.

"I don't know what you're talking about," Lucy heard Clive say, and her heart almost burst. For she realized now that Clive was innocent and therefore in terrible danger. But in those fateful few seconds she spent wrestling with the option of warning him or not, another evil was about to be done.

"You need to get out of here," Clive went on. He was coughing deeply and his voice was strained. "Dragons are emerging from hills and mountains all over the world. This is a predestined site. Run, Ms. Gee. These tunnels aren't safe. Even if the rigs don't collapse from her movements, you're going to be poisoned by the stench of her urine." (Urine. That was the smell. Lucy covered her mouth and quashed a rush of bile.) "After several thousand years of nonrelease, there are certain things a hibernating creature needs to do. Now, is Hannah down here or not? Hannah!"

"Idiot," Ms. Gee said coldly.

"What?"

At that moment, Lucy decided to give herself up. What else could she do to save Clive's life? But just as she began to call out, her exclamation was quickly abridged by a loud and lingering gurgling sound emerging from Clive's throat. It was followed by a cocktail of spurting liquid, tightening muscle, and a strangely hideous popping noise. Lucy sank back in terror. She knew right away that Clive was dead, but could only imagine what horrors the sibyl must have committed. She heard the fatal slump of his body, followed by Ms. Gee's brief snort of contempt. With it, all hope of escape seemed to fade. To make matters worse, Bella was arching up in her lap, doing her utmost not to sneeze. Lucy quickly turned the cat into her body hoping to soften the sound against her clothes, but the tiny expulsion of air sounded like the crash of a hundred dishes. In the tunnel, she saw a light beam rise. Ms. Gee had picked up Clive's flashlight.

Within seconds, their hiding place was flushed with light. "Out," the sibyl snarled. "And bring that ungrateful girl with you."

The cat hissed. Lucy cradled her tighter. Though she couldn't be sure which of them Ms. Gee was addressing, she boldly shouted, "Why? Why are you doing this? Why did you turn Bella into a cat?"

"Because she's unruly, like you," the sibyl growled. "I find young girls become more . . . polite for the experience, especially when they know what will happen to their parents if they should betray me or try to leave. I trust you're listening, Bella?"

The cat shivered. Lucy stroked her head. "Why her? Why pick on Bella?"

There was a triple thump and the Tor shuddered. The stench of urine grew even stronger. Lucy turned her head. The soil beside her was sweating with the stuff. In the space behind Ms. Gee, the air was also beginning to mist, giving the appearance of fine rain.

Even so, the sibyl kept talking. "She's a red-headed innocent, born of dragons. I brought her here to calm the creature — and, as luck would have it, the unicorn. But you and she are from the same stock, which makes one of you dispensable — or perhaps you both are." Lucy didn't like the sound of that. A smug sibyl was a seriously dangerous one. From Ms. Gee's lips came more words of magick. Lucy tensed herself, half-expecting she would be padding along like Bonnington from now on. Yet, as the spell ended, nothing much seemed to have happened. Then she saw that Ms. Gee was holding an unstopped vial, into which a few drops of liquid were falling. Lucy touched her cheeks. They were hot and dry. The old witch had stolen her tears.

"What are you doing?" Lucy gasped.

"Oh, come, girl. I don't have time for history. Didn't the sibyl that delivered you teach you anything? Your tears are the purest form of the dragon essence within you and the safest means of identifying yourself to them." She stoppered the vial and waggled it in front of her evil face. "If I'm correct — and I usually am — one drop of this thrown into the eye of the Glissington cairn will spread out and form a mirror to reflect moonlight back over Scuffenbury Hill. The light wakes the unicorn, the unicorn frees the dragon. Perfect. You really are quite useful, you girls. All I need now is your beautiful red hair. Oh, and for your insolence, child, I will try to make this as painful as possible — before I kill you, that is." She twisted a hand.

"No!" Lucy screamed as her hair began to rise. Every root protested in agony. Her scalp tightened and the skin above her ears was tugged to tearing point. But just when it seemed she would be sick with the pain (and stripped of her chief claim to beauty), she heard the sibyl herself give out a sharp screech.

Lucy's hair fell back into place. Looking up, she saw Ms. Gee flapping a hand. A wisp of smoke was rising from her fingers.

"Gwendolen," Lucy whispered. She spotted the little dragon zip around behind the sibyl and let loose another quick tongue of flame.

"Agh!" the sibyl cried. Her bun of gray hair crackled alight and frizzled into a blackened prune. She staggered back against the tunnel wall. But by now she had set her evil glare on her assailant and the next exclamation to leave her mouth had venomous intent wrapped all around it. The spell left Gwendolen frozen in flight.

Ms. Gee fumbled by her feet for a stone. "You pathetic excuse for a dragon," she sneered. "I'll smash you into pieces, scale by scale . . ."

"No-ooo!" Lucy screamed. And as if her cry of woe had ignited a charge, the Tor lurched and part of the main tunnel collapsed.

Ms. Gee looked up. The last thing she saw was the ceiling splitting open and a flood of stale urine pouring down upon her. Within five seconds, its toxic acidity had stripped the clothing and flesh from her bones, leaving nothing but her skeleton standing. The frail whimper she'd managed to elicit just before the stinking deluge engulfed her became a sad and eerie echo for mercy. Mercy, there was none. Her bones wobbled then collapsed into the poisonous stream, fizzing like magnesium strips as they were carried away with the flow.

And though she could have been imagining it, Lucy thought she heard a high-pitched cackle of laughter rushing through the tunnels — as if the ghost of Mary Cauldwell had finally had her revenge.

At the same time, the spell holding Gwendolen was broken and she tumbled into a heavy spin. Lucy cried out, but could do nothing to stop her beloved special dragon falling headlong into the waste. The splash gouged a chasm in Lucy's heart and drove her scrabbling to the edge of the stream. Only Bella's tight claws and yowling protests prevented her from wading in to try to save the dragon. Lucy's arid skin wetted with tears again.

But then came a remarkable turn of events. The

wastewater parted and Gwendolen rose up, shaking herself dry in midair. She spat out something Lucy cared not to imagine and coughed an important hurr. *Dragon,* she said.

Lucy looked at the yellow-green flow. "You mean it won't hurt us?" She tweaked Bella's ear.

Gwendolen nodded. She dipped her paw into the urine and stroked Lucy's hand. The fluid ran away. No burning. No scars.

Lucy gulped, closed her eyes, and dipped one foot in up to her ankle. Here was a journal entry to top all others: Dragon urine feels inexplicably warm and has the density of a milky paste, but it's safe to descendants of Guinevere and Gawain. "Lead the way," she said, holding Bella safe in her arms.

Within a minute, and with tunnels collapsing as they went, Gwendolen brought them back to the cellar. Letting Bella go, Lucy pounded up the steps and fell to her knees in the kitchen, taking in enormous gulps of air. Gwendolen immediately landed beside her carrying Ms. Gee's vial, which had washed up by the cellar steps. She put it down beside Lucy, whose first thought was to dash it against the tiled floor. Bella came up and eyed the vial intently, as if she'd had the same idea. The two females exchanged a green-eyed look, and for some reason she couldn't explain just then, Lucy changed her mind and put the vial into her pocket. Bella slunk away and leaped onto the sink, to look through the window at the rumbling Tor.

Lucy stood up and rested her hand on the table for support. In doing so, she began to appreciate the magnitude of what was happening. Anything that could move within the house was rattling. Lights were swinging. Doors were banging open and shut. Cans of vegetables were dancing on their shelves. Apples were tumbling off their pyramid in the fruit bowl.

Yet, despite the threat of destruction, the situation seemed to have peaked. For the Tor was still standing and the cairn at its zenith was visible again. It was as if the dragon had risen so far but could go no farther until the right word was spoken or the right action was completed. This was confirmed when a bellow of despair rushed through the house with the physical impact of a cannon blast.

Meow! Bella's fur stood on end. She turned her head and stared at Lucy.

Lucy in turn looked at Gwendolen. "Did you hear that?"

Gwendolen nodded. Every dragon from here to Wayward Crescent would have heard that.

The great matriarch, Gawaine, had spoken. *Free me,* she had said. *Teramelle, free me.*

CLOSE CALL

A soft, warm shower. A long, luxurious soak in one of Zanna's herbal bathing lotions. A stimulating foot spa. A rubdown with a damp cloth. Even five minutes beneath a leaking gutter. Lucy would have jumped at any of these chances to improve her personal hygiene, for she stank like nothing she could ever describe. But for once she put aside her private needs in favor of an urgent phone call home.

"Hello. Lucy?"

David's voice. Her spirits lifted. She began to unload everything to him. The words came out in a breathless gabble, as if she were speaking through a tumbler of water. "You've gotta come. It's all shaking. You've gotta come, NOW. The hill's going to crumble.

Tam's . . ." The pain nearly knifed her to the farm-house door. "Tam's . . ."

"Lucy, slow down. Speak calmly if you can. Are you safe?"

"I think so."

"Right, tell me what's happened."

"We went into the Tor," she jabbered. "It was a trap to kill Tam. She buried him in a tunnel."

"She? The sibyl?"

"Mm."

"Where is she?"

"Dead. I got away from her. Bella led us out."

"Bella?"

"She's a girl. The sibyl turned her into a cat. I touched the dragon, David. It's trying to wake up." Another restless thump from the Tor shook the whole guesthouse, spreading cracks along the plaster ceiling. Lucy winced as the kitchen light fizzed out, its chandelier fittings half-breaking away and swinging precariously on their chains. Bella jumped down off the sink and ran to find shelter under the table.

"I hear crashing. Where are you?"

"In the guesthouse. In the kitchen. It's like an earthquake!" Deep inside the house, something made of glass fell over and shattered. "The dragon's crying for the unicorn to free it. What shall I do?"

"Nothing. You do nothing. Find a safe place and — hang on, Zanna wants to tell me something."

Lucy sighed and turned away in frustration. She looked into the dining area and saw Gwendolen on one of the breakfast tables, creeping gingerly toward the window, as if she had spotted something in the garden.

"Lucy, are you there?" David's voice came through again.

"Yes."

"Listen, something's happened here. Zanna's just told me your mom's coming around."

Mom. In all the trauma, Lucy had forgotten her guiding light. Her anxiety once again gathered pace. "Is she all right? Is she asking for me?"

"She's not talking yet, but Zanna says she's calm. I'm going to stay here a little while longer to make sure the situation's stable, but I'm sending Grockle down to protect you."

"Grockle?"

"Yes. Go outside. Let him see you. Is Gwendolen there?"

With the phone pressed hard to her ear, Lucy headed for the dining room. Gwendolen was now on the sideboard where the cutlery was kept. Her ears were fully pricked. *What?* Lucy mouthed at her. David spoke again. "Luce, did you hear me?"

"Yeah, she's here."

"Good. Tell her to put out a beacon. It'll help Grockle find you. He can travel across time planes as easily as you or I could look through a window. He'll be in the general area before you know it. You can speak to him in dragontongue. Takes a bit of tuning, but you'll get it. OK?"

Lucy nodded blindly. "What about Tam?"

There was a pause. David said, "We'll find him. I promise."

A slow tear cut across Lucy's cheek. "But —"

"I'll come as soon as I can," David said. And he ended the call.

Lucy clamped her phone shut, one-handed, and buried it into her jeans pocket. "Spread your auma," she said to Gwendolen. "We're going to have company."

Hrrr! went the dragon.

Lucy screwed up her face. "Listen? To what?"

Gwendolen cocked her head. She was sure she could hear a distress call somewhere. Not aimed at her, but the frequency was —

The next heartbeat moved the house sideways a foot, shifting the furniture at least the same distance. The windows in the upper sash shattered and photographs of Scuffenbury flew off their hooks. High above, Lucy could hear what she thought was brickwork crashing against the roof. A shower of roof slates beyond the French windows and a bungee-jumping TV satellite dish convinced her. It was time to get out.

"Gwendolen, fly!" she cried. She hurried into the kitchen for Bella. The cat was poised and ready to run. "Through the hall, out the front door!" Lucy panted, not sure if Bella would understand. But the language of falling masonry was common: Wherever Lucy ran, Bella would run, too. Within moments they were breathing in the garden air, where the ground was just as active as the floors of the house but there was far less danger of injury.

But a greater threat was perched less than twenty feet away. In her hurry to escape, Lucy had fled toward the one place in the garden she thought would be stable: the dead, gray tree. Little did she know that Mary Cauldwell's gallows still harbored evil, past and present. If Gwendolen had finished her calculations, she would have concluded that among the tainted branches was another dragon. Unlikely as it seemed, a Pennykettle dragon. And if she had turned her ears from the mayhem, she would have heard that dragon's warning *hrrr!* For Glade had seen Lucy emerging from the house and had measured her captor's eagerness for slaughter in the subtle tightening of its ruthless claws. From lungs that contained less air than an envelope, Glade had bravely cried out. Her call was eclipsed by the raven's wings as it swooped to make an ugly mess of Lucy's head. What saved the girl was a falling chimney. It thundered to the drive like a spent red rocket, clipping both handles of the empty wheelbarrow and flipping it through the air like an autumn leaf. The raven was lucky to avoid the turning metal, luckier still that the dust and debris created by the crash enabled it to swerve away without detection. Halfway through its plunge, it had sensed a major ripple in the fabric of the universe and knew there could be only one reason for that. Lucy Pennykettle had felt the rift, too, and was holding her breath in expectation. She was not to be disappointed. Once the clouds had settled, sitting astride the mess of bricks was the most magnificent creature she had ever seen.

The bronze-scaled juvenile dragon, Grockle. Fearless, breathtaking, and huge.

THE RIGHT TO DISOBEY

W ow . . . "

In the circumstances, Lucy could think of nothing more fitting to say. The last time she'd seen Grockle, five years ago, he'd been something of a kitten in dragon terms. Impressive, yes. Classically prehistoric. Charming. Frightening. Humbling. Vulnerable.

Now he was simply mesmerizing. Ten times the size she remembered. And though he possessed all the strength and characteristics of a predatory monster (his incisor teeth were as long as her shins), there was a gentleness about him that Lucy had only ever seen before in the likes of cuddly, domestic animals. And he was beautiful. The soft scales that had covered his body back then had thickened up into roughened plates, though it was clear from his able versatility of movement that their pliability was almost fluid. When Lucy raised her hand to touch his chest the scales tensed in a kind of autonomic way, interlocking like a row of Roman battle shields. But as they measured her warmth and sensitivity, maybe even his kinship with her, the plates yielded and their hardness reconfigured, until her palm was gliding smoothly over him and the scales were changing color to the pressure of her touch without ever losing their glistening bronze base.

But it was his eyes that enthralled her the most. In his youth they had resembled plain lizard eyes. Slitted, scary, and uniformly yellow throughout the iris. Now his iris, like his scales, had deepened and developed. The general shade was still predominantly yellow, but there was a richness in its textured layers as appealing to Lucy as amber gemstones. And behind the iris, in the darkly mysterious oval of the pupil, was a world that Lucy could only dream of. Here she saw unparalleled beauty. Incredible complexity. Extraordinary history.

Her true destiny.

She decided she would formally introduce herself. But before she could initiate a dialogue, Grockle jerked back and raised his head. With his ears extending in a stacking motion, he stretched his neck and turned to sniff the air. His nostrils dilated so widely that Lucy could see a fragile membrane of pale gray tissue rippling like a sail inside his snout. Above his wonderful triangular eye sockets, the bony ridges pressed themselves into a scowl.

"What's the matter?" she asked. Something was clearly wrong, but she could see no dangers in the garden or beyond.

Even so, Grockle lifted his tail, turning his isoscele like a rudder. An angry growl sounded in his serpentine throat.

"Grockle, what's the matter?" Lucy asked again.

The dragon stared at Mary Cauldwell's tree. He blew a line of smoke that was all the colors of Bella's fur. With a rasp like a butcher's knife, his claws emerged from the leathery pouches at the ends of his toes. He flushed his wings and prepared to fly. So great was the draft of air that it swatted Lucy's face away to one side.

"WAIT!" she commanded in (loud) dragontongue. To her amazement, the dragon stalled.

His eye patterns switched again, reinventing the human definition of "confused."

"David sent you to protect me," she said, with just a hint of truculence shading her voice.

Grockle tilted his head.

"Can you understand me?"

Hrrr, he replied, in a low bass register that made her red hair lift off her shoulders. She even felt the rumble deep in her diaphragm and realized to her amazement that she could interpret the vibrations just as accurately there as she could in the bones of her inner ear. But then, the word was easy to render. He had spoken her name.

"Don't leave me," she said. "We need your help."

Grockle sucked in through a tiny row of air vents just to the rear of his lower jaw. His jeweled eyes flashed toward the ancient tree. The scent of a raven hung in its branches, on a trail that was rapidly diminishing. *Help us do what?* he heard a small voice say. With near-preternatural speed, he swung back and peered intently at Gwendolen, realigning his nostrils like a double-barreled gun. From the sanctuary of Lucy's shoulder, Gwendolen waved a wary paw.

Lucy pointed at Grockle's claws. "There. That's what we need."

Gwendolen's eye ridges mirrored Grockle's.

"His claws," Lucy said. Perfect for digging. "We're going to go and search for Tam."

THE COMING
OF GAWAINE

Hrrr? said Gwendolen. Had the girl gone mad? Tam would be as dead as the tree by now. Crushed. Suffocated. Drowned in pee.

"He might have found a pocket of air," Lucy argued. "If we wait for David, it might be too late."

She noticed Grockle tilt his head again and wondered for a moment if he'd read her thoughts. The dragon rumbled, but didn't say a word. One eye swiveled toward her pocket as she opened it and showed him the vial of tears. "This will help," she said, jiggling the vial so he could see its contents. She watched his extraordinary, multilayered pupil undergo a series of focal adjustments. Right at its center, a tiny floret of light appeared.

"The moon," Lucy whispered. She spun quickly on her heels and found it in the afternoon sky. A fragile rice-paper disk of light, sitting over the Vale of Scuffenbury.

"That's it," she breathed. "That's what I need to do." Her destiny was right here, bottled in her hand. She swung back to face Grockle again. "Take me to the top of the Tor!" She pointed to her chest, then the sky, and flapped her hands. "I want to go close to the cairn."

Gwendolen questioned the wisdom of this.

"I'm not giving up on Tam," Lucy said. "He wouldn't have given up on us. We're going to do this, Gwen. We're going to make the mirror with my tears and let the moon reflect in it and" — she trapped a nervous bubble of air and looked back at the restless Tor — "we'll have a better chance of finding him once the dragon's free."

Meow. For the first time in Grockle's presence, Bella made herself known. She stepped out from the shelter of an ornamental mushroom and sat down in plain view of the dragon. Her canny gaze swept toward the vial of tears and Lucy wondered, yet again, if the cat could be trusted. Maybe Bella had her own agenda? Maybe she had come to "claim the dragon"? Grockle, too, seemed equally wary. His keen sense of smell had detected the existence of a warm-blooded animal at ground level near to Lucy, but he'd assumed it would be nothing but a harmless feral creature. Bella's swaggering arrival made him reconsider. Once again, his nostrils prepared for a strike.

Lucy raised her hand. "No, she's my friend. You protect her as well." *For now*, she thought. She put the vial deliberately into her pocket, making sure that Bella knew that her trust was under scrutiny.

Grockle gave the cat an extended glare. He growled but appeared to have understood. Leaning forward, almost kneeling, he rested one paw on the ground next to Lucy.

"I'm supposed to climb on?" she asked. Not quite the romantic carriage she'd hoped for. In the movies, the princess always rode on the dragon's shoulder. But laying vanity aside, she pressed herself into the contours of his "hand," wincing as his claws closed around her in a cradle. The smell of them almost made her heave. In the quick between toe and claw were remnants of dried blood and rotting meat. It made her wonder how dragons had ever come to suffer persecution.

With a whoosh, Grockle extended his wings, making shadow puppets on the trembling ground. Lucy clicked her fingers. "Bella, come on." The cat swished her tail and bolted up. In one leap, she bounced off Lucy's thigh and settled herself in the crib of the girl's arms. Gwendolen, a little more sedately, opted for a pocket of Lucy's coat.

I will not squeal. I will not be sick, Lucy told herself, though she nearly committed both in the first three seconds after takeoff. They were above the house in half that time, looking down on a vast depression of splintered timbers and broken roof slates. Surprisingly comfortable in Grockle's grip, and shielded from the wind by his skillful use of air-deflecting scales, she was able to view her surroundings with ease. She was praying that she might see a lonely figure staggering around the base of Glissington Tor. But though there were cracks in the grassy strata in the area nearest the rear of the guesthouse, there was nothing human moving among them.

Grockle banked and the ground rushed away in a blur. Up they climbed, into colder, paler skies until, with a slight breathtaking jolt, Grockle backswept his wings and went into a kind of angelic hover. The next sensation Lucy felt was akin to traveling down in an elevator. Lower, lower, until Grockle brought her level with the Glissington cairn. Lucy was impressed. As "rides" went, it beat anything a carnival had to offer. The whole flight had taken less than fifteen seconds.

"Take me nearer," she said.

He moved her forward, until the "eye" was as close as a basketball hoop. Bella turned her head, chattering in the way that Bonnington often did whenever he was slightly unsure of something. Lucy ignored her and peered into the tear-shaped hole. There was nothing to see, other than a snippet of the far horizon at the end of a long, long carpet of green. She could not find the moon and that panicked her briefly, until she remembered that it must, of necessity, be above them and behind. It always struck her as strange that the moon could sometimes be seen in a sunlit sky.

With more than a hint of nervousness, she repositioned Bella and put her hand into the pocket containing the vial. This, she warned herself, might be the biggest anticlimax of all time. She was no sibyl. She knew not a word of mirror-forming magicks. All she had was her ancestry — and faith.

"Please work," she whispered, and drew the stopper.

She had been expecting drama, of course, but nothing of the sort that was about to follow. As she lifted the vial, Bella immediately slashed at her hand. A fine trail of scarlet scratch marks manifested quickly on Lucy's wrist. Even before Grockle could react to her scream, the cat had struck again, this time targeting the vial itself. The result was that Lucy let go of both. Bella twisted through the air, righting herself, narrowly avoiding the sweep of Grockle's tail as he attempted to spear her with his isoscele. She landed, as cats often do, on all fours and ran into the shadows at the base of the cairn, before turning her sequin green eyes to look up. No doubt she was confident of seeing the vial come tumbling down to its destruction after her. But that was not to be. For at the moment Lucy had pulled the stopper, Gwendolen had fluttered out to watch the proceedings. It was a simple task, when Lucy dropped the vial, for Gwendolen to zip down and catch it.

Lucy saw the cat's face and the fury in it. But what concerned her more was the added look of fear. She saw Bella's frightened eyes suddenly flick sideways. Gwendolen was nearing the cairn.

Bella wailed as though her life depended on it.

"Wait!" Lucy shouted. But Gwendolen, thinking she was saving the day, had flown to the eye and tipped the vial. The glass fell away, shattering on the hard gray stones below, but a droplet of its contents was drawn into the opening. It glittered like a jewel at the absolute center. And nothing, Lucy knew, would draw it out.

Suddenly, there was a neon blue flash. The light made Lucy blink and lose focus. When she was able to see again, a film of shimmering water, as delicate as the surface of a bubble, was stretched right across the eye of the cairn.

"Move me away," she said to Grockle, though her voice was somber with uncertainty. As Gwendolen returned and settled in her pocket, Lucy looked for a final time at Bella. The cat was transfixed, staring at the moon. It was in position over Scuffenbury Hill.

Lucy ordered Grockle to take her there and set her down close to the white horse carving. The flight took less than thirty seconds. She had barely put one foot on the slope when the mirror across the vale began to shimmer erratically and a burst of silver light was drawn down from the moon and redirected onto the hill. It hit the horse precisely where Rupert Steiner had predicted it would, at the point on its head where the horn grew out.

Lucy gasped and stood back a pace. The beams of light were done within an instant, but on the hillside the chalky figure was ablaze. Any normal fire would have left Lucy baked. But this was like the fire that David had written about. The blue-white fire that melted no ice. "The fire of creation," he sometimes called it. And it was powerfully at work on the hill. As it raged, the flames leaped up and froze, each one changing to a solid strand of flesh. Layer upon layer, thread upon thread, until they had formed the shape of a unicorn.

For a moment or two, there was absolute stillness. The Vale of Scuffenbury waited in silence. Then with a tremendous snort of air the creature bucked its hind legs and scrambled to its feet. It tossed a mane that still retained sparks of white fire and opened its eyes. They were pure violet.

A soft breeze played around Lucy's face, picking up a few loose strands of her hair. In an instant, the unicorn had her scent. "Stop!" Lucy shouted, sensing it would run. But it turned and fled so fast that a ghost trail of replicates was left in its wake. There was nothing between Lucy and the legend now but an ordinary, windswept grassy hill.

But the unicorn had not deserted the hill. It was Grockle who saw it next, standing on the peak, facing Glissington. He snorted at Lucy, who was just in time to see the creature lower its head and point its celebrated horn at the Tor. A jagged bolt of white light crackled across the valley and struck the ancient burial mound. The Tor exploded like the shell of an egg, spraying sods of earth in a shuttlecock arrangement back toward Scuffenbury Hill. Lucy yelped and covered her head, though none of the pieces had the range to reach her. When she looked again, Glissington Tor had broken into four distinct mounds, and rising from its smoking center was the most terrifying dragon she had ever seen.

It was green, savage, and at least three times the size of Grockle. When it threw out its wings it blocked the sun and seemed to draw the landscape around it like a blanket. From nostril to tail it must have measured half a small field. For a moment or two it kept its head folded into its chest, but when it raised its snout and Lucy saw the redness in one eye, the bones at the base of her spine turned to jelly. The dragon had been horribly attacked at some time. Or maybe something had failed with its fire tear? Or the eye had become diseased in some way? She couldn't tell. Nor could she bear to look at it for long. But little did she know she would soon be forced to. For just as the unicorn had sensed her presence, suddenly the dragon seemed to scent her as well. The scales around its neck came up in a frill and black smoke gushed from its long, narrow snout. Paying no heed whatsoever to Grockle, it turned its damaged gaze on Lucy. At first she told herself it couldn't have seen her. She had to be a mile and a half away, at least. But with a wallop of wings that tickled the blades of grass around her feet, the thing took off and headed their way. In mid-flight, it uncoupled its jaw and let out a squeal that sounded like a pig being forced through a grinder. Lucy saw Grockle tense. The squeal gathered force and grew into a roar, which seemed loud enough to shatter the dome of the sky. Lucy covered her ears and screamed.

The Queen of Dragons was coming for her.

And she intended to kill.

WAYWARD CRESCENT, TEN MINUTES EARLIER

So what brought about the change?" asked David, following Zanna up the stairs to Liz's room.

"I don't know," she said. "I got a shout from Arthur while you were talking to Lucy and went to check Liz out. She's been mumbling incoherently and her temperature's up, but nothing out of the normal range for her."

She swept into the bedroom with David close behind. He immediately sat down and picked up Liz's hand. Her eyes were still closed. And though it looked from her expression that she was dreaming again she didn't appear to be unduly disturbed.

"Anything? Any words?" David said to Arthur.

The professor was on the other side of the bed. He, too, had taken hold of one of Liz's hands. "Nothing I can make any sense of," he said.

David frowned and bent close to her ear. "Liz," he said in dragontongue, "if you can hear me, squeeze my hand."

A second passed. Zanna held her breath. The potions dragon, Gretel, flew off Liz's pillow and positioned herself by David's knee. Together, they saw Liz's knuckles lift.

"Yes," said Zanna, clamping her hands together in relief. "She responded."

Gretel raised an eye ridge and whizzed to the bedside table, there to dip her paw into one of the many small crucibles she'd been brewing her concoctions in. She settled like a feather on Liz's chest, then smeared her patient's lips with a pale blue liquid. No one questioned what was in the potion, but it seemed to work. Like a shoot breaking out of its seed, a word passed across Liz's lips: "Lu-cy."

Gretel knocked her paws together in triumph. David

touched the dragon's spine in gratitude. He bent toward Liz's ear again. "Lucy's fine," he said (he saw Zanna grit her teeth). "She'll be here soon."

A vein pulsed in the side of Liz's neck. She turned her head to one side, nestling into Arthur's outstretched hand. The professor rolled his eyes across the bed toward David. Despite silence and blindness his message was clear. *Is this true?*

David patted Arthur's shoulder and motioned Zanna to the door. "I need to talk to you in the den," he whispered.

Zanna drilled him with one of her famous stares. She cast a glance at Liz and stepped out onto the landing. "How could you say a thing like that about Lucy? Arthur's not stupid. He can sense you're lying. Maybe Liz can, too."

"I'm not lying, Zanna."

"No. You're just being 'economical with the truth,' as usual. It sounds to me as if Lucy's in a heap of trouble. And what about Tam? Is he . . . ?" She couldn't bring herself to say the word.

"I don't know," David said, gesturing her to keep her voice down. "Somehow Lucy got away from the sibyl. She was helped by its familiar."

"What?" Zanna was right in his face again. A sprig of hair jumped from where it had been tucked behind her ear. "And you let that pass? Have you learned nothing about these women? How do you know Lucy's not been tricked?"

"Grockle's there now. She's safe," he said.

She drew a breath. "That's what you said about Tam."

Before either of them could speak again, Alexa emerged from the Dragons' Den holding two dragons out in front of her.

"Lexie?" said her mother. "What are you doing with them?"

The child was carrying Liz's cherished dragon, Guinevere, and its male companion, which they appropriately called Gawain. In all the time Zanna had known the family, neither of these dragons had ever been removed from the den, though Lucy had once told her how David had managed to break Gawain during his first few months in the house, while he was still innocent of Liz's gifts. Of all the special dragons these two were arguably the most important, certainly the most mysterious, for they were always present when a new dragon was kilned. Yet no one ever really talked about them — and Zanna had never heard either of them speak. To see them being carried along the landing was an oddity indeed.

Alexa merely said, "Aunty Liz needs them."

"In what way?" Zanna asked, but David touched her arm, indicating she should leave it.

Together they watched Alexa drift away, as though she were a bridesmaid going up an aisle. She turned at a stiff right angle into Liz and Arthur's room. And that was that.

Zanna shook her head and slipped into the den, where the atmosphere seemed to be remarkably composed. No board games today. Strangely, no chatter. "Tell me about this familiar," she said.

"It's a cat, called Bella."

"Bella?" Zanna paused.

"Is that a problem?" he asked.

Zanna narrowed her gaze. "There was an e-mail from someone named Bella — on Lucy's computer. Some days earlier than the others, I think." Her worried eyes found his.

"Check it," he said.

She folded her arms and backed out of the room.

David, in the meantime, turned toward Gwillan. The little dragon was still on the workbench. He tapped his foot as David approached, as though he'd been waiting for this moment for some time. David glanced around the shelves and noticed the absence of Gruffen, G'reth, and Gollygosh — all of them last seen doing housework (Golly had been shining the bathroom taps). But where on Earth was Groyne? His orders had been to stay with Gwillan.

"You look well," David said, drawing up a stool.

Hrrr, agreed Gwillan, swishing his tail.

David reached forward and touched his thumb to the side of Gwillan's snout. The dragon looked down his nose at the digit, thought about biting, and pulled away.

"How do you want me to address you?" asked David. He watched the scales around Gwillan's neck change color. Interesting. Was the youngster reading his mood?

Gwillan lifted his shoulders.

"Are you Gwillan or Joseph Henry?"

The dragon chewed its lip. *Hrr-rr*, he replied. *Both — sometimes.*

David nodded. The irony made him smile. "Your mother isn't well."

That made Gwillan look beyond him, as if he could stare through the walls at Liz. His handsome eye ridges crumpled a little. His violet eyes gave a blink of concern.

"She's using all her strength to protect you, isn't she?"

Gwillan tilted his head.

"To control the darkness?"

The little dragon contracted his claws.

"If you let me take you north, they won't hurt you, Gwillan. The illumined dragons can help you to the light, just like they once helped me. Then Liz will be free again — and so will you. That is what you want, isn't it?"

"David!" Zanna's voice rang out from Lucy's bedroom. Gwillan lifted his head, focusing hard on the direction of the sound. "David, get in here. You need to look at this."

David put his hands between his legs and pushed himself leisurely off the stool. "Soon, there won't be any choice, Gwillan. You go with me — or the natural dragons take you. Don't let Liz suffer."

With that he went next door, where Zanna was peering hard at the computer.

"Mmm, glasses," he said. "I'd forgotten how cute you look in them."

"Shut up," she said. "This is important." She turned the flat screen through forty-five degrees, so they could both read the e-mail there. "This is from a girl who signs it 'Bella.' See that?" She pointed to the header. "'Tales of Gawaine.' She knows how to spell it."

"Go on," he said.

Zanna scrolled down. "She gives a lot of basic stuff we already know about Glissington, but this is the crucial bit, here. She describes this as a legend, but it's beginning to sound horribly real." Her finger traced a paragraph of highlighted text. "'At the end of the last great Wearle, Gawaine, the Queen of Dragons, came to the valley in search of the unicorn, Teramelle. She (Gawaine) was heavily pregnant and injured from a conflict with forces of darkness that had driven her from her eyrie in the ice lands of the North. The unicorn, Teramelle, protected her and tried to heal her wounds. What strength the queen had, she put into bearing her eggs.'"

"Eggs? Plural?" Now David was fully awake.

"Hang on," said Zanna. "It gets worse. 'The birth weakened the matriarch further. Knowing she would have no strength to rear the wearlings, and fearing she would die if she did not enter' . . . I don't know this word: coelacanthis?"

"Stasis," David said.

"Stasis," she repeated, "'before the wearlings could be hatched, she entrusted the eggs to the sanctuary of two agents of Teramelle. One, the eagle Gideon. Two, the red-headed girl who combed the creature's mane and looked to its needs. Gideon flew his egg back to the ice lands where some say the wearling hatched and lived secretly for a time among humans untainted by the darkness. But the girl was murdered by the forces who sought to end Gawaine's life. A black witch' — sibyl, anyone? — 'dressed in the likeness of the girl, stole the second egg, blinding the queen in one eye with the girl's poisoned tears so that the dragon could not easily pursue her. The egg was broken and spilled in sight of the queen. Distraught, she lay down to die, but was kept alive by the wishes of the unicorn which also chose to lay down close by' . . . blah, blah, blah . . . Do you know what this means?"

David was already backing toward the door. "A

black witch dressed in the likeness of the girl. When Gawaine sees Lucy she's going to remember how she was betrayed."

"Hurry, David," Zanna said, tears breaking from the corners of her eyes. "Please hurry."

He clicked his fingers and the narwhal tusk materialized on Lucy's bed. He closed his hand around it and shook it three times.

"I love you," he said to Zanna.

Then he was gone.

Union

Grockle took off a second too late. Perhaps it was his juvenile inexperience. Perhaps he was awed to be in the presence of a dragon so mighty. Most likely he simply believed there was no real reason for Gawaine to attack. It was the scent of hydrocarbons coming up from her throat (too subtle for any human to detect) and the vast suck of oxygen as she bore toward the hill that convinced him she did not intend to simply fly by. He flew to intercept her, and for several seconds the advantage was his. He had lifted off, silently, on her blind side, and was gaining on the matriarch faster than she was gaining on Lucy. But the olfactory senses of the queen were profound, and as she closed in on the girl she supposed to be a traitor she grew fully aware of the counterattack. Claws spread, Grockle merely intended to pinion her body and carry her aside. But with the agility of one many years her junior, Gawaine tilted (with no disruption to her wingbeat) and struck the young dragon behind the ear, not with open claws, but with a strong, closed fist. In terms of weight, it was little more than a cuff. But the effect on Grockle was spectacular. She had knocked out his center of balance, located (like humans) in the inner ear. The more he flapped, the dizzier he became. He spiraled down through a palette of greens and browns and crashed onto the hill forty yards away from Lucy. The impact righted his senses a little, but as he adjusted his pineal radar and prepared to fly back to reengage the queen, he saw Lucy engulfed in a yellow cone of flame. Too late. It was over. The girl was surely dead.

But amazingly, she wasn't. Grockle blinked and tested his optical triggers, hardly able to believe that the child was on her feet and apparently unharmed. One switch of his wings took him back to within six yards of her. The queen had flamed from twice that distance and was standing, dumbstruck, her fire receding in bright orange scribbles underneath her tongue. She turned her head and spat viciously at Grockle. In a strange, archaic variant of dragontongue she ordered him to come no nearer. Wary and unbalanced, but mildly optimistic, he bowed and turned his gaze on Lucy.

She was quivering and in shock, making the pathetic whimpering noises humans were so fond of. But not a jot of her, not even the garments she was wearing, had been ruined by the matriarch's fire. The same could not be said of the surrounding grass, which bore a scorch mark as long as Grockle's tail. It would not grow again for many a year, he thought.

A guttural noise rumbled deep inside Gawaine's throat. Her anger had lessened, but not her curiosity. She blew a thick gobbet of phlegm onto the ground. It sizzled like a hot wet coal, consuming yet another patch of land. Grockle stood by, reverent and inert, praying that the queen would not lose patience and chew the girl's head off in one quick bite. In truth, he could have done little to stop her. But the sight of her cleansing her nostrils gave him hope that all Gawaine intended was to scent the girl — though, he reminded himself, a dragon liked to smell its food before it ate.

Gawaine's head swanned down and her giant breathing holes scanned the full length of Lucy's body, plucking so much air from around the girl that she was pulled forward a step onto the cindered earth. Where she had stood, the green shape of her feet remained.

The Queen of Dragons reared back in confusion.

Once again she swept her nose over the girl, concentrating now on two distinct areas: a single pocket of Lucy's coat and then her thick red hair. To Grockle's despair, he saw the matriarch flip her tail so the isoscele was pointing like a blade. One quick thrust and Lucy would be opened like a gutted rabbit. He leaned closer, ready to launch a final, probably fatal, defense. But in an act of supreme tenderness, Gawaine passed her tail right around the quaking girl (making the shape of a G) and touched the isoscele to her heart.

Making a sound between a stifled scream and the need not to choke on the dragon's breath,

Lucy finally uncovered her face. At the same time, Gwendolen climbed out of Lucy's pocket and settled in Lucy's hands. Whatever fate awaited them, awaited them both.

Traumatized and held on her feet by terror, Lucy somehow found the will to look into the penetrating eye of the monster, then down at the dagger tip pressed against her heart. She closed her eyes again, certain she would die. But the monster simply tilted its head, twitched its nostrils in disgust at Gwendolen, and spoke to Lucy, saying, *Where is my son?*

"Here," said a voice.

David Rain materialized at Lucy's back.

Gawaine roared and instantly retrieved her tail. With fury bleeding into her eyes, she looked set to chop the intruder in half for a moment. But as Lucy turned around and sank into his arms, the dragon paused and concentrated hard on David. In him she had a new challenge to unravel: how anything in the shape of a human could possess the scalene eyes of a dragon or resonate so strongly with the auma of her dynasty.

"There is no time to explain to you," he said, speaking her dialect, nodding with respect, "but you will know that a mother cannot flame her young. This girl is your kin, through Gawain, your son. His auma is bound to this Earth and we to it. You must leave here, Gawaine. Fly north to the ice lands. The Wearle await you. He awaits you."

"Ohh . . ." Lucy's head suddenly rolled on David's shoulder.

Gawaine's eye ridges shortened at the sound.

"Lucy, what's the matter?" David said. He put her head between his hands and looked into her eyes.

"They're here," she whispered.

And Gawaine knew it, too. Rising up to her full height, she turned and looked back toward Glissington Tor.

Hrrrrr, she said.

A long, low snarl, and yet the translation was very short.

Ix.

MIRROR, MIRROR

A second adversary. A female. A savage. Radiating hatred. Seeking revenge. How terrifying must it have seemed to a solitary raven, with a solitary hostage, to witness the release of a foe more threatening than the hunter that had slain the rest of its flock? It must have been counting its remaining wingbeats no greater than the number of claws on its feet. How could it escape or expect to cheat death? Its chances were nil. Hopes of mercy, none. Expectations of surrender, zero. For driven as it was by an irreversible mania to morph into a darkling and possess dark fire, there would have come a moment of reckless exposure when it would have put its evil life in peril. And that life would have been rubbed out in a snip. For vicious as it was, evolving in strength and cunning as it was, it was still no match for a champion like Grockle, and compared to Gawaine it was nothing but a gnat.

But it was due for a change of luck. Fortune was about to glint in its eye.

When Grockle had arrived in the garden of the guesthouse, the raven had escaped, still holding Glade, and flown to the far side of Glissington Tor. It had witnessed the hunter come down near the cairn and all the events that had followed, culminating in the release of the queen.

The one thing it had not seen was Gawaine's attack on Lucy. The reason for this was simple: When the Tor had erupted, the bird had experienced an urgent need to flutter out of hiding (from underneath a row of hedges, of all things). The displacement of earth was no threat to it, but a hundred pounds of broken cairn flying through the air and landing with a twig-shattering thump certainly was. The bird had given a malicious squawk and turned to spit venom at the fallen stones. That was when it saw the eye of the cairn, and Lucy's tear still glistening across it.

Hopping onto the ledge of the eye, it tilted its head and studied its reflection. What it saw was the profile of a raven. Blueberry-eyed. Severe. Feathers lacking gloss. Harsh, but not frightening. Mean, but not cruel. Large, but not brutal. Basically, a gnat. It hissed in disappointment. Something was wrong. It was losing strength. Reverting to its dismal genetic origin. It shuffled its feet and felt Glade drag against the rough gray stones. Angered by her presence, it hauled her up, almost throttling her for fun as it held her over the shimmering tear. Not for the first time, it pecked at her ivy. Why was it black when the rest of the pathetic little object was green? It spat into her eye. *Cry,* it carked. But Glade turned her head and merely let the bird's saliva run off her snout. It dripped onto the tear below. And that was when everything changed.

There was a fizz as the fluids met. The raven switched its gaze in a flash and saw what appeared to be a battle for supremacy between the glob of spittle and the surface of the water. The water was victorious. It rapidly assimilated the spit, burning the impurities out of it before the surface calmed again.

The raven waggled its tongue. Though its experience of dragons and their auma was minimal, it sensed power in the water and took a step nearer. It remembered how this mirror had been touched by the moon, energized by its feeble light. Could it be a weapon to be used against the dragons?

Those hopes were reinforced when it noticed that Glade was extending her tail and trying to dip her isoscele into the water. It immediately lifted her and squeezed her throat again, this time until her head had lolled and her breathing had stopped. It tossed her into the grass.

Strangely, the moment the bird let her go it felt a surge of energy, a new rush of growth. Checking its dark reflection again it saw that its ears were already swelling, back toward the bunched-up size they'd been when it had captured Glade from the car. Had the miniature dragon been drawing its strength? It snarled and would have stepped across the grass and slit her throat, had it not believed she was already dead. It stared once more at the glistening film, and this time dipped its toe.

Once again there was a minor conflagration. But on this occasion the raven sensed that the tear was trying to resist invasion and did not have the means to overpower it. A strange, primeval lust for power began to juggle with the bird's senses. What would happen if it *drank* the water?

A roar came down from Scuffenbury Hill. With it came the scent of a gallon of fire. The bird grizzled. What did it have to lose? It plunged its beak into the tear — and sucked.

Right away, the water came together in a droplet, as if it was nothing but a silken handkerchief being delicately plucked off a tabletop. Down the raven's throat it went. And there, in the stomach of one bird's small alimentary system, the birth of a darkling began.

What happened next came about largely by association. The evil that had stained the bird on Farlowe Island instantly connected to the auma trails defining Lucy's heritage. It recognized Gawain. It recognized Guinevere. It found memories of a cold obsidian knife and the flame inside, which it coveted so much. Above all, it homed in on a part of Lucy's auma she had never been able to remove or cleanse: her encounter with the agents of darkness, the Ix. As fast, ironically, as the speed of light, the raven formed a conduit to them.

The transformation was swift. The bird gave a *caark* of triumph, but that was the last it would ever utter. As the Ix streamed in and formed a Cluster within it, the raven died in an instant. For a moment it simply stood transfixed, as if it had been dipped into a subzero liquid, its feathers iced, its eyes locked into a bewildered stare. Then one clenched foot rose vertically upward, shuddering as it tucked itself against the body. For several seconds the bird remained balanced on one leg. Then the body toppled forward and struck the ground. From beak to tail, it divided into two clean husks.

In the remains was a hunched-up gargoyle, covered in mucus and slithering innards. It, too, remained balanced for several seconds. Then its wings went out with a click, like blades, and it quickly tripled in size. Rocking forward, it let itself stand on bowed but deceptively brawny legs, unwrapping with them a sinuous body that was somewhat apelike in its suppleness. It jolted any stiffness out of its shoulders, setting off a ripple that vivified most of its crosshatched scales. Unlike a dragon's they did not change color, but their semifoiled blackness glinted at the moon, as if they were somehow taunting its light. With a slapping noise the monster turned its head. Its hideous face, thickened by stubs at the frontal lobes, looked with disdain at the mess it had grown from. And then it *ate* the mess it had grown from, sucking the corpse into an *o*-shaped mouth haunted by a filter of needle-shaped teeth.

The last thing it did before it took to the air was to swing across to Glade, who was nestling, barely alive, in the grass. With one dreadful swipe of malice, it stripped the ivy from around her neck. But this was more than a deed of senseless cruelty; it was an act of war. Kicking poor Glade right into the hedges, the darkling tied the ivy around its wrist. Then, like the raven had done before it, it tapped into Lucy's family history, via the auma of a Pennykettle dragon. With consummate greed, it gathered in their means of parthenogenesis and absorbed their capability for self-replication.

Thus were the Ix made manifest upon the Earth.

First, there was one.

And then there were two.

THE BATTLE OF
SCUFFENBURY HILL

There were four by the time they chose to show themselves. By then, Lucy had reported her sensations to David, and Gawaine was turning back toward the Tor. The darklings, already highly attuned to the auma trails pouring off Scuffenbury Hill, were soon aware that their presence was known. Between them they swiftly assessed their enemy, dismissing any threat from the unicorn. It intrigued them, yes, but its pacifistic tendencies were highly transparent. Likewise, their respect for the matriarch was minimal. She was old, poorly sighted, and had surrendered her wits to her wild fury. Her judgments, as a result, would be rash. They were confident of killing her first. Then there was the agent of the Fain and his dragon. Him they feared, for his mind was trained. They suspected he might be newly illumined to the younger dragon at present making its obeisance to the queen. He would be hard to infect with the darkness, though his weakness might be found in the dragon-human hybrid he was so clearly keen to protect. All this they picked up at the speed of thought. Yet, as the moment arrived when they were forced to cease their replication and engage in battle, there was one auma source they had failed to measure or readily identify. It was unlike anything the Ix had ever encountered. A tiny nucleus of dark energy, wrapped inside a skin of malleable . . . clay? Intrigued, greedy, and a little frustrated, the alpha darkling sent out an impulse to the others: Find that energy, scan it — and absorb it.

Then they rose.

The moment David saw them coming he called to Gawaine not to battle them without him. But the Ix had read the matriarch correctly and she lifted off the hill without paying heed. David gripped Lucy by the shoulders, shook her, and told her what was going to happen.

"Take the tusk," he said, pressing the narwhal bone into her hand. "Think of home and shake it three times. Tell Zanna there are darklings here and I'm sending a message to the dragons in the North. They'll come for Alexa. Zanna must obey their will." He pulled her forward and kissed her head. "Your work is done, Lucy. Now go home — to your mom."

In the vale, Gawaine's fearsome roars cracked the air. The darklings had surrounded her like a flock of bats.

"What about Tam?" Lucy said, her eyes full of pain. In her pocket she could feel Gwendolen quaking.

"No time," David said, as Grockle whooshed in and posed, wings spread, at David's back.

Lucy shook her head in fear. "Wh-what's happening?"

Go, David mouthed, stepping backward and raising his arms high and wide. His eyes had turned scalene; their irises, violet. He retreated for two more steps, until Grockle's wings looked like a huge vampiric cape. And then, right before Lucy's eyes, he merged into Grockle's body.

They were in the air before Lucy could gasp, moving so fast that she'd lost them before she could complete a half turn. A mile away, a belt of flame ripped across the vale. One part of it flared up and blew into a fireball. That was one darkling fewer, she guessed. Despite her loathing of all things gruesome, she found her spirits cheered by its death.

But then the contest switched the other way. Gawaine let out a piercing scream and began to lash her head back and forth with great force, as if some demon had squirmed into her brain. She rolled into a dangerous spin, with one wing locked and her tail in spasm, her volatile claws turned firmly in. Lucy saw the queen drop a good thirty yards and feared she would break her twisting neck on the hard, unforgiving fields below. But just when the matriarch's life seemed doomed, from nowhere Grockle swept under her body and joined the descent, fixing himself to Gawaine's undersides as if he intended to cushion her fall or maybe even drag her down faster. Seconds from the ground they broke apart, and though Lucy had no idea what had passed between them, both dragons miraculously pulled out of the spin. One banked east, the other west, before both turned in to face the darklings again.

At the same time Lucy glanced to her left and saw the fretful unicorn bleating out a warning. It was gone like a glint of sunlight, but the object of its caution was not. Lucy looked up and saw one of the darklings flying toward her. When it was less than fifty yards away, its nauseating o-shaped mouth somehow defied the laws of physics and widened to the size of her head. The needle teeth retracted into their sockets, ready to spring out and pierce her from every angle. Meanwhile, in her hand, the narwhal tusk was buzzing as if it was eager to get into the fray. But Lucy was taking no chances. She shook it three times as David had said and, with one massive burst of concentration, pictured the house at Wayward Crescent.

The fabric of the universe ripped and she was gone. She felt the sickening tug of interspace travel and opened her eyes, confident of seeing her bedroom again.

To her horror, she was still at Scuffenbury. All that

had changed was her perspective on it. Somehow, she had jumped across the valley and landed, not in Scrubbley, but on the turmoil that used to be Glissington Tor. High above her, darklings and dragons fought. To her right lay the rubble of the Gray Dragon guesthouse.

"No," she protested and shook the tusk again.

This time, there was no sense of travel, but something did free itself from her hand.

"Groyne?" said Lucy, opening her eyes. A Pennykettle dragon was hovering in front of her.

It turned and blew a confident smoke ring.

Not Groyne.

Gwillan.

AN UNWELCOME RETURN

I love you.

The words pricked at Zanna's heart. There was no passion in the way he'd said it. No lasting promise in his dark blue eyes. What he'd left her with were memories of that day in the Arctic.

I love you.

Like a soldier, going to war.

She sat in the kitchen making origami roses from a white paper tissue. In the front room, the news reports kept on coming. Verifiable footage of "Steiner" dragons was now being beamed across every continent, backed by endless eyewitness accounts of dragons emerging from "spiritual" sites all over the Earth. Colonization. A true "New Age." A revolution in consciousness. Was this it? Was this what her life had amounted to? To see the world reinvented from a lonely kitchen and humankind divided into wonder or madness? What did all this mean for her, when everything she cared for was under threat and might, at any moment, be taken away?

On that thought, Alexa walked into the kitchen and spontaneously gave her mother a hug.

"Talk to me," Zanna said. "Tell me what you are."

"I'm your little angel," Alexa said.

Zanna bent forward and quietly cried.

"I want to go into the garden," said the girl.

Zanna folded her tissue away. "No. Stay inside today."

"But there's a squirrel. I want to talk to it."

"Squirrel?" said her mother. She couldn't see one — but she didn't look hard.

"It came yesterday," Alexa said. "It's very smart."

"I'm sure it is," said Zanna, standing up. "But you're not to go into the garden, is that clear?"

Alexa sighed and plonked her white horse on the table. Zanna glanced at it and did a double take. A horn had emerged on the sculpture's forehead. She pointed to it. "Did you do this?"

"It just came," said the girl. "Please can I go out and see the squirrel? It does tricks, Mommy."

Zanna shook her head. How could a horn just happen like that? "No ... run upstairs and talk to Gwillan."

"I can't." This time, the little girl stamped her foot.

Zanna stared down at her. Bad temper in Alexa was extremely uncommon. "Why not?"

"He's gone away, with Daddy."

"Don't be silly, Alexa. Gwillan's in the den."

"No, he isn't," she insisted, letting her black curls sweep across her back.

"Zanna!" Arthur's voice called down from the bedroom. Strident. Urgent. Needy.

Alexa said, "Can I go and play with Bonnington, then?"

"What? Oh ... yes, if you want to," Zanna said. She got up and strode into the hall, stopping just once to look back into the kitchen. Alexa was juggling

Bonnington's favorite toy: a plastic ball he liked to chase around.

"Mommy?"

"Yes?"

"You've got to do something for me."

"I'm in a hurry, darling. What is it?"

"My horsey wants to sit with Gawain and Guinevere."

The unicorn. Zanna came back and picked it up. "Tell me again how this happened, this horn?"

"It doesn't matter," said Alexa.

No, thought Zanna. *It never does.* "Be good," she said and rushed upstairs.

Alexa smiled and gave a little girl wave. Then she dropped the ball into Bonnington's bed and quietly opened the kitchen door.

At the top of the stairs Zanna shouted to Arthur, "I'm on my way! Need to check something first!" She burst into the den and went straight to the bench. No Gwillan. No guard. Groyne fast asleep. A hint of panic rippled through her chest. Her hand shot straight to her phone.

The line to David was dead. But by then he and Grockle were in the air above Scuffenbury, fighting under the name of their i:lluminus, G'lant. There was no connection to Lucy's number either by the time Zanna had swept into the bedroom. "Take my phone," she said to Arthur, thrusting it at him. "If Lucy answers, give it back to me."

Alexa, for reasons known only to herself, had put Liz's dragons on the dressing table, spookily facing the mirror. Zanna put the unicorn down between them and sank onto the bed. Liz was drenched in sweat and had thrown aside the bedspread, spilling most of Gretel's potions to the floor in the process. From her shaking mouth was coming one word, "No."

"Nothing," said Arthur, offering the phone back.

"Keep trying," Zanna said, damping Liz's forehead. "Gwillan's gone. He's tricked us. I think he's stolen Groyne's powers, maybe some of the others."

"Gone? Gone where?"

"To Scuffenbury — I don't know!" Her temples reddened under pressure from her fingers. "We've got to warn them. If the dark fire —"

Arthur held up the phone. "The line is dead."

Zanna groaned and hammered her thigh in frustration.

"You must go," he said. "Use your power, like before."

"I can't. I can't leave Liz like this."

Arthur leaned over and gripped her arm. "If you don't warn David, it may not be just Liz who's in trouble."

"But I can't leave her."

"You can," he said. "You told me Agatha Bacon gave you a card — so that you could contact her."

Agatha. Of course. Zanna foraged in her pocket. She pulled out the card and ran her thumb across it. Agatha's picture came up right away. "I don't know how to use it."

"The image may be all that's required," said Arthur.

And it was. Right at that moment, the door-bell rang.

Zanna pounded downstairs, already pushing back her sleeve to expose the mark of Oomara on her arm. She yanked the door open.

"You called?"

On the step was the figure of Agatha Bacon.

Zanna threw her arms around her. "Oh, you don't know how pleased I am to see you!"

Agatha pushed her gently back. "Invite me in, girl. The magicks can't work without your wish."

"I wish," said Zanna.

A smile of satisfaction spread across Agatha Bacon's face. She stepped over the threshold into the hall. The two sibyls exchanged places.

"Can't explain now," Zanna continued. "In a kind of rush. Liz needs your help. She's in the bedroom. Arthur's with her." She fed her fingers into the scars.

Agatha nodded. "Where is your daughter?"

"I'm not sure. Playing with the cat, I think."

"Then waste no more time here. Be gone, girl, be gone." The old woman waved good-bye and the door closed quickly in Zanna's face.

For a moment, Agatha stared at her surroundings. Then, with a smile, she raised her chin and set off briskly toward the kitchen. She stood by the window, looking out.

"How delightful," she said to herself. The cat and the girl were both distracted by the squirrel she'd magicked. The only opposition would be the blind fool upstairs.

She locked the kitchen door and took her time going up, wondering briefly why the idiot dragons were all engaged in domestic cleaning duties. At the bottom of the stairs, she stopped to break apart a missed cobweb, putting its tiny creator out of its misery by scooping it onto her snaking tongue.

As she entered the bedroom and looked down at Elizabeth, she saw no reason to maintain her disguise. It had been a simple matter to intercept messages to Agatha Bacon and appear in another sibyl's image: a modest deception to guarantee unchallenged entry to the house. But now she yearned for her "natural" look. Arthur Merriman was aware of the deception anyway, tipped off by a cry from her old familiar, Gretel.

"You," he said, fumbling for any kind of weapon. He tried for the bedside lamp but in his panic only knocked it onto the floor. One click from the sibyl's fingers threw him backward into his chair.

"Sit there, don't move, and I will let you comfort her when I'm done."

"What do you want?" raged Arthur, gripping the chair until his knuckles drained of color.

From a pouch at her waist, Gwilanna drew out her most treasured possession, the isoscele of the dragon, Gawain. "What do I want?" she sneered, testing its point, noting its sharpness, reveling in its ancient power. She cast her eyes down again and smiled. "What I always want, Arthur. I've come to attend to Elizabeth. . . ."

ON HEROISM AND DEATH

D A-VIDDDD!"

Lucy's call thinned out across the valley, far too weak to attract his attention. In the sky he was twisting, shadowing Gawaine, while the darklings continued to strafe the queen. Meanwhile, Gwillan, having flown from Lucy's hand, was hovering a short distance away. The movements of his head suggested he was following the fight with keen interest, as if he were assessing the strength of both sides before committing himself to the skirmish.

Lucy plunged a hand into her pocket. Her phone was there — but the signal wasn't. She threw it down in dismay. Her other pocket was suddenly a bundle of movement as Gwendolen fought to be released and get a look at what was going on.

Gwendolen!

Lucy yanked her out. "I need you to be brave," she whispered to the dragon, anxious that Gwillan should not hear.

Gwendolen's gaze swept warily upward. A roaring burst of flame sucked the cold out of the air.

"I know it's dangerous," Lucy went on, "but I need to tell David that Gwillan's here."

Gwendolen's eye ridges came together.

"Please," said Lucy, her voice cracking.

There was a squeal in the distance. Gawaine again. Hurt.

Gwendolen turned a circle or two (her favorite activity when she was thinking). She came back with a long, slightly gabbled hurr. *David is fighting. Distracting him might be fatal. There might be a better way to warn him.*

"What? Tell me."

Gwendolen fluttered down to the phone. She hurred at length again. *The Pennykettle dragons can communicate over distance through a listener,* she said.

"Yes, yes," said Lucy, urging her to hurry.

Gwendolen pointed at the discarded phone. If she used it to boost her auma, she said, she could bypass the listener and send a message directly to . . .

". . . Gadzooks," gasped Lucy, catching on. "And he'd know how to reach David." She looked up. Gwillan had disappeared. "Do it," she said. "Do it. Now."

If the conflict over Scuffenbury Hill had been waged on strength and size alone, the darklings would have been mapped and destroyed long before Gwendolen began to transmit her SOS. But the tactics of the Ix did not rely solely on the venom and wounding power of their creatures. Their modes of attack were far more devious. They knew, for instance, that the unicorn, Teramelle, would not attempt to come to the rescue of the dragons and would only defend itself if attacked.

Therefore they simply left it aside — a bonus, a treat, once the dragons were eliminated. They were also aware that Gawaine (and possibly the Fain i:lluminus) could be weakened if they could reach inside her mind. So the matriarch became their first target. One darkling, the first of the replicates, was given the privilege of destroying her.

There were two ways the Ix could disrupt the dragon's wits. First (and most commonly) a breakaway Cluster could invade through her sensitive pineal gland. This would provide a neural highway into the spongy cells of her brain. Once inside, they could rip her consciousness apart until her motor functions were lost or frozen. They could then torment her or simply bring her down. The union of gravity and ground would do the rest.

In order for the leap to be effective, however, the darkling had to be in the dragon's eyesight. At the optimum point of transfer (usually when the dragon was confident of a kill) the Ix Cluster would rapidly detach from its host, leaving the darkling temporarily unruddered and as vulnerable as paper to the chemistry of fire. In short, it was a suicidal lunge. Annihilation was a likely and acceptable forfeit, but a minor sacrifice if it left the quarry addled. Such a transference called for skill and precision, but it had been achieved by the replicate darkling — just before Gawaine had turned it to ash.

At that triumphant juncture, with the queen in a spin, the three remaining darklings were preparing to focus their attention on the juvenile, only to see him fly to the queen's aid. They watched him commingle with the failing matriarch and must have been alarmed to see her recover. He had cleansed her mind and restored her sanity. She would be stronger for it and learn from the experience. To terminate her now would require real cunning.

The squeal that Lucy had heard while she was talking to Gwendolen was partly a result of their renewed assault. For the second, more dangerous, means of transference required a darkling to attach itself to its prey so it might poison the blood as well as the mind.

To maximize their chances, the darklings separated. The alpha (that born from the gut of the raven) sped toward G'lant, hoping to draw him away from the queen. The Ix Cluster controlling the creature was in no hurry to engage the Fain i:lluminus, certainly not on the battleplanes of thought, even though he was probing, willing them to try. Instead, the beast rolled under him, crying out as a length of its stringy tail was half consumed by G'lant's well-aimed arc of fire. It retaliated swiftly by spitting a cloud of venom at his feet. The object: to get inside the pouches of his claws where the muscles were unprotected by scales. G'lant hissed in pain as the venom struck home, but still managed to coil his tail and tangle the darkling within its loops. Using a violent whipping motion, he attempted to shake the creature giddy. But the Ix were reinventing their host creature with each new act of aggression they faced. On the second beat of G'lant's tail, the darkling dissociated its atomic structure and slipped through the prickly coils like water. By the time G'lant was aware of the escape, the darkling had reconfigured its shape and was back alongside him, pouring its toxic breath into the run of spiracles by his jaw, hoping to infect his secondary airways. Choking, and almost driven wild by the irritation in his claws, G'lant swerved away from Gawaine. Mission accomplished. The other two darklings moved in on the queen.

While one of them led her in a zigzagging chase (back toward Lucy, still watching from the Tor) the other creature came in silently above her, dropped swiftly, and clamped itself to her left shoulder. She saw it as she fully unveiled her eye, but could do little to shake it off. She could reach it with her tail, she was certain of that, but to attempt that maneuver during flight would destabilize her balance and send her tumbling earthward again. Her only hope was that G'lant would come to her aid again. But for the moment she could not see him. And the darkling was wasting no time.

Its objective had been to puncture her spine or dislocate the bones of her ear canal. But as the steady reinvention of its wickedness continued, it considered a far more hateful attack. Bringing its two front feet together, it found it was able to merge its claws and make a jagged cutting tool, not strong enough to carve up a dragon's scales, but easily able to tear through a wing. . . .

Gawaine squealed in agony as the claws went in. Realizing what was happening, she found a supportive thermal and glided into it, knowing that to beat her wings with any thrust might result in a rip that would not only leave her helpless in the air but negate any chance of a safe landing. The creature dug again and she heard the awful high-pitched whistle that was air rushing through her punctured sails. In desperation she flipped upside down, not a position she could hold for very long, but long enough, perhaps, to throw the creature off. The darkling wobbled but did not fall. It snarled in annoyance and clamped its teeth into the kitelike bones that framed her wing, gnashing back and forth until one of them cracked. Sickened and dizzy, Gawaine was forced to right herself. Even then the beating did not stop. The darkling stamped on the bone repeatedly, gargling with pleasure as it snapped clean through. The pain was almost unbearable, but by now the queen was forming an idea. One slim chance of escape. She turned again and dipped the injured wing, knowing that the sharper angle of roll would throw the darkling toward the front boom. She felt the creature stumble and she instantly struck, throwing out one of her retractable stigs (the thorns that decorate an adult dragon's skeleton, particularly along the wings). The stig itself had no physical receptor, but the mulching sound of perforated flesh and the lurch of weight to the front of her wing told Gawaine her aim had been true. With a roar of pain she shed the stig and watched it sink to the green fields below. Every instinct encouraged her to chase down and burn it, and not stop until a well of fire raged in the Earth. But her wounds were severe and there was poison in her blood. She had no option but to land.

As horrific sights went, the sight of a darkling impaled on the curving stig of a dragon wouldn't have been far out of Lucy's top ten. She shrieked and jumped back in terror, even though the stig had landed yards away, point-first into a chunk of the Tor. She saw the darkling's body convulse. Black fluid oozed like oil from its mouth. Its legs and tail hung as limp as a willow. Its staring eye still shone as brightly as a doorknob.

She yelped again as its death tremors slid it down the stig. It came to rest in a pool of vital fluids, stopped by and draped across the broken earth, its repulsive head thankfully turned away from her.

Picking up a rock, she stumbled toward it. Why she chose to, only she knew. Maybe a desire to kill beyond doubt.

Gwendolen was stupefied beyond comprehension. *Hrrr?* she cried. What was Lucy doing? The message to Gadzooks was sent. They should just wait now. Wait — and hide!

But Lucy pushed on, her feet slipping sideways as she climbed the mound of soil. She stopped a few paces from the twitching beast. The rock felt cold and heavy in her hand. The creature's head looked easy to crush.

She lifted the rock. As she did so, she spotted a movement to her right. Uttering a gasp of fear, she turned and almost brained Bella instead.

"You!"

Meow, yowled Bella, limping forward, coming to stand between the darkling and Lucy. The cat was filthy, covered in dirt. A thick yellow discharge was weeping from a half-closed, bloodshot eye. Her tail hung low between her legs. One of her paws had been dislocated or broken.

She's frightened, hurred Gwendolen, flying forward. What the catgirl had actually said was, *Help me.*

Lucy let the rock fall out of her hands. She looked at the open scratches on her wrist, but realized now that Bella had only been trying to warn her about Gawaine's fury. She sank to her knees and opened her arms.

The cat hobbled forward. In that moment the darkling gave a vitriolic snort and rolled its head toward them, neck bones cracking, eyes on fire, teeth primed. One of its snapped arms flapped toward Bella.

"No!" Lucy screamed.

Bella jumped around, her hackles raised. But for all her hissing bravery she would have been dead — if the soil had not erupted and thrown her aside. Lucy screamed again and tumbled backward. She got up and scrambled back to Bella, but Gwendolen stopped her with a single hurr: *Look.*

To Lucy's astonishment, a human hand had emerged from the ground and taken the darkling by the throat. The creature, still impaled, was turning white and shuddering as if it were coming to the boil. With a pop it imploded and turned to water, soaking the hand and the earth around it. The soil broke again and a head and a pair of shoulders came through.

Lucy dived forward to get her arms around him. "Tam!" she gasped, clearing his face of dirt, as if she couldn't believe that it was him.

He coughed and spat a small stone onto the ground. "I'll say one thing for David: He knew what he was doing when he fixed me up with bears — they're good at surviving in dens. And this one" — he raised his right hand and turned it, showing once again the image of Kailar — "really does not like ravens. . . ."

The Healing Touch

If Professor Rupert Steiner had ever found the means to investigate the "ice lands" of the North, he would have made some astounding discoveries, including several faded cinder glyphs describing the last great encounter on Earth between dragons, men, and the strange life form known as the Ix (shown as a swarm of dots). Among the pictures he would have found at least one record, maybe more, of dragons suffering. And being a man of sensitive disposition, he would have concluded there was nothing more pitiful than the sight of such a magnificent creature mortally wounded and ready to cry its water of life. This is how it was with Gawaine just then, on the opposite side of the valley from Lucy.

The queen, when she landed, could not even kneel. The pressure on her lungs was far too great. The darkling's poison had spread into her windpipe and all her auxiliary bronchial chambers. She could feel their multi-layered linings peeling. It could only be a matter of time before her veins burst open and the ichor running through them flooded her lungs. She was going to drown in her own blood. She was going to die.

Gawaine, like any dragon, had no fear of death, but what irked her as she lay there gasping for breath was that she did not have the power to make a final, sacrificial impact on the fight. The brave G'lant had swept over her twice. She absorbed his despair as she collapsed onto her side with her maimed wing stretched out, pathetic and useless. It was her flag to him to say that she was done. He must abandon her; let them torture her, even. All that mattered was that he prevailed. She could help no more.

There was an outcome, however, that Gawaine had not considered: that her injuries might be cured. When Teramelle came to look over her its distress was even

greater than G'lant's. It put its head down and repeatedly nudged the queen, as if it hoped she would take
some elixir from it or weave some magicks and save
herself. But the enigma of unicorns was really quite
simple. They were a fertile cornucopia of healing, but
could not wield any curatives themselves. The legends
of red-headed maidens were correct. But it was not a
girl with red hair that came to save Gawaine. It was
a sibyl. And her name was Zanna.

In choosing her destination, Zanna had focused on
the white horse of Scuffenbury, expecting to arrive
inconspicuously in the general locality. The magicks,
however, had interpreted her wish as a need to be close
to the unicorn itself. *Whoosh*. There she was. Right
before them both. Almost dropped into the jaws of a
dragon. The unicorn bolted. Despite the searing pain,
Gawaine raised her head. Justifiably suspicious, she
summoned up what fuel was left in her fire sacs and
drew in the oxygen she needed to light it.

Two things saved Zanna's life. Though her body was
largely paralyzed with awe, her dry mouth managed

to spill a word of dragontongue: *Gawaine?* The pronunciation was poor, but good enough to make Gawaine hold apart the ignition nodules on her tongue which, if ground together, would produce the spark to light the incendiary mixtures in her throat. She was closing them again, prepared to take no chances, when Teramelle whinnied and begged her to stop.

The unicorn, now on the other side of Zanna, tilted its head and looked at the girl. Its violet gaze lighted on the mark on Zanna's arm, literally coloring her skin the same shade. Zanna knew she was being scanned, but still couldn't help but give a gasp of surprise when Teramelle's voice came into her mind. *We are one*, the unicorn said. And it sounded, for all the world, like Alexa.

Slowly, careful not to panic the creature again, Zanna reached out and stroked its neck. Her fingers glided through its silky mane. It responded by leaning its head against her shoulder. It was then she saw something that shocked her deeply and made her understand what its words had meant. Every picture she had ever seen of a unicorn painted its horn as a spiraling cone. But the whipped up, cotton candy image was wrong, probably because very few observers had ever come this close to see or tell the truth. The horn was nothing more than a plain ivory tusk, just like the horn of the seagoing narwhal. (The associations with Groyne did not occur to her right then.) What made the horn seem spiraled was a carving etched repeatedly in it, flowing around and around from base to tip: the three-line shape that the Inuit called the mark of Oomara. The mark that Zanna had been branded with.

A cry from above made her look up suddenly. In the sky she saw Grockle (or so she thought) hovering between two evil-looking gargoyles as if they had him suspended on wires. Turning quickly back to Teramelle she said, "You have to help me. I came to deliver a warning . . ." But maybe it was too late for that? She heard another squawk. The gargoyles were circling, but Grockle hadn't moved. And nowhere was there any sign of Gwillan — or David.

With a wretched groan, Gawaine keeled onto her

side again. Zanna ran to her and knelt by her head. Small wisps of steam were issuing from vents along the dragon's neck. Zanna looked along the body to the shattered wing. "I have healing abilities," she said to Teramelle. "Can we help her? With magicks?" She raised her arm.

The unicorn walked forward and lowered its horn. *You must be swift*, it said. *The great fire is coming.*

"Great fire?" asked Zanna. "What do you mean?"

The unicorn looked toward the peak of the hill. The moon was almost directly above it.

In that instant, Zanna knew the answer to the question that had nagged her several days ago in the kitchen: why a unicorn should choose to roam the Vale of Scuffenbury. The hill was on a vast intersection of ley lines. *X* marked the spot, many, many times over. They were sitting on a gateway to the Fire Eternal. A conduit directly to the center of the Earth . . .

An Unexpected
Outcome

Gwilanna, stop! You mustn't touch her!" Once again Arthur tried to lunge forward, and once again the sibyl's magicks threw him back. This time, for his trouble, she put a constriction spell around his throat, leaving him to choke for several seconds before snapping her fingers and releasing him. He slumped down, gasping for air. Gretel risked the sibyl's wrath and went to his aid.

"Pathetic," Gwilanna sneered. She turned her attention back to Liz.

"Please, you don't understand," Arthur spluttered. "There was an accident. The dark fire was freed from the obsidian. It went into Elizabeth."

That *did* make Gwilanna pause. "Ah, so that's what called me," she muttered. "I sensed a deep change in Elizabeth's condition, that naturally required my presence, of course, but I didn't expect a bonus like this." She turned the isoscele and held it flat, passing it twice over Liz's body. "Yes, it's here," she purred in delight, "but I can detect no trace of it in the child."

"There's more," Arthur panted, regaining his breath. "Something unusual has happened with the boy. He's extended his auma into one of the dragons."

"Preposterous," Gwilanna snorted. "The Fain's experiments with the transference of consciousness always ended in failure. You expect me to believe that an unborn child and a stupid clay dragon could achieve what they couldn't? Show me which one."

"I can't," Arthur said. "He's gone to join David."

"David," the sibyl repeated scornfully. "Why does that name *always* make my fingernails curl? You're lying," she snapped. "Now, be silent. You're wasting my time, *Professor*."

Arthur raised his hands. "Forgive me. I'm pleased

you're here," he said, in a tone designed to appeal to her vanity. "Who better than you to nurse Elizabeth? So . . . you can definitely confirm my son is safe?"

"Yes," she murmured. "Do you really think I'd let a child of *his* potential come to any harm?"

Probably not, Arthur thought. Even so, the avarice embedded in those words was a clear enough warning that Gwilanna had every intention of stealing the child one day. That, if nothing else, strengthened Arthur's resolve to keep her away from him now. Seizing upon the chance to keep the sibyl talking, he leaned forward slightly and said, "But you told us the boy was of no importance. A natural born. Why are you even bothering with him when there's no dragon in his blood?"

Gwilanna laughed. Her feet scuffed the carpet. Arthur guessed she had turned away from the bedside. The arrogant old bird had always liked to stroll through her moments of triumph.

"The descendants of Guinevere, those females born from a quickened egg, have tried many times to have children with humans, but the genetic fusion has always failed. You should applaud yourself, Arthur Merriman. Your child is not only alive and well, but he's also survived the Ix's obsidian and now appears to be shielding himself from the most destructive force in the universe. That makes him of *very* great interest to me."

Downstairs, the back door rattled.

Gwilanna was immediately on her guard. "What was that?"

Arthur's heartbeat quickened. He knew at once what had made the sound, but tried to show no surprise in his face. "The wind . . . it moves the mailbox sometimes."

"At the *back* of the house?" The floorboards creaked. Gwilanna, Arthur realized, had taken steps toward the landing. "It must be the girl," she said, "trying to get in."

"You wouldn't hurt her?" said Arthur, wiggling his fingers to bring Gretel close. The potions dragon fluttered to his shoulder.

"I don't need to," Gwilanna said. "I locked her out." She whipped around. "What are you saying to Gretel?"

"I just asked her to soothe Elizabeth," he said. "I may not be able to see her, Gwilanna, but her distress is plain to hear. May I give her something to drink?" Without waiting for permission, Arthur fumbled beside him for a bottle of water. He picked it up but didn't unscrew the cap.

The bedsprings took the sibyl's weight. "Stay where you are," she said. "It's time."

Arthur ran a hand inside his collar. "Time? Time for what?" he asked, trying to remain as calm as he could. "You might at least explain to me what you're going to do."

Gwilanna sighed with exasperation.

"I'm a scientist. It's my nature to understand procedures."

"It's your nature to interfere," she hissed. "It cost you dearly in the past, as I recall."

For a moment, Arthur was a young man back in Cambridge, remembering how Gwilanna had tricked him into ending his courtship with Liz — something he'd never forgiven the witch for. "At last," he heard her drool. "At last I can claim what's rightfully mine."

"You can't mean the baby?" Arthur said, shocked. He could hear the tinkle of a bell on the stairs. At any moment, Bonnington would be in the room.

Gwilanna, in her irritation, had missed it. "Of course I don't mean the baby!" she snapped. "I'm taking what David stole from me on Farlowe. I'm taking the fire."

"But . . . that's madness," Arthur mumbled. And fearful of what this would mean for Liz, his fingers tightened around the bottle of water.

At that moment, the sibyl exclaimed, "What the —? How did that fur ball get in here?"

"Through the cat flap," said Arthur, pausing as Bonnington jumped onto his knee. He immediately lifted the cat in one arm and turned its eyes toward the bed.

"No matter. Keep it under control."

"Oh, believe me, I will," Arthur said. He stood up silently as Gwilanna bent forward to attend to Liz.

With a heavy *thwack* he brought the water bottle down across the sibyl's shoulders, close to the side of her scrawny neck. Gwilanna groaned and slumped across Liz's body, still clutching the triangular isoscele. Arthur put Bonnington down, grabbed the sibyl's arm, and flipped her over. "Gretel," he panted. "Can you keep her unconscious?"

Gretel flew forward. *My pleasure,* she hurred.

But as she dipped into her quiver for the flowers she needed, the isoscele pulsed in Gwilanna's hand and a shock of energy raced up the sibyl's arm, restarting her brain as if a match had been struck. Her eyes opened like submarine hatches. Her body jackknifed up. Her cold glare fell upon Arthur. Without hesitation, she issued a spell.

Behind him an armoire door flapped open and several shirts flew off the rail. Arthur was catapulted into the space, as if a cannonball had caught him in the gut. He was clutching his heart as he crumpled from the impact. The armoire door slammed shut.

"Go to him and you die," said Gwilanna.

Gretel was hovering, uncertain what to do.

"And stop that stupid animal whining or I'll stuff it with mushrooms and eat it for my lunch."

Gretel cocked her ear toward the den. Bonnington was in there, making a lot of racket.

"Do it!" snapped the sibyl.

Gretel rattled her scales — and flew to the cat.

"Now," said Gwilanna, rubbing her withering hands together, "let me relieve you of your discomfort, my dear." With that, she threw the blankets aside and placed the isoscele of Gawain over Liz's heart. Then she whispered a sinister spell. Immediately, the isoscele began to turn, around and around like a spinning arrow. As it gradually gained momentum, sparks of light began to flash from its points. They landed like the embers of burnt-out fireworks, planting themselves across Liz's nightdress to form a network of crisscrossing light trails, all arcing away from their centrifugal origin. Liz, powerless to prevent what was happening, jerked and tossed her head to one side. She cried out weakly, though it seemed to be more in distress than pain.

"Calm yourself, my dear," Gwilanna said, and with her fingers stretched above the spinning scale she moved it by levitational force into the region of Liz's forehead.

Liz responded with a sudden stiff jolt. Her neck muscles hardened. Her small fists clenched. Half a second later, her eyes flew open. The irises were huge and flooded with color. Green, violet, green, violet, tumbling at the speed of slot machine reels. Gwilanna gave a nervous shudder of excitement and turned her hand once, a few degrees to the right, as if she were opening the lock to a safe. The left eye calmed down, then the right. Until they were a uniform color: black.

Instantly, the isoscele came to a halt. Its point tipped forward, divining the power. For a second or two it quivered and rocked as some grand magnetic struggle was fought. Then with a flash that sucked heat and moisture out of the air, the darkness freed itself from Liz and was absorbed into the isoscele, turning it black.

With a squeak of triumph, Gwilanna snatched at it — only to find that her ancient fingers had closed around nothing: The isoscele had moved. When she looked for it, it was hovering menacingly at her eye level. The sibyl gulped and stumbled back in dread. It crossed her mind, bizarrely, to hide in the armoire. But that was full of Arthur Merriman's body. Instead, she issued a restraining spell, still hopeful she might contain the fire. A force field shimmered around the scale — and quickly popped like a weak soap bubble.

Then, right before the sibyl's eyes, the most terrifying apparition appeared. It grew so swiftly, raising itself from the tailpiece of the dragon, that Gwilanna probably had time to feel her heart stop and might have been quietly grateful that it had. A vaporous creature had filled the room, appearing from the neck up only. It was a starkly hideous inversion of Gawain. A shadow beast with all the power of a dragon and many times the evil of a darkling.

Gwilanna's eyes glazed. She sank to her knees. Her body twisted sideways and crashed to the floor. Her head struck a carpet littered with Gretel's crucibles and flowers. One tiny droplet of sweat dripped from the end of her crooked old nose. Her work as a dragon midwife was done. And no one, neither human nor dragon, would mourn her.

As quickly as the shadow beast had formed, it now collapsed inward to a concentrated spark of dark fire. The ancient, magical scale of Gawain shriveled to a crisp and fell apart in ash. The fire drifted over Liz's heart and noted that its host of several days was beginning to regain her independence and consciousness. It considered terminating her, but spared her and moved to the dressing table mirror, letting its dark reflection play across the glass. Gawain and Guinevere were solid, in prayer. The fire could read great power in their aumas, but it sensed far more in the elegant creature standing between them. Something had created a portal there. It hovered by the tip of the unicorn's horn and went through the portal at the speed of its own dark light, off to find its purpose in a battle taking place above a faraway hill.

When it was done, the two clay dragons came out of stasis. They stared into the mirror, as if they were looking at a different world. In fact, they were looking no farther than the garden, through the telepathic mind of Alexa's unicorn. They saw three dragons as tall as trees land on the lawn in front of Alexa. Two of them were dark red. Guardians. Dangerous. The third was a pure white ice dragon. It bowed toward the girl and she to it. Then she turned and raised her arms in the very same manner her father had. But rather than commingle with the ice dragon's body, Alexa's top ripped open at the back and two small wings emerged through the fabric. Within seconds, she and the dragons had gone. The garden was still, save for a few green leaves dancing energetically on the grass.

Gawain and Guinevere bowed their heads.

They reached behind the unicorn, and quietly joined hands.

THE RETURN
OF GADZOOKS

With the queen dragon grounded and seemingly no threat, the two remaining darklings concentrated their attack on the Fain i:lluminus, G'lant. This time their Ix masters, confident of victory, chose to accept the dragon's enticement to engage in battle on the high-vibrational dark energy thought planes. It must have seemed a strange encounter indeed to anyone, like Lucy, watching from the ground.

"What are they doing?" she said to Tam. Several times now, G'lant and the darklings had come to a kind of midair standoff. On each occasion they would hover in close proximity for a while, before the challenge broke down and each reappeared again in a new and more aggressive spatial formation.

"I don't know," Tam said, still brushing soil from his clothes and hair. "But if that really is David fighting up there, believe me, it's no ordinary contest. How's Gwendolen doing?"

Lucy knelt down. The IT dragon was deep in concentration and had plugged her tail into Lucy's phone again. Suddenly, her eyes popped open and she gave a little snort.

"What is it?" said Lucy.

Gwendolen gulped and peered across the vale.

"Did you get a reply from Gadzooks?"

Gwendolen nodded. *Hrrr,* she said.

"What's the message? I missed it," said Tam.

Lucy stood up, cradling Bella. "Gadzooks is coming. And he won't be alone. . . ."

In the sky, G'lant was finally aware of Gwillan's escape. The little dragon suddenly appeared in the sensory matrix between G'lant and the third cloned darkling. The matrix instantly dissolved and the darkling pressed forward with a physical assault. Teeth bared, front legs stretched, it clicked out its claws, ready to make short work of the intruder. G'lant, still in balance with the alpha darkling, could do little to intervene. But he had no need to. With a flash of blue sparks, Gwillan and the darkling came together. When they were seen again, Gwillan had somehow increased his mass and was holding the darkling in two slightly oversized paws . . . just like the paws of a wishing dragon. The energy matrix reformed around them, and something odd began to happen to the darkling. It didn't lose its color as the others had done, but it did change shape, until it was a mirror of Gwillan himself. He had created a small black dragon.

Gwillan, look to the light, said a voice. David's voice, inside Gwillan's head.

The young dragon cast its gaze down. At the place called Scuffenbury, a column of pearlescent light had formed between the moon and the peak of the hill. All around it the ground was beginning to move as flame-filled cracks sawed through the green fields. Gwillan — Joseph Henry — turned his head and saw a host of dragons descending from the clouds. One of them was not a dragon at all, but the child, Alexa, who had played with him. He watched her open her arms and saw the effect this had upon the Earth. The center of the hill simply crumpled inward creating a large, saucer-shaped caldera. In its midst was a well to the Fire Eternal, the greatest creative force in the universe. The boy inside Gwillan filled up with joy. He looked at the black dragon he'd created and embraced it. And what had been evil was now made pure.

But as this remarkable transcendence was happening, the alpha darkling was also going through changes. In response to the sudden appearance of Gwillan, yet more of the Ix had poured into their creature, committing themselves in vast numbers. With an impulse that stunned G'lant's neural core, leaving him overwhelmed and momentarily helpless, they broke the matrix and gave their darkling physical expression again. It reared back ready to rip G'lant's throat — but it dwelled half a second too long.

It felt a rush of air and turned just in time to see a perfect view of Gawaine's yellowing, broken *moyles* — the final rows of teeth at the back of her jaws. Even as she clamped down and swallowed the beast whole she was banking back toward Scuffenbury Hill. She closed her wings and put herself into a spin. The Ix worked through her, terminating muscles, freezing synapses, unhinging her mind. She was probably dead and certainly insane by the time she plunged into the Fire Eternal, but the disorientation created by her dive had prevented the Ix from escaping her body. What was left of the evil in the skies above the vale she took with her to the center of the Earth. The will of her Wearle was finally done. And she had claimed revenge for the loss of her sons.

But there was still one dark twist to come. For as Gawaine's body was accepted by the Fire, witnessed by a ring of praying dragons — including Alexa, holding

Gadzooks — Teramelle, who had done so much to restore the queen, was overcome by a series of extraordinary fits. Zanna, temporarily overwhelmed by the sight of her daughter hovering like an angel, came to her senses and ran to it. She cried out as it tossed her brutally aside. David, now parted again from Grockle, rushed to her and gathered her into his arms. Gwillan was at his shoulder.

"What happened?"

"Its eyes," she panted, "look at its eyes."

But the unicorn had gone, leaving fiery black prints anywhere its nimble hooves touched the ground. It crested what remained of Scuffenbury Hill and it, too, plunged into the Fire Eternal.

The white light reaching the moon went out. Those dragons on the ground, including Grockle, spread their wings, anticipating conflict. But the darkness that emerged from Scuffenbury Hill could not have been fought by a thousand dragons. It was a shadow, an inversion of the Fire Eternal, a force that could fold both space and time. It appeared to them as a darkling with a unicorn's horn, but only inasmuch as it needed a shape through which it might be duly recognized and feared. The two dragons that went to engage it were obliterated before their fire sacs had opened, their atomic structure crushed into a single point of matter — dark matter, quickly absorbed into the shadow.

From the ground, Gwillan let out a brave *hrrr!*

"Gwillan, no!" David shouted. But the shadow had heard him and turned.

A twisting bolt of dark fire burst through the air. But at the moment when it should have hit the little dragon's snout and turned him into particles of dark matter, too, it crackled to a halt and was suddenly snapped sideways.

"What's happening?" said Zanna, still trying to recover. A great wind blew, making trails of her hair. "Where's Alexa? I want to be with Alexa."

"Close your eyes," David said, covering her head, pressing it firmly into his chest.

"Alexa?" she cried out. "Where's my little girl?"

"She's here with us," said David, almost having to

shout. The ground was tearing up in strips around them. "You'll see her again, but things might be different. Trust me, Zanna. Just hold on tight."

"No! What's happening?" Zanna demanded. She kicked out and finally struggled free.

Alexa was now kneeling beside her parents, with Gadzooks sitting on her outstretched palm. Her wings were folded, her blue eyes closed in deep meditation. Her delicate fingers were resting on the ridges of the dragon's spine, keeping Gadzooks both focused and calm. The dark fire flowing out of the shadow had been directed to the end of his pencil. Despite the turbulence the shadow was creating, he was keeping it there as he wrote on his pad. Alexa was mouthing every letter he wrote. Zanna saw the *s* and the *o* and the *m* before she shut her eyes and clung against David.

"Will I still know you?" She gripped his shirt.

"Yes," he whispered, and kissed her head.

And then they were gone, all of them. David. Lucy. Tam Farrell. Zanna. The catgirl, Bella. The watching dragons. Gone like a wind to another world.

Thus it would be written in the Chronicles of Dragons:

In the new beginning was the Word.

And the Word of Gadzooks was . . .

Sometimes

Chris d'Lacey is the author of several highly acclaimed books for children and young adults, including the other books in the Last Dragon Chronicles, *The Fire Within, Icefire, Fire Star,* and *The Fire Eternal.* He is also the author of the early chapter book series The Dragons of Wayward Crescent.

In July of 2002, Chris was awarded an honorary doctorate by Leicester University for his services to children's fiction. Chris lives with his wife in Leicester, England.

Visit www.icefire.co.uk to learn more
about Chris d'Lacey's books.